CW00373442

GENESIS I.

Also by Paul Adam

UNHOLY TRINITY
SHADOW CHASERS

GENESIS II

PAUL ADAM

LITTLE, BROWN AND COMPANY

A *Little, Brown* Book

First published in Great Britain in 2001
by Little, Brown and Company

Copyright © 2001 Paul Adam

The moral right of the author has been asserted.

All rights reserved.
No part of this publication may be reproduced,
stored in a retrieval system, or transmitted, in any
form or by any means, without the prior
permission in writing of the publisher, nor be
otherwise circulated in any form of binding or
cover other than that in which it is published and
without a similar condition including this
condition being imposed on the subsequent purchaser.

*All characters in this publication are fictitious
and any resemblance to real persons, living or dead,
is purely coincidental.*

A CIP catalogue record for this book
is available from the British Library.

HARDBACK ISBN 0 316 85748 3
C FORMAT ISBN 0 316 85747 5

Typeset in Palatino by
Palimpsest Book Production Limited,
Polmont, Stirlingshire
Printed and bound in Great Britain by
Clays Ltd, St Ives plc

Little, Brown and Company (UK)
Brettenham House
Lancaster Place
London WC2E 7EN

www.littlebrown.co.uk

ACKNOWLEDGEMENT

I would like to thank Dr Alan Hay and Amanda Parker for their help in the research for this book.

They went in at dawn, the wind howling low across the Fens, the horizon rent by the seeping wounds of the distant sunrise. There was something symbolic about the time, choosing the birth of a new day for what was essentially a mission of death.

Jake was in the first group, ten of them piling out of the back of the transit van and running for the high wire fence around the perimeter of the field. They were all identically dressed: white anti-contamination suits, the hoods pulled up over their heads, faces partially concealed by surgical masks. Clean, sterile, their individuality hidden beneath the protective clothing, they raced towards the fence in a straggling line. Jake was near the front, watching his feet as they crossed the strip of bare uneven land next to the road. He could feel his breath warm on his face under the mask, a tightness in his stomach that was part nerves, part exhilaration.

The leader reached the fence and dropped to his knees, a pair of boltcutters in his hands. Coolly, without haste, he snipped the wire strands and bent them back to form an opening big enough to crawl through. Jake went after him and straightened up on the other side, glancing back towards the road. Two more transit vans had pulled in and were disgorging their passengers. Fifteen or twenty hooded figures clad all in white came sweeping across the strip of earth like some Ku Klux Klan horde run amok.

Jake turned back to survey the shadowy field. The oilseed rape was waist high, rustling and swaying in the breeze. The flowers – wet with the morning dew – were just beginning to open. He could smell their sweet, sickly perfume. In another few days the area would be a sea of vivid yellow. If the crop was allowed to live that long.

Grasping a few stalks in his gloved hands, Jake wrenched the plants up from the soil and tossed them down, moving forwards across the field. The others fell in beside him, each taking a narrow band and stripping it bare of vegetation like voracious insects. The new arrivals ducked down through the hole in the fence and joined in, ripping the rape up frantically, knowing that time was not on their side.

It was growing lighter now. The ground was still cloaked in gloom but the horizon, far out beyond the endless mosaic of fields, was glowing pale yellow, the clouds above it laced with streaks of watery sunlight. The wind whistled across the plain, gusting through the rape, tugging at the material of Jake's anti-contamination suit, but he barely felt its bite. Underneath the thin cotton he was already running with sweat.

They were fifty metres into the crop when the security guards came for them. Six uniformed men emerged from the research centre on the far side of the field and hurried across the inter-vening car park to the fence. They were middle-aged and out of condition, their black tunics stretched taut over their flabby bellies. One of them pulled out a bunch of keys and unlocked the access gate in the fence. Then they ran through, flattening the oilseed rape as they charged towards the line of ghostly white figures.

The figures scattered, splitting up and heading in all direc-tions, still tearing up plants. The guards gave chase, disorgan-ised, unsure who to tackle first. The figures danced around them, taunting them, waving severed stalks in their faces before darting away unscathed. The guards floundered through the vegetation, impotent and hopelessly outnumbered. The figures, younger and more agile, were enjoying the game. They shouted abuse, crowing at the red-faced, panting security men as they stumbled around the decimated field. The ground was littered with torn-up plants, whole swathes lay crushed and broken and even the rape still standing was criss-crossed with tracks.

A guard came for Jake, lunging at him aggressively. Jake twisted sideways, easily avoiding the outstretched arms, and hared away across the field, gleefully ripping up more plants as he ran. The group leader, a man in his late twenties Jake knew only as Dan, came up beside him and drew breath. They watched the guards regroup and revise their tactics, all six of them now going after just one figure.

'To the vans!' Dan yelled, sensing the moment to get out.

The figures flitted back quickly through the rape, retreating towards the hole in the fence. The security guards pursued them doggedly.

Dan turned to Jake, his voice muted by the mask across his mouth. 'This is too easy. You want a real challenge?'

He gestured towards the car park. 'Let's hit them where it really hurts.'

Dan took off across the field, outflanking the guards. Jake followed him without thinking, through the open gate and out into the car park next to the three-storey glass-and-concrete research centre. Dan paused for a moment to look back. The hooded figures were scuttling away through the hole in the fence and heading for the transit vans. One of them was pulled to the ground by a security guard but managed to wriggle free. Another, caught inside the field, was clinging to the top of the fence while two more guards attempted to drag him off.

'Come on.'

Dan jogged away across the car park and round the corner of the research centre.

'Where are we going?' Jake asked, running alongside.

Without replying, Dan came to a halt by a door, a fire exit in the side of the building. He unzipped his anti-contamination suit and rummaged inside, pulling out a short steel jemmy which he inserted between the edge of the door and the frame. He leant his weight on the jemmy, forcing it back with a sudden jerk. The lock snapped, releasing the door. Almost immediately an alarm went off, a piercing clang that could probably be heard for miles around. Dan whipped open the door and stepped inside. Jake hesitated, aware that he was crossing an important boundary in more than just the literal sense.

'Let's go,' Dan said. 'Move it!'

He grabbed Jake's arm and pulled him inside. A long dark corridor stretched out before them, doors on either side. Dan seemed to know where he was going. He ran on a few metres and tried one of the doors. It was locked, but the jemmy had it open in seconds. Beyond it was a wide open-plan laboratory, benches lined up down the middle, a series of floor-to-ceiling windows on the far side overlooking the car park and the fenced fields at the rear of the building.

Dan stepped across to one of the benches and swept a tray of glass beakers off on to the floor. They shattered with a jarring crash that echoed around the room. The noise had barely died away before there were more explosive impacts as Dan raced along the benches hurling equipment to the floor. Test tubes, retorts, complex structures of pipes and glass bottles smashed into glittering fragments so the tiles looked as if they were layered with crushed ice.

'What the fuck're you standing there for?' Dan shouted at Jake, picking up a metal bar and hammering it down on a stack of plastic Petri dishes. 'This'll show the bastards we mean business. You gonna help or not?'

Jake ran to the other side of the lab. The vandalism had taken him by surprise but he wasn't squeamish about destroying property. Plants, fences, laboratory equipment, what difference did it make? It all belonged to the enemy. He picked up a large glass jar full of clear liquid and hurled it across the lab. The liquid showered out as the jar shattered on the floor. Another jar followed, then another. The chemicals hissed together forming a cloud of noxious vapour. Shit! Jake backed off, knocking more containers over. Botanical cultures, bottles marked with complex chemical formulae, trays of samples. Jake didn't know what any of them were but he was on a high, the euphoria of destruction coursing through his veins like a drug.

Dan was down at the far end of the lab, forcing open another door that led to a glass-walled office containing a desk and rows of filing cabinets. He took the jemmy and began to break the locks on the cabinets, taking out the papers inside and strewing them across the floor.

'Hey, give me a hand here,' he yelled.

Jake ran down the side of the laboratory, toppling more shelves, opening the door of a refrigerator and tipping it up so the contents slid out and smashed. The floor was awash with glass and plastic and puddles of strange fluids. Through the windows he saw three of the security guards panting back across the car park. He realised the alarm bell was still ringing.

'They're coming,' he said to Dan, stepping through the doorway.

'Get your finger out. Take these cabinets here.'

Dan wrenched open the drawers and moved on to the next cabinet.

'I think we should go,' Jake said nervously.

He looked back at the trail of destruction they'd left across the lab. The elation he'd felt earlier had waned, anxiety taking its place.

'Do the fucking cabinets,' Dan snapped.

'The guards . . .'

'I *know.*'

Dan tossed some files on to the floor. He was holding others in his hand, riffling through the papers. Jake grabbed a handful of documents from the nearest drawer and flung them on to the pile that was rapidly accumulating behind them. The security guards would be round the side of the building by now. Coming in through the fire exit.

'Dan . . .'

'Yes, *okay.*'

The door at the far end of the lab banged open and the three guards burst into the room, pausing to take in the carnage.

'Dan . . .'

Jake looked round urgently. Dan had his back to him, doing something with one of the filing cabinets.

'They're here. Dan . . .'

Dan broke away from the cabinet and pushed Jake aside, diving back out into the lab. He tore open another door next to the office and they ran through into a second laboratory almost identical to the first. Jake heard the guards coming after them but didn't dare look round. His stomach was seized by a spasm of nausea and fear, his breath coming in shallow gasps that made him feel dizzy.

They reached a door at the other end of the room. It was locked. Dan fumbled for his jemmy. *Come on, Dan.* The guards were racing through from the first lab. Forty, maybe fifty metres behind. *Come on.* Dan rammed the jemmy into the gap next to the jamb and heaved the door open, half ripping the lock out of the wood. The corridor on the other side was the same one they'd entered earlier. Glancing left, they saw a fourth security guard coming in through the broken fire exit.

'This way,' Dan snarled, turning right.

They sprinted down the corridor. Ten metres on it took a

dog-leg to the left. Skidding round the corner, they saw another fire exit ahead of them. The guards were in the corridor now. Jake could hear the heavy thud of their boots, even the rasp of their breath, they were so close. He accelerated after Dan who slowed just a fraction as they approached the fire exit, slamming into the metal quick-release bar with both hands and erupting through the door on to the driveway at the front of the building.

The road was only a few metres away, a patch of dense woodland beyond it. Dan sped across the deserted carriageway and plunged into the trees. Jake kept behind him, risking a quick glance back as the undergrowth closed around them. The guards were out on the driveway, bent double, hands on knees, recovering. One of them was pointing at the woods, saying something to his colleagues. Then from round the side of the building came the throaty rumble of an engine. Jake saw headlights, the unmistakable outline of a Land-Rover, before the shrubs and bushes blotted out the view. He looked around for Dan. There was no sign of him.

'Dan?'

He ran on, peering through the low branches, the thick curtain of leaves.

'Dan?'

He suppressed a sudden gut-churning flutter of alarm. He was alone. Looking back again, he thought he caught a distant glimpse of figures coming into the wood. The Land-Rover engine seemed closer but he couldn't place its exact location. Where the hell was Dan?

A branch whipped him in the face, stinging his cheek above the surgical mask which was still strapped across his mouth and nose. He ducked, pushing aside the vegetation, running instinctively though he had no idea where he was going.

A figure broke through into a small clearing ahead of him. For one terrifying second Jake thought it was a security guard.

Then he noticed with relief the white anti-contamination suit. He changed direction and headed after the figure, stumbling over the dark, pitted forest floor. Traces of weak sunlight lanced in through the canopy above him but in the shadowy depths it was difficult to find a clear path. He caught his foot on a root and fell headlong, slithering across the damp ground. The front of his suit snagged on a protruding rock and tore apart, exposing the T-shirt he wore beneath it. He picked himself up. His suit was smeared with dirt and moss.

Dan was further in front now, not bothering to wait. Jake chased after him. He sensed the guards closing in on them, heard the snap of twigs, the rustle of leaves behind. The harsh throb of an engine was also drawing nearer though Jake couldn't see any sign of the Land-Rover. There must have been a track somewhere, hidden beyond the ranks of silver birch and beech.

More branches lashed into his face. He lifted a hand, pushing them aside. He saw a trace of grey sky in the near distance. The wood was coming to an end. Dan was slowing, getting his bearings. Jake narrowed the gap between them, aware of his own laboured breathing, the rustle of his clothes against the undergrowth, the roar of an engine getting louder. *The engine.* Something glinted through the trees, light reflecting off glass, off metal. Jake almost shouted. But he was already too late.

Dan broke out from the wood, not seeing, not listening, a rutted track just below him. He slithered down the steep earth embankment, struggling to keep his balance. His eyes were fixed solely on the slope. At the last moment he turned his head, sensing something, but his feet slid from under him and he fell, toppling out over the track.

The Land-Rover hit him before he reached the ground. Took him in mid air, the radiator smashing into his torso. Lifting him high, limbs flailing, his body crumpling like a bonfire guy.

Jake stopped dead at the top of the bank. Watching, a cry choked off in his throat. Watching as the figure arched up into the air, glowing white in the beam of the headlights, and came slowly, almost floating, down on to the muddy track.

2

The call came shortly before 7 am. Madeleine was a light sleeper, even more so the nights she was on the rota, but she still found it hard to force her eyes open and reach out for the telephone. It was the Duty Solicitor agency. Madeleine had a brief conversation, then rang Parkside police station, speaking first to the custody sergeant then to each of the suspects in turn – explaining who she was and how she was independent of the courts and the police and that they had a right to have any solicitor of their choice represent them. Did they want her? The words flowing out automatically, a part of her hoping they'd say no and save her the trip into town. But they never did. No one ever said no.

She dragged herself out from the covers, pulled on a dressing gown and stumbled wearily through into the bathroom. She washed quickly, the water waking her up, then put on her make-up and got dressed. There was no time for breakfast, but she'd see if she could scrounge a cup of tea from the police. They always had a kettle on the go somewhere.

Graham was stirring when she poked her head around the door to look in at the bomb-site that passed for his bedroom. There were dirty clothes all over the floor, school books and papers scattered across the desk. He was sprawled under the duvet, one large pale foot sticking out over the edge of the mattress. She was struck once again by how big he was getting. The room had a masculine smell to it, of sweat and grubby socks and rampaging hormones. A pungent man's smell she found strange, yet not so strange, in her little boy.

'You awake? I've been called out,' she said.

He grunted.

'See you later.'

Another grunt. He specialised in grunts, each one subtly graduated in pitch and intonation, but all meaning basically the same thing: leave me alone.

Madeleine went out to her car and drove down Mill Road and up over the railway bridge, one of so few inclines in the city that she'd even seen lazy students getting off their bikes to push up it. The central police station was just on the other side of the Gonville Place roundabout, a charmless four-storey concrete edifice overlooking Parker's Piece. She could probably have walked there in less than fifteen minutes, cycled in five, but she preferred the professional dignity of arriving by car to the undoubted health benefits of leaving it at home.

The city was only just stirring. The grass and lime trees on the Piece were misty in the morning light. A group of young men in university tracksuits was jogging energetically along one of the paths, and over the far side an elderly Chinese man in singlet and shorts was performing t'ai chi exercises by himself. Madeleine felt very tired just watching them.

She turned and went into the police station. A uniformed constable escorted her from the front desk to the interview rooms at the back where the custody sergeant was preparing breakfast for the inmates of the cells – pre-packed trays of Cumberland sausage, baked beans and fried potatoes heated up in a microwave. The smell made her wish she'd snatched a quick snack before coming out.

''Morning, Miss King,' the sergeant said amiably. 'We must

stop meeting like this.' He said the same thing every time she came to the police station.

'Hello, Sergeant Hall.'

She'd been there often enough to know most of the officers, certainly all the custody sergeants. Some were hostile and uncooperative, imbued with an inbred resentment of defence solicitors, but most were sensible enough to see her as almost an ally, a necessary part of the criminal process that could make their jobs easier: smooth the procedures, the legal requirements. The whole messy business was draining enough as it was without adding a dose of antagonism to the mixture.

Jim Hall was a big, phlegmatic man with the calm aura of a twenty-five-year veteran, a copper who'd seen it all and not been remotely surprised by any of it.

'You'll be wanting a cup of tea, I imagine,' he said, removing a steaming tray from the microwave and depositing it on the table.

'Please.'

'Milk, no sugar, right?' Hall glanced at the uniformed constable. 'Jump to it, lad. And one for me too.'

Then he pulled out the custody records, filling Madeleine in on the facts as she read through the sheets, noting down the details.

'They were picked up at the Transgenic Biotech research centre. You know, out beyond Waterbeach.'

Madeleine nodded. She'd already been given the gist of the story over the phone.

'Cut through a fence and pulled up a field of oilseed rape. There was a whole crowd of them, but the security guards only caught three.'

'So what're we looking at, criminal damage?' Madeleine said.

'And burglary for this one.' Hall touched one of the sheets with his finger. 'Jake Brewster. Broke into the research centre itself and smashed up a lab. I mean really smashed it up, according to the DC who went out to check the scene. Two of them took the place apart apparently.'

'Two of them? What happened to the other one?'

Hall put another breakfast tray into the microwave and set the timer.

'He got hit by a company Land-Rover that was chasing them. Brewster's pretty shook up. They're just kids, you know. Stupid kids. They don't know what they're doing.'

'Hit? Was he badly hurt?'

'Taken to Addenbrooke's. We haven't had a condition check yet.'

'What about bail?' Madeleine asked.

'These two, yes. Brewster, no. He did ten, maybe twenty thousand pounds worth of damage in the lab alone. You want him first? Go on through, I'll bring him in for you.'

Madeleine walked down the corridor and took a seat in the interview room: a drab, windowless cubicle that was neither welcoming nor particularly intimidating. It was simply functional, like a dentist's waiting room.

Jake Brewster was brought in a couple of minutes later. Sergeant Hall asked him if he wanted breakfast and he shook his head. Tea? Nothing. He sat down on the other side of the steel-framed table, and Madeleine examined him carefully, practised at assessing a prisoner's state of mind. Sergeant Hall was right. He was just a kid. Not much older than her son. The date of birth on the custody sheet made him twenty-two years old but he looked younger. Boyish, fresh-faced, she would have called him if it weren't for the cuts and scratches on his cheeks, the dark purple bruise under one eye and the faint traces of stubble on his jaw. He looked tired, and perhaps a little scared.

Madeleine tried to put him at ease, introducing herself and

explaining to him what the procedure was. He nodded weakly but didn't say anything.

'What happened to your face?' Madeleine asked.

'My face?'

'The cuts, the bruise.'

'I was hit in the face by some low branches in the wood. Running away.'

'The bruise too?'

He touched his eye tentatively. 'They did that.'

'They? The police?'

'The security guards.'

'They beat you up?'

'Not exactly. They just knocked me about a bit when they threw me in the back of the Land-Rover.'

'Have you seen a doctor?'

'No. I'm okay.'

'I want you examined,' Madeleine said. 'That's assault.'

Jake shrugged, quite calm about it all. 'I smashed up their lab, ripped up a field of rape. They were pretty pissed off.'

'That doesn't give them the right to beat you up.'

'What's the point of complaining? Where will it get me?'

Jake pulled open the front of the grubby white anti-contamination suit he was still wearing. It was hot in the airless room and he was beginning to sweat, his spiky black hair sticking together in clumps. There was something distant, lethargic about his manner. He seemed dazed, not fully aware of what was going on.

'Have you been in custody before?' Madeleine said.

Jake hesitated. He lifted a hand and fiddled with the gold ring in his left ear.

'You'd better tell me,' Madeleine continued. 'I need to know. If you've a record it will be on the Police National Computer.'

'Once,' he said. 'Two, three years ago.'

'For what?'

'Obstruction. They were going to cut down some trees to build an out-of-town shopping centre. I was with a group trying to stop them. We didn't succeed, of course.' He gave a twisted smile. 'We never do, do we?'

'Were you charged?'

'Cautioned. Lectured by some pompous copper and sent home like a little boy.'

'They're going to charge you this time,' Madeleine said. 'Criminal damage and burglary. Those are serious offences.'

For a moment he became more animated, leaning towards her over the table.

'Do you know what they're doing out there? In that research centre.'

'No.'

'That's the problem, neither do they. They're experimenting with things they know nothing about, playing God with the environment and our futures, all in the name of profit. That's why we pulled up their fucking plants.'

'And the lab?'

Jake glanced away, uncomfortable. 'Yeah, well, that wasn't part of the plan.' He looked back, defiant now. 'But I don't regret doing it. Anything we can do to stop them is a good thing in my book. What we did was in the public interest. It was absolutely justified.'

The outburst seemed to drain him for he slumped visibly in his chair, his chin dropping to his chest.

'Jake,' Madeleine said, 'I want you to tell me exactly what happened this morning. I need the facts before the police interview you. Are you listening?'

He looked up, his face drawn, an expression of weary resignation in his eyes.

'They're going to stitch me up anyway, aren't they? Why do I need a solicitor?'

'No one's going to stitch you up. I won't let them, you can be sure of that. The police will interview you. The interview will be taped and I will be present throughout. You don't need to say anything at all if you don't want to. Then they'll charge you, take your fingerprints and photograph and a swab from your mouth for DNA analysis.'

His head jolted up. 'What? DNA?' He was roused now. 'What do they want that for?'

'Genetic fingerprinting. It's standard practice. They have a DNA database they cross-check against.'

'Christ, they're all at it. Messing around with genes, with stuff they should leave well alone. What do they think I am, a rapist, a murderer? Well, they're not getting any bloody DNA sample from me.'

'They have the right to use reasonable force to take one,' Madeleine said.

Jake stared at her, then his lip curled and he shook his head. 'And they call this a free fucking country.'

Madeleine was inclined to agree with him. It was always the thin end of the wedge, the slow erosion of rights – the right to silence, to jury trial, to personal privacy – that tilted the scales against a defendant. When sex offenders and killers could be identified from their DNA, who could reasonably object to the taking of a sample? If you were innocent, what did you have to hide? But liberty wasn't an absolute. It was always hedged about with provisos, qualifications, with boundaries which were constantly changing. It was like a boulder on the seashore that seemed so solid, so permanent but which, over time, was eaten gradually away until nothing was left. And no one could remember what it had originally looked like. She could see ahead, not too far ahead, to a time when everyone would be DNA-typed at birth and their genetic coding held on computer by the police. It worried her, but she was a solicitor. It was her

17

job to work within the law no matter what she thought of it.

'Are they keeping me in custody?' Jake said.

'Yes. But I'm going to make a bail application to the Magistrates' Court. You'll appear later this morning, or maybe this afternoon.'

'Magistrates? They won't give me bail. They're in the pocket of the police.'

'That's not true.'

'Are they going to try me as well?'

'That depends. Burglary is triable either by magistrate or by jury. Criminal damage is a summary offence unless you've caused more than £5,000 worth of damage, in which case it can go to the Crown Court. The police claim you did a lot of damage. They haven't got an exact figure yet.'

Jake gave a sour smile. 'More than five grand, I bet. We had a fucking ball in there.'

He was a curious mixture of naivety and cynicism, of nerves and occasional flashes of bravado. Madeleine regarded him seriously.

'I wouldn't take this too lightly,' she said.

'Me? Lightly? Why not, it's a joke, isn't it? I was there, remember. I stood on the top of a bank and watched them run Dan over. They could have stopped, they could have braked but they just ploughed straight on. Hit him – bang! – like that.' He hammered his fist against the palm of his other hand. 'Tossed him into the air. And when he hit the ground they got out and stood there looking down at him. Arseholes with shit for brains. They just stood there as if they'd run over a fucking hedgehog or something. So, yeah, let's all have a good laugh about it.'

He swallowed hard and rubbed the side of his nose, up near the eye socket. Madeleine saw a tear-drop on the tip of his finger. She wondered what the symptoms of shock were.

'I'm getting you a doctor,' she said.

But there was a knock on the door before she even stood up. Sergeant Hall came in with her mug of tea. He glanced at them both. Madeleine could tell from his expression that he had something to say to them.

'We've just had a call from Addenbrooke's,' he began grimly. 'Your mate, Dan Cruickshank. He's died, I'm afraid. They didn't even get him into surgery. I'm sorry.'

Jake looked at him expressionlessly for a long time, as if he hadn't taken in any of the words. Then he turned his head and stared at the wall of the interview room, his eyes unblinking, his face a hard, impenetrable mask.

There had been a time – so long ago now she could barely recall it – when Sandy Harrison had enjoyed the start of the day. When she could sip her tea slowly without scalding her mouth, eat a piece of toast without bolting it, sit back for a moment and gaze out of the window without a knot of tension in her stomach. Those distant days seemed so unreal now she wondered sometimes if they had even existed. Were those weekend lie-ins just a figment of her imagination; those cups of coffee with the papers and croissants warm from the oven merely dreams that had come and gone in her sleep?

'Mum, where's my bag?'

'Mum, can I have some more milk?'

'Mum, my bag . . . Mum?'

Always that word, constant, whining, demanding. The noise ringing in her ears, impossible to ignore.

'Muuum . . .' Lucy coming in, petulant and cross. 'Did you hear me? It was in the hall. Somebody's moved it.'

'*Mum*, the milk.'

Sandy glanced at the clock, wondering why it always ran faster in the mornings. She put the pan on the ring, opened the fridge door for the bacon and eggs. Jeff would be coming in soon, wanting his breakfast.

'Mum . . .'

'What's that over by the door?'

'Who put it *there*?'

'Get a move on, you'll miss the bus.'

'I *am*.'

'Mum, the milk.'

'Yes, yes, for goodness' sake.'

Hearing herself, short-tempered, fraying. Snapping like a sheepdog at the heels of her recalcitrant flock. She got the bottle from the fridge, topped up Tim's glass. Put the bacon on to fry and pulled a lock of damp hair out of her eyes, feeling bedraggled, feeling her age. More than her age.

She looked around for her tea, took a sip. It was cold, undrinkable. She put the kettle on. There was time to make a fresh pot. No time to drink it, but Jeff would want a cup. The bacon sizzled in the pan, the fat spitting angrily over the sides.

'Lucy . . . the bus.'

'I *know*. I'm looking for my pass.'

'It's on the mantelpiece.'

Sandy went through, following her daughter. Finding her bus pass and ushering her out, a brief kiss on the cheek before Lucy went running down the drive, her coat flapping over one shoulder.

Sandy dashed back in, catching the bacon before it burnt, putting the eggs in to fry.

'Hurry up, Tim. You have to clean your teeth.'

'I *am* hurrying. Have you got my dinner money?'

'What? Oh, sh . . . sugar.'

She found her purse and took out a note, then rummaged for change. Why did they always have to have the exact money? She heard Jeff come in and start to wash his hands in the scullery sink. The eggs! She whipped the pan off. Too late. Damn. Jeff hated his eggs all leathery, but there was nothing she could do. She tipped them out on to a plate with the bacon, then filled the teapot with water from the kettle.

'Have you finished, Tim? Your teeth.'

'I'm going.'

Sandy turned to accompany him.

'Phoebe?'

She'd only just noticed the small figure at the far end of the long farmhouse table. Overlooked, as always, sitting forlornly in her chair, her Weetabix untouched in the bowl in front of her.

'What's the matter? You haven't eaten anything,' Sandy said in exasperation.

'Don't want it,' Phoebe said quietly. 'Hurts.'

'What hurts?'

'Here.' Phoebe pointed.

'Your neck?'

'Yes.'

'Do you mean your neck, or your throat?'

'Yes.'

'Which?'

'Don't know.'

'Is it inside or outside?'

'Inside.'

Sandy sighed. One of the three children was always going down with something. There was hardly a week in the year when they were free of colds and coughs.

'Let's get your shoes and coat. I'll have a look when we've dropped Tim at school.'

She picked her daughter up and carried her out. Phoebe felt limp in her arms, resting her head on her shoulder.

'You want to stay here today? With Daddy?'

They came back through the kitchen. Jeff was at the table, mopping his plate with a slice of bread. He reached out to kiss Tim and a pale, listless Phoebe.

'She's got a sore throat,' Sandy explained. 'Can I leave her here with you?'

'Fresh air'll do her good,' Jeff said. He liked the kids out of the way when he had breakfast. He chewed on the bread and wiped his mouth with the back of his hand.

Sandy went out and loaded Tim and Phoebe into the car. Late, as usual. She knew the memories of those long-lost mornings ended where the memories of the children began. A time gone for ever, never to be regained. Yet the core of her didn't want to go back. It was just that sometimes . . . She glanced round at Phoebe, slumped sideways in the car seat with her eyes closed. Why was there always something to worry about?

David Seymour stepped through the doorway into the lab and came to an abrupt halt, staring around at the wreckage. He'd been prepared for a shock, but nothing quite this bad. The room looked as if a tornado had hit it. The walls and ceiling were intact but just about everything else had been smashed or hurled on to the floor. There was glass everywhere, the crystal shards glinting in the sunlight which flooded in through the windows. Pools of liquid had gathered by the benches and there was a smell in the air he couldn't identify: a mixture of sulphur and acid and God knows what.

He took a few paces into the room, watching where he trod. The police had already left, the damage inspected, photographs taken, but their report would not even begin to describe exactly what had been destroyed. For the real wealth of the laboratory lay not in the equipment that had been vandalised, but in the work that had gone on there. Glassware, centrifuges, chemicals could all be replaced. But the months, the years of research, too intangible to quantify purely in monetary terms, would perhaps never be recovered.

Seymour picked his way through the debris, his shock giving way to anger. The electric propagators had been overturned and he could see tiny seedlings scattered over the floor, plants dying in the toxic soup swilling about on the tiles. He picked up a couple and cupped them in his hands. He'd bred them, nurtured them. They were living things and he abhorred the wanton destruction of life. It was so unnecessary, so ignorant. These people knew nothing of what went on here. They knew nothing of its value, its potential for doing real good out in the burgeoning world where only science had any hope of alleviating malnutrition and starvation.

Seymour believed in his work. He believed in it as a force for progress and human wellbeing. But the people who had done this were hooligans, fanatics fighting reason and science with violence, their heads full of scare stories and ill-informed paranoia. He was a quiet, gentle man but seeing his work demolished like this made him want to smash the culprits the way they had smashed the laboratory.

A figure was moving around in the glass-walled office at the far end of the room. Seymour recognised the silvery beard and balding head of the research director, Dennis Baxter. He was picking up files from the floor and sorting through them on his desk. Seymour walked down past the benches and paused on the threshold of the office. Baxter took a moment to sense he was there, turning around and looking at him briefly before resuming what he was doing.

'Check the lab,' Baxter said curtly over his shoulder. 'Give me a full damage assessment.'

Damage assessment? Seymour thought. I can tell you that now. Everything. Every bloody thing down the toilet.

'They got in here too?' he said.

Baxter gave no sign that he'd heard the question. He went to one of the filing cabinets and combed quickly through the contents, looking for something. He seemed agitated.

'Can I help?' Seymour said.

'What? Oh, no. Start cleaning the place up. See what you can salvage.'

Baxter flicked through the papers on the desk, then checked the cabinet again. He scanned the floor. All the documents had been picked up. He went back to the cabinet, looked inside it once more.

'Where do I begin?' Seymour said, thinking aloud. He stepped back as Baxter pushed roughly past him.

The research director hurried away without responding, almost running down the laboratory, his shoes crunching noisily on the carpet of broken glass.

'Look how long it took them,' McCormick said furiously, jabbing a finger at the television screen. In the bottom right-hand corner of the shadowy black-and-white picture a digital clock was ticking away, second by second.

'Four and a half, nearly five bloody minutes. Where were they all that time?'

Rick Cullimore shifted awkwardly in his seat. He didn't know the answer, but that wasn't the point of the question. McCormick was going to answer it himself anyway.

'I'll tell you where they were. Sitting on their arses drinking tea and playing cards or whatever they do all night instead of earning their fucking pay.'

Cullimore felt obliged to reply although he knew there was no placating the managing director.

'They'd checked the field only ten minutes earlier. They were caught off guard.'

'Caught off guard?' McCormick repeated incredulously. 'Are

you kidding me? They're security guards. They're never supposed to be off fucking guard.'

He looked back at the screen, his smooth tanned face
congested with anger. The dim, grainy picture, taken from a
CCTV camera high up on the rear wall of the research centre,
showed the security guards opening the gate in the fence and
chasing the hooded protesters around the field.

'I never knew we'd hired the Keystone Kops,' McCormick said
scathingly as they watched the guards' clumsy attempts to catch
the white-clad figures. 'They must have flattened more rape than
those bloody kids did.'

'They caught three of them,' Cullimore said, realising it was
a mistake as soon as he opened his mouth.

'Three!' McCormick spat the word across the desktop. 'Don't
give me fucking three. Three out of thirty, you think that's good?
And we killed one.'

Cullimore winced, narrowing eyes which were too small for
his fleshy face. His skin, the colour and texture of lard, seemed
paler than ever.

'It was an accident. The kid deserved it. What do they expect,
coming in and smashing up the place like that?'

'I know he deserved it. That's not the point. The point is we
look like killers. The press will throw us to the lions. Corporate
murderers, they'll call us. Some shit like that.'

McCormick turned his head away from the screen as if he
couldn't bear to watch the scene, the protesters fleeing to their
distant transit vans, tiny white specks flickering to and fro like
dancing moths; the guards pursuing them, ungainly lumps humi-
liated and defeated.

'We're going to have to work overtime to limit the damage
on this. It's a fucking mess. What were they doing anyway,
knocking him down?'

Cullimore pressed the pause button on the remote control.

'Like I said, it was an accident, Cliff. You seen enough of this? There's something I want to show you.'

He leaned over to eject the tape, anxious to move on. To make amends for the incompetence of his security team. McCormick held up a hand, stopping him.

'Ten minutes, you said.' The MD was frowning. 'They arrived ten minutes after the fields had been checked?'

'Coincidence.'

'Bollocks. They knew the routine.'

This wasn't something Cullimore wanted to get into.

'Maybe,' he conceded.

'From inside?'

'Not necessarily. They know what they're doing, those people. They could have watched us for a few days. Noted when the patrols went out. That wouldn't have been difficult. There are public roads all round the site.'

McCormick wasn't convinced. 'Check it out.'

Cullimore nodded and pulled the tape out of the video machine. He inserted another cassette.

'You should see this.'

He pressed the start button. Just as the tape began to whir the office door opened and Dennis Baxter burst in.

'Cliff . . .' Baxter began.

McCormick waved him to a seat, his eyes fixed on the television screen. Another CCTV security camera mounted on the wall of the laboratory had captured the two protesters entering the room and smashing up the equipment. With their hooded suits and surgical masks it was impossible to identify exactly who they were.

'Cliff, we need to talk,' Baxter said.

'Hang on a second,' Cullimore interjected. 'This is important. Let me find it for you.'

He fast-forwarded the tape, watching the blurred picture intently.

McCormick glanced at the research director. 'What's the damage?'

'Well, the field is ruined. What's left of the oilseed rape isn't worth having.'

'Not the field,' McCormick said tersely. 'The field's a cover, you know that. I meant the lab.'

'It's bad. We didn't expect the lab to be a target. We've lost a lot of cultures, seedlings. And worse . . .'

'This is it,' Cullimore broke in. He pressed the play button on the remote control and talked them through the images. 'There's one kid out in the lab, trashing the place. Ignore him. Look in the background, the other one's in the office. You see him?'

He adjusted the contrast, the brightness, trying to make the picture clearer.

'Watch what he's doing. Opening the cabinets, forcing the locks with something, looks like a jemmy. Then he's tossing the files out on to the floor, making as much mess as he can. This bit. He's looking for something. Here. You see that?'

'See what?' McCormick said.

Cullimore wound the tape back and played it again.

'These files he's not tossing out, he's looking through them. Now watch here . . . I've looked at this several times, only noticed it the fourth or fifth time. There. That file. He doesn't throw it down or put it back.'

McCormick shuffled to the edge of his chair and leaned forward across the desk, peering at the television. The figure in the office was a long way from the camera and he had his back to it so it was difficult to make out what he was doing. But his right elbow was raised, his arm sliding across the hidden front of his body.

'He's slipping the file inside his clothes,' Cullimore said.

'Stealing it?' McCormick was bolt upright now, tense. 'These are the two who were chased through the woods, aren't they? Which is the one who was killed?'

'I don't know,' Cullimore said.

'Find out, Rick.'

McCormick turned to Baxter. 'You'd better check to see what's missing.'

Baxter had his thumb in his mouth, chewing anxiously on a nail.

'I already know,' he said.

3

Madeleine had spent three years at university, a year at law college and a further two years in articles, thinking she was training to become a lawyer. It was only when she'd qualified and begun to practise that she realised she was actually a kind of glorified social worker.

The surface trappings of her job, the court appearances, the pleadings, the paperwork were legal enough in nature, but nearly everything underneath, the fundamentals, had nothing at all to do with the law. Almost all her clients were damaged individuals. Almost all had problems which underpinned and went well beyond the particular criminal offence which brought them into contact with her. Drugs, alcohol, mental instability, clinical depression were all so common that most of the time Madeleine felt she was a counsellor, a confidante, a shoulder to lean on first and a solicitor last.

It was exhausting, and very often immensely frustrating, but she'd gone into it willingly and with her eyes at least half open. She'd known early on at university that she was going to specialise in criminal law. Other subjects, tort, contract, constitutional law, international law – but not property, she'd loathed that – had interested her, but they were somehow abstract, detached. They were concerned with bits of paper, clauses, disputes that nearly always, in the end, came down to money. Only criminal law dealt with real people, with questions which, although trivial in many cases, made a vital difference to someone's future. A fine, a prison sentence, a criminal record could tarnish a person and shape or distort the rest of their lives.

Madeleine felt the responsibility that came with her job, but the legal side was the least of her worries. Criminal procedure was easy; trying to cope with the emotional and personal problems of her clients much harder. Poverty, drink, heroin, violence and abuse, these were problems so intractable that no matter what she did they never went away. They never would, of course, until the individuals sorted them out for themselves. It was up to them. But most didn't try and those who did seemed doomed to failure from the start. Doomed to repeat all the mistakes that had landed them in trouble in the first place.

There was no shortage of clients – Madeleine acquired new ones virtually every day of the week – but what was depressing was the old ones who kept coming back on a regular basis. Clients like Tina. Twenty-one years old, on the game since before she was sixteen, back in court for the sixth time in as many months. This time for breach of bail conditions: failing to report to her local police station as laid down by the magistrates on her previous appearance, charged with loitering for the purposes of prostitution. Madeleine had talked to her in the courthouse custody cells half an hour earlier.

'What happened, Tina? I thought you understood the conditions. You have to report twice a week, Mondays and Thursdays between ten am and noon. What happened?'

'I felt sick,' Tina said feebly.

She didn't look well. Her skin was white and pasty, her hair lank and she had a hollow-eyed permanently bruised look, not from any specific injury, but from the battering life had given her. Madeleine couldn't believe that any man would want to have sex with her, never mind pay for it, but men were strange creatures.

'You felt ill?'

Tina nodded. 'Morning sickness.'

'*What?*' Madeleine tried to keep any hint of condemnation out of her voice, but she could barely conceal her exasperation. Tina already had three children, aged four, two and nine months. All by different men. All taken into care by Social Services. 'Are you sure?'

'Yes.'

'Who's the father? A client?'

'No.'

'Wayne?' Wayne was her pimp.

'I think a friend of his. Came home one night with Wayne. I didn't want to but . . .'

'He raped you?'

Tina didn't reply.

'Did he force you?'

'It happened.'

'Tina, did this man rape you?'

Madeleine knew the question was pointless – Tina would never go to the police, never give evidence – but she had to ask, to establish the facts in her own mind. She had a relationship with this young girl. A professional relationship, it was true, but also one which went beyond the boundaries of solicitor and client. Madeleine wanted her to know that one person cared what happened to her.

'Did he?'

Tina grimaced as if in pain, shaking her head. 'Leave it.'

'Did he? You have rights, you know, Tina. People can't do that to you.'

'Can't they?' Tina said bleakly.

Madeleine dropped the subject, moving on to practical issues that Tina would be more comfortable with. They were none of her business, but she knew no one else was likely to bring them up.

'Are you going to keep it?'

'Dunno.'

'How many weeks pregnant are you?'

Tina shrugged. 'Ten, twelve weeks. I dunno exactly.'

'Have you seen your doctor?'

'No.'

'I'm going to call her for you, fix up an appointment. You need to see her, Tina. You need to talk to her. Will you do that if I arrange it for you?'

Tina nodded, probably more to shut her up than because she intended to keep the appointment. Maybe this time she'd take some notice, Madeleine reflected optimistically. It hadn't happened before but there was always a first time.

Sometimes she wondered why she bothered. Why she always seemed to be on the phone to Social Services, probation officers, bail hostels, drug rehabilitation centres, trying desperately to resolve the irresolvable, to rebuild the safety net of the welfare state which had collapsed underneath her clients leaving them swinging over a precipice. It was a thankless task, rarely appreciated by the people she represented. They'd slid so far down the vicious spiral of despair that they neither noticed nor cared when someone tried to help them. But Madeleine did it for herself, because she couldn't just take care of the legal questions and ignore everything else. Her conscience wouldn't let her.

She was tired. She'd been up since 7 am, been at Parkside police station until nearly 9 o'clock, then down to the Magistrates' Court where she'd seen several other clients in the cells before coming into the courtroom for their bail applications. Now there was Tina, her third application of the morning.

The young girl was in the dock at the side of the court, leaning forward in her chair, elbows on knees, her head bowed. She'd been there so many times before, the routine should have been familiar to her, but she looked bewildered, unsure what was happening. Trusting in Madeleine. 'You take care of it, Miss King.' That's what they all said.

Tina lifted her head and smiled weakly at someone in the public seats at the back of the courtroom. Madeleine glanced round. It was Wayne, Tina's pimp, a grinning, swaggering thug with long greasy hair and mean eyes. He gave a cocky wave and a reassuring nod which seemed to say, 'It's okay, baby, I'm here, just leave it to me.' As if he'd ever done anything for her except pocket her earnings to pay for the flashy yellow BMW convertible he cruised around in. Madeleine turned away in disgust. If there was any justice, it would have been Wayne in the dock not this feckless, exploited girl.

The magistrates were on their raised dais, beneath a plaster relief of the royal coat of arms – the lion and the unicorn and the *Dieu et mon droit* motto which most of the people who appeared in the dock could not read, much less understand. This morning the bench consisted of two elderly men and a middle-aged woman in the chair. Well dressed, elegant, she probably spent more on having her hair done than Tina had to live on for a week.

Madeleine listened while the Crown Prosecution Service solicitor outlined the facts of the case, then she stood up and explained about the pregnancy, the morning sickness. The Chair asked a couple of questions then the three magistrates retired to discuss their decision. There was no telling which way they'd go. Madeleine was even on the day: one bail application granted, one refused. The process was a lottery, determined as much by the combination of magistrates and their moods and prejudices as by the facts of the case.

Madeleine stretched her legs, wandering over to the table

where the CPS solicitor, Colin Miller, was sorting through an enormous pile of files. They knew each other well. Madeleine had a professional respect for him, but she didn't like him. He was a bore. Old-maidish, pernickety, a shirt so stuffed you could have put him in the Natural History Museum.

'I wanted to talk to you about Flash Harry,' she said. 'Harry Longstaff,' she added, giving the name that would have been on the CPS file.

'Longstaff?' Miller said, checking through his pile. 'The burglary?'

'That's the one. You're not seriously going through with it, are you?'

Flash Harry was one of her regular clients. The nickname was ironic: he was a filthy old tramp, a familiar figure around the streets of the city who slept rough on Midsummer Common and carried his worldly goods in a couple of Sainsbury's bags. Two days earlier, on Saturday afternoon, he'd been found in the Senior Common Room of Magdalene College, helping himself to the dons' malt whisky. The police had been called and Harry had been charged with burglary and held for two nights in the cells.

Miller checked through his file, reminding himself of the details.

'He's admitted the offence to the police, what's the problem?'

'The problem,' Madeleine said, 'is the charge. He went in there for a kip. He's not a burglar, he's a harmless old tramp. He didn't break in, he did no damage. He had a couple of drinks and went to sleep.'

'Half a bottle of Glenlivet, I believe,' Miller said pedantically. 'And he stank the place out so much the college had to disinfect the room.'

'So? Being dirty and smelly isn't a criminal offence, even in a Cambridge college. There was no intention to steal.'

'But he stole nevertheless.'

'A bit of whisky worth, what, a fiver at the most? He's already spent two nights in custody. Isn't that enough?'

'You want him bailed? He has no fixed abode and a record of offences.'

'Nearly all drunkenness. I want the charges dropped.'

Miller shook his head. Madeleine stepped back a little to avoid the overpowering scent of his aftershave. Why did men wear the stuff? Did they not realise it smelt like toilet cleaner?

'The college wants to press charges. As a deterrent,' Miller said. 'He's a thief.'

'Oh, come on. Half a bottle of whisky? What's that to Magdalene College? You think I haven't been inside a college, seen the High Table set for dinner with three different wineglasses for the meal alone? And that's not counting the sherry they have beforehand and the port and Madeira afterwards. You think the dons pay for any of it?

'You press a burglary charge and I'm going to take it to the Crown Court and tell the media in advance. The tabloids will have a field day. I'll call all the kitchen staff, the bursar, the college servants and get a full picture of how hard life is for our impoverished academics. You think a jury will convict a seventy-year-old man who rummages in litter bins for his meals and sleeps under a tree in the snow and rain?'

Miller sighed. 'He's an old tramp. Why are you getting so worked up about it?'

'He's a client. And he shouldn't be in custody. But go ahead, if you want to make the CPS look foolish. Let's go to trial on this one.'

Madeleine walked away. The clerk was coming back in, followed by the magistrates. The Chair announced their decision. In view of the circumstances, Tina would be released on bail again on the same conditions. But if she broke them again, she'd be arrested and brought back before the court. Madeleine went over to the dock and exchanged a few words with the girl before she was allowed to leave. Then they went out into the vestibule where Wayne was waiting for them.

'She needs looking after,' Madeleine said to the pimp. 'I want you to make sure she goes to the doctor as soon as possible. Do you understand?'

'Fuck off,' Wayne said. 'It's none of your fucking business. Come on, baby.'

He took hold of Tina's arm and led her away. Madeleine watched them, incensed but not surprised. She knew it wouldn't be long before Tina was back.

Flash Harry was in the dock when Madeleine returned to the courtroom. He'd been cleaned up a bit by the police, but the pungent ripeness of his body odour permeated the whole room.

'Mr Longstaff is charged with burglary, Madam,' the clerk said to the Chair. 'Mr Miller?'

Miller stood up and fiddled with his files, avoiding Madeleine's eye.

'The Crown Prosecution Service is offering no evidence in this case,' he said. 'The charges are dropped.'

Madeleine kept her face expressionless. She didn't have many victories, and when they came they were always small. But, God, they felt good.

'Just try a little bit. One bite.'

Phoebe shook her head listlessly. Even that one small movement seemed to tire her.

'Is it still your throat?' Sandy said.

Phoebe didn't reply. She was slumped over the table, her cheek resting on her arms. Her face was flushed and her breathing quick and shallow. Sandy put a hand on her forehead. It was burning hot. Sandy went out of the kitchen and ran up the stairs to the bathroom. She found the forehead thermometer in the cupboard and took it back downstairs. Phoebe hadn't moved. Sandy picked her up and put her on her lap, then she held the thermometer to her daughter's forehead, counting silently to fifteen. The little circles on the heat-sensitive strip changed colour one by one. Thirty-five, thirty-six, thirty-seven, thirty-eight, creeping up to thirty-nine, then forty degrees Celsius. That was as high as the thermometer went.

Sandy put it down. Forty degrees. That was a hundred and four Fahrenheit. None of the children had ever had a temperature as high as that. Sandy carried Phoebe through into the sitting room and laid her down on the sofa. She undid the buttons on the child's blouse and pulled it off, knowing she had to cool her down. Phoebe's whole body felt red hot. Her eyes were closed and she was moaning and holding her stomach.

'Does your tummy hurt? Phoebe, does it hurt?'

Phoebe gave a slight nod. Sandy put her hand gently on her daughter's stomach, to reassure her rather than because she had any idea what to feel for. Phoebe winced.

Sandy stared down at her, feeling sick. *Jesus, what do I do*?

Phoebe moaned, pulling her knees up and hugging them. The temperature, Sandy thought. Get that sorted out first. She sprinted up the stairs and came back with the bottle of Calpol. She propped Phoebe up and poured some of the thick liquid into a spoon.

'I've got some medicine here, to make you feel better. Open your mouth. Phoebe, open your mouth.'

Phoebe didn't seem to hear. Or didn't have the energy to respond. Sandy prised her mouth open and forced the plastic spoon in, tipping the Calpol down her throat. A second spoonful went in the same way then Sandy fetched a beaker of water and held it to Phoebe's lips.

'Try, Phoebe,' she pleaded. 'It will make you feel better.'

Phoebe took a long gulp, then another. Her head rolled sideways. She retched. Her body convulsed and she was sick. The vomit, tinted pink by the Calpol, spewed out on to the cushions of the sofa.

Oh, God. Sandy hesitated, almost paralysed by anxiety. What was it? A simple stomach bug, some kind of viral infection? Phoebe had never been like this before. Sandy hurried through into the kitchen, found a damp cloth and returned to mop up the vomit. Phoebe was still curled up in a ball, holding her stomach. Where was Jeff? Sandy looked at her watch. It would be half an hour before he came in for his lunch. He was probably over on the other side of the farm. She was on her own. She looked down helplessly at her daughter, then went to the table by the window and picked up the telephone.

To Madeleine, there was something unreal about Cambridge. The colleges, with their quadrangles and hidden courtyards, their private chapels, baroque architecture and manicured lawns on which only Fellows were allowed to tread, were like some large academic theme park; a tourist resort populated by a cast of actors pretending to be eccentric dons and loud-mouthed students. It all seemed so theatrical. The quaint, picturesque setting, the punts on the Backs, the sit-up-and-beg cyclists rattling past with the wind tugging at their gowns. It was easy to imagine that it was all put on for the coachloads of visitors who snaked around the narrow streets with cameras and guidebooks, wallowing in the picture-postcard ambience of Olde Englande.

But there were parts of the city where the pervasive, alluring air of academe was not allowed to penetrate. Where people lived and worked who had nothing to do with the dreaming spires. The Lion Yard precinct off Petty Cury which housed both a shopping centre and the Magistrates' Courts was one such enclave.

Built in the sixties and seventies, it appeared to have been constructed as an extreme reaction to the tranquil perfection of the colleges, countering the ancient brick and stonework with a concrete monstrosity of quite staggering banality. It was as if the town planners, patronised once too often by the university, had decided to spit in the eye of the heritage lobby and stamp the mark of the twentieth century on a city whose most distinguished institution had yet to emerge from the nineteenth.

There was a small tea bar in the Magistrates' Courts, run by the WRVS, but with baffling logic it closed at lunch-time, precisely the time people might want to use it, so Madeleine went out to a coffee bar in Petty Cury which she regarded almost as a second office – preparing cases there, scribbling notes, making calls on her mobile in between mouthfuls of sandwich. It was a dull, characterless area of the city. Once it had been dominated by coaching inns and stables, by cobbled alleyways teeming with barrow boys, pickpockets, thieves and whores. The thieves and whores were still there, safely contained within the barred cells of the Magistrates' Courts, but the alleyways and street traders were long gone, replaced by a pedestrian precinct and the Disney Store.

The coffee bar was crowded that lunch-time; with solicitors, defendants, witnesses, probation officers, all the human flotsam of the criminal process. Madeleine paid for her ham roll and tea and looked around for somewhere to sit. There was a spare chair at a two-person table near the door. She walked across and looked down at the other occupant.

'Hello, Frankie. Mind if I sit here?'

Frankie Carson lifted his head and smiled. A sincere smile containing a genuine warmth which Madeleine didn't see that often around the courts.

'My pleasure,' he said.

Madeleine sat down and gave him a quick glance. Then a

second, more considered look. A cursory inspection was never enough to fully take in Frankie's striking appearance. He was a flamboyant character. Well built, with a trencherman's girth and a balding head giving way to a luxuriant pony-tail which gave the impression that his pate had somehow slipped back-wards, taking all the hair with it. He had the dress sense of a colour-blind American tourist and was sporting a pair of baggy maroon trousers and a vivid orange and luminous green shirt, the kind of shirt you see in department stores and wonder, who on earth would buy a shirt like that?

'How are you, Maddy?' he said.

'Tired,' Madeleine replied.

She didn't need to ask him the same question. Frankie was fat, but he always looked in the pink of good health, quite liter-ally so for he had a soft, smooth complexion the colour of a new-born piglet's belly.

'What's that you're reading?' she asked instead, seeing the Penguin Classic in his hand.

He showed her the cover: *King Solomon's Mines*.

'Good?' she said.

'Tosh, but entertaining. Doesn't take too much concentration. All that *Boy's Own* stuff, chasing around Africa searching for diamonds.'

He closed the book and put it down on the table. Then he gave her a sly look, half smiling.

'You know, I was reading the introduction. Tells you a bit about Rider Haggard. Apparently, he was a complete dunce at school. Hopeless. He failed the entrance exam for the Army, was too stupid to get into the diplomatic service, so you know what he did? He became a lawyer.'

'They didn't have private detectives then, Frankie,' Madeleine said. 'So his first choice was out.'

Frankie grinned at her and took a sip of his coffee. Madeleine ate some of her ham roll. The bread was dried out, the ham tough and fatty. She pushed it to one side.

'So what brings you into town?' she asked.

Madeleine had used Frankie on a few cases in the past. He was good. To look at him you'd think he was too conspicuous to be a gumshoe, but his outrageous style was one of his great assets. He just didn't look like a detective. He was likeable, disarming. People talked to him, they revealed things they would never have divulged to someone who looked like a snooper. And information and careless talk were Frankie's business.

'Custody case in the Youth and Family Court,' he said. 'I was due on this morning but they haven't called me yet. Acrimonious divorce dispute. Husband wants custody of the kids because his wife left him for another woman. Took the kids with her. He says she's unfit to be a mother.'

'And is she?'

'What do I know? He hired me to follow her around for a couple of weeks. I was hoping for some kind of dyke orgy at the very least but she just went shopping at Sainsbury's, took the kids swimming, picked them up from school, took them to ballet, to piano lessons. Christ, it was boring. If I was a middle-class suburban couple with kids, I'd have to have myself humanely put down.'

Madeleine smiled. She didn't know much about Frankie's private life – didn't want to know – but she was aware it was less than conventional. He'd been a police officer once, but left the force after some undisclosed sexual indiscretion. She couldn't imagine him as a copper, conforming to all the rules, the prejudices.

'But get this,' Frankie continued gleefully. 'The wife found out I was tailing her and subpoenaed me to give evidence on her behalf – to show what a clean, healthy life she's leading.

The husband is really pissed off. He's paid my fee and now my evidence is being used against him.' Frankie made a wry face. 'Beautiful, isn't it? How about you? Anything interesting?'

'The usual,' Madeleine said. 'Something a little different this afternoon. An eco-protester, a young lad, pulled up crops, smashed up a lab out at Transgenic Biotech early this morning.'

'I heard about it on the radio on my way in. One was killed, wasn't he?'

Madeleine nodded. 'Knocked down by a Land-Rover.'

'What a waste. I hope you get the other one off. Those biotech companies are a bloody menace.'

'You don't like them?'

Frankie gave a short, cynical guffaw. 'They're only interested in profit, in controlling agriculture. They'll destroy the planet if we're not careful.'

He finished his coffee and checked his watch.

'Sorry, I have to be going. I'm on at two. I'll see you around.'

'I love the shirt, Frankie,' Madeleine said. 'I just hope the magistrates are wearing sunglasses.'

It was five miles from the farm to the nearest doctor's surgery, the medical centre in Great Dunchurch, and there was not a single yard of it that Sandy remembered driving. Not a single minute of the journey when she couldn't hear her own throbbing heart, feel the taut sickness in her guts.

Why the hell didn't doctors make house visits any more? All the money they earned and they couldn't even be bothered to come out unless you were at death's door. Bring her in, we'll have a look at her, the medical centre receptionist had said. I'm not sure she's up to travelling, Sandy had replied. Can I speak to the doctor? He's out on call, an emergency, the receptionist had said in her snotty way. This *is* an emergency, Sandy had felt like screaming, but she hadn't. She didn't want to make a fuss.

She didn't want to get hysterical on the phone. Maybe it wasn't an emergency. Maybe I'm overreacting, she thought. She didn't know what it was.

Phoebe was strapped in the car seat in the back. Sandy kept turning round to check her. She was slumped sideways, half asleep, shifting occasionally. She was still boiling hot, breathing rapidly. Sandy had checked the symptoms in the Family Health Digest before she left, terrified it was meningitis. The vomiting, the temperature, the drowsiness, the dislike of bright light all matched the illness, every parent's worst nightmare. But some of the other classic symptoms weren't present. There was no rash on Phoebe's stomach and she was curled forwards. That was a good sign. Sandy knew that with meningitis children arched their spines the other way. So what was it?

She waited five minutes at the surgery, Phoebe twitching feverishly in her lap, before the doctor returned. He saw them immediately. He took Phoebe's temperature, her pulse and blood pressure, examined her chest and back through a stethoscope and checked her stomach and eyes and ears. There was nothing exceptional about the examination. Sandy had watched the doctor do it nearly every time one of the children had been ill. But there was something different about it today – the doctor's manner, his movements, the expression on his face. There was an urgency about it she hadn't seen before. For the first time she knew the doctor was worried.

He went quickly through the symptoms with her, scribbling notes. When had Phoebe started feeling ill? When had she been sick? What did the vomit look like? Had she eaten anything unusual? Did she have a headache, a sore throat, stomach pains? Sandy answered as best she could, then the doctor excused himself and left the surgery. He was back within a minute.

'I've sent for an ambulance,' he said calmly. 'Your daughter needs to be in hospital.'

'Hospital?' Sandy said, her voice going hoarse. 'What's the matter with her?'

'I don't know,' the doctor admitted. 'But she's not well. They'll take her to Cambridge, to Addenbrooke's.'

'I can take her in the car.'

'An ambulance is better,' the doctor said.

Sandy called Jeff from the phone in reception, telling him what had happened, asking him to collect Tim from school. Then she sat with Phoebe, holding her on her knee, feeling faint with anxiety until the ambulance arrived. The paramedics were big, gentle men. Quiet and reassuring. One of them carried Phoebe out to the ambulance. Sandy wanted to go in the back with them, but what would she do about the car?

'You follow on behind,' one of the paramedics said. 'We'll look after her.'

Sandy saw them lay Phoebe down on a stretcher and place an oxygen mask over her face. Then the doors clicked shut. She ran to her car and followed the ambulance out on to the main road.

'How are you feeling, Jake?' Madeleine said.

'I'm okay.'

He was looking a little better, less pale and drawn than he had at the police station. His anti-contamination suit had been taken away for forensic analysis and he was wearing a clean T-shirt and trousers brought in by a friend Madeleine had rung for him when she'd left Parkside.

'Are you sure you don't want me to let your parents know?' Madeleine said. He'd already said no when she'd asked him at the police station, but she thought he might have changed his mind. A few hours in a cramped police cell often made people more appreciative of family support.

But Jake was having none of it. 'They won't care. They live in Dorchester anyway.'

'This is going to be on the news, you know. They'll find out. Your name will be in the papers.'

'The papers? Why would they be interested in me?' he said naively.

'These kinds of protest aren't new, but no one's been killed during one before. That's the difference. Your friend Dan died.'

'He wasn't my friend,' Jake said indifferently.

Madeleine was surprised. 'He wasn't?'

'I only met him this morning. I didn't even know what his surname was until that copper came in and said he was dead.'

Jake's manner had changed since Madeleine had last seen him. The signs of shock seemed to have gone. He was in control of his emotions, apparently untouched by the accident he'd witnessed.

'Did you know any of the other protesters?' Madeleine said.

'A couple. Most of them I'd never seen before. It was all fixed through the Net.' He saw her blank expression and explained. 'You know, the Internet. If you know where to look and understand the codes you can find out about things like this. It tells you where to meet, what to bring. No one knows who's organised it so the police can't pin the blame on any one individual. And it moves so quickly they don't know where we're going to strike next.'

'How come it was just you and Dan in the lab?'

'I was the only one he asked.'

'It was Dan's idea?'

'Yes. What does it matter now?'

Madeleine was making notes on her A4 pad. She looked up.

'You're probably facing a custodial sentence, Jake. Anything we can use in mitigation is going to be useful. It might get the sentence reduced.'

'You mean blame Dan? I don't want that.'

'You said it was his idea.'

45

'Yes, but I didn't have to go with him. I take full responsibility for what I did. I'm prepared to stand up and be counted. That's what this is all about. Direct action.'

Madeleine sighed. 'Have you ever been in prison, Jake?'

'No.'

'Believe me, it's not pleasant. I'd advise you to do everything you can to get your sentence reduced.'

Jake turned his head away, looking around the bare walls of the Magistrates' Courts holding cell. He was different from most of Madeleine's other clients. He was educated, middle-class. He had a job, somewhere to live. What he'd done had been out of idealistic principle, not necessity. But Madeleine had dealt with hundreds of young men his age. Whatever the bravado, she knew they were all scared children underneath.

'I'm here to help you, Jake,' she said. 'I'm on your side.'

'What are my chances of bail?' he asked.

'Reasonable. You don't have a record, you're in stable employment, you have somewhere to live. You're not likely to abscond or interfere with witnesses. You caused a lot of damage, which will be held against you, but if you agree to certain conditions you have a fair chance of getting bail.'

'What conditions?'

'I'm going to suggest a number to the bench. That you continue to live in your bedsit; that's not a problem for you. And you report to a police station at regular times during the week. That's a standard condition of most bail arrangements. In addition, you'll have to agree to go nowhere near any property or building owned by Transgenic Biotechnology. The Crown Prosecution Service will insist on that. Will you accept those conditions?'

'I don't think I did anything wrong, you know,' Jake said. 'Companies like them are evil. They're the criminals. They're tampering with nature, redesigning life itself. It's wrong. They should be in court, not me.'

'Let's deal with the practicalities first,' Madeleine said firmly. 'Will you agree to those bail conditions?'

Jake thought for a long time, then he shrugged.

'Yeah, okay. I agree.'

Phoebe had already been taken upstairs into the Paediatric Intensive Care Unit by the time her mother found somewhere to park and then located the Casualty Department at Addenbrooke's. A nurse took Sandy up in the lift to the first floor. They went through a secure door and down a corridor to a room cluttered with medical equipment: machines and tubes and monitors.

Phoebe was on the bed, whimpering deliriously while two doctors in white coats examined her. The doctors glanced round as Sandy approached the bed.

'Are you the mother?' one of them said. She was in her thirties, with short blonde hair and a security badge indicating that she was a Registrar.

'Yes.' Sandy reached out for her daughter. 'It's all right, sweetheart, Mummy's here.'

She took hold of Phoebe's left hand. It was hot and sticky and limp. She stroked it, murmuring softly, trying to reassure her daughter. Phoebe's eyes were closed, her head turned to one side, the fringe of her hair damp with sweat. The other doctor, a younger man – Senior House Officer, his badge read – was inserting something into the back of Phoebe's right hand and taking a sample of blood. Phoebe didn't seem to feel it. She was like a ragdoll lying there all floppy on the bed.

'How old is your daughter?' the Registrar asked.

'She's four. What's the matter with her?' Sandy said. 'Is she going to be all right?'

'We've brought her in here as a precaution,' the Registrar said. 'We're going to keep her in overnight.'

'Can I stay?'

'We can arrange for a bed for you, yes. Come and sit down, I need to ask you a few questions.'

The Registrar steered Sandy out of the room to a chair by the nurses' station. She repeated all the same questions the GP at Great Dunchurch had asked.

'What's the matter with her?' Sandy kept asking. All other questions seemed irrelevant. But the Registrar didn't answer.

'Has your daughter eaten anything unusual?' she said. 'Berries? Any pills or medicines?'

'No,' Sandy replied. 'Why?'

'Excuse me a minute.'

The Registrar moved away as an older man with rimless glasses came down the corridor. His badge read: 'Dr J. Cornwell, Consultant Paediatrician.' They went into the room and began to converse in low tones. Sandy watched them helplessly through the open door, feeling excluded, useless. Finally, she stood up and went across to confront them.

'You have to tell me what's happening. I need to know,' she said. There was a lump in her throat and she was trying desperately not to cry.

'We don't know exactly what's wrong with your daughter,' the consultant said smoothly. 'We're taking samples of blood to check in the laboratory and we're going to give her a dose of activated charcoal. It'll be mixed with fruit yoghurt to make it more palatable but we'll probably need your help in getting your daughter to swallow it.'

'Activated charcoal? What's that?' Sandy said.

'It binds together a variety of drugs and chemicals in the system,' the consultant explained. 'It's quite harmless.'

'But what's it for?'

48

'From your daughter's symptoms, we think she may have been poisoned.'

Madeleine pushed open the door and stepped over the threshold into the hall. From the eerie silence she knew her son was not at home. Graham did nothing quietly. His every activity, from brushing his teeth to doing his homework, was accompanied by either the relentless throb of pop music or, worse, his own feeble vocal attempts. But she called out nevertheless.

'Graham? You in?'

She went through into the kitchen. The clock on the wall read 8.15. There were dirty pans and a plate by the sink. Madeleine inspected them, noting the strand of cold spaghetti in a puddle of congealed tomato sauce. At least he'd had a proper meal.

He was old enough to cook for himself, but Madeleine still felt guilty for not being there to do it for him. In the early days she'd always made sure she came home in time to make them both dinner. She'd enjoyed those shared moments, the intimacy of evenings alone with her son. But over the last couple of years it had all slipped. She found herself working later, seeing clients, doing paperwork after office hours because she was in court all day. And Graham was just as busy, always off out somewhere, to friends', playing sport. They were drifting apart. Madeleine saw that as inevitable, as healthy, but the house seemed very empty without him.

She put the kettle on and a slice of bread in the toaster, too tired to think of cooking something for herself. There was no note. She wondered where Graham had gone. He knew she worried about him, she'd told him often enough, and he usually left a note. Perhaps he'd forgotten this time. Or perhaps it was his way of punishing her for not being there.

She went upstairs and changed out of her work suit. On her way back down she made a detour into Graham's bedroom, telling herself she was simply going in to pick up the dirty clothes he never put in the laundry basket, but in reality going for a nose around. She hated herself for it. Yet, as he never told her anything voluntarily, it was her only way of keeping tabs on his life. His surly uncommunicativeness drove her mad. He seemed to regard even innocuous questions as a form of interrogation, either flying off the handle or clamming up entirely when she tried to start a conversation with him.

It was normal for a teenager, of course, but Madeleine – maybe her job had something to do with it – was paranoid about making sure he kept out of trouble. Graham was lazy. He'd never been very conscientious about his schoolwork. His GCSE results the previous summer had been a lot worse than she thought they should have been and she was determined he wasn't going to blow his A-Levels as well.

She checked his desk. It looked the same as it had that morning. No sign that any work had recently been done at it. Madeleine sighed. She'd ask him later – if she was still up when he came in. She went back downstairs, feeling despondent now. Professionally, it had been a very successful day. But the job meant nothing to her when her personal life was going awry. She knew she wasn't a good mother. Just as she hadn't been a good wife.

The first thing Jake did when he got home was take a shower, swilling away the taint of the police station and the courtroom. He was glad to be out. Relieved too. The prospect of several months on remand before his trial had terrified him. The solicitor woman – what was her name? Miss King – had done her job well. She knew her stuff all right. He'd been impressed by the way she'd argued his case, the way she'd outflanked the wanker in the suit, the CPS solicitor. He'd never believed he'd get bail, not after the police refused, but the magistrates had retired for twenty minutes – each second of it an agony for him – and returned to say he was free, provided he kept to the conditions Miss King had suggested. Two of them were a cinch: living at a fixed address and reporting to Parkside police station Mondays and Thursdays after work. The third, going nowhere near any Transgenic Biotech property, was tougher. He'd have to think about that one.

He watched the six o'clock news on TV: the protest and the death of Dan was one of the headlines. There was even a clip of Jake emerging from the Magistrates' Court, saying nothing, of course, on the instructions of Miss King. That had been hard. He'd wanted to go on camera and put the case against the biotech industry but he was glad he hadn't. Television companies edited what you said, distorted it. And where did talking ever get you?

Miss King had made a brief statement, saying that they would be bringing assault charges against the company's security guards. Jake liked that. She was feisty, a real fighter. Then there was a short interview with some PR man from the company who spouted the usual bullshit about how GM crops were perfectly safe, no threat to people or the environment. The final clip was of the Minister for Agriculture standing outside MAFF headquarters in Whitehall, defending the biotech industry. 'We offer our condolences to the family of the young man who was killed. This was a terrible, senseless accident which highlights the risks protesters take when they engage in these unlawful activities. The Government's policy on GM crops remains unchanged. They must be properly and rigorously tested to ensure they are safe to grow and eat. The biotech companies involved in GM research have our full support. This kind of violent protest against them is counter-productive and, as today's events show, can lead to tragic consequences.'

Jake swore at the screen and switched the television off. Politicians, they were all the same. He opened a can of beer and went over to the electric stove in the corner of his bedsit. He stir-fried a few vegetables with some chilli sauce for his dinner, then put on his jacket and went out. He'd called a couple of mates, arranged to meet them at a pub off the Newmarket Road.

He was ten minutes away, over the other side of the railway line, cutting through the backstreets near an MOT service garage, when he realised he'd left his wallet behind. Shit! He'd put it on the chest of drawers when he changed his clothes after the shower and forgotten to transfer it to his new trousers. He turned round and walked back to his bedsit.

Nearing the front door of the two-up, two-down terraced house – each floor converted into two tiny bedsits – he paused. Something wasn't right. The ground-floor front room curtains were drawn and there was a light on behind them. He knew for certain he hadn't pulled the curtains or switched on the light. It was only now getting dark outside.

Jake took out his front door key and weighed it in his hand, wondering if he should call the police. But he'd had enough of the law for one day. He'd handle this himself. He inserted the key quietly into the lock and turned it, pushing open the door. He took a few steps down the hall and stopped outside the door to his bedsit. He listened. He could hear sounds inside. Very carefully, he used his Yale key to unlock the door and swing it open. Two men were searching methodically through his things, examining his possessions and replacing them exactly where they'd found them.

'Who the fuck are you?' Jake said angrily.

The men turned. Jake saw their faces clearly. Thick-set, beefy men with short-back-and-sides haircuts; wearing suits and black leather gloves. They stared at him for an instant, then charged at him. They were unexpectedly fast considering their size. Jake had no time to get out of the way before they knocked him to the floor. His face hit the edge of the skirting board, opening up a gash in his cheek. A foot thudded into his stomach, once, twice. Winded, Jake took a few seconds to drag himself to his feet and run after them. They'd gone out the back way, across the yard and through the gate on to the street at the rear of the houses. Jake heard car doors slamming, an engine kicking into life. He stumbled out on to the street and saw a dark blue Rover saloon, its number plate obscured by mud, racing away. It turned hard left towards the railway line and was gone.

4

Jeff Harrison had been farming for the best part of fifteen years so the long hours and the sheer physical grind of the job were drawbacks to which he'd grown accustomed. He'd got used to getting up at dawn, to seeing to the animals before the rest of the household were stirring. The cold, the darkness, the wind which never seemed to stop blowing across his fields were discomforts he'd learnt to live with. Most mornings he barely noticed them. But he did today.

He'd had a bad night. Worrying about Phoebe in hospital, missing the warmth of his wife's body next to him in bed. Sandy had telephoned him from the hospital the previous evening. *Poisoned*! he'd exclaimed. What do they mean, poisoned? They don't know, Sandy had said, but Jeff didn't believe it. Doctors always kept things from you. Told you half the story. So he'd been awake most of the night, thinking about Phoebe, half expecting another phone call to say she'd got worse. That was what the mind did when you were starved of information, too far away to ask questions and demand answers. He'd wanted to go in to Addenbrooke's, to be there with his daughter too. But there were Lucy and Tim to consider. Someone had to stay with them.

He'd slept fitfully, and when he awoke there was a heaviness in his limbs which he initially put down to tiredness. He swung his legs out of bed. The muscles, from the thigh to the ankle, all seemed to ache. He had a sore throat too. He took a sip of water from the glass on the bedside table and forced himself to get dressed. This was more than tiredness. Lack of sleep alone wouldn't have accounted for the groggy way he felt. He dosed himself with a couple of paracetamol tablets from the bathroom cabinet and went downstairs. He was shivering violently. He put on a heavy jacket. It was summer but the house was always cold at this time of the morning. Going outside into the yard, he had to steady himself momentarily against the wall before he felt up to attempting the walk across to the pigshed. The fresh air seemed to revive him a little but he still felt feverish and weak. It occurred to him fleetingly that he might be going down with whatever Phoebe had – the children's illnesses invariably ended up infecting the whole family in turn – but that didn't make sense. Poisoning wasn't contagious, was it?

The pigs were awake and ready for their morning feed. Jeff filled their troughs with a mixture of cereals and potatoes and an organic protein supplement. Marsham Grange was an organic farm. Potatoes were the main crop, but they also grew brassicas and kept hens and a few pigs. Jeff replenished the water in the drinking bowls and leant on the metal railing around the pen. He felt faint. His head ached now, a sharp pain behind the eyes that seemed to penetrate deep into his skull. He wondered if he was going to be sick.

He noticed a couple of the pigs were off their feed. They were still lying down on the straw outside their wooden ark. One of them had mucus trickling from her nostrils. Jeff felt too weak to open the gate for a closer look. A hot and cold wave surged through his body. He knew he had to lie down. He went out of the shed and stumbled across the yard.

Lucy and Tim were still upstairs in bed. Jeff staggered through into the hall.

'Lucy!' he called weakly. 'Lucy!'

He just had enough strength to call out a third time before he collapsed to the floor.

When Madeleine was a university student, she'd found what purported to be an old legal aphorism in a book of quotations. 'Justice is about truth, law is about lying', it read. It had appealed to the cynic in her, and when she started to practise she'd had it written out in copperplate script and framed and had hung it on the wall over her desk, much to the disapproval of her older colleagues.

She still had it in her office. She found it helped her to keep what she did in perspective. The law was a very smug, grand institution, but it had never concerned itself much with the truth. The English legal system was accusatorial in nature, not inquisatorial. It was not the court's duty to uncover the truth of a matter, but simply to decide whether on the evidence an accused person was guilty. Proof beyond all reasonable doubt was all that was required. Not absolute proof. Just enough proof to convince a jury. Truth was a vague, lofty ideal that floated around the cloistered groves of academe, but which, had it accidentally strayed into a courtroom, would soon have been sent packing. Assuming anyone even recognised it, that is.

Lying, however, was anything but a stranger in the courtroom. Witnesses did it, defendants, occasionally lawyers though Madeleine had never knowingly told an untruth in court. It wasn't her job to lie for her clients, most of them could do that quite well by themselves, but nor was it her job to do the prosecution's work for them. They had to prove their cases. It was her role to make sure they did it properly.

She was conscientious about it, preparing her cases as thoroughly as she could, though she knew a lot of it was wasted effort. A large number of her clients pleaded guilty, the evidence against them was often incontrovertible, and all she could do was try to mitigate the sentence.

The evidence against Jake Brewster was pretty damning. If he'd wanted to be difficult, he could possibly have denied being in the laboratory. He'd been wearing a hooded anti-contamination suit and mask so the security guards would have been hard-pressed to identify him specifically. But Jake didn't want to deny it. He was proud of the fact that he'd smashed up the place. Those were his colours, and he wanted them pinned firmly to the mast.

'I don't recognise what I did as an offence,' he told Madeleine once again, slouching back in the chair on the other side of her desk.

It was nine o'clock and she had roughly forty minutes to fill in all the Legal Aid forms and get him to sign them before she was due in court.

'If something is wrong, and what that company and all the rest of them are doing *is* wrong, then you have a moral duty to oppose them, even if it means breaking the law yourself. It's civil disobedience. Socrates was all in favour of it.'

Madeleine looked up from her forms. None of her clients had ever quoted Socrates at her before. 'Do you have any savings?' she said.

'What?'

'Savings. If you have more than £3,000 in capital you're liable to pay a contribution towards your legal costs.'

'Three grand?' Jake said. 'Do I look as if I have three grand in the bank?'

'I have to ask.' She paused. She'd just noticed the new cut on his face. 'You didn't have that gash yesterday, did you?'

Jake fingered his cheek. 'I got it last night.' He told her what had happened.

'Did you report it to the police?' Madeleine asked.

'I spent half the day in a police cell,' Jake replied. 'I wasn't too keen on having anything more to do with the bloody police. And besides . . .'

Madeleine waited for him to go on. 'Yes?'

'No, you'll think I'm being paranoid.'

'What is it, Jake?'

'Well, I think they *were* the police.'

Madeleine frowned at him, wondering if she'd misunderstood. 'You think the burglars were police officers? Are you serious?'

Jake shrugged. 'They had that look. You know. There's something about a copper. Their size, their haircuts, the way they carry themselves. You can always spot them.'

'Are you sure?'

'Of course I'm not sure. They could have been anyone. But they didn't look like ordinary burglars.'

'What does an ordinary burglar look like?'

'You know, kids. Smash your back window and climb in. Nick your video and CD and scarper. They're inside only a couple of minutes. These blokes were in their thirties, maybe older, wearing suits and gloves. And they didn't break anything. Even the locks on the doors were intact.'

'You should report this.'

'Come on, what for? You think the police are going to take it seriously? To them, I'm just an irresponsible vandal. Anyway, they didn't take anything.'

Madeleine studied his face. 'Jake, I have to ask you this. Are you mixed up in anything else that might bring you to the attention of the police?'

'Like what?'

'I don't know. Anything criminal. What were those men doing there?'

'Looking for information, I'd guess,' Jake said. 'Names,

contacts in the Green movement. There were more than thirty of us in that field yesterday. They only caught three. They'll want to know who the others were, won't they.'

He seemed remarkably sanguine about the whole thing. But Madeleine, though she had few illusions about the police, was genuinely shocked. 'They can't do that,' she said, knowing she sounded uncharacteristically naive.

'But they do,' Jake said. 'It's not worth bothering about. They won't find anything in my bedsit. Now what else do you need to know? For the forms.'

Reluctantly, Madeleine turned back to the Legal Aid application, filling in the relevant sections and getting Jake to sign them.

But after he'd gone, she stayed seated at her desk for a time, thinking through everything he'd told her; at Parkside police station, in the cells at Lion Yard and now in her office. Then she looked up a telephone number in her contacts book and punched it in.

'Frankie? It's Madeleine King. I wonder if I could ask you a favour?'

'Thanks for coming, Karl. Take a seat.'

John Cornwell gestured towards the cheap moulded plastic chair to one side of the door. Karl Housman sat down on it awkwardly. He was six feet seven inches tall. His rangy figure swamped the chair, making it look as if it had come from a child's playhouse. There was a third man in the room Housman didn't know. Cornwell introduced them to each other.

'Chris Webster. Chris is a Registrar in General Medicine but he has an MRC project on the go, doing research into toxicology – principally the effects of drug overdoses on the body. Karl is a virologist, consultant in infectious diseases.'

The two men shook hands, then waited for Cornwell to continue. He gave a brief outline of Phoebe Harrison's symptoms, addressing Housman alone. Webster already knew the background.

'The headache, the vomiting, the ataxia, drowsiness and respiratory depression were all consistent with some kind of poisoning so I asked Chris to do a toxicological analysis,' Cornwell said. 'Chris?'

Webster turned to Housman. 'We did all the usual checks, for salicylates, paracetamol, iron, ethanol and lithium. The child's mother said she hadn't accidentally taken any pills, but you can never be absolutely sure with kids. They all came up negative. So we did an assay. And found a huge level of glycoalkaloids in her bloodstream.'

Housman adjusted his glasses. The metal frame on one side was held together with Sellotape. Toxicology wasn't his field but he knew what a glycoalkaloid was. 'Which ones?' he said.

'Principally solanine. That made me think of two possible sources, both plants in the family *Solanaceae* – *Solanum dulcamara*, the woody nightshade, and *Solanum nigrum*, the black or garden nightshade.'

'She's eaten deadly nightshade?'

'That was my first guess, ' Webster said. 'But the other glycoalkaloids didn't fit that hypothesis. With *Solanum dulcamara* I would have expected to also find traces of solaneine, solaceine and dulcamaric acid. I didn't. Similarly, with *Solanum nigrum* there should have been traces of tropeine and tropane. Negative in both cases. But what I did find was a high level of chaconine.'

'Indicating what?' Housman said.

'The only member of the *Solanaceae* family containing both solanine and chaconine is *Solanum tuberosum*. The common potato.'

Housman blinked. 'She's suffering from potato poisoning? Is that possible?'

'It's happened. Potato leaves, of course, are known to be

poisonous. So are the tubers if they're exposed to light and turn green, or if they're stored incorrectly. But the levels of solanine and chaconine I found . . .' Webster gave a bewildered shrug. 'She'd have to have eaten one hell of a lot of green potatoes.'

'What's her condition?' Housman asked Cornwell.

'Stable. We've given her activated charcoal. She's in the ICU on a drip and ventilator. We would have expected her to be showing signs of recovery by now.'

'But she isn't?'

Cornwell shook his head. 'Which is where you come in, Karl.'

What was it about doctors, Sandy wondered, that made them so bad at handling people, so oblivious to the emotions, the distress of those around them? Was it the nature of the recruitment process? That the teenagers who made it into medical school were all fundamentally insensitive? Or did that arrogance and casual indifference come later, as the routine of dealing with the sick and dying destroyed part of their innate humanity, inuring them to the suffering that was an unavoidable adjunct to their jobs?

There were three of them examining Phoebe now. Standing around her bed, touching her, prodding her, checking all the bits of equipment that were fastened to her tiny body. Sandy had been asked to move away and she watched them from a distance. She was Phoebe's mother but she might not have existed. She'd sat by her side for half the night, her thighs and legs numb from the rock-hard chair, until one of the nurses had finally persuaded her to retire to the bed they'd made up for her in the adjoining room. Yet they treated her as if she weren't there, these three men in white coats who strolled in and chatted coolly together in loud voices while her daughter twitched and sweated in a semi-coma before them. Sandy was angry, her anger fuelled in part by an anxiety so intense she felt permanently sick. She'd slept for a couple of hours only, exhaustion eventually getting the better of her fears. She was worn out, terrified, and now they ignored her.

Dr Cornwell, the consultant paediatrician, she recognised from the previous evening. The other two she was pretty sure she'd never seen before. Certainly the tall one was too striking to forget. A giant of a man in his early forties, quite good-looking but unkempt. The collar of his shirt was frayed, his mop of brown hair untouched by a comb and was that really Sellotape holding his glasses together? The second newcomer was a little younger, and obviously junior to the other two. Sandy could tell from his deferential manner. In hospitals, the pecking order of doctors was as strict and regimented as in the Army. He looked round at her, discussing her with his colleagues, then all three walked over.

'Mrs Harrison?' the younger man said. 'I'm Dr Webster. I've been doing a toxicological analysis of your daughter's blood. It shows a very high level of toxic substances known as glyco-alkaloids. Has Phoebe eaten any potato leaves by accident over the last twenty-four hours?'

'Potato leaves?' Sandy struggled to understand what the doctor was talking about. 'Of course not. Why on earth would she eat potato leaves?'

'It's just that the particular glycoalkaloids we've found are present in potato leaves. They're also found in green potatoes, though in much smaller quantities. Has she eaten any green potatoes?'

'Well, she had potatoes last night, for her tea. But they weren't green.'

'Sometimes poor storage or fungal infection can increase the level of glycoalkaloids. Where did you get the potatoes?'

'They're our own. We have a farm.'

'How were they stored?'

'They weren't. They were fresh from the ground.'

'What about sprays and pesticides?'

'We don't use any. It's an organic farm. Look, are you saying Phoebe was poisoned by *potatoes*?'

'It's a possibility,' Webster said.

Sandy was incredulous. 'But we eat them all the time. So does everyone else in the country. How can she have been harmed by something as healthy and natural as a potato?'

Webster was used to people equating natural foods with safe foods. But some of the most toxic substances on earth were 'natural'. Too much solanine could kill. So could too much caffeine, or carotene or tomatine in tomatoes. People drank comfrey tea, you could buy it in health food shops, yet comfrey was a deadly poison. It was quantity, and balance, that counted.

'How many potatoes did she eat last night?' he asked.

'I made chips. She had a good helping, though . . .' Sandy had just remembered. 'She did say they tasted a bit funny. I gave her some tomato ketchup to put on them. That seemed to make them better. But she didn't eat all of them. And they were cooked.'

'I'm afraid cooking doesn't destroy glycoalkaloids,' Webster said.

'So how ill is she?' Sandy asked, a sense of guilt adding to her worries. They were accusing her of poisoning her own daughter.

It was Dr Cornwell who answered. 'It may not be just the glycoalkaloid poisoning that your daughter's suffering from. There may be something else, a virus of some sort. That's what Dr Housman here is going to look into.'

'A virus?' When doctors didn't know what something was, they always said it was a virus. It was her GP's favourite cop-out. 'It's probably a virus, there's nothing I can do,' was what he always said when she took one of the children to the surgery.

But Sandy wanted more than that. This was a hospital. These people were supposed to be experts.

'What sort of virus?'

'It's impossible to say at the moment,' Housman replied. He had a deep bass voice, warmer than she'd expected. 'But you can rest assured that we're going to do everything we can for her.'

'Do what? What are you going to do? She's very ill, isn't she? You have to *tell* me.'

Sandy brushed away a tear. She didn't want to cry in front of these men, but she was close to cracking. 'What are you going to *do* for her?' she implored.

The doctors glanced at one another, uncomfortable at this display of emotion. But they were spared the necessity of answering by a nurse who came into the room, her eyes roving over their faces, then coming to rest on Sandy.

'Mrs Harrison?'

'Yes.'

'Your daughter told the ambulancemen you were here.'

'My daughter?' Sandy said, puzzled. 'Lucy? Oh, God, she's not . . .'

'It's not your daughter,' the nurse broke in. 'It's your husband. He's just been admitted to Casualty. I think you'd better come with me.'

When Frankie Carson had first set up in business as a private investigator, he'd had an office in the centre of town, a cramped, dingy little place near the old Corn Exchange which looked as if it hadn't been decorated, or even cleaned, for half a century. It had rickety stairs leading up from the street, dark wood panelling on the walls and a fusty, decrepit atmosphere redolent of a television adaptation of Dickens. It was meant for clerks with quill pens and fat men in waistcoats and stovepipe hats, not a progressive, high-tech investigation agency. The only modern thing about it was the rent, an extortionate sum levied monthly by the landlord – one of the better-endowed colleges – who believed strongly in the ancient virtues of thrift, godliness and screwing your tenants for every penny you could get.

Frankie had stayed there for six months, believing misguidedly that a central location was essential for any serious enterprise, before he realised that it made no difference to his flow of work. There was no passing trade; he acquired most of his business through word of mouth and the Yellow Pages. Also – and this was the crucial deciding factor – there was nowhere to park his car. With his build, he wasn't ideally suited to walking and he certainly wasn't going to make an exhibition of himself on a bicycle. So a car was essential, both to his well-being and the proper servicing of his clientele.

He now had an office above a take-away pizza parlour in Cherry Hinton, on the south-eastern side of the city – a convenient location as he had only a few stairs to negotiate to reach his lunch. It had parking at the rear and enough space for his own desk and a second for an assistant who was mentioned frequently to clients and whose work was billed accordingly but who had yet to appear on the company payroll.

Frankie was not a great adherent of the Protestant work ethic. He did just enough to get by and support his relatively modest lifestyle, which was why he happened to have a few hours free when Madeleine King telephoned him.

He liked Maddy. She was straight, down-to-earth and she worked her bollocks off for the bunch of drop-outs and losers she always seemed to represent. Frankie wouldn't have put himself out for many other solicitors in the city but Maddy was different. She'd earned a few favours.

'I'll see what I can do,' he'd said. Then he'd made a couple of phone calls, the first to the Coroner's Officer, the second to an old police crony he knew from his days on the Cambridgeshire force. Then he went downstairs and out to his car.

He drove north across the city and over the Elizabeth Way bridge, pulling off the main road to check his *A–Z*. This was an affluent, middle-class suburb, the houses set back from the road with mature bushes and trees overhanging the pavements. He'd had a client out here recently: a married woman who'd found a pair of red and black lacy silk knickers in her husband's car which didn't belong to her. Convinced her partner was being unfaithful, she'd hired Frankie to check him out. Frankie had tailed him for a couple of days but, discovering nothing suspicious about his behaviour, had begun to wonder about the knickers. They were size 18, enormous. The wife was slim, good-looking. Had her husband got bored with her and opted for a fling with some sixteen-stone shot-putter? Or was there another explanation?

Frankie had searched the client's house and found a trunk in the garage containing a whole selection of female lingerie: knickers, bras, teddies, corsets, basques – all classy and expensive. And all size 18. And the husband was a big guy. The wife had been first stunned, then livid as the realisation sank in. 'He's a pervert,' she'd said to Frankie. 'But, you know, what really pisses me off is that he's got a better bloody wardrobe than I have.'

The address Frankie was looking for was down by the river, a small block of luxury flats in its own compound with landscaped gardens and a private six-berth marina. Frankie drove in through the open gates and round to the main entrance to the block. He parked in an empty space and studied the flats for a time. Was this really the right address? The flats were only a few years old. They had big picture windows and balconies overlooking the river. A glossy lawn fringed with beds of begonias, salvia and lobelia stretched down to the water's edge where an opulent cabin cruiser was tied up to one of the moorings.

The Cam at this point was pretty enough, but it had none of

the carefully maintained charm of the Backs. No one punted in straw boaters out here. The river was deep and cloudy, fringed with the college and university boathouses. There was an Eight out training on the water; big, muscular young men straining against the oars. Frankie watched them, admiring their physiques, their bulging thighs and biceps. Then he sighed ruefully and climbed out of his car.

He walked across the parking area to the entrance to the flats. There were six bells on a panel by the front door, a name card beside each one. Dan Cruickshank was in Flat 4 on the first floor. Frankie rang his bell. Cruickshank was dead but you never knew, he might have had a live-in lover or a lodger.

There was no reply. Frankie examined the front door. It was made of heavy steel and had a sturdy-looking lock which he knew from experience would be difficult to pick, and even harder to force. Besides, force wasn't Frankie's style. He preferred to use his head.

He made a note of the other names on the bell panel. They were just surnames and initials, no indication of gender. Frankie had seen an elderly woman at the window of one of the second-floor flats when he approached the entrance. He checked the names. Flats 5 and 6 were occupied by L. Pargeter and K. Lim respectively. Lim, that sounded oriental. The woman had definitely looked English so he put her down as Pargeter. Then he went for a stroll around the back of the block, trying not to draw too much attention to himself but peering in through the ground-floor windows. Flat 1 was occupied by a man, he could tell from the colour scheme, the furniture, the personal belongings scattered around. Flat 2 had a more female ambience; china ornaments on a table, potted plants on the window-sills, a pink duvet cover on the bed. Frankie referred to his list of names. The occupant of Flat 2 was S. Carlisle.

Returning to his car, Frankie drove round to a row of shops

on Milton Road and bought a bouquet of flowers from a florist's. Then he went back to the block of flats and rang the bell for Pargeter in Flat 5. A woman's voice crackled over the intercom.

'Yes?'

'Interflora,' Frankie said. 'Delivery of flowers for Carlisle, Flat 2. There's no answer. Could I leave them with you?'

'Well, I'm not sure about that. Can't you come back later?'

'It's okay, I'll leave them here on the doorstep. Not to worry.'

'No, someone will steal them. You'd better bring them up.'

The front door lock clicked open. Frankie went inside, pausing to scribble a note on the card with the bouquet: 'You were great last night, darling', followed by an illegible signature. Then he went upstairs to the second floor. He left the bouquet with the elderly woman and walked slowly back downstairs, listening for the sound of her door closing.

On the first-floor landing he stopped outside the door to Dan Cruickshank's apartment. He tried the handle. He didn't need to depress it. The door swung inwards a few inches of its own accord. Frankie pushed it wider with his foot. There was a hallway inside with doors opening off it. Through one of them he caught a glimpse of an armchair and a television set.

'Hello?' Frankie called.

He looked down at the mortice lock. He'd worked ten years in CID, but it didn't take a detective to see that the lock had been forced – so cleanly it wasn't apparent from the outside. He slipped on a pair of thin cotton gloves he had in his pocket and wiped the door handle. Then he went inside.

It was a two-bedroom flat with a kitchen, bathroom and living room.

It was expensively furnished, thick carpets on the floors and Italian marble tiles in the bathroom and space-age kitchen. It didn't seem the kind of place an eco-protester would live.

Frankie went slowly through the rooms, trying to figure out

who'd been there before him. Not a common thief for sure: the television, a CD player, VCR and several stacks of compact discs were untouched in the living room. Not a cleaner nor a relative either. There was still food in the refrigerator – cheese and bacon and a carton of rancid milk – and clothes and other possessions in the main bedroom. Those were the first things someone would have cleared out, or at least sorted through after a death. And anyway, a cleaner or relative would have used a key to get in.

The second bedroom was more interesting. It contained book-shelves and a desk and chair. Frankie looked around from the doorway. Something about the room wasn't quite right. It was too empty. He knew from his phone calls that Dan Cruickshank had worked from home as an 'Environmental Consultant', what-ever one of those was. Yet this room didn't look like an office. There was none of the equipment he would have expected to find. There was a phone socket but no phone, a four-socket adapter plugged into the electricity supply but nothing plugged into the adapter.

Frankie crouched down and peered across the surface of the desk. A thin film of dust covered the whole top, except for a patch about eighteen inches square at the left-hand side. Frankie stood up and examined the empty shelves next to the desk, noting more distinctive patterns of dust. Then he pulled open the desk drawers. There was blank stationery, some headed note-paper and compliments slips in the top drawer. The other two drawers were empty.

Frankie sat down in the chair and stared thoughtfully out of the window. He had a clear view of the boathouses on the far bank of the river. The one immediately opposite was painted blue and white. It had long sloping eaves and a wooden balcony running the full width of the building which made it look like a dilapidated Swiss chalet. Below the balcony, on the ground floor, were three sets of double doors, one of which was open to reveal the rowing boats stacked inside. A lean young man in shorts and vest was carrying out a single scull and a pair of oars. He went down the concrete slipway and lowered the scull into the water. Frankie's eyes flickered back to the boathouse, noting something on the brick wall just above the doors.

He hauled himself to his feet and left the room. He gave the flat a quick final inspection to ensure he'd left no signs of his visit, then went out on to the landing, pulling the door to the way he'd found it.

Downstairs in the entrance hall, he was about to open the front door when he noticed some envelopes in a mesh mailbox on the external wall. The postman had been while he was upstairs. Frankie opened the box and fingered through the letters. Something for Pargeter, something for Miss Susan Carlisle – a copy of the *Catholic Herald*, so he hoped she'd appreciate the card he'd left with the flowers – and a long white envelope for Dan Cruickshank. Frankie slipped the envelope into his inside jacket pocket and went out.

It was a breezy day. The wind was chopping at the surface of the river, breaking it up into rippling slivers. The young man glided past in the single scull, his oars barely disturbing the surface of the water. A sudden gust caught Frankie's pony-tail, blowing it over his shoulder. He flipped it back and checked the strands of hair were still fastened together. It had always been a tricky decision, working out what to tie his pony-tail back with. Young girls could use coloured ribbon, grown women a metal or tortoiseshell clasp, but what did a man use? He'd tried a simple rubber band but that looked cheap. He'd tried threading it through a boiled sheep's vertebra – a throwback to his days as a Boy Scout when it had been cool and trendy to use a sheep's backbone instead of a woggle, and the hills of the western Peak District had teemed with spotty teenage boys searching for ovine remains – but that was somehow macabre. In the end he'd settled for a plain antique silver napkin ring which was smart but not overly ostentatious.

He climbed into his car and drove back over the Elizabeth Way bridge. Turning off down a side street, he located the university boathouses and parked a short distance away. He strolled along the river and stopped outside the open doors of the boathouse. He looked up. There was a CCTV security camera positioned at an angle on the wall so that it could cover a large swathe of ground in front of the building. Frankie stood underneath it and tried to estimate exactly how much ground.

A narrow boat was heading downstream, its wash lapping over the bottom of the slipway. Frankie waited for it to pass, then slipped inside the boathouse, the professional in him despairing at how easy it was. They'd spent all that money on a surveillance system, then a student came along to train and left the doors wide open because he couldn't be fagged to close them. Frankie peered up at the inside wall, tracing the ducting for the camera cable as it descended to a wooden cupboard near the floor. The cupboard was locked but the flimsy bolt was easily snapped back with the blade of the Swiss Army knife he always carried in his pocket. Inside was a black metal box with a slot on the front. Frankie had seen many like it before. The big CCTV systems, in city centres and on industrial sites, transmitted their pictures to a central control room. But this camera had its own video recorder attached. The tape would only be looked at if and when something happened to require it: a break-in, an incident of vandalism or something like that. The tape didn't even need to be changed. It ran for a period of hours – usually twenty-four – then automatically rewound and recorded over the previous day's pictures.

Frankie ejected the tape from its slot. It was a digital cassette little bigger than a cigarette packet. He slid it into his pocket and walked away from the boathouse.

*   *   *

An acquaintance had once unkindly remarked of Karl Housman's appearance that it looked as though he had a charge account at Oxfam – an unfair comment considering there was never anything in a charity shop that fitted him. Had there been, he might well have been tempted, for neither clothes nor the way he looked had ever been of much concern to him. What he wore was dictated almost solely by his bodily dimensions.

He took size fourteen shoes, a fitting unobtainable in virtually every shop in the country so he had to have them specially made by a small manufacturer in Northampton at £150 a pair. His inside leg measurement was thirty-nine inches, again a size unheard of in the High Street. His trousers, and jackets and shirts too, had to be personally tailored to his build. When he purchased any he always did it in bulk, buying three or four of each item at a time. And he made damn sure he got a lot of wear out of them before he threw them away. Which was why his clothes, as well as being several years behind the fashion – a consideration of no consequence whatsoever to him – were also threadbare and tatty to the point of indecency. He didn't look quite as if he'd come in off a park bench, appropriated a white coat and passed himself off as a doctor, but he wasn't far off it.

This morning it was uncomfortably hot in the laboratory of the Infectious Diseases Department. Housman had removed his jacket and tie and was wearing his stained lab coat over his creased white shirt. His hair, worn a little long because he could rarely be bothered to get it cut, was flopping down into his eyes and sticking to his damp forehead. His glasses were beginning to steam up as his breath, collecting behind the surgical mask he was wearing, rose upwards behind them.

Removing his spectacles, Housman adjusted his position on his stool and peered through the eye piece of the electron microscope. Below the powerful lens, magnified a hundred thousand times, was a glass slide containing a sample of Phoebe Harrison's nasopharyngeal fluids. Housman had taken specimens from both the little girl and her father who was now in the adult intensive care unit, conscious but suffering from a high temperature, headache and generalised aches all over his body – the classic symptoms of some kind of viral infection.

Housman took a long look at the sample on the slide, adjusting the focus to bring the image up sharp. He stayed like that for maybe half a minute, not a muscle of his body moving, his eyes fixed intently on the sample. It was only when he sat back that he realised he'd been holding his breath. He took a deep gulp of air and swallowed. Then he had another look through the microscope.

'Jesus Christ,' he whispered.

He pulled away and stood up, automatically moving a few paces back from the bench. His gaze was still riveted on the slide beneath the microscope lens. He wiped his forehead with his sleeve. The perspiration now was due to more than just the temperature in the lab. He was aware of a dryness in his mouth, a slight constriction of his breathing.

Maybe he was wrong. Nothing was perfectly sterile, even in a hospital. There was just a possibility the sample might have been contaminated, either in the Intensive Care Unit or in the lab when he made up the slide. He hoped that was all it was.

He walked away down the lab, putting some distance between himself and the microscope. He pulled off his surgical mask and dropped it into the waste bin for incineration. Then he swapped his lab coat for a surgical gown, put on a new clean face mask and rubber gloves and returned to the microscope. Very carefully, he removed the glass slide and slid it into a hermetically sealed plastic container. He took the container to the refrigerator and labelled it with Phoebe Harrison's name and the instruction, 'Do Not Touch', the word 'not' underlined three times. He placed the container on the top shelf of the refrigerator and lifted out another sealed tube containing the nasopharyngeal swabs he'd taken from Jeff Harrison.

He prepared another slide and put it under the electron microscope. He paused. Part of him didn't want to look, but another part – the professional, clinical side of his nature – could hardly wait. He was excited. And perhaps a little scared. This was why he'd become a virologist.

Taking a deep breath, he sat down on the stool and looked through the eyepiece. He took his time, studying different bits of the sample very slowly, very thoroughly. He wanted to be sure. Then he took the slide out and put it in another hermetically sealed container. He labelled it and placed it in the fridge next to the first container. He could feel his pulse throbbing violently inside his head.

There were technicians in other parts of the lab, going about their routine work. Housman didn't notice them. Their voices, their footsteps, their movements didn't impinge on his consciousness. He was in an environment as tightly sealed as the samples he'd stored in the fridge.

He went to the phone and dialled the switchboard. He asked for John Cornwell. There was no answer from his extension.

'Could you bleep him please? Ask him to call me immediately.'

Housman gave his extension number then rang the hospital Isolation Unit and spoke to the sister in charge.

'I'm transferring two patients,' he said calmly, his hand clammy on the telephone. 'One from the Paediatric Intensive Care Unit, the other from the adult ICU. Phoebe and Jeff Harrison, father and daughter. I want them in separate rooms, full barrier nursing. I'll be there as soon as I can.'

'What's wrong with them, Doctor?' the sister asked.

Housman licked his dry lips, reluctant to admit to fallibility.

'I'm not sure, Sister,' he said. 'I wish I were.'

5

Frankie found a café in Chesterton which did a fry-up – sausage, chips, baked beans and a garnish of grease – with bread and butter and a pot of tea for under three quid. He passed a leisurely half hour, eating and chatting casually to the man at the next table, a rep for a company described by the salesman as 'Britain's foremost recreational garden sculpture suppliers' which turned out to mean plastic gnomes, then he drove out along Milton Road to the Cambridge Science Park.

Silicon Fen, as the press had dubbed the Park, was a sprawling estate of office buildings and high-tech research laboratories, many of them spin-offs from the academic research conducted by the university. The dons, for all their unworldly, fuddy-duddy image, were strangely adept at making money out of their intellects. Frankie doubted there was a single science professor who didn't have shares in, or a part-time position with, one of these thrusting new companies.

The building he was looking for was at the back of the Science Park, sandwiched between a computer software company and a pharmaceutical research consultancy. Frankie parked outside the front door, his rusty F-reg Cavalier looking shabbily out of place amongst all the BMWs, Mercs and Porsches, and went into Reception. The leggy blonde behind the desk had the front cover off the system unit of her PC and was fiddling with the circuits inside, a screwdriver clenched between her teeth. Even the receptionists out here had PhDs in rocket science.

'Hello, Ellie.'

The girl removed the screwdriver from her mouth. 'Hi, Frankie.'

'You busy?'

'Just changing the jumpers on my motherboard. Upgrading my CPU to an AMD K6-21 266 Mhz.'

Rocket science and double Dutch.

'Eric in?' Frankie asked.

'In the back. Just go through.'

Frankie pushed open a door and walked down a corridor. Through the glass panels on either side he could see the workshops and benches where technicians were designing and putting together a variety of complex electronic equipment. The company specialised in miniature recording apparatus and cameras which they sold to television production companies and the corporate security market. They made cameras the size of a matchbox, some even smaller, which could be fixed to the stumps in a cricket match for a worm's-eye view of a batsman being bowled, in a briefcase for an undercover reporter or on the cockpit of a Formula One racing car.

But their biggest market was paranoid employers who wanted to spy on their workforce by putting concealed miniature cameras all around their offices. To see who was reading the newspaper, who was playing computer games in work time, who was groping whom by the coffee machine. They could put a camera almost anywhere without anyone knowing. In a door handle, a light fitting and – their most popular spot – in a fake fire sprinkler which was attached to the ceiling. All of it perfectly legal.

Eric Barclay was in his office adjoining the workshops, talking to a client on the phone, when Frankie walked in. He gave a nod and waved at a chair. Frankie sat down. Eric was a geeky sort of bloke: crooked teeth, glasses so thick they looked bullet-proof and enough dandruff on his shoulders to fake a blizzard. It was a source of constant amazement to Frankie that this kid, who looked as if he could barely tie his own shoelaces, owned a company worth five million pounds.

'Hello, Frankie,' Eric said, putting down the phone. 'What brings you out here?'

Frankie showed him the videotape he'd borrowed from the boathouse. 'Any chance I can take a look at this?'

Eric examined the tape. He knew what it was but he knew better than to ask where Frankie had got it. 'Sure, you can use one of the edit suites. I could copy it on to VHS for you if you like, but it would take a long time.'

'I just want to run through it,' Frankie said.

'Come with me.'

Housman was worried. And he wasn't worried very often. As a specialist in infectious diseases he was used to seeing patients who were seriously ill: travellers returning from abroad with malaria, hepatitis, very occasionally yellow fever. He'd seen people with tuberculosis, on the increase in Britain despite the immunisation campaign to eradicate it altogether, and during his time in Africa as an epidemiologist he'd even encountered cases of haemorrhagic fevers such as Ebola and Lassa which were nearly always fatal.

But in all those instances he'd known what he was dealing with. The virus – and it was usually a virus – had been identi-fied, and though that didn't mean there was necessarily a cure for it, it was nonetheless reassuring. The worst thing about medi-cine was not knowing. He was a doctor, trained, conditioned to heal the sick. Yet if you didn't know what the ailment was, how could you treat it? With Jeff and Phoebe Harrison the problem was he didn't know exactly what was wrong with them.

They were both in the Isolation Unit now, as secure as the hospital could make them. Separate rooms, experienced nurses who were practised at dealing with contagious diseases. There was very little more they could do except wait and see what happened. Laymen thought that medicine was all about intervention, that there were drugs and treatments for everything. But in Housman's work there were occasions where all he could do was stand by and hope that the body's own immune system kicked in and dealt with the problem itself.

Both father and daughter were very ill, the father worse than the little girl which surprised Housman. He was a grown man in his forties, apparently fit and strong. Phoebe was only four, her immune system still immature and her body was also having to deal with the effects of the glycoalkaloid poisoning. The toxicological analysis of Jeff Harrison's blood had shown no abnormal traces of solanine or chaconine. What he had was simply a viral infection. Phoebe had the same thing too, but she seemed to be coping better with it than her father. Their temperatures were still dangerously high. They were feverish, delirious, sleeping restlessly, but Phoebe's respiratory system was less congested.

'What's the matter with them?' Sandy Harrison asked him again as she accosted him outside the Isolation Unit. She'd placed herself directly in front of him and wasn't going to let him pass until she had a satisfactory answer.

Housman weighed up the options in his head. How much to reveal, how much to conceal, that was a doctor's perennial dilemma. Some patients, some relatives didn't want to be told everything. They preferred to hope and pray in ignorance. Others needed to know every detail because information helped them to deal with their anxieties. Sandy Harrison was in the latter category, Housman surmised. She would ask, and keep asking, until she got a response.

'I think, and I must emphasise I'm not absolutely sure,' he said, 'that they're suffering from some kind of influenza virus.'

'Flu?' Sandy said. She was relieved. She knew what flu was, she'd had it herself. In her imagination she'd conjured up something far more terrifying.

'It's still serious,' Housman said. 'We don't yet know what strain of influenza it is.'

'If it's only flu, why are you taking all these precautions? Thousands of people get flu.'

'Because we don't want anyone else to catch it. Influenza is transmitted through the air. Your husband and daughter's breath, their mucus and saliva will contain the virus. We're trying to ensure it doesn't spread.'

Sandy watched Housman's face, his eyes. She didn't trust the medical profession. They were a secretive, protective cartel who looked after their own and treated everyone outside the Brotherhood with an arrogant disdain. But Housman appeared to be being open with her.

'There's nothing you can do here, Mrs Harrison,' he said. 'You're not allowed in their rooms. Why don't you go home and get some rest? We'll let you know immediately if their condition changes. You've given the nurses a contact number, haven't you?'

'Yes.'

'Then go home.'

Housman understood her fears. He could see why she didn't want to leave her four-year-old daughter. But he knew she didn't really fully comprehend what influenza meant. 'Only flu', she'd said, exhibiting the ignorance and complacency she shared with most of the population. Housman didn't disillusion her, she was worried enough already, but influenza was a killer. Over the centuries it had probably accounted for more deaths than any other disease known to man. Four thousand people a year still died of it in the United Kingdom, yet no one in the general population took it very seriously. Employees took time off work saying they had flu when all they were suffering from was a common cold. Even most of those with genuine influenza generally only had a few days in bed followed by a few weeks of feeling weak before they were fully recovered. It was the elderly, and patients with heart or respiratory conditions, who were most vulnerable. They were the ones who died, but no one really cared about them.

Housman did. He cared what happened to them. Not because he had a personal involvement in their fate – you couldn't survive long as a doctor if you felt any real attachment to patients who died – but because he had a professional interest in the virus that killed them. He was able to separate the person and the disease and it was the disease that really interested him. Like a lot of doctors, he looked on patients as sort of living Petri dishes, a perfect environment for the culture of all manner of fascinating microbes. That they were people too was of secondary importance, for his vocation was to study the cause of their illness and find a way of treating it.

Jeff and Phoebe Harrison were of particular interest to him. The virus he'd found in their nasopharyngeal fluids looked like influenza. He was almost certain it *was* influenza, but it had certain characteristics which gave him cause to doubt the diagnosis. Over the years he'd examined thousands of flu virions but he'd never seen any which looked quite like these. And that was disturbing.

Influenza was one of the great survivors. It had a supreme ability to adapt – to different hosts, to different environmental conditions. It could mutate, evolve. It could vary its structure by recombining with genome fragments from other, different influenza viruses. It could reassort its genes by exchanging them with other flu viruses, producing new variants against which the human body had no immunity. What Housman was seeing in Jeff and Phoebe Harrison was some kind of mutant virus. Exactly how virulent it was remained to be seen.

Back in his office, he sat down at his desk and thought hard for a long while. He needed to identify the strain of virus, but he knew he didn't have the facilities at Addenbrooke's. He needed a secure lab, a supply of different reagents which were not available in the hospital. He needed outside help.

He picked up the telephone and dialled a London number he knew by heart.

'Ian Fitzgerald, please,' he said to the switchboard operator who answered. 'My name is Housman.'

He waited, then a new voice came on the line. A rich, throaty voice with a strong, unmistakable Birmingham accent.

'Karl, where are you? In town?'

'At work.'

'Oh, shit. What're you doing there? It's been a long time, Karl. Too long.'

That was one of Fitzgerald's more endearing characteristics, wearing his emotions on his sleeve. But when he said something you knew he meant it.

'I might be coming in,' Housman said. 'But not for a social visit, I'm afraid.'

'Really?' Fitzgerald's professional curiosity was aroused. 'You've got something for us?'

'Influenza virus.'

'Influenza? What's the problem?'

'Two things,' Housman said. 'On the surface of the virion there's something I've never seen before. There are the haemagglutinin and neuraminidase antigens but also something else. Some other kind of growth I don't recognise.'

'You've ruled out bacterial contamination?'

'I haven't done a culture, but it doesn't look bacterial. Whatever it is, it goes right through the lipid bilayer into the matrix protein.'

'What's the second thing?'

'The genome has nine segments of RNA.'

'*Nine*? You sure? In every virion?'

'Every one I've examined.'

Fitzgerald said nothing for a time. Then his voice came back, sober, controlled. 'You should really take this to the Public Health Lab at Colindale. You know that.'

'Yes, but I want the best, Ian. You're the best.'

'Have you got a micrograph?'

'Yes.'

'Fax it to me. I'll call you when I've looked at it.'

Housman put down the phone and went out into his secretary's office. He'd been back to the lab and taken a micrograph – a hugely magnified photograph – of the virus under the electron microscope. He slid the print into the fax machine and watched it transmit, then returned to his desk to wait.

The call came less than a minute later. Fitzgerald sounded tense. He wasted no words. 'You've isolated your patient, I assume?'

'Of course. What do you think?'

'I've never seen anything like it either. You'd better bring it in. And, Karl, I know I don't have to tell you this. But be very careful.'

Frankie didn't watch much television, partly because there was nothing on worth watching, but mostly because he had better things to do with his spare time. He remembered reading an article in the paper about a scientific study which had discovered that the brain was actually more engaged and active when you were staring at a blank wall than when you were watching a television programme.

That was the way he felt now: brain dead and bored. He'd been watching the security tape from the boathouse for two hours without a break. He hadn't watched every minute of it, he'd skimmed through large chunks, but there were still several hours left to view. And no guarantee that it wasn't all a complete waste of time.

He'd been right about one thing though. The position of the CCTV camera on the boathouse wall, its angle and the fish-eye lens with which it was equipped, gave it a huge field of vision, covering not just the area outside the boathouses and the slipway leading down to the water but also the river itself and a strip of land on the other side. In the background of the pictures on the tape was the apartment block where Dan Cruickshank had lived.

Frankie fast-forwarded through another segment of tape, then pressed 'play'. The time code at the bottom indicated that it was 6 pm the previous evening. Another group of well-built students was opening up the boathouse and going out training on the river. Frankie reminded himself what he was supposed to be doing and tore his eyes away from the young men to concentrate on the car park outside Cruickshank's apartment block. Nothing much had happened throughout the day. Cars had come and gone, one or two people had entered and left the flats, but that was about all. It was no more interesting now. Frankie yawned and looked at his watch. Half the afternoon had gone and he wasn't even being paid. I'll give it another hour, he thought, then call it a day.

He watched a bit more, fast-forwarded, then watched again. A couple of teenagers strolled past, hand in hand. They stopped by the boathouse wall and started to kiss. Dusk was falling. The street lamps had come on and the surface of the Cam was etched with shimmering light.

Frankie looked beyond the river. A dark-coloured Rover saloon had pulled in outside the apartment block. Two men climbed out and walked up to the main entrance. Frankie didn't pay much attention. He picked up the remote control and whizzed on a bit. He pressed 'play'. The time code now read 8.11 pm. The Rover was still parked outside the flats. As he watched, the two men emerged from the front door and walked over to their car. Frankie sat up.

Wait a minute.

One of the men was carrying what looked like a black bin-liner. The other had something in his arms which, from the way he was walking, was obviously heavy. Covered with a large towel, it was about the size of a television set. Or about the size of a PC. Like the one that had left a clean space behind in the dust on Dan Cruickshank's desk.

Frankie studied the screen. The men loaded the objects into the boot of the car and went round to the front. They were too far away to be anything other than indistinct shapes. Their faces, their features were just a blur. The car lights came on and it drove away around the side of the block. Frankie stopped the tape and opened the door of the edit suite.

'Eric, you got a minute?' he called.

Eric came out of his office.

'I want you to look at this.'

Frankie wound back the tape a little and played it again for Eric. 'You see the car? When they turn the lights on . . . there.' Frankie paused the tape. 'The licence plate light comes on too. But it's too far away to read. Can you do something with the tape? Blow it up, enhance it in some way so I can get the number?'

'I'm not sure,' Eric said doubtfully. 'It's very dark and those CCTV tapes are not exactly state of the art.'

'But you are, Eric,' Frankie said, patting him on the back. 'If anyone round here is state of the art, you are. A technical genius like you should be able to do it.'

Eric didn't look keen. Frankie went for his Achilles heel. 'It's a challenge. If you can't do it, maybe one of your technicians can?'

'I didn't say I couldn't do it,' Eric said quickly. 'But it won't be easy. And I won't be able to do it today.'

'Whenever you can fit it in,' Frankie said. 'Just give me a call.'

It was a few years since Housman had last visited the National Institute for Medical Research in Mill Hill, north London, but it still looked the same. A big, ugly brick building with a green copper roof and a high spiked metal perimeter fence, it resembled a maximum-security prison or a sweatshop textile mill. It had been built to last, to survive a couple of centuries of harsh British weather, but the diseases they studied inside the building would long outlive it and all the scientists who worked there.

It was here that the human influenza virus was first discovered in 1933. It was still the leading flu research establishment in the UK and one of four key World Health Organisation flu-monitoring stations around the world.

Housman had worked here for ten years, doing research into flu and other viruses after he'd completed his medical studies. He still felt a certain nostalgia, an attachment to the place, but had no desire to return other than as a visitor. He'd served his time. He enjoyed being at Addenbrooke's, loved the clinical side of his work. Pure research was no longer so important to him. And, besides, a hospital consultant earned a hell of a lot more than a researcher and didn't have to scrabble around perpetually for funding to preserve his job.

Ian Fitzgerald was waiting for him at Reception. He was in his mid-sixties, close to retirement, a tall, heavy man with a shock of grey hair and pallid skin which looked as if it needed a holiday in the sun. They greeted each other warmly. They were a generation apart but friends despite the difference in their ages. Fitzgerald had been Housman's mentor during his early years at the Institute and something of that teacher-student relationship would always be present. But they were more colleagues now, two professionals working in different places with a mutual interest and respect to link them together.

Fitzgerald was a world authority on influenza. He was one of the select group of experts who met each spring at the WHO in Geneva to discuss what strain of flu was likely to strike the following winter and decide on the vaccine which would then be manufactured by drug companies in the intervening months. He'd spent close on forty years studying the virus. If anyone could help Housman, it was Ian Fitzgerald.

'How are you, Karl?'

'I'm fine. You?'

'I'm not complaining. Come on.'

They moved off towards the lift and Housman noticed the change that had come over his old friend. Fitzgerald was walking with difficulty, a stick in his right hand to help him. The shock must have been visible on his face for Fitzgerald gave a nod and smiled wryly.

'I know,' he said. 'It's got worse very quickly. Osteoarthritis. It's damned inconvenient.'

'You've seen a doctor?'

'It's not a medical problem, Karl. It's old age.'

'Knees or hips?'

'Hips mostly. I sometimes use a wheelchair to get around the corridors upstairs but I wasn't going to come down in one. Makes me look like a cripple.'

'You can get replacement joints. They're pretty good these days,' Housman said.

'Stop being a bloody quack,' Fitzgerald replied, pressing the button for the lift.

They went upstairs and down the corridor to one of the laboratories, Fitzgerald shuffling along with his wooden stick. Housman was carrying an insulated bag containing a stainless-steel canister surrounded by dry ice. Sealed inside the canister were the nasopharyngeal samples from Jeff and Phoebe Harrison.

The laboratory was a Bio-Security Level 4 facility, intended for the study of lethal viruses like Ebola, Marburg and Lassa. Influenza was not generally classed in the same deadly league as those diseases, but Fitzgerald and Housman were taking no chances with the samples inside the bag.

They changed into thick protective barrier suits and sterile rubber boots, then put on gauze masks and three pairs of latex gloves. They said very little. The time for small-talk had passed. They were focused on their task, both tense, apprehensive.

At the entrance to the lab they passed through an airlock lined with microbe-killing ultra-violet lights. The air in the lab itself had a negative pressure, lower than outside, so that if there was a leak, the air and any viruses in it were sucked in, not blown out. Housman carefully removed the steel canister from his bag and placed it inside a glass-walled glove box. The box was hermetically sealed, the air inside it sucked upwards through a duct and past ultra-violet scrubbers and microscopic filters fine enough to remove even the tiniest virus – and viruses were very small, about a hundred times smaller than a bacterium.

Fitzgerald looked at him. 'You ready?'

Housman took a deep breath and nodded.

If, and when, global warming led to the melting of the polar ice caps and a rise in the sea level around the coast of England, Frankie Carson's house would be one of the first to be engulfed. The water would sweep down from the Wash, drowning King's Lynn before racing up the plain of the Great Ouse to submerge Downham Market, Ely and finally Cambridge. Frankie's two-bedroom cottage, ten feet below sea level, in the middle of nowhere on the Fens, would not stand a chance. The water would swallow it whole, smashing the walls and roof into frag-ments and tossing the timbers into the angry surf of the tidal wave as it turned this part of East Anglia into a shallow lagoon.

Not that Frankie cared. The global environment didn't concern him unduly, which was surprising given how assiduous he was in maintaining his own local environment. He'd bought the cottage for its isolation, and for its garden, half an acre of lawn and mature shrubs leading down to the marshy fringes of a lake where coots and ducks and moorhens glided in and out of the reeds.

Gardening was one of Frankie's passions. He'd grown up in the urban confines of Manchester, starved of open spaces and fresh air, and when he'd moved south, transferring from the Greater Manchester force to Cambridgeshire because he couldn't stand the weather in the north-west, he'd promised himself that when he'd saved up a bit of money he'd buy himself a garden to tend. It had taken him a while, but now that he'd acquired it his every spare moment was spent in that garden. He'd planted trees, perennial shrubs, built a summerhouse with a verandah, added gravel paths and an ornamental pond and reserved an area near one of the side boundaries for his other great passion – bee-keeping.

His grandfather had been an apiarist. He'd lived in New Mills in Derbyshire and kept his hives out on the heather-clad moors. Frankie had vivid boyhood memories of cycling out to look at the hives, then returning to Grandpa's house for hot toast dripping with melted butter and honey. The countryside and bees were inextricably linked in Frankie's consciousness so it seemed natural, inevitable even, that when he moved to the Fens he should acquire a few hives of his own.

He had eight now, the original single hive multiplying as the bees swarmed and established new colonies. Looking after them wasn't hard; getting rid of the honey was the problem. Each hive produced a hundred pounds of honey a year, about a hundred and thirty standard-sized jars. Frankie sold most of it to a health food shop in Cambridge to supplement his income and gave the rest away. The Carson family and friends always knew exactly what they were going to get for Christmas and birthdays every year.

When he came home from work, the first thing Frankie did was stroll down the garden to inspect his bees. It unwound him, helped him forget whatever job he'd been doing that day. This evening it was warm and clear, a pale blue sky filling the horizon. That was one of the things he liked about the Fens: the way the sky seemed to envelop the landscape, saturating it with light.

He got his veil and smoker from the shed and walked down across the lawn and through the shrubbery. The hives were in a line in front of a low beech hedge. You could buy modern hives made of plastic, but Frankie preferred the old-fashioned wooden variety. The cedar frames needed regular treating with preservative but they looked so much better in a garden.

The bees were coming and going through the entrances to the hives, off foraging in the surrounding fields. Frankie watched them for a time. Then he noticed something peculiar.

On the grass in front of the furthest hive were a number of tiny dark brown bodies. He went over and looked down. They were dead worker bees, perhaps twenty or thirty of them. Frankie picked a couple up and studied them on his hand. There were several diseases that attacked bees. The parasite varroa was another hazard which could kill whole colonies over a period of years, but this didn't look like varroa.

Frankie lit the touchwood inside his smoker and let it burn for a moment, squeezing the bellows gently until it was smouldering nicely. Then he lifted off the lid of the hive and looked inside. He puffed in some smoke to drive the bees out and removed the upper honey super. He examined the frames. They seemed normal enough. He squirted in more smoke and took off the lower super to expose the brood chamber underneath.

There were workers crawling all over the brood frames. Frankie looked more closely at the dense clusters of bees. They weren't making honey. They were coating more dead bodies with propolis, the sticky brown resin bees gathered from trees, and pulling the bodies out of the frames to eject them from the hive.

Frankie had never seen anything like it before. Bees had no immune system. To keep the hive free of contamination they killed intruders, then coated them with the sterile propolis and tossed them out. They did it to their own dead brethren too but never in this quantity. Frankie had never known so many bees to die at the same time.

He replaced the supers and inspected his other hives. They seemed to be all right. He went back up the garden and into the cottage, removing his jacket and tossing it down on to a chair. He was disturbed. His bees weren't pets like domesticated animals, they were working insects. But he didn't keep them just for the honey. He kept them because he was fascinated by their world; their social organisation, the way they communicated, navigated, bred. He was attached to them and anything that harmed their welfare was upsetting to him.

He opened a can of beer from the fridge and sat down to think what the problem might be. Bees were susceptible to infection. The sprays and insecticides farmers used on their fields – and in this part of the country they used a lot – were all toxic, and potentially lethal to a worker out gathering pollen. With forty thousand bees in a hive it didn't usually matter if some died prematurely. That's probably all it was – an isolated incident of insecticide poisoning.

Frankie put his can of Carlsberg down on the table. Something had fallen out of his jacket on to the floor. He reached down and picked it up: it was the envelope addressed to Dan Cruickshank he'd taken from the mailbox at Cruickshank's apartment block. Frankie tore it open. There was a single sheet of paper inside with a black horse at the top and the heading Lloyds TSB. It was a bank statement.

Frankie glanced down the list of withdrawals and receipts to the final balance, an enormous £46,220. Stunned at the amount, he examined the entries in more detail. They were all itemised and dated, the cheque numbers printed beside each withdrawal. There were payments to Sainsbury's; to filling stations, presumably for petrol; a standing order to the Abbey National, almost certainly a mortgage payment on his flat; to AOL; to a department store and a few other names Frankie didn't recognise – an ordinary boring list recording the everyday expenses of modern life.

The column headed 'Receipts' was almost blank. There was only one entry, for exactly £50,000. Frankie looked at the source of the payment and pursed his lips thoughtfully. Now that was interesting. It put a whole new complexion on Dan Cruickshank. Frankie slipped the statement back into its envelope and returned it carefully to his jacket pocket.

Although the influenza virus had only been discovered in the twentieth century, the disease itself had been around for thousands of years, possibly millions.

Ancient peoples had been baffled by it, attributing its debilitating symptoms to some malign, supernatural influence – hence the name they gave it. Considering the size of the virus, it was hardly surprising that no one had identified it until the invention of the electron microscope. About a hundred nanometres – a thousand millionth of a metre – in diameter, the virions were so small you could fit a million of them on a pinhead and still have room left over.

They were basically very simple micro-organisms, consisting of the genome – a core of nucleic acid – surrounded by a protective protein coat called the capsid. There were three species, imaginatively labelled A, B and C, of which only the first two were significant in the infection of humans. Influenza A viruses were designated according to the two protein antigens, haemagglutinin and neuraminidase, which protruded from the outer surface of the capsid. It was these two proteins that were the virus's main weapons of attack.

Influenza, like all viruses, was metabolically inert. Left by itself it did nothing. It could multiply only inside the living cells of a host organism. Once inside a human, it locked on to the cells in the respiratory tract using its haemagglutinin like a grappling hook – binding with the sialic acid on the surface of the cells. The virus then fused with the human cell, uncoating itself to allow its nucleic acid to replicate. The new virions then broke free of the cell, using the neuraminidase to ease their departure past the sialic acid molecules, and moved on to infect the neighbouring cells.

This was all kindergarten stuff to Housman and Fitzgerald, but it formed the basis of everything else they'd learnt over the years and was the key to identifying what kind of influenza virus they were dealing with. One of the first things they had to do was 'type' the virus according to its haemagglutinin and neuraminidase antigens, alloting a number to each so that it could be labelled: H1N1, H2N2 and so on through a combination of fifteen known haemagglutinin antigens and nine neuraminidase. Types H1, H2 and H3 were generally human or – in a slightly variated form – swine influenzas. H4, H5 and H7 were avian.

The problem with the virions they'd obtained from both Phoebe and Jeff Harrison's nasopharyngeal fluids was that there was something else on the surface of the capsids – something that shouldn't have been there.

They inactivated a sample of the virus isolate to make it safe and Fitzgerald looked at it under the electron microscope. The haemagglutinin antigens were most obvious. There were more of them and they looked like triangular tent pegs sticking out from the spherical virion. The neuraminidase antigens were fewer in number and mushroom-shaped. Then there was a third type of protrusion, smaller than the others and distributed at random over the capsid. They looked a bit like tiny mottled balls on short stalks.

'You see them?' Housman said.

Fitzgerald pulled his eyes away from the microscope and nodded.

'I've never seen, or heard of, a flu virus with a protein like that on the capsid. Maybe it's not a protein. We'll have to culture some with antibiotics to rule out bacterial contamination.'

'It could be a reassortment. Antigenic shift.'

Influenza mutations were sometimes only slight, minor structural alterations to the virus which could result in small outbreaks of the disease in a population that was already partially immune to the original virus.

But occasionally the change was more marked and antigenic shift occurred. A host cell, often in an animal or bird, as well as humans, became infected simultaneously with two different flu viruses so that their progeny contained genes from each parent virus. If this reassortment of genes led to a new combination of haemagglutinin and neuraminidase, the result was a strain of flu against which the human population had no immunity at all.

'And the genome?' Housman said. 'What do you make of that?'

'It's peculiar. I don't know what the hell's going on there.'

The influenza genome was made up of eight discrete strands of RNA. But the virus from Jeff and Phoebe Harrison had nine strands.

'There seem to me to be two possibilities,' Fitzgerald said. 'Either one of the strands has split into two and the resulting change in the RNA accounts for those strange growths on the capsid . . .'

'Or?' Housman said.

'. . . or we have an additional strand of RNA. In which case we're looking at an entirely new kind of flu.'

The two men moved away from the bench. It was cool in the laboratory, but they were starting to sweat under their gowns and masks and gloves. Housman could feel tiny flapping wings in his stomach, a nervous excitement that was transmitted directly to his muscles. He had to make a conscious effort to remain calm. In contrast, Fitzgerald seemed unnaturally composed, but Housman knew that had to be an illusion, a product of an iron self-control. Inside, Fitzgerald had to be as much in turmoil as Housman was. They both sensed they were on the edge of a precipice every scientist one day hoped to reach in their career. Standing precariously above the drop, preparing to launch themselves out into the swirling vortex of discovery.

'What's the condition of your patients?' Fitzgerald asked.

'Serious.'

'But not critical?'

'Not at the moment.'

'Any unusual symptoms?'

'In the father, no. The daughter, yes. She's had the additional problem of glycoalkaloid poisoning.'

Fitzgerald stared at him quizzically. 'Glycoalkaloid?'

'Solanine and chaconine. The toxicologist reckons it has to have come from green potatoes.'

'Does this have any connection to the virus?'

'Not that I can see. The father's clear. It looks like an unrelated illness.'

Fitzgerald lowered himself awkwardly on to a stool, supporting himself on his stick. Housman felt a pang of . . . what?

Not pity. He would never feel pity for Ian Fitzgerald. Concern, distress maybe. Why did the human body and brain never seem to age at the same rate? You could keep your faculties while your body fell apart around you, or you could stay physically healthy and go slowly senile. It was hard to know which was worse. Fitzgerald's mind was as acute as ever, but his body was deteriorating rapidly. And the terrible thing was he knew it.

'Leave this part of it to me,' Fitzgerald said.

'No way,' Housman replied quickly. 'I'm seeing this through.'

'Karl, Karl,' Fitzgerald lifted a hand in a calming gesture, 'I'm not taking anything away from you. You know I would never do that. We're not rivals.'

'I know we're not,' Housman said a little sheepishly. 'But you can't do it all on your own.'

'I don't intend to. But this is lab work. Sedentary work. I can do this. What I can't do any more is go out into the field. You know what has to be done.'

Housman nodded reluctantly. 'You'll let me know the second you discover anything?'

'Of course I will. You're a bloody good epidemiologist, Karl. Go back to Cambridge and isolate the source. You have to find out where this virus has come from.'

It was almost dark by the time Housman located the farm. All the tracks in the windswept fenland countryside looked the same, and few farmers seemed to believe in erecting signs to identify their properties. After two wrong turnings, Housman finally found Marsham Grange, driving up the stony, unmetalled drive and pulling in outside a two-storey brick house. Even then he wasn't absolutely sure this was the right place. It was only when Sandy Harrison came out on to the doorstep that he relaxed. She showed him through into the big, stone-flagged kitchen and made him a mug of tea. Housman could see she was under a terrible strain. The lines of worry were chiselled into her pale face.

'Phoebe, my husband . . .' she began.

'They're in good hands,' Housman said, resisting the temptation to fob her off with reassurances he knew were not honest. He would have liked to have said they were both doing fine, both on the road to recovery, but neither was true. They were still seriously ill, holding their own but showing little sign of improvement.

'I was there till after lunch. Then I had to come home, to collect Tim from school,' Sandy said. 'I should be there now. What's happening?'

'You're better off here, Mrs Harrison. Your son needs you. Do you just have the two children?'

'Three. There's Lucy as well. She's eleven. She makes her own way home.'

'Have either of them shown any signs of illness?'

'No, they seem okay.'

'And you?'

'Me? I'm exhausted but I don't think I'm ill. Touch wood.' She reached out and laid her thin fingers on the edge of the pine table. She wondered why he was there. Hospital doctors didn't make house visits. She was starting to worry now. 'You didn't come all the way out here to tell me how they were, did you?'

'Tell me,' Housman said, 'have your husband or Phoebe been in contact with anyone recently who was ill with flu-like symptoms?'

'Not that I'm aware of.'

'Does Phoebe go to school?'

'No, she doesn't start till Christmas. But she goes to playgroup three mornings a week.'

'I'm going to need the names of people to contact. At the playgroup. At your son and daughter's schools. The headteachers.'

'This isn't normal flu, is it? You wouldn't do all this for common-or-garden flu.'

'There's no such thing as "normal" flu,' Housman said. 'Some strains are commoner than others, that's all. If it stayed the same, we'd all be immune to it by now.'

'Is this a serious strain?'

Housman considered his answer carefully, knowing his reply could have a significant impact on her mental state. 'I don't know. That's the honest answer. We haven't yet identified what kind of influenza it is. The effects of flu often depend more on the fitness of the patient than the strain of the virus. Neither your husband nor Phoebe has asthma or heart problems. People with either of those are the most vulnerable groups.'

'They're going to get better then?'

'At the moment, I see no reason why not. Now, can I ask you something? You told us at Addenbrooke's that Phoebe had potatoes on Sunday evening.'

'That's right.'

'Did all the family have them?'

Sandy had to think for a moment. 'Well, no. Jeff and I ate later. A curry with some of the left-over joint. We had rice.'

'And the other children?'

'Now you mention it, I don't think they did. Tim went to a friend's house for tea and Lucy – well, Lucy is worried about her weight. Can you imagine it? Eleven years old and she's watching her figure. No, she didn't have any potatoes. Are the potatoes relevant?'

'I'd like to take some away with me, if I may. Where do you store them?'

'Some in the kitchen, most in the barn. We keep a pile of rejects in the pigshed too.'

Housman put down his mug of tea slowly. 'You keep pigs?'

'Just a few. Why?'

'Where are they?'

'I'll show you.'

Sandy stood up. Housman gestured her back down. 'Don't show me. Just tell me where I can find them.'

Sandy took in the expression on his face and didn't argue. 'Across the yard. The big silver galvanised iron door.'

Housman went out of the kitchen. He saw the pigshed on the far side of the farmyard. He walked across quickly and slid back the door.

The stench from inside almost knocked him out. Fetid, pungent, it had a putrid rawness that turned the stomach. He was no farmer, but he knew it wasn't the normal smell of a pig.

It was gloomy, almost dark in the interior. Housman reached out and clicked on a light switch. The pigs were in three separate pens at the back of the shed. Housman covered his mouth and nose with his handkerchief and walked over to the pens.

The pigs were dead. Every last one of them. Sows and weaners lying on their sides in the straw, their snouts and mouths smeared with thick yellow mucus and pinkish dried blood.

Housman turned and headed for the exit. He slid the heavy iron door back into place and started to run across the yard.

6

Sandy and the children were confined to the farmhouse. Lucy and Tim went to bed but Sandy remained downstairs in the kitchen, watching through the window as the stream of vehicles arrived.

It was less than an hour since Housman had come sprinting back across the yard, bursting into the house and asking brusquely for the telephone. Sandy had been bewildered by his manner, the urgency in his voice, the peremptory way in which he'd ordered them to stay inside. She'd tried to question him, but he'd ignored her concerns and shut himself away in the sitting room, making a series of phone calls. He'd been no more communicative when he emerged, simply asking her if they kept any other animals.

'Some hens,' Sandy had said.

'Where?'

'The other side of the barn.'

She'd started to give him directions but he'd pushed her aside and run back out into the yard. The yard that was now filling up with vans and cars and men in white overalls.

Sandy watched them with a curious fascination, both physically and mentally detached from what was going on. She could only guess who they were, why they were there. But she knew it had to be something serious. Housman was talking to them, gesturing towards the pigshed and barn. The men strapped white surgical masks over their faces and opened the rear doors of their unmarked vans. They took out what looked to Sandy like heavy plastic bags and a folding stretcher similar to the ones she'd seen ambulancemen use. Then they went inside the pigshed.

Housman stayed in the yard, talking now to a man in a suit who'd arrived just after the vans. It was dark but the exterior lamps on the wall of the farmhouse and above the barn doors were on, illuminating the scene with a harsh white light.

The two men broke off their conversation and moved aside as a couple of the men in white overalls came out of the pigshed. They were pushing the stretcher, one at either end, struggling a little over the rough surface of the yard. On top of the stretcher, swollen by some bulky object inside, was one of the heavy plastic bags. From the size, Sandy knew it had to be a sow. And it was dead.

Another two men in overalls emerged from the pigshed and assisted with the stretcher. It took all four of them to lift the body bag into the back of one of the vans. Then they returned to the pigshed.

Sandy lost track of the number of trips they made, how many bags they brought out. She was too shocked to count them. Then they disappeared behind the barn, coming back with a number of smaller bags, all bulging. They placed them in another van, separate from the pigs. So the hens were dead too. Sandy felt a jolt of alarm. This was much worse than she'd expected.

'What's going on, Mum?'

Sandy turned. Lucy was standing in the kitchen doorway in her pyjamas. 'Go back to bed.'

'Who are all those men? I've been watching them from upstairs.'

'You should be asleep.'

'What are they doing? All those bags. It's the pigs, isn't it?'

Sandy nodded. 'I don't know any more than you.'

'Are they dead?'

'I think so,' Sandy replied, though she had no doubts. She just didn't want to upset her daughter with the cold truth.

'Why?'

'Lucy, go back to bed.'

Lucy padded across the kitchen in her bare feet and peered out of the window over the sink. One of the men in white overalls was putting on plastic goggles and a gas mask. He slipped the straps of a mesh harness containing a metal cylinder over his shoulders and picked up a long rigid spray hose which was connected to the cylinder. He headed towards the pigshed but was stopped outside the door by Housman who said something and handed him a clear plastic bag. The man nodded and went inside the shed, emerging moments later with the bag dangling from his fingers, now filled with something dark and lumpy. Sandy realised it was potatoes.

Housman took the bag in his gloved hands to one of the vans while the man went back into the pigshed and closed the door behind him.

'Bed, Lucy,' Sandy said firmly. 'Now.'

She took her daughter's hand and led her out of the kitchen and upstairs to her bedroom, deflecting all further questions. She didn't know the answers to them and, in any case, had a feeling they wouldn't have been suitable for a sensitive eleven-year-old girl. Sandy was a farmer's wife. She wasn't squeamish about animals and their fate in the business of agriculture, but something had happened that was outside her experience. Individual animals had died before but never anything on this scale.

When she got back downstairs to the kitchen, Housman and the man in the suit were just coming in from the yard.

'Mrs Harrison?' the man in the suit said. 'My name is Manville. I'm from the Cambridgeshire Public Health Department.'

'Public Health?' Sandy said. 'What are you doing? Who are those men?'

'They're from the Ministry of Agriculture. Your pigs and hens are all dead. We don't yet know the cause of death but it may be some kind of influenza.'

'Influenza?' Sandy began. 'My husband and daughter . . .'

'I know,' Manville broke in. 'Dr Housman told me. The carcasses are being taken away to be examined and your pigshed and chicken coop are being disinfected. What we have to ensure, Mrs Harrison, and I'm sure you understand this, is that whatever killed them doesn't spread to the surrounding area.'

'Of course, yes.'

'Your farm is going to have to be sealed off. Placed in quarantine, if you like, until the risk of contamination has been eliminated. Were those your only animals?'

'Yes,' Sandy said. She was in a daze, still trying to take in the implications of what he'd said.

'What about our potatoes? We have a lorry coming tomorrow to take some away.'

'Cancel it,' Manville said. 'Nothing comes in or goes out until the scientists give the all-clear.'

'But this is our livelihood. You can't stop us selling our potatoes.'

'I'm afraid we can, Mrs Harrison. We have power to make an order forbidding movement of any agricultural produce from your farm.'

Sandy slumped down on to a chair, feeling slightly faint. Did these men not realise what that meant to a small operation like Marsham Grange, a business that, like most farms, lived on overdraft for half the year and depended on a good harvest to pay it off? With no savings to fall back on, any restriction on sales spelt financial ruin.

'I think you should keep your children away from school as well.' It was Housman speaking.

Sandy looked up sharply. 'Are they at risk?'

'It's a precaution. To protect them and other children in the area. Did they have much contact with the animals?'

'Not the pigs, but they help collect the eggs from the hens. Are you saying my husband and Phoebe have caught flu from the animals?'

'We're saying nothing until after the autopsies,' Housman replied. 'But it's best to err on the side of safety. May I use your phone again?'

Sandy nodded, overwhelmed and confused. She didn't know what to ask next, what to do next. If only Jeff had been there. She depended on him so much.

Housman went through into the sitting room and closed the door behind him. He rang Mill Hill. It was ten o'clock at night but he knew Fitzgerald would still be in the lab.

'Ian, it's Karl. Where are we?'

'I've done a complement fixation test,' Fitzgerald said. 'Checked the "S" antigen. It's a type A influenza virus all right. We're going to culture some to test with antisera.'

Housman told him what had happened at the farm, describing what he'd found in the pigshed and then the henhouse. The pigs had almost made him throw up but the hens had been worse. They'd bled from every orifice of their bodies, their insides haemorrhaging and turning to jelly. He'd never seen anything so disgusting in his life.

'Hens *and* pigs?' Fitzgerald said. He swore softly.

'I hope to God I'm wrong,' Housman said. 'But it looks to me as if it's jumped species.'

Frankie's Fenland cottage had two bedrooms upstairs, one at the front and one at the back. The front was the bigger of the two rooms but Frankie chose to sleep at the back because it over-looked his beloved garden and because it faced almost due east and he liked the morning light. The curtains over the window were deliberately thin and unlined so that the rays of the sun penetrated deep into the room. In summer they woke him early, playing softly over the duvet and pillows. Frankie would doze in their warmth, waiting until the room was bathed in light before he got up.

Breakfast was always the same: a pot of tea with buttered white toast and his own honey which he kept in a large glass jar in the kitchen and replenished regularly from his hives. If the weather was fine, he would sit outside on the patio in the sunshine and eat his toast, then go for a slow meander around the garden.

He was too much of a pragmatist to believe in any true concept of communion with Nature – that seemed an affecta-tion of New Age travellers and tree-hugging middle-class Aga owners – but there was definitely something spiritual about gardens. Frankie would have scoffed at the very idea of trans-cendental meditation, but what he did in his garden was almost the same. The process of contemplation as he wandered along the paths seemed to cleanse his mind. Occasionally he would pause and wonder what he'd been thinking about, only to realise he'd been thinking of nothing at all. His subconscious was a complete blank.

He wasn't a fan of formality in a garden – he preferred the wild profusion of dense shrubberies, cluttered borders and haphazard lines – but he'd considered turning a corner of his plot into a Japanese Zen garden; using stones and water and raked gravel to create an oasis of calm. He'd read books about such gardens and the stark, rigid nature of their design was somehow appealing. As in everything else Japanese, there were rules to be followed, customs to be observed. It turned gardening into a form of religion and while Frankie had no denominational faith, he was quite prepared to see the hand of God in his garden.

This morning, as every morning, he finished his tour with an inspection of the bees. Seven of the hives were throbbing with activity, the foragers constantly on the move, but the eighth hive, the one he'd checked the previous evening, was strangely quiet. Frankie studied it from a distance. Not a single bee came or went through the entrance. That wasn't just unusual, it was a biological impossibility unless for some reason the hive entrance was blocked, or it was empty inside. Bees were never dormant during the honey-making season, they were programmed to gather pollen until they dropped dead from exhaustion. And they never left the hive en masse unless the queen departed.

Frankie walked over to the hive. He didn't bother getting his veil from the shed, he wasn't going to need any protection this time. He bent down for a closer look. The hive entrance was clean and unobstructed and he knew there was no reason for the bees to have swarmed. With some trepidation, he lifted the lid and removed the supers. The bees were still inside, in the honeycombs and clustered together around the brood cells. But they were all dead.

Frankie lifted each frame in turn and inspected it, hoping to find some small sign of life, something he'd missed. There was nothing.

He reassembled the hive, putting the bees back into their cedarwood mausoleum, then picked the whole thing up and moved it away from the other hives. Bees were colonial insects. They stayed loyal to their own queen, their own group. There was no mixing between hives. But Frankie didn't want to risk any possibility of cross-contamination.

He went back into the house and washed his hands, puzzled by the death-toll. What had caused it? And why only the one hive? There was little he could do. With human sickness you consulted a doctor, with animals a vet, but who cared about insects? He telephoned the secretary of his local apiarian association, a retired pharmacist who'd been keeping bees for fifty years, to ask for advice and see if anyone else had experienced the same problem. The secretary was out so Frankie left a message with his wife and rang off.

By now it was gone nine o'clock. Frankie went out to his car and drove to the Cambridge Science Park. Eric Barclay took him through to the edit suite and sat down at the console.

'Did you manage it?' Frankie asked.

'Take a look at this first.'

Eric pressed a button and a picture appeared on one of the screens above the console. It showed what looked to be some kind of public toilet, a brightly lit room with cubicles down one side and a row of washbasins on the other. As they watched, the door to the toilets opened and two smartly dressed women came in, chatting to each other. They took a cubicle each and went inside. Every sound was crystal clear: the bolts clicking shut, the rustle of clothing.

Frankie looked away, feeling uncomfortable. 'Why are you showing me this?' he asked.

'We did a trial for an employer in the City,' Eric said, his eyes not leaving the screen. 'Good, isn't it? The camera's about the size of a torch battery, the lens less than a centimetre across. But look at the picture quality. And the sound. Sound's always the problem, but we're developing a non-directional mike that can pick up almost anything within a radius of ten yards. And it's smaller than a five pence piece. What d'you think? Any of your clients interested in upgrading?'

Frankie did some work as a security consultant, advising firms on anything from alarms to surveillance methods and staff vetting. He'd put quite a bit of business Eric's way in the past but you had to draw a line somewhere.

'It's a ladies' toilet,' he said in disgust. 'You put a camera in a ladies' toilet? I don't believe that.'

'We put them everywhere else. Why not the toilets?'

'Don't you think people deserve a bit of privacy?'

'You can't see into the cubicles. It's tastefully done,' Eric said defensively. 'Besides, it's what his staff were doing in private that the employer was worried about.'

'It's none of his business what they do in private.'

'Snorting cocaine? In work time? That was the problem. This is a City trading firm. You know the kind of money those people deal with, Frankie. If you were an employer, would you want your employees, handling millions of pounds' worth of transactions every day, to be high on coke?'

Technology always had an answer. Frankie had noticed that. Whatever new invention you came up with, there was always a valid reason for using it. Micro-cameras in the workplace: it stops employees stealing or taking drugs. Surveillance cameras on the street: it cuts down crime. Smart cards for everyone: it stops fraud. But no one – no one in authority, at least – worried that the technology might be misused. To keep tabs on dissenters, to check their bank accounts, tap their phone lines, spy on their lives. A camera in every public place and a few private ones too. That was the future. If a ladies' toilet was acceptable, why not a sauna, a brothel, the honeymoon suite at the Dorchester? Frankie could see there would be quite a market for Eric Barclay's latest high-tech gizmo.

'What about the tape I left?' Frankie said.

Eric sniffed and jabbed at a couple of buttons on the console. Frankie knew he'd offended him. These Silicon Fen whiz-kids were all the same. Kids was the right word. They were like little children, constantly wanting praise, a grown-up's approbation. They never seemed to conceive that their genius should be restrained by any kind of moral parameters.

A different picture appeared on a second screen. It was a freeze-frame shot of the Rover saloon outside Dan Cruickshank's apartment block.

'I've done some work on it,' Eric said, launching into a complicated explanation about pixels and digital enhancement.

Frankie let him talk. Eric always had to let you know how he'd done something. Frankie never paid any attention to the technical gobbledegook. All he was interested in were the results. The image on the screen had been enlarged so that the rear section of the car filled the picture. The licence plate was blurred, but if you studied it closely it was possible to make out the numbers and letters.

'What's that last letter – P?' Frankie said when Eric finally shut up.

'B,' Eric said. 'You can see the shadow here. The plate's dirty so some of the letters are fuzzy. But it's a B.'

Frankie wrote down the number in his notebook. 'Thanks, Eric. That's a big help. Any chance of a still of that frame?'

Eric pulled a face. 'How many favours do you want?'

'Just one more. Can you put the tape in your safe for a few days?'

It was a gut decision, based on nothing except a faint sense of unease. But Frankie, in his work at least, was a careful operator.

Sandy knew now what it felt like to be under house arrest. Manville, the man from the Public Health Department, had been very low-key and diplomatic about it, but he'd left her in no doubt that she shouldn't leave the farm unless it was absolutely essential. Housman, too, had stressed the need for caution, repeating his advice that she should keep Tim and Lucy away from school. There'd been no coercion; it was much more subtle than that. No one could stop Sandy from leaving, or from sending the children to school, but the 'advice' had been framed in such a way as to make it clear she would be acting irresponsibly if she did.

And yet – and this really annoyed her – they weren't prepared to give her the full picture about what was happening. They wanted her to be responsible, but they treated her like a child, withholding information as if they thought she was too stupid to understand it.

The men from MAFF had driven away in their white vans at 11 o'clock the previous evening, leaving strict instructions that no one was to go anywhere near the pigshed or chicken run. They'd fenced off the yard with red and white plastic tape, the way Sandy had seen the police sealing off the scene of a crime on the television news, and there was something about their officious manner that made her feel as if they regarded her as a criminal.

Housman had left around the same time. She'd questioned him repeatedly about the deaths of the pigs and the chickens but he'd been as evasive as Manville. They wouldn't know what exactly had killed them until after the autopsies, he'd said again. And in the meantime, what should she do? What should she do if Lucy or Tim started to feel ill? Keep an eye on them, let me know immediately, was all he had to say on that.

A different group of men arrived in the morning. Sandy assumed they were also from the Ministry of Agriculture, Fisheries and Food, though since they didn't have the courtesy to introduce themselves, she couldn't be sure. They brought with them another white van, more protective clothing and a trailer bearing a small mechanical digger.

They checked the area around the farm buildings, then one of the men came into the kitchen in his dirty boots and said abruptly: 'The field outside the pigshed, what's it used for?'

'The pigs,' Sandy replied. 'They used to come in and out. We didn't keep them penned up except at night.'

'We're going to dig up a corner of it, to bury the waste.'

'What waste?'

'The straw, the slurry, the feedstuffs. Everything inside the pigshed and chicken coop has to be buried.'

He wasn't asking her permission, he was simply telling her what they were going to do. Sandy was nothing more than a spectator.

They were there all morning, excavating a deep hole with the mechanical digger, filling it with waste and covering it up with soil. Then they disinfected the inside and outside of the pigshed and chicken run again and told Sandy to keep away for at least forty-eight hours.

When they'd gone, she sat at the kitchen table and tried desperately not to cry, fighting back the tears because she didn't want to upset Lucy and Tim who were in the living room next door. Everything was getting too much for her. Jeff and Phoebe ill, the pigs and hens dead, the farm grinding slowly to a halt. She had no idea what to do. Jeff had always taken care of the agricultural side of the business. She didn't know what needed doing. She couldn't even drive a tractor. And Jeff wasn't there to ask.

She wiped her eyes on a piece of kitchen towel and composed herself. She went into the living room. Tim was on the floor building something out of Lego, Lucy on the sofa reading a book. It all seemed so innocuous, so normal that Sandy was momentarily taken aback. Perhaps it was as well the children didn't fully understand what was happening. She went to the telephone and rang the hospital.

The Isolation Unit sister was calm and professional. Her daughter had had a good night.

'And my husband?' Sandy asked.

The pause was infinitesimally small but Sandy was tuned in to even the slightest hesitation.

'Is he worse?'

'He's in a stable condition,' the sister said.

'Can I see him?'

'I'm afraid not. No visitors for the time being.'

'I have to see them.'

'I'm sorry, they're in strict isolation.'

'I don't care if they're contagious. Whatever they've got, I've already been exposed to it.'

'It's the doctor's orders, Mrs Harrison.'

Housman again. What right does he have to stop me seeing my own husband and daughter? Sandy thought angrily as she put down the phone.

'How are they?' Lucy asked, looking up from her book.

'No change,' Sandy said. 'What about you two? How are you feeling?'

'You keep asking us that, Mum. We're fine, aren't we, Tim?'

'Yes.'

That was something, at least. Housman had said the standard incubation period for influenza was one to four days. Phoebe had started feeling ill on Monday morning. It was now Wednesday morning – was it really only two days? – and there were no signs of any symptoms in either herself or the other two children. Perhaps we'll be lucky, Sandy thought. Two out of five is enough. Perhaps the rest of us will be spared.

No one knew for certain where the influenza virus came from. Scientists had discovered that it lived quite happily in the intestinal tracts of aquatic wildfowl without making the birds sick. The problems only arose when the virus attacked other types of bird, particularly domestic hens and chickens, or when it jumped species and infected some other animal, notably pigs whose respiratory tracts were susceptible to both avian and human strains of flu and who provided a perfect breeding ground for viral mutation.

Housman's personal view – and he wasn't alone among virologists – was that influenza type A, which caused pandemic outbreaks of the disease, originated in southern China where large numbers of people lived in close proximity to both pigs and ducks and where there was considerable scope for genetic reassortment. Influenza viruses were found in duck faeces and in pond water. They circulated constantly in swine without necessarily producing any adverse symptoms. But when they transferred to humans they could be deadly.

The 1918 flu pandemic, which killed more than forty million people worldwide, was almost certainly an H1N1 influenza strain which probably started in China. The 1957 outbreak of 'Asian flu' was an H2N2 of Chinese origin and the next pandemic, in 1968, was an H3N2 dubbed 'Hong Kong flu' because of where it was first isolated. All three strains were killers, but all three were essentially variants of the human influenza virus. Avian influenza had been around throughout the period but had only ever killed birds. No human had ever caught it – until Hong Kong in 1997.

In March of that year, chickens started dying in the New Territories – dying in their thousands in the most excruciating way imaginable. The avian influenza strain responsible was identified as an H5N1. In an attempt to contain the outbreak, the Hong Kong authorities destroyed every bird on the farms affected.

Two months later, a three-year-old boy fell ill with a sore throat and fever which gradually worsened, becoming viral pneumonia. Twelve days after he was admitted to hospital the boy died. His doctors believed he'd been suffering from an H1 or H3 human strain of influenza, but extensive laboratory analysis showed it had, in fact, been an H5N1.

The scientists were stunned. No one had ever seen an avian flu virus mutate sufficiently to infect a human. Panic set in. All eight gene segments of the virus were wholly avian. If it spread, there was not a person on earth who would have a natural immunity to it.

The Hong Kong Department of Health and a team from the Influenza Branch of the Centers for Disease Control and Prevention in Atlanta, Georgia, the world's largest viral research agency, tried to find out if the dead child had had any contact with chickens. They discovered that his playgroup had had a pets' corner containing chicks and ducklings which had died shortly before the boy fell ill. But they found no trace of the virus itself. The infection was put down as a one-off freak.

Then, in November, another child from a completely different part of Hong Kong got sick with a sore throat and fever. He was admitted to hospital but recovered within two days. His illness was identified as an H5 influenza. A fortnight later, a thirty-seven-year-old man from Kowloon contracted the disease, then a thirteen-year-old girl, then a fifty-four-year-old man. None of the victims had had any contact with each other. The girl and the fifty-four-year-old man both died of pneumonia and multiple organ failure.

By Christmas, a total of eighteen people had caught the disease. Of those, six were either dead already or dying, a huge mortality rate of one in three. And the disease wasn't only killing the very old and the very young; it was taking fit, strong people in the prime of life.

The people of Hong Kong and the territory's health authorities were terrified. Their one consolation was that the virus didn't seem to be able to transmit from human to human. In all cases, it had been contracted from chickens or chicken droppings. But the influenza was evolving fast – faster than any of the scientists had ever seen. If by chance it met and mixed with a human flu strain and the genes reassorted, the mutant virus that resulted was likely to kill thousands.

The health authorities did the only thing they could to stop the disease in its tracks. Every chicken in the colony was slaughtered. In a three-day period nearly two million birds were gassed before being buried in mass graves. The measure seemed to work for there were no more reported cases of H5 influenza in humans thereafter.

Karl Housman hadn't been there, but he'd talked to virologists who had. They were all of the same opinion: if the birds hadn't been destroyed, the virus would almost certainly have spread like a plague through the population of Hong Kong. It was an apocalyptic hypothesis but one based on a deep knowledge of how the virus multiplied. Influenza wasn't like other infectious diseases that tended to be confined to the tropics, like malaria or haemorrhagic fever, or were spread by sexual contact like AIDS. All you had to do to catch flu was breathe. One sneeze in the departure lounge of Chek Lap Kok airport and you had a possible global pandemic on your hands.

They'd been lucky in Hong Kong, but Housman knew it was only a question of time before the disease resurfaced. The infected chickens had probably come across the then border with mainland China. There was no doubt that it was still present in China, lying dormant in some vast animal reservoir. And when it reemerged . . . Housman didn't like to think of the consequences.

He'd speculated about it with colleagues, but the one thing he'd never imagined was that it would show up in his own back yard. He didn't know with any certainty that it *had*. They didn't yet know what exactly had killed the hens and pigs at Marsham Grange or what had infected Jeff and Phoebe Harrison. But the signs weren't looking good.

He called Mill Hill from Addenbrooke's first thing in the morning. Ian Fitzgerald was back in the laboratory, assisted now by some of his colleagues and PhD students. He'd worked until

2 am, gone home for a few hours' sleep, then returned to his bench at eight. He hadn't yet identified the influenza strain but it was a long process. You couldn't 'type' a virus just by looking at it under an electron microscope. You had to culture the virus in canine kidney tissue and observe it for haemagglutination or haemadsorption with human group O erythrocytes. You then identified its type by treating the virus with specific antisera and measuring for haemagglutination inhibition. The process could take several days to complete.

Housman and Fitzgerald talked briefly – idle chatter was valuable worktime lost – then Housman hung up and left his office. He went down to the Isolation Unit and spoke to the nursing staff before going in to examine his patients. Phoebe Harrison was first. She was showing distinct signs of improvement. She still had a high temperature but she was taking fluids by mouth and breathing more easily. Housman finished his examination and stripped off his disposable apron, mask and gloves and dumped them in the incinerator bin just inside the door of Phoebe's room. Then he went out, put on a fresh apron, mask and gloves and went into her father's room. Jeff Harrison had deteriorated. He was on a ventilator, the thin plastic tubes threaded into his nostrils like transparent worms, and he needed all the help he could with his breathing. His temperature was forty degrees Celsius and he was bringing up globs of yellowish mucus.

Housman took a sample of the mucus. He was concerned. Influenza alone wasn't usually fatal. It was the complications that killed: primary influenzal pneumonia which was viral in origin and fairly rare, and the more common secondary bacterial pneumonia in which the lungs were invaded by *staphylococcus aureus* or other bacteria. Housman feared that bacterial pneumonia had already set in.

He sent the sample to the lab and rang the chief technician to request a priority analysis. If it *was* pneumonia, there wasn't very much he could do except pump Jeff Harrison full of antibiotics and cross his fingers.

Frankie was an old hand at identifying the owner of a vehicle from its licence plate. During his years in the police force he'd done it innumerable times, and without any difficulty. It was much harder now he was a PI, but it was still possible if you had the right contacts.

The Cambridgeshire force had tightened up the security around DVL – Driver and Vehicle Licence – checks. Every request was now logged on computer and the details passed to the duty inspector. The days of getting a mate to run a quick check in his meal break were long gone: there had to be a valid reason for every enquiry and it had to stand scrutiny by a senior officer.

But there were loopholes, weak points in the system. The trick was not to do the check from a police station, where the control room staff could ask awkward questions, but to call in the enquiry from a patrol car out in the field somewhere. To make it urgent, to relate it to some trivial road traffic offence that had allegedly been committed. The staff were less likely to query such a request and if there were problems afterwards, it was easier to concoct some plausible excuse for the check.

Frankie used a number of former colleagues to help him out when he wanted a vehicle identification. He didn't like to ask too many favours of the same person, and it was wiser to spread the backhanders around. He always paid. Put the matter on a business footing. It didn't do to presume too much on old friendships.

He'd known Ken Bowyer for nearly fifteen years. Bowyer was not far off forty and still a uniformed constable – one of the stolid footsoldiers who would retire at the same rank at which they'd joined the force. He'd tried for sergeant on several occasions but failed each time. He'd applied for a transfer to plain clothes at least twice but always been turned down. He'd given up now, tired of the humiliation. He was serving out his years without much enthusiasm, embittered by his failure to win promotion and looking forward to the day he could begin to draw his pension. Frankie sympathised with him. Who wanted to spend their entire career at the bottom of the heap, saluting patiently while their superiors shovelled the shit on top of them?

They were sitting in Bowyer's patrol car, parked facing west behind a row of empty tourist coaches at the side of Chesterton Road. The Cam was below them to the left. Through the branches of the willow trees they could see swans swimming on the river and a lone angler sitting on the bank. People were walking or cycling along the footpath on the far side, and on Jesus Green a group of teenage kids was sprawled on the grass drinking Pepsi and Coke from cans. Foreigners. Frankie could tell by their complexions and their clothes, not to mention the bright yellow rucksacks they'd all been given, emblazoned with the name of one of the city's many language schools.

Frankie handed Bowyer the number of the car written down on a page torn from his notebook, and a twenty-pound note. Bowyer slipped the money into his tunic pocket and reached for the radio. He called in the number, claiming that a pedestrian had made a complaint against the vehicle, accusing it of jumping a red light and nearly knocking her down. They only had to wait ten seconds for a reply.

'Access denied,' the voice on the radio said. 'Authority of Superintendent required. Are you sure the number is correct?'

'It may be wrong. I'll check and confirm,' Bowyer said quickly. 'Over and out.'

He jammed the mike back into its slot with enough force to break it and turned his head to glare at Frankie. 'What the fuck are you playing at?' His narrow face was pinched with anger. 'You heard that?'

'I didn't know,' Frankie said. 'I'm sorry.'

'Don't give me that shit. You know it's logged. You think they won't want to know what I was doing? I'll be on the Super's fucking carpet before the end of my shift.'

'Take it easy, Ken. Just say it was a mistake. The woman got the number wrong. It's no big deal.'

'It's not your pension that's on the line,' Bowyer snapped back. 'Never ask me to do this again, you got me?'

He screwed up the piece of paper and tossed it into Frankie's lap. 'Get out.'

'Look . . .' Frankie tried to placate him.

'Piss off. I'm a fucking idiot for having anything to do with you.'

Bowyer turned the key in the ignition. Frankie sighed. He was genuinely contrite, but he could see Bowyer was in no mood for either apologies or explanations. Frankie pushed open the door and climbed out. He barely had time to shut the door behind him before the patrol car sped away into the traffic.

Frankie walked back along the road to his own car and got in, unfolding the piece of paper and studying the number. He knew it was correct. Things were starting to slot together now. They were beginning to make sense.

He called Madeleine's office on his mobile. Her secretary said she was down at the Magistrates' Court. Did he have her mobile number? Frankie said yes and rang off. This wasn't something he wanted to do on the telephone.

He drove into the city centre and left his car in the multistorey at Lion Yard. The Magistrates' Courts were above the car park, accessed through the same bank of lifts. Frankie went up to the top, trying to shut out the stench of urine that the lift exuded, and found Madeleine in Court Number Three, making a submission on behalf of a client to the Bench. He sat down in the deserted public seats at the back of the room and watched her. She was probably the best defence solicitor in the city, and Frankie had had personal experience of just about all of them. She was clear and lucid in her advocacy and always seemed on top of her brief, even when she'd only met the defendant for the first time in the cells ten minutes earlier. She could think on her feet and had a knack of unsettling the CPS solicitors arrayed against her who had too vast a pile of cases on their hands to deal with any of them thoroughly. Frankie, at least the ex-copper in him, had no great love for defence solicitors – whom the police generally regarded as troublemakers intent on freeing obviously guilty criminals – but he had to admire the conviction and tenacity Madeleine brought to the aid of her clients. If he was in the dock himself, she would be the lawyer he'd want out front fighting his corner for him.

The magistrates stood up and retired to discuss their decision. Madeleine gathered her files together and, glancing round, saw Frankie at the back of the courtroom. He pointed to the exit and she nodded. Frankie went out first and waited for her in the lobby area.

'Tell me,' Frankie said as Madeleine sat down next to him on one of the hard moulded plywood seats. 'What exactly made you wonder about Dan Cruickshank?'

'Just a feeling,' Madeleine replied. 'The raid on the research centre. The other protesters thought they were just targeting the field. That's what the purpose of it all was. But Cruickshank seemed more interested in the research centre itself. He got Jake Brewster to come with him and I wondered why. Jake had never met him before, didn't know who he was.'

'Strength in numbers?' Frankie suggested.

'So why didn't he get more of them to join him? I think Cruickshank wanted a fall guy – someone who could be sacrificed if things got hot. He had it all planned. He seemed to know where he was going, how to get into the building. He had a jemmy with him to break the locks.'

'He could have brought that for the gates to the field. It was fenced in, wasn't it?'

'He used boltcutters on the fence. He didn't need a jemmy for that. It all seemed a bit odd. Then Jake found a couple of guys in his flat, searching the place.'

'Two men?' Frankie said sharply.

'Does that mean something to you?'

'I went to Cruickshank's flat. Someone had been there before me. Broke in, removed his PC and files. A video camera across the river taped them coming out to their car.'

'A video camera?'

Frankie took out the still of the car he'd got Eric Barclay to make from the videotape. He showed it to Madeleine.

'I got a contact to check out the licence plate. It wasn't listed. Or rather, it *was* listed but access to the registration details was restricted.'

'You're losing me,' Madeleine said. 'What are you talking about?'

'The details of every licence plate in the country are held on computer. But certain types of number are protected. They're unavailable, even to the police, without the specific authority of a senior officer – superintendent and above. There's a block put on them to prevent identification.'

'What types of number?'

'Home Office numbers.'

Madeleine stared at him without blinking. 'Shit,' she said softly.

'Certain Foreign Office vehicles are also protected,' Frankie continued. 'And Special Branch. It could have been any of them.'

'But why break in? Special Branch could easily get a warrant.'

Frankie shrugged. 'There's something else too.'

He looked around the lobby. A man with heavily tattooed arms was sitting next to a woman with a pushchair, watching a small child tottering around on the carpet. They were paying no attention to anyone else. Frankie took out a white envelope from his pocket and handed it to Madeleine. She looked at the contents.

'It's Cruickshank's bank statement,' Frankie explained. 'Look at the receipts column. He was a freelance environmental consultant. You see the figure, fifty thousand pounds? A credit transfer to his personal account from Xenotech UK.'

'The American multinational?' Madeleine said.

'Agrochemicals company, based in Chicago. But they have a biotech division over here doing research into genetically modified organisms.'

Madeleine lifted her head from the paper, lowering her voice instinctively. 'He was working for one of Transgenic Biotech's rivals? Is that what you're saying?'

'Looks like it to me,' Frankie said. 'Fifty thousand is a lot of money. Now what do you suppose they paid him that for?'

Madeleine studied the statement again. 'How did you get hold of this?'

'You don't want to know.'

Frankie took the paper from her fingers and slid it back into the envelope.

'Can I keep that?' Madeleine asked.

Frankie looked at her with an intense, uneasy concern. 'I like you, Maddy,' he said. 'Before you go any further, are you absolutely sure you want to get into this?'

7

Each time Cliff McCormick visited Whitehall, he had to make a conscious effort to remind himself which century he was living in. The Civil Service, despite the efforts of its political masters to modernise every public institution in the country, still seemed to be resolutely rooted in the traditions and working ethos of the Victorians. The buildings were of that time, of course; huge stone temples to the ambitions of Empire. McCormick could understand that. They were impressive, functional edifices, ideally located at the centre of the political firmament. It would have been pointless vandalism to knock them down simply because they were the relics of another age. What he couldn't understand, however, was why the people who worked inside them were also artefacts from a bygone era. To McCormick, accustomed to the relentless innovation of the business and scientific worlds, central government seemed a parallel universe populated by strange living anachronisms who, though recognisably human, seemed to have dropped in from another planet.

People like Tristan Allardyce. McCormick was about the same age as him – mid-forties – and they were both succumbing to the gentle ravages of middle age: shrinking hair and expanding waists. But there the resemblance ended. McCormick was restless, ferociously ambitious, always looking for a new challenge on which to expend his enormous reserves of energy whilst

Allardyce, though ambitious in his own way, was diffident and lazy, an academically gifted individual who'd never had to work hard to succeed. He and his colleagues in the Ministry of Agriculture, Fisheries and Food reminded McCormick of clerks from the pages of a Trollope novel: idle young men from public school and Oxbridge who loafed around, making obscure jokes in Latin and discussing in which country house they were going to spend the weekend.

McCormick had once believed that the English class system was changing, that the Establishment was loosening its grip on the reins of power. But he knew that was an illusion. In ten years of dealing with various Whitehall departments he'd never once heard a marked regional accent, never once encountered a senior civil servant who'd been to a comprehensive school. It was a closed shop, open only to those from a particular caste. At the beginning of the twenty-first century, McCormick found that both unbelievable and profoundly depressing.

'Tea?' Allardyce asked.

'Coffee,' McCormick replied, knowing it was an unforgivable solecism in the corridors of power to drink coffee at four o'clock in the afternoon.

He would have preferred something stronger, to fortify himself for the meeting that was about to begin, but that was no doubt an even greater social *faux pas* than rejecting tea. Somewhere in Whitehall, across the road in the Admiralty perhaps, there was probably a yard-arm with a flunkey in attendance to measure the angle of the sun and send out the official notice specifying at exactly what hour the whisky decanters were permitted to be deployed.

'Two teas, and a coffee,' Allardyce said to his secretary, coming out from behind his kneehole mahogany desk. 'Gavin's coming over from the House, he should be here shortly. We'll wait, shall we? He'll be jolly miffed if we start without him.'

Allardyce smiled at McCormick, revealing a set of perfectly white teeth. McCormick gave a shrug, not caring one way or another whether they waited for the minister's Parliamentary Private Secretary. He wanted only to get down to business and then back to Cambridge as soon as possible. But Allardyce seemed in no hurry to do anything much. He never was, McCormick had noticed.

Allardyce tugged his trousers up over his knees and sat down in one of the two leather armchairs in the informal discussion area at the side of his office. There was a brown leather sofa there too, its cushions soft and polished from the thousands of well-upholstered bottoms that had sat on it over the years. McCormick settled himself in one corner and studied the ghastly cream wallpaper and the crystal chandelier hanging from the ceiling, rehearsing in his head what he was going to say when they finally started the meeting.

The drinks had come in by the time Gavin 'It's pronounced Smythe not Smith' Smyth arrived from the House of Commons, bursting in, all breathless and fired up as if he'd run all the way along Whitehall instead of being chauffeured there in the minister's official Jag.

'My apologies,' he said insincerely. 'I'm snowed under at the moment, absolutely snowed under. Is that tea?'

He helped himself to a chocolate digestive and waited for Allardyce to pour him a cup from the pot. Then promptly sat down in the other armchair to make sure the civil servant had to stand up to bring him the tea.

'Thank you, Tristan,' he said graciously, their respective status in the governmental pecking order reaffirmed. 'Have you started?'

'We were waiting for you, Gavin,' Allardyce said dryly.

'Were you? Well, fire away.' Smyth turned to McCormick and added confidentially, 'Of course, I'm not here. Not officially, you understand. Watching brief, that's all. It wouldn't do to get the Minister too involved, now would it?'

McCormick half expected him to wink conspiratorially, but Smyth merely took a bite of his biscuit and chewed it, the crumbs drifting down to settle like dust on his immaculately pressed trousers. McCormick wasn't sure which of these sub-species he found more distasteful, the upper-class pen-pusher or the vain, posturing PPS. There wasn't much to choose between them.

'Over to you, Tristan. This is your show,' Smyth said, brushing the crumbs off his trousers.

Allardyce gave an ingratiating smile. 'Thank you, Gavin.' He turned to McCormick. 'Now where are we with this unfortunate business out in the Fens?'

'You know where we are,' McCormick replied, a trace of irritation in his voice. Was this why he'd been summoned to London, to discuss something they'd already talked about on the phone?

'It's for me, Cliff,' Smyth said. 'We have to keep the Minister up to speed. Put it on the record.'

'I thought this was all off the record?'

Smyth's thin lips twitched as if they'd been dabbed with acid. 'I think you know what I mean.'

McCormick turned his gaze back to Allardyce. 'It was my understanding that you were handling this.'

'Was it?' Allardyce said evasively.

'That's what you said. Aren't you?'

'We're obviously taking a certain interest in the matter. But it's not our responsibility entirely.'

McCormick could sense the shifting sands under his feet. He'd had enough experience of Whitehall to know how things worked. How civil servants slowly and imperceptibly moved the ground beneath you so that before you realised it you were perched precariously on the edge of a cliff. And no one was going to throw you a rope if you went over.

'Have you located it yet?' McCormick said.

Ask a direct question: one that had a simple answer. But it wasn't in Allardyce's nature to give simple answers.

'That's difficult to say.'

'You either have or you haven't.' McCormick pressed the point. He wasn't going to allow them to put him on the defensive. You rolled over for these people and they'd chew your entrails for *hors-d'oeuvres*.

'We're still looking. Unfortunately, the object is proving rather elusive,' Allardyce said.

'What Tristan is trying to say,' Smyth interjected, talking a lot for someone who officially wasn't there, 'is that we're doing our best. But this whole ghastly mess is not of our making.'

The implication was obvious, but McCormick had no intention of conceding the point. 'You're in a better position to take care of it,' he said. 'You have the resources, the personnel. You can do things a private company like ours can't.'

'We can't work miracles,' Allardyce said. 'If it doesn't turn up soon, we may have to reconsider our position.'

'I don't think it's quite that easy,' McCormick said.

The others looked at him, sensing some new undertone in his voice.

'Whatever do you mean?' Smyth asked sharply.

McCormick chose the more diplomatic route first, using the kind of ambiguous language they all spoke down here. 'I'm sure we all understand what's at stake. It's in all our interests that it be found, and found quickly. But apportioning blame isn't going to help.'

'You were negligent. Let's not forget that,' Smyth said. 'You can't expect the buck to stop with us. It was your research centre, your file.'

McCormick put down his cup and saucer on the coffee table in front of the sofa. It was time he spelt it out for them. 'Let's cut all the crap, shall we? We're in this together. If this leaks out, we're all going to be up to our necks in shit.'

Smyth winced, whether from the sentiment itself or the crude way in which it had been expressed, McCormick couldn't tell. These people never said what they meant or meant what they said. That way no one could ever pin anything on them.

'I hope that's not a threat?' the PPS said icily.

'It's a fact,' McCormick replied. 'You gave the go-ahead for this programme. Everything we've done had your approval.'

'Unofficial.'

'You think that makes a difference?'

'It makes it deniable,' Smyth said.

McCormick's cold blue eyes came to rest on the PPS. He knew quite a lot about Smyth. It was his practice to make discreet enquiries about people with whom he had business dealings. That was only sensible. Gavin Smyth was a young man in a hurry; another Oxbridge graduate who'd moved effortlessly into the cushy world of political lobbying and from there to the Westminster Old Boy's Club without having to soil his hands on a proper job in between. He'd been appointed a Parliamentary Private Secretary in only his first term in the House and made no attempt to conceal his relish at this early taste of influence. A PPS was only a bag carrier, a mere cockroach on the scale of political vermin, but he acted as if he was already in the Cabinet. He craved power, but responsibility was someone else's concern. McCormick despised that in a man.

'I hope you're not getting any silly ideas, Gavin,' he said. 'We sink or swim together. The programme may not be official – we all know the reasons why not – but, if anything, that makes it harder to wash your hands of it. You've concealed it as much as we have. Your guilt is the same as ours. You throw us to the wolves and I promise you one thing, I'll make sure you're torn to shreds too.'

The ensuing silence was so absolute McCormick could hear the faint tap of a computer keyboard in the secretary's office outside. Smyth's boyish face was flushed with a mixture of anger and embarrassment. Allardyce allowed him to dwell on his humiliation for a fraction longer than necessary before stepping in to smooth the waters.

'I think mutual cooperation is the way forward here, don't you? We gain nothing by recriminations.'

He glanced at McCormick, looking for some sign of agreement. McCormick deliberately didn't give him any. He knew that for all the atmosphere of urbane affability civil servants liked to cultivate, there were more ruthless assassins in Whitehall than there were in Palermo.

Smyth recovered some of his composure, tugging at the cuffs of his shirt to expose a pair of silver cufflinks adorned with the portcullis emblem of the House of Commons. 'Quite,' he murmured. 'This kind of thing will get us nowhere. Perhaps we should move on to the other topic.'

'What other topic?' McCormick said, perhaps a little too hastily. He didn't like being caught unprepared.

Allardyce stood up and walked over to his desk. He picked up a sheet of paper and brought it back to his armchair. Some sixth sense told McCormick that they had a surprise in store for him, and he wasn't going to like it.

'Marsham Grange Farm, near Great Dunchurch, Cambridgeshire. Have you heard of it?' Allardyce asked.

McCormick shook his head. 'Should I?'

'It's a potato farm north of Cambridge. They kept a few pigs and hens too. Yesterday evening all the livestock were found dead. First signs would seem to indicate an outbreak of influenza. The veterinary people are examining the carcasses to check.'

'What has this to do with me?'

'The pigs were partly fed on potatoes which were grown on

the farm. Some sample tubers have been examined in our lab in Cambridge.'

Allardyce paused and handed the sheet of paper to McCormick. 'You'd better see this. The potatoes – not all, but some – were found to be genetically modified.'

McCormick froze. He gazed intently at Allardyce, his brain racing, trying to fathom why he was being told this. 'You know all our farms,' he said. 'Marsham Grange isn't one of them.'

'It's a bit of a puzzle, isn't it? Made more puzzling by the fact that Marsham Grange is an *organic* potato farm.'

'What are you saying?' McCormick asked, his brow furrowing. 'That the farmer has been growing GM potatoes and selling them as organic?'

'I suppose that's possible,' Allardyce conceded. 'Who can really tell the difference between the two without a laboratory analysis? But I don't think it's likely, do you? The farm is Soil Association accredited. They're pretty thorough with their checks.'

'I repeat, it's not one of our sites.'

'You haven't been conducting unauthorised field trials, have you?' It was Smyth who spoke, just a hint of pleasure in his voice. Now it was McCormick's turn to squirm a little.

'No, we haven't,' McCormick replied vehemently. 'Why the hell would we do that? We don't need to conduct unauthorised trials anywhere.'

'So that leaves two other possibilities,' Allardyce continued. 'Firstly, that the farmer was carrying out unlicensed trials for some other biotechnology company. That question hasn't been put to him yet, but we're going to investigate it over the next few days.'

'And the second possibility?' McCormick prompted.

'That the potatoes were somehow contaminated by GMOs from somewhere else. The only people, to our knowledge, who are growing GMOs in that area are you.'

'We have no sites within ten or fifteen miles of Great Dunchurch,' McCormick said heatedly. 'There can't possibly have been any contamination from us. There has to be another explanation.'

'You can take that report away,' Allardyce said. 'Let your scientists look at it.'

'And we want you to check your potato sites, every one of them,' Smyth added. 'Make sure everything is as it should be.'

'You're not making this public?' McCormick said.

'What do you take us for? Do you think we want a panic on our hands, more of a backlash against GMOs? You know our policy. Transgenic crops are the food of the future, Britain's way of staying at the forefront of biotechnology research. The last thing we want is uninformed speculation about this kind of thing.'

Smyth paused, looking directly at McCormick. 'But I promise you one thing,' he went on, smugly echoing McCormick's earlier words, 'and I have the full backing of the Minister on this. If we find there are any questions surrounding the safety of Genesis II, we're shutting it down immediately.'

The lab report came back in the late afternoon, confirming all Housman's fears. The mucus sample from Jeff Harrison contained large quantities of the bacterium *staphylococcus aureus*: the farmer had secondary bacterial pneumonia.

Housman went straight to the Isolation Unit and donned his protective gear to go in and examine the patient. Pneumonia could set in very quickly, and when combined with a viral infection like influenza, the mortality rate was high. Harrison's condition was worse than it had been that morning: high temperature, acute respiratory distress. Housman prescribed a course of antibiotics then went back to his office and called Ian Fitzgerald.

The Mill Hill team were still trying to culture enough virus to test with antisera.

'Have you managed to identify the other growth on the plasmid?' Housman asked.

'No. But it's not bacterial contamination. We did a culture in antibiotics. The virus looked just the same. We're not going to identify it either, you know that, Karl. Not in the time we've got available.'

Housman was all too aware of what Fitzgerald was up against. It had taken scientists years of intensive research to isolate and identify the haemagglutinin and neuraminidase proteins on the influenza virus. There was no way they were going to identify the other strange protrusion on the capsid overnight. It just wasn't possible.

'How're your patients?' Fitzgerald asked.

'The girl's stable. The father's got bacterial pneumonia.'

'Ah.' Fitzgerald was never a man to overreact, but the very brevity of the reply carried more impact than a string of fiery curses.

Housman stared at the wall of his office. He'd had electron micrographs of various viruses blown up and framed: smallpox, hepatitis, rabies, meningitis, half a dozen others. Minute organisms that were so primitive they could hardly be classified as life forms. Yet they could kill a human being. They were morbid decorations for a room but they had a certain beauty Housman could admire.

The influenza micrograph – an H1N1 – was next to the window. The magnified virions looked like the heads of maces, tiny spheres covered in spikes that could tear apart a cell wall with even greater force than that crude medieval weapon. The mushroom-shaped neuraminidase antigens seemed to burst from the surface of the capsids like small nuclear explosions –

an accurate, if chilling, metaphor for the damage they could wreak on the human body.

'How long do you think you'll need?' Housman said, knowing it was a question Fitzgerald couldn't answer. Knowing also that it was of academic interest as far as Jeff Harrison was concerned. The type of virus that had knocked him out no longer mattered now another, equally dangerous, infection had taken over.

'Impossible to say,' Fitzgerald replied. 'It's not proving easy to culture.'

'Keep me posted, Ian.'

Housman rang off. He removed his glasses and rubbed his eyes. The left arm of his spectacles was starting to wobble again as the Sellotape holding it to the rest of the frame became brittle and lost its adhesion. He picked off the old tape and replaced it with a new piece which he wound tightly around the broken hinge. He'd been meaning to get the glasses repaired for weeks. He'd written it down several times on the list of things to do he scribbled periodically on scraps of paper. He was good at making lists. The trouble was, he always lost them before he could carry out any of the reminders.

He went across to the window and stretched his long frame, reaching up with his arms and arching his spine backwards. He knew he was acquiring a stoop – an occupational hazard when you were six feet seven inches tall and had to look down at almost everyone you encountered – and did his best to exercise whenever he could to correct his poor posture. He was flexing his shoulder muscles, opening out his ribcage and breathing deeply when the telephone rang.

'Karl Housman,' he said, picking up the receiver.

'This is Manville,' a clear, pleasant voice announced.

Housman sensed bad news, hearing nothing specific in the public health official's noncommittal tone, but feeling it somehow as if his subconscious were wired into the telephone line. He waited.

'We've got another case,' Manville said. 'Notified to us by one of the GPs we faxed the alert to this morning. A forty-five-year-old woman from Great Dunchurch.'

'You're sure it's flu?'

'The symptoms are the same. High fever, muscle aches, sore throat, headache.'

'Where is she?'

'An ambulance is bringing her in now.'

'I need to know two things,' Housman said. 'Whether she's had any contact with the Harrisons, and whether she's been in recent contact with hens or pigs.'

'I'm already looking into it,' Manville replied.

Housman put down the phone and called the sister in charge of the Isolation Unit to tell her to prepare another room. Then he rang the hospital dispensary and spoke to the senior pharmacist.

'How are we fixed for amantadine?'

'I'll have to check.'

'I want twenty doses sent up to the IU now. And another hundred doses ordered in.'

'You're expecting a flu epidemic?'

'I hope not,' Housman said.

The debris had been cleared up, the broken glass taken away, the spilt chemicals disposed of safely. The floor and benches had been thoroughly scrubbed with disinfectant and soap and water and new equipment brought in to replace the apparatus destroyed in the raid. The laboratory looked pretty much the way it had before the weekend, but to David Seymour its soul had been shattered along with the test tubes and retorts. It would be a long time before it was restored to its original state.

He felt as if he were in shock still. The surprise, the horror and then anger he'd experienced on first seeing the wreckage had subsided. But in its place had come a sort of numbness, mental rather than physical. His body had been untouched by the destruction of the lab, but his mind had received a blow which had left it bruised and sluggish. He couldn't summon the mental energy to begin again.

He knew his colleagues were suffering from a similar lassitude. Even Dennis Baxter, the research director, who normally possessed a contagious energising drive, was subdued, depressed by the amount of work that had been destroyed. Seymour watched him in his glass-walled office, sitting at his desk for long periods at a time. That was abnormal behaviour for a man who loathed the administrative part of his job and was usually out in the lab getting involved in some hands-on research whenever he could.

Baxter was on the phone now. Seymour could see his lips moving behind the glass but not hear what he was saying. The research director replaced the receiver and stood up from his desk, looking out through the window into the laboratory, his eyes meeting Seymour's. He beckoned with his right forefinger. Seymour walked across and pushed open the office door.

'Sit down,' Baxter said, coming out from behind the desk to close the door.

Seymour glanced round. Baxter had an open-office policy. His door was always ajar for any of his researchers to walk in and talk to him. The only times it was shut were during the annual round of confidential staff appraisals and when a member of the team had to be reprimanded for some transgression. Staff appraisals were in November, five months away, so that left only one possibility. Shit, I'm in for a bollocking, Seymour thought.

'I've just been speaking to Cliff McCormick,' Baxter began.

'He's been at a meeting with MAFF in London.' The research director returned to his chair and sat down heavily. His face was pale and taut, the shadows under his eyes so pronounced they looked like used tea bags. 'He wants someone to go out to Eastmere and check the potato crop.'

Seymour waited for Baxter to continue, but the research director appeared to have finished. It was a strange request. The potato crop was under constant scrutiny. Someone from the team was always out at the site, doing tests, taking samples to bring back to the lab for analysis. Cliff McCormick knew that.

'Is there a problem?' Seymour asked. The managing director didn't usually get involved in the fine detail of the plant breeding programme.

Baxter considered his reply, fingering his patchy grey beard which was uneven around the edges, as if it had been gnawed by one of the lab rats.

'You've found nothing out of the ordinary, nothing that might give rise to concern, have you?' he said.

'Like what?' Seymour replied.

'Anything.'

The research director seemed distracted, unusually vague. Seymour sensed he was being given only a part of the picture. 'You need to be a little more specific, Dennis,' he said. 'We've done all the regular tests. You've seen most of the data. Until the end of last week everything was going exactly as planned. Has something happened?'

Baxter pursed his lips, musing on something, then he stared hard at Seymour. 'This mustn't go beyond this room.'

It was such a melodramatic cliché that, but for the research director's earnest tone, Seymour might have been tempted to smile. Instead he nodded, waiting for Baxter to elaborate.

'There's been an outbreak of what looks to be swine or bird flu on a farm near Great Dunchurch. Marsham Grange,' the research director said at last. 'Tests on some of the potatoes fed to the pigs have shown them to be transgenic.'

'Great Dunchurch?' Seymour said. 'We have nothing anywhere near there.'

'That's what McCormick told MAFF.'

'No one's suggesting a link between the potatoes and swine flu, are they?'

'No, no, that would be absurd. They were checked simply because the farmer's daughter is in hospital with glycoalkaloid poisoning. The tubers, as well as being genetically modified, also contained abnormally high levels of solanine and chaconine. MAFF have given McCormick the report. That's not something we've ever detected at Eastmere, is it?'

'No. We've had no problems at all. Every test we've conducted has shown our potatoes to be substantially equivalent to non-transgenic potatoes. You know how thorough we are, Dennis.'

'McCormick's concerned. I want you to go out to Eastmere immediately and take a random sample across the fields. Check the glycoalkaloid levels in them.'

'Does MAFF think the potatoes were ours?' Seymour asked.

'Apparently they were grown on the farm itself. Mullen's not playing silly buggers, is he? Selling seed on the side.'

'He doesn't have any seed. We harvest it all. Besides, he just wants our money. That's all he's interested in. He's not going to do anything to upset us.'

'Get out there, David. Let's put our minds to rest on this.'

The road ran straight as an arrow across the broad open plain, a landscape so perfectly flat it seemed unnatural. But nothing here, despite its bucolic vista, was the way Nature had designed it. The fields, with their rich dark soils and neat rows of vegetables and cereals, had once been treacherous marshland: a waterlogged wilderness of pools and streams and muddy bogs into which man ventured at his peril. Like almost every other wilderness in England, it had been tamed, its resources yoked to the greed and necessity of its human residents. The marshes had been drained, many of them stamped with the signature of the Dutch engineers who centuries ago had brought their expertise, their windmills and their dykes to the area and reclaimed the land from Nature's uncivilised embrace.

The fields stretched to the horizon in a rectilinear pattern, their edges marked by deep drainage ditches fringed with swaying reeds. The uniformity of the panorama was interrupted only by scattered farm buildings and, in the distance, highlighted against the skyline, an earth embankment leading up to the High Fen Lode which took the water drained from the surrounding countryside south-west to the confluence of the Cam and the Great Ouse.

Seymour had driven out here many times, but was always struck by the strangeness of the landscape. It was only a few miles from Cambridge, yet it had a feeling of isolation as if it were part of a different country. Heading out along the potholed road, its asphalt crumbling from decades of winter frost, you came across remote farmhouses and the occasional brick cottage standing on its own at the edge of the fields, woodsmoke trickling from its chimney. And you wondered who lived there in such a lonely, desolate place.

The inhabitants had a reputation for oddness, and worse. Peculiar individuals, many of whom had barely journeyed outside their home parishes in their lives, they'd inbred over generations, creating a limited gene pool from which strange mutations were said to emerge. Seymour had heard terrible stories of incestuous relationships, of deformed babies being born: babies with two heads, with six toes, with no eyes, who were hidden away in attics or secretly drowned in the waterfilled ditches, their bodies never to be found. They were no doubt fabrications with only a slender basis in fact, but there was definitely something creepy about the Fens, some atmosphere of menace and maleficence that Seymour felt whenever he went there.

Eastmere Farm was a ramshackle collection of tumbledown buildings: an ugly main house with rotting window frames and broken gutters, a corrugated iron barn so rusty it was orange all over and a brick workshop in such a fragile state of dilapidation it looked as if it would collapse if a sparrow landed on it. The yard in between these architectural hazards was cluttered with discarded bits of machinery, leaky oil drums, black plastic bags and a cannibalised old tractor of uncertain pre-war vintage – devastating proof that the wellbeing and beauty of the English countryside could never safely be left in the hands of farmers.

Barry Mullen came out of the farmhouse as Seymour drove into the yard and parked next to a mound of ripe straw and dung. It was a warm afternoon and the farmer was wearing just a cream vest with his work boots and faded baggy jeans. The front of the vest was soiled with grease.

The accuracy of all the myths and half-truths about Fenland dwellers seemed to be confirmed by this curious figure, a walking example of the dangers of inbreeding. Mullen was short and stocky but there was something odd about his proportions. His torso was very long for his height, his legs truncated to give him a simian appearance that was exacerbated by his long, muscular arms, covered with hair from wrist to shoulder, which looked as though they'd been borrowed from a gorilla and stuck on as a joke. His head was too big for his body, swollen out at the top like an inverted pear and when he opened his mouth he revealed gaps where teeth should have been – the result not of decay but of a congenital defect that had left two incisors and his upper canines missing. Seymour found his appearance disturbing, his manner even more unsettling. He was like the issue of a union between a rustic peasant woman and Piltdown Man.

'Hello, Barry,' Seymour said.

Mullen gave a grunt of acknowledgement but didn't utter anything discernible as speech. Conversation, even a few basic civilities, wasn't his strong point. From Transgenic Biotech's point of view that was a distinct advantage. When the company had been looking around for land to use, Mullen's monosyllabic truculence had been an attractive characteristic. He would take their money, do as they told him but not blab about it down at the pub. A bachelor who lived alone and appeared to have almost no social contact with other people, he was the perfect overseer for their operations.

Seymour pulled on his wellingtons and gloves and spent the next two hours taking samples of potato flowers, leaves and tubers from different parts of the 15-hectare crop. When he'd finished he returned to the farmyard and loaded his trays and boxes into the boot of his car. Mullen came out and watched him from the threshold of the house with his unnerving porcine eyes. Seymour packed everything away as quickly as he could. He lived in dread of being invited into the house and being forced to attempt to converse with the farmer, but fortunately Mullen never showed any inclination to socialise. So long as the monthly cheques kept coming into his bank account that was all that concerned him.

Seymour held up a hand in a gesture of farewell and drove away down the pitted track, thinking about what Baxter had told him in his office. They'd been cultivating transgenic potatoes on this plot for three seasons without any significant problems. The potatoes, genetically modified to provide protection from the potato leaf roll virus which caused net necrosis – black spots – in the tubers, had been as safe to eat as non-GM varieties and there had been no adverse effects on the surrounding environment or insect life.

The incident at the farm near Great Dunchurch puzzled him, and worried him slightly – particularly the glycoalkaloid poisoning. In the initial lab trials he'd conducted for the company they'd had problems with increased glycoalkaloid levels in the GM tubers, but that was a risk inherent in all potato breeding, not just GM. In the 1970s, the United States Department of Agriculture had bred a potato cultivar called Lenape by conventional cross-breeding. The cultivar was found to have glycoalkaloid levels several times higher than normal and it was withdrawn from release. Glycoalkaloids were not necessarily dangerous, but they made the tubers too bitter to be palatable. Incidents of poisoning were very rare; so rare that when they occurred it was worth sitting up and taking notice.

Seymour knew for certain the potatoes at Marsham Grange had no connection to Transgenic Biotech – Baxter's suggestion that Barry Mullen might have been lifting GM seed potatoes himself and selling them was, frankly, laughable. Mullen wasn't that devious and he had a lot more to lose than gain by doing such a thing. But any problem with a genetically modified organism had a knock-on effect, tainting every other GMO and every other biotech company with the same blight. Seymour was more than curious to know where those poisonous GM potatoes had come from and who had bred them.

He took his samples back to the research centre and placed them in the refrigerator in the lab. The other staff had all gone for the day and he felt disinclined to work any later than he already had so he called his wife and then left. On the way home he stopped off at the corner newsagent's near his house and bought a copy of the *Cambridge Evening News*. He sat in the car and leafed through the newspaper.

On page five there was a short report on the flu outbreak at Marsham Grange Farm. Seymour read through it, noting that the farmer and his daughter had also contracted flu. Baxter hadn't mentioned anything about that, nor that all the hens on the farm had also died.

Seymour folded the paper carefully and placed it on the passenger seat next to him. Then he stared out of the windscreen at the passing traffic. He was uneasy. He couldn't be sure, but parts of all this were beginning to seem eerily familiar.

8

For once, Madeleine was home before seven o'clock. She closed the front door behind her and dumped her bulging briefcase in the hall, then went through into the kitchen. The bottle of Argentinian red wine she'd opened the evening before was on the worktop. She pulled out the rubber stopper and poured herself a glass, listening to the dull throb of music that was coming from upstairs. So Graham was in. Normally her son's constant background noise irritated her, but tonight she found it comforting. She didn't want to be alone in the house.

She went back into the hall and up the stairs.

'Graham?' she called out, giving him some warning of her presence though she doubted he'd hear her over the beat of the drums and the wailing vocals. His taste in music was a mystery to her, but she knew from her own youth that that was the whole point. If it didn't alienate your parents, why bother listening to it?

'Graham?'

She knocked on his door and waited for a reply. He was very touchy about his privacy.

'Yes?'

Madeleine pushed open the door. 'Hi.'

Graham was sitting at his desk, his school books open before him. One elbow was bent, his hand propping up his head as he leaned forwards, holding his pen. Madeleine got the impression he'd assumed the pose just seconds before she entered. There was something studied about it, and the pad of paper in front of him was completely blank. Why am I always so suspicious? she wondered.

'What are you doing?' she asked. She'd said it to open a conversation, but it came out more curtly than she'd intended.

'Nothing. Just my homework.'

He was on the defensive already. Madeleine smiled, trying to defuse the resentment she could sense was starting to smoulder under the surface. 'What subject?'

'Why?'

'I'm just interested, that's all.'

'Economics.'

'Oh.'

He looked back at his books. Madeleine waited awkwardly in the doorway, wishing he would talk to her more, wishing she could think of things to say that didn't sound like parental inter-rogation. Their lives hardly ever seemed to intersect. They were like satellites in different orbits around the same planet, com-municating intermittently from a distance, occasionally crossing paths for a brief instant yet never truly meeting. And the time wasn't far away when Graham would break free altogether and go shooting out into space in search of a new planet. Madeleine didn't like to think what she'd do when that happened.

'Well, I'll make us something to eat, shall I?' she said.

Graham nodded indifferently without looking up. Madeleine hesitated, watching his profile, the tight set of his jaw.

'I'll give you a call when it's ready.'

She went across the landing into her bedroom and changed out of her work clothes, sipping her wine as she hung up her black suit and slipped on a pair of jeans and a T-shirt.

It was only as she went back downstairs that she realised she had no idea whether there was any food in the house. Shopping and cooking were two chores she loathed, along with cleaning and ironing and everything else domestic that was traditionally labelled 'women's work'. Left to herself, she would quite happily have lived on toast and omelettes but Graham required something a little more substantial and varied. Madeleine cooked for him, but she always seemed to do it on the fly, as if there were a part of her which was determined to avoid it until the very last moment. Every so often, and it wasn't very often, she would get herself organised and plan a week's meals in advance, buying in all the ingredients at the same time. But the sheer effort involved was exhausting and she soon went back to her habit of grabbing a few things from the corner shop on her way home from work.

There was nothing in the fridge. Not even any eggs. There was passata and spaghetti in the cupboard but they seemed to have pasta almost every night. She checked the freezer. Tucked underneath a packet of frozen peas was a pepperoni pizza. It must have been there weeks, if not months. Madeleine brushed the frost off the plastic wrapper and inspected the sell-by date: 6 March. It was now the beginning of June. Three months, that was okay. She removed the pizza from the packaging and put it in the oven. Then she tipped some of the frozen peas into a pan of water and placed it on the hob to boil. It wasn't the most imaginative meal she'd ever devised but she was too tired to care.

The dirty dishes were still in the sink from breakfast. Madeleine contemplated washing them up for all of half a second before deciding they could wait. Her mother would have called her a slut, but then her mother had never had to spend a day listening to rubbish in the Magistrates' Court. Madeleine topped up her glass and went through into the sitting room and collapsed into an armchair.

The relentless pulse of pop music continued to vibrate down the stairs. How Graham could work with that din in his ears was anybody's guess. Madeleine suspected he didn't. His room was his refuge, his sanctuary. She'd forbidden him to have a television set in there, despite all his pleas, because she didn't want a hermit for a son. She felt he should watch television downstairs. She didn't want to vet the programmes, but she thought it important for them to do at least one thing together in the evening. It hadn't made any real difference. He still had a CD system and a computer in his bedroom and he simply shut himself away and played with those.

Madeleine sometimes wondered if this reclusiveness was all her fault. If she'd done something to drive him away. If things would have been different if she and his father had stayed together. She knew Graham wasn't unusual, that other boys his age were exactly the same, but that wasn't much of a consolation when you were stuck in your sitting room gazing at the wall and your only son was in voluntary exile just up the stairs.

Madeleine reached out and pushed the door to, muting the sound of the music. She thought about what Frankie Carson had told her in Lion Yard that afternoon. It was disconcerting. There was no doubt in her mind that the two men who'd burgled Dan Cruickshank's apartment were the same two men Jake Brewster had caught searching his flat. It was too much of a coincidence to be otherwise. That they were most probably working for Special Branch or the Security Service wasn't surprising. You had to be very naïve to think the authorities didn't keep tabs on environmental campaigners.

What she could do about it was another matter entirely. Jake Brewster wasn't going to make a complaint, he'd made that clear already, and Dan Cruickshank was dead. There was no evidence she could legally use, in any case. Frankie's videotape had been acquired under circumstances that no court would regard as admissible, whatever it proved. As a solicitor, she was extremely wary of having anything to do with it. The same applied to Dan Cruickshank's bank statement, which she knew Frankie hadn't come by legitimately. She was relieved that she'd eventually decided not to take it from the private detective. It would have been unethical, as well as illegal to handle something that might well have been stolen. But that didn't mean she couldn't make use of the information.

If Cruickshank really had been working for a rival biotech company, that put a whole new slant on the break-in at the Transgenic Biotech research centre. It moved it from the realm of eco-protest into the even more contentious area of industrial espionage. What had Cruickshank's motive been? Merely to smash up a lab and set back Transgenic Biotech's research programme, or had he had another reason for breaking in? Either way, it had an impact on Jake Brewster's role in the incident and Jake was her client. If she could portray him not as a willing co-participant in the criminal damage, but as an innocent idealist who'd been duped by a cunning industrial spy, then that might make a significant difference to the sentence he received.

Suddenly she smelt burning. The pizza! She leapt to her feet and ran into the kitchen, grabbing the oven gloves and pulling the pizza out. It was charred around the edges but the middle looked just about edible. The peas had almost boiled dry. She salvaged them before they burnt the pan. She served up the distinctly unappetising meal and called Graham, wishing she was one of those perfect mothers – if there really were such a mythical beast – who could work all day and come home to rustle up a cordon bleu feast in minutes.

Graham made no comment about the singed excrescence on his plate. Madeleine was grateful. They ate in a silence relieved by short bouts of stilted conversation.

'What did you do at school today?'

'The usual.'

'What's that?'

'You know.'

'No, I don't.'

'Oh, it's too boring.'

'I'm interested.'

'No, you're not.'

Help me out here, Madeleine wanted to scream. I'm *trying*, for God's sake.

'Have you had your results?'

Bad choice, Madeleine thought, seeing the barriers clamp shut over her son's face. He'd finished his Lower Sixth exams a few weeks earlier but the marks had not yet been given out. So he said. She wondered if he'd actually tell her when they were or hope she'd forget.

'Have you?' she asked again. She wasn't going to be deterred by his hostile expression.

'No.'

'It's taking a long time.'

'They've a lot of papers to mark.'

'So when are they due?'

'I don't *know*.'

He left the edges of his pizza crust on his plate. Madeleine didn't blame him, but she still took it as a pointed reminder of her failure as a mother. I'm getting as touchy as he is, she thought, as she scraped the blackened dough into the kitchen bin.

Graham was putting on his jacket in the hall.

'You're going out?' Madeleine said.

'Round to Craig's.'

'Have you done your homework?'

'*Yeees.*'

'What time will you be back?'

'I don't know.'

'Don't make it late.'

He turned away, zipping up his jacket.

'Graham, I mean that. No later than eleven. You've school tomorrow.'

He scowled and went out. Christ, I'm a nag. No wonder he doesn't talk to me. But someone has to be responsible for him. Someone has to ask him these questions.

Madeleine threw the plates into the sink, angry with herself, with him, with everything. Sod it, she thought. She picked up the bottle of Argentinian red and went through into the sitting room.

The autopsy results from the Ministry of Agriculture veterinary lab at Weybridge were faxed through to Housman's office at ten minutes past eight in the evening. He read the five-page preliminary report at his desk, eating a tuna mayonnaise sandwich he'd bought from the hospital canteen. Both the pigs and hens that had died at Marsham Grange Farm showed post-mortem characteristics consistent with influenza and pneumonia, though the veterinary pathologists had not yet been able to identify any particular strains of virus in the animals' tissue and blood. The hens had suffered massive internal haemorrhaging and the lungs of the pigs were swollen and choked with fluid. Accustomed though he was to the gory realities of an autopsy, Housman found some of the details nauseatingly repugnant. He took his tuna mayonnaise sandwich and dumped it in the bin.

It was a brief, but thorough report. As well as the internal damage, the pathologists had noted severe swelling on the neck of one of the hens. Closer inspection had revealed the presence of a bee sting in the centre of the inflamed flesh.

Housman put the report down on his desk and took a sip of his coffee. The dead animals weren't his responsibility, but if an infection was somehow being transmitted from them to the human population it was imperative that it should be stopped. He dug out the business card Stephen Manville had given him and picked up the telephone. He was about to punch in the public health official's home number when his own hospital pager began to bleep. He checked the number. It was the Isolation Unit. He called them instead. They took a long time answering.

'Yes?' The young female voice sounded rushed, under pressure. One of the staff nurses.

'This is Dr Housman.'

'Oh.'

'What's happening? I was bleeped.'

'It's Mr Harrison . . . His heart's failed. Dr Firth's in there with him now with the defibrillator . . .'

She broke off. Housman heard voices in the background, sounds of activity, a door closing. He recognised the Welsh lilt of Sarah Firth, his Senior House Officer. Then the nursing sister came on the line.

'Dr Housman? Mr Harrison has died.'

'I'm on my way,' Housman said and hung up.

He stayed in his chair for a time, staring into space. Feeling suddenly weary, diminished by the loss. Looking ahead with a sense of foreboding. Then he stood up and walked slowly out of the office and down the corridor. There was no hurry now.

9

The clock on the laboratory wall read 7.45 am when David Seymour walked in through the door and threw his jacket and leather briefcase down on to one of the benches. The early-morning sun was still low in the sky, but the lab was already starting to warm up as the rays burned through the large panes of glass that ran down one side of the room. Seymour walked across and opened several of the windows, letting in a refreshing breeze. The lab was always stuffy, too hot in both summer and winter. Some of the scientists liked it that way and there was a constant, niggling dispute between the window closers and the fresh-air fiends. Seymour was in the latter camp, but there would be no arguments this morning, at least not for a while. He was the only person present.

He walked down the room past the benches and pushed open the door to Baxter's office. Like most other staff, the research director didn't usually come in until half past eight. Seymour glanced up at the clock again. That gave him just under three-quarters of an hour to find what he was looking for.

He went to the filing cabinets and pulled out one of the drawers. Under normal circumstances they would have been locked, the key safely stowed in Baxter's jacket pocket, but the locks had been damaged beyond repair during the break-in and new cabinets had not yet been delivered. Seymour checked through the files, looking under D for Derapur. The file wasn't there. He moved to a different cabinet, searching under I for India. He drew a blank there too. He knew the file existed, he'd seen parts of it three years earlier, though he'd never read the whole of it. What would it be filed under? The two most obvious classifications had been empty, but Baxter was notoriously eccentric in his system. Looking for the obvious was not always the best approach.

Thinking laterally, Seymour looked under 'Asia' and 'Third World'. There were plenty of files in those categories but none of them the one he wanted. Momentarily nonplussed, Seymour opened a few drawers at random and searched through them. He tried the P drawer, pulling out the general files on the potato breeding programme. There were too many to inspect in any detail, but he riffled through them and was pretty sure the documents he was seeking weren't there. He moved from the general to the specific, checking under the names of particular cultivars. Nothing there either.

He looked up at the clock once more. It was a quarter past eight. Baxter would be here in fifteen minutes. He might already be on the site, parking his car. Other staff might also be arriving any minute. It was too risky to remain in the office.

Seymour closed the cabinet drawers and went back out into the lab. Perhaps the file had been removed for some reason. Maybe one of the research scientists had taken it out to consult. Baxter himself may have been reading it but Seymour didn't think so. It certainly wasn't on the research director's desk because he'd checked, and even Baxter wasn't allowed dispensation from the company prohibition on files being taken out of the building. It was possible it had been inadvertently lost – that wasn't a completely unknown occurrence at Transgenic Biotech – or put away somewhere in a drawer and forgotten. Or it might just have been transferred to Central Records. It was four years old. There was a limited amount of space in Baxter's office. Periodically, he cleared out the older files to give room for the current research data. That was a possibility worth exploring.

Seymour picked up his jacket and left the laboratory. Central Records was downstairs in the basement. The archivist wouldn't be in yet, but Seymour obtained the keys from the security guard at Reception and went down the steps into the storage room which, despite its vast size, he always found claustrophobic. The ceiling was very low and it was crammed with metal filing cabinets and high metal bookshelves bearing cardboard boxes of papers. There was little room to move, no windows or natural light and the close, oppressive atmosphere seemed starved of air. Seymour rarely ventured down into this subterranean cavern and when he did, he tried not to linger.

Switching on the lights, he went across to one of the computer terminals and logged on. The Central Records files dated back forty years and more. Transgenic Biotechnology International, as an entity, was only fifteen years old, but it had been built on the foundations of a much older traditional plant breeding company which had been sold off in the 1980s by its parent corporation, a multinational engineering company which had acquired it by default. Most of the paper stored on the shelves and in the cabinets dated from before the sell-off, but no one had bothered to sort through it or throw it away. When Transgenic Biotech moved to their new, purpose-built research centre outside Cambridge the old files had been moved along with everything else and simply dumped down here to gather dust. The information in them was hopelessly out of date and so poorly indexed it was almost impossible to use. More recent information was thoroughly classified on computer, with the files shelved and labelled for easy access. These days, only a tiny fraction of the data was actually printed out on to paper. The DNA and genome material on the various breeding programmes –

potatoes, oilseed rape, sugar beet, maize, wheat, rice – was so huge it would run to hundreds of thousands of pages. It would only ever be stored, and read, on computer.

Seymour punched in his password and asked the system to search under the key words 'Derapur' and 'Potatoes'. There were fifty-six entries. He scrolled through the short-form listings: analysis of soil type; agrobacterium-mediated transformation and chlorosulphuron resistance; application of Cry3A protein from *Bacillus thuringiensis*; assessment of blight and other fungal diseases; environmental effects; gene transfer; glycoalkaloid levels in transgenic cultivar PLRV6/2397 . . .

Seymour stopped. That looked promising. He typed in the number next to the listing and the full catalogue details appeared on the screen: 'Preliminary report on glycoalkaloid levels in potato cultivar field trials for Potato Leaf Roll Virus resistance, Derapur, India, 1997.' A classification number followed which Seymour scribbled down on a scrap of paper. He should have come down here first rather than wasting time in Baxter's office.

'Do you need any help, Dr Seymour?'

Seymour started and spun round in his chair. The chief archivist, Patricia Grey, was standing by her desk just a few metres away.

'I'm sorry, I thought you heard me come in,' she said, seeing his reaction.

'No, I . . . hello, Pat. Yes, I'm okay, thank you. I just need something from the stacks.'

He logged off and stood up, moving away into the rows of shelving. He found the file without difficulty. It was a thin blue cardboard folder containing fifty or sixty sheets of paper. He scanned a few of the pages, the contents coming back to him. This was the one. It wasn't a project with which he'd been directly involved, but he'd been told something of it at the time because it had a bearing on the research he was doing in the UK. He put the sheets back into the folder and tucked it under his arm.

He was nearly out of the stacks when something made him pause. Some strange sensation that left a pinprick of unease on the nape of his neck. He held the folder out in front of him and studied it thoughtfully. His instincts told him to be cautious. He looked up. The archivist was out of sight. He could hear her moving around over near her desk. As quietly as he could, he retraced his steps, then turned down one of the cross aisles into a different row of shelves containing more recent reports on the work out at Eastmere. He lifted down a boxfile he'd referred to in the past and opened it, slipping the Derapur folder inside. He closed the lid and carried the boxfile out from the stacks.

The signing out book was on the archivist's desk, a dog-eared pad with columns for the date, the title of the item withdrawn and the name and department of the person borrowing it. Seymour appended his signature, had a brief, inconsequential chat with Patricia Grey and went out with the boxfile.

Upstairs in the lab, Baxter and a couple of his colleagues were engrossed in a discussion beside one of the benches. Seymour walked past them to his desk and put the boxfile down. Unobserved, he removed the Derapur folder and slid it quickly into his briefcase.

'David?'

Baxter was staring at him. Seymour held his gaze, suppressing an involuntary shudder of guilt. What am I doing? he thought. 'Good morning, Dennis.'

'Did you go out to Eastmere?'

'The samples are in the fridge.'

Baxter nodded approvingly. 'Good. Get to work then. Let me know what you find.'

Sandy could hear the nursing sister's words repeatedly inside her head, knew she would always be able to hear them: *I'm afraid*

I have some bad news, Mrs Harrison. She'd thought at first it must be Phoebe, her precious little four-year-old Phoebe, and she remembered – with a feeling of intense guilt and shame now – the sense of slight relief she'd experienced when the nurse explained it was Jeff, not her daughter. How did you choose between the two, a child and a husband?

She'd emitted a howl, more animal than human. A sudden, sharp ululation that was like a death cry itself, full of a pain, an agony that had no coherent human expression except as a noise that said nothing yet conveyed everything. It was an atavistic, instinctive response, going back to the time before language when every emotion had its own undisguised sound, a small, universal vocabulary of love and fear and grief.

She'd sunk on to the edge of an armchair, the telephone clutched to her ear, and from there she'd collapsed to the floor, the sister's words almost inaudible over the spasms of sobbing: *complications . . . pneumonia . . . organ failure . . . I'm very sorry.*

Sandy had taken in none of the details. All she knew was that Jeff had gone. Everything else was of no consequence. Then for an instant she'd stemmed the flood of tears, a sudden terror jolting her upright.

'Phoebe . . . my daughter . . .'

'Your daughter is fine,' the sister had said. 'She's in no danger.'

'You're sure?'

'I'm sure. Now, I know this is a difficult time, but is there someone – a friend, a relative – who could bring you in?'

The rest was just a haze now. Sandy had a vague recollection of calling her sister, and a neighbour to come round and babysit. Then she broke down again, sagging in a heap on the living room floor, weeping inconsolably.

She'd gone in to Addenbrooke's, her sister with her, and collected Jeff's things and the death certificate, a flimsy piece of paper signing away her husband's life. He'd still been in his bed in the Isolation Unit, cleaned up and arranged by the nursing staff. Sandy had been allowed in to say goodbye. His hands, his face were still warm. She'd touched his cheek, shaking with emotion, her tears running down into the surgical mask they'd insisted she wore. Then she'd left the room, too overwhelmed by grief to remain long. She'd gone to the adjoining room and peered in through the glass window in the door. Phoebe was asleep. She looked as peaceful as Jeff. The deceptiveness, the cruelty of the image was like a knife blade in Sandy's heart. Appearances meant nothing. One was there, the other was gone.

Sandy had pushed open the door. The nurses had tried to stop her but Sandy was not going to be deterred. She was going to see for herself. She'd gone to Phoebe's side and held her hand, leaned over to hear and feel her breathing. Then the nurses had led her out and closed the door on the tiny, fragile figure in the bed.

Later, Sandy had cried herself to sleep, physical exhaustion overriding the agonised turmoil in her mind. Daylight had brought it all back but there were things to be done. A pale, uncomprehending Lucy and Tim to console, the death to be registered in Cambridge, funeral arrangements to be made. A long list of requirements which seemed to have been designed with the object of preventing the bereaved from dwelling too much on their loss. Sandy's sister stayed with her, the children too, all struggling to come to terms with what had happened. Sandy hugged them continually, finding solace in human contact, in the knowledge that she had to bear up and keep going for Lucy and Tim and Phoebe's sake. They were all she had left.

There were four of them seated around the table in the conference room on the first floor of the Cambridgeshire Public Health Department offices. Housman knew Stephen Manville, but the other two were strangers, introduced to him as Will Burbank from the MAFF Veterinary Service and Tristan Allardyce from MAFF headquarters in Whitehall.

It was Manville who opened the proceedings, recapping briefly what had occurred at Marsham Grange Farm – more as a courtesy, a way of starting the ball rolling than because any of the men didn't know the facts. Then he turned to Burbank, the vet.

'The autopsies on the pigs and hens. What's the latest information you have?'

'Pretty much the same as in the preliminary report, which I believe you've all seen,' Burbank replied. 'We've completed all the autopsies now, but our findings are the same. Without exception, the animals died of influenza. Type A. We don't know the exact strain yet, but it appears to be a reassortment of some kind. We haven't managed to type the haemagglutinin and neuraminidase antigens.'

'And what exactly does that mean?'

It was Allardyce who'd spoken. He was sitting a little apart from the others, leaning back in his chair with his jacket thrown open to reveal a pale pink shirt and a dark blue tie held in place by a Wallace and Gromit tie-pin, the sort of jokey fashion accessory that in the stuffy ranks of the civil service gave you a reputation as 'a bit of a character'.

'It means we don't know the exact nature of the virus that killed them,' Burbank explained. 'And that could have a significant impact on how we deal with it.'

'Is it going to spread?' Allardyce asked.

'It's quite possible.'

'Have we had any other outbreaks in the animal population?'

'Not so far.'

'It's just the one farm at the moment?'

'That's correct.'

Allardyce gave a thoughtful nod and stroked the underside of his chin. Housman looked across the table at him. The

Whitehall man was the odd one out in the group, the only one who wasn't local, who wasn't directly involved in the case. Housman wondered what he was doing there. His manner was a mixture of arrogance and diffidence that Housman suspected masked a departmental infighter of considerable skill. You didn't get to his rank in the civil service without having learnt something of the finer points of stabbing a rival in the back.

'And three people,' Manville added. 'It is still only three, isn't it, Dr Housman?'

Housman nodded.

'Three?' Allardyce said, screwing up his face a little as if he wasn't sure he'd heard right.

'Yes, three,' Manville confirmed.

'It's hardly an epidemic. Three cases.'

'Three very unusual cases,' Housman said. Allardyce's attitude was already starting to irritate him.

'So?' Allardyce asked. 'Flu's a common enough illness. Thousands of people get it every year. What's so special about this?'

'The strain,' Housman said. 'And the fact that it has probably been transmitted from animal to human.'

'The strain? I thought you didn't know what the strain was?'

Allardyce was looking at Burbank, but it was Housman who answered.

'We know enough to see that it's not a strain we've encountered before. And that makes it potentially very dangerous.'

'I'm glad you said potentially,' Allardyce remarked. 'You have no evidence yet that it is *in fact* dangerous.'

'Jeff Harrison, one of the three infected patients, died last night. Another, Caroline Malcolm, is in a critical condition.'

'But it's still only three people.'

'It will almost certainly be more if we don't take steps to prevent it spreading,' Housman said. 'If this breaks out, it could be very serious indeed.'

'Mmm.' Allardyce didn't sound convinced.

'Perhaps Mr Allardyce needs a more scientific explanation about the virus,' Manville said. 'To help him understand.'

'Christ, no,' Allardyce said, holding up his arms in a mock gesture of surrender. 'No science, please, I'm a civil servant, remember.'

It was a joke, but it was too close to the truth for the other three men to find very funny. They'd all had dealings at some point with Whitehall, the last bastion of British amateurishness where expertise of any kind – particularly scientific – was looked on with horror. Only in this country, Housman reflected, would the civil service be proud of their ignorance.

'The problem with a new strain,' Housman said, giving Allardyce the explanation whether he liked it or not, 'is that no one in the population will have acquired an immunity to it, because they will never have been exposed to that particular form of the virus before. And with influenza it's particularly hazardous because of the ease with which it is transmitted. Now at the moment we don't know the exact strain, but there's a strong probability it's avian in origin because the hens at Marsham Grange all died from it.

'Jeff Harrison had contact with the hens, his daughter collected eggs and played around the farmyard. The virus can live in hen droppings and on the shells of eggs contaminated by droppings. The third victim, Caroline Malcolm . . .' Housman paused and looked at Stephen Manville.

'I got the information this morning,' Manville said. 'She bought some free-range eggs from Marsham Grange on Sunday afternoon. She lives in Great Dunchurch. Apparently she buys her eggs from the Harrisons on a regular basis.'

'So all three of our victims have had contact with hens,' Housman said. 'That's reassuring news. For the time being, at least.'

'Meaning?' Allardyce asked bluntly.

'Meaning that, as far as we know, the disease has only been transmitted to people from either hens or pigs. If that remains the case, the outbreak may be very limited because most people never have any contact with farm animals. What worries me, though . . .' Housman glanced around the table, making sure he had everyone's full attention, 'is what happens if the virus finds a way to pass from person to person.'

'Is that possible?' Allardyce said.

'It hasn't happened before with an avian flu virus. But it was very close in Hong Kong in 1997. Influenza is infinitely adaptable. Give it the right conditions and I have no doubt an avian virus will mutate or reassort sufficiently to be transmissible between humans.'

'You make it sound very cunning.'

'It is.'

'Cunning' wasn't a word Housman would have chosen to use, but he knew what Allardyce meant. It was a human word, a man-made concept that had no application to Nature. The influenza virus was in many ways, and to use another human concept, a very stupid virus. It had survived so long because in its natural reservoir, the intestines of aquatic wildfowl, it had formed an asymptomatic relationship with its host. Both could live quite happily together without causing any adverse effects. When the virus transmitted to a human host or to pigs or domestic hens, however, it lodged in the respiratory tract to which it was not perfectly suited. The result: fever symptoms and, in some cases, the death of the host, neither of which were desirable outcomes for the virus. Killing the host was particularly bad news because the virus died with it, and creating illness in the host was also 'stupid' because it prompted the production of antibodies whose sole purpose was the destruction of the virus.

Imperfectly adapted to human beings, the flu virus had to keep constantly on the move to survive, jumping from host to host, changing its shape to thwart the deadly antibodies. Housman thought of it as a thief in the night. It broke into your house, smashed up the contents and then slipped away to do the same to your neighbour's house, assuming new disguises to prevent the police apprehending it.

'We have to ensure we don't give the virus those right conditions,' Housman continued.

'What are you suggesting?' Manville asked.

'We have to do what the Hong Kong authorities did. Eliminate the source of the disease.'

Burbank leaned forward in his seat, his gaze fixed on Housman. 'They destroyed every chicken, every duck in the colony.'

'I know,' Housman said.

'Now wait a minute.' Allardyce was alarmed. 'What are we saying here? You're proposing we have a cull on chickens?'

'And pigs,' Housman said.

'That's pretty extreme. For one outbreak, on one farm. A few pigs and chickens and only three people infected by it. I repeat, *three* people, and you want to kill every hen and pig in . . . well, where?' Allardyce ran his eyes around the group. 'How big an area? The other farms near Marsham Grange? Cambridgeshire? East Anglia? Let's think this thing through properly.'

'I have thought it through, believe me,' Housman said calmly. 'Let me give you some history. The 1918 flu pandemic, the worst the world has ever seen, killed somewhere between twenty and forty million people, maybe more. No one knows the exact figure. That was two per cent of the earth's population at the time. More people died in that one year than were killed in the whole of the First World War. More people died in that year than have so far been infected with AIDS in two whole decades. And no one knows why. No one knows exactly what it was about the 1918 virus that made it so deadly.'

'It's not 1918 now,' Allardyce retorted testily. 'We've moved on since then.'

'Unfortunately we haven't. We know more about flu than we did then, but in terms of treatment almost nothing has changed. There's no cure for flu, almost no drugs that can really alleviate the symptoms. If there's another global pandemic – and on past incidence we're about due one – then the effects will be catastrophic.'

'This *isn't* a global pandemic,' Allardyce snapped. 'It's completely irresponsible to talk like this.'

'It's irresponsible to do nothing when the virus could spread,' Housman countered.

'You're exaggerating, being unnecessarily alarmist.'

'Have you been listening to anything I've just said?' Housman demanded. 'If this virus gets loose in the general population, thousands of people will get it. Many of them will die. The NHS will implode.'

'This is just scaremongering,' Allardyce replied angrily. He wasn't going to be lectured to by some gangly doctor with Sellotaped glasses.

'Gentlemen, gentlemen,' Manville said, trying to take the heat out of the atmosphere. 'Let's just take a brief pause here. Fill up our coffee cups.'

He lifted the coffee pot that was on a tray next to a plate of biscuits in the centre of the table and offered it around. Housman held out his cup to be refilled. He didn't want any more, but he felt he should support the chair's diplomatic attempt to prevent the meeting getting out of control. Allardyce waved the pot away.

'Let's take another view on this,' Manville said a moment later. 'Mr Burbank?'

Burbank squinted at his cup of coffee, taking his time. Then he said slowly: 'I agree with a lot of what Dr Housman has said. I've seen this virus. I've seen what it did to those animals. I don't think we can afford to be complacent.'

'Who's being complacent?' Allardyce interjected.

'Let him finish, please.' Manville glared at Allardyce who shook his head in irritation and looked away.

'We don't know where the virus came from,' Burbank continued. 'And we don't know what it is, which is worrying. We've already notified all the other farms in the Great Dunchurch area to be extra vigilant. They have instructions to contact us the moment any of their livestock show symptoms of influenza. I'm not sure how much further we should go at the moment.'

'Can't you test the pigs and hens on other farms?' Allardyce asked. 'See if they're carrying the virus.'

'It could run to thousands of animals. We don't have the manpower or the laboratory facilities for that.'

'Besides,' Housman added, 'by the time you've tested and waited for the results more farmers, their children, their customers, may have gone down with the disease.'

'What about vaccinating those most at risk?' Allardyce asked.

'You can't even think about a vaccine until you know what strain the virus is,' Housman replied.

'And when will you know that?'

Housman shrugged. 'The virologists at the NIMR are studying it, but there's still a long way to go.'

'You haven't answered my question. When will you know?'

'I can't say.'

'Well, maybe someone should get their finger out and give us a result.'

'I know the people there,' Housman said, his temper flaring. 'The scientist in charge, Ian Fitzgerald, is one of the foremost authorities on influenza in the world. They're working around

166

the clock to identify this virus. If they haven't done so yet there's a damn good reason for it. As I've already said, this is not a virus anyone has encountered before. Slagging off the people who are busting a gut to crack it is unjustified and, frankly, a disgrace.'

'If we can go back a little way,' Manville broke in quickly, holding out his arms as if to keep the two men apart across the table. 'We were discussing the question of a cull. What is your proposal, Dr Housman?'

Housman took a deep breath. 'That all pigs and hens within a certain radius of Marsham Grange should be destroyed. Say, ten miles. The figure is arbitrary, but it has to be set at something.'

'Do you realise the implications of that?' Allardyce asked forcefully. 'Killing what may be healthy animals. The farmers will want compensation. The public will be alarmed. The last thing we need is another food scare or people panicking about some mystery flu bug.'

Housman knew it had been a mistake to lose his temper. Whatever he said now would be implacably opposed by Allardyce.

'We can't brush this under the carpet,' he replied. 'The public will be concerned, but then they have a right to be concerned. Doing nothing isn't an option.'

'Mr Burbank?' Manville said. 'Your opinion as a vet.'

'Avian flu is nasty and highly contagious,' Burbank said. 'We shouldn't take chances with it. Particularly if it's spreading to the human population.'

Allardyce shook his head. 'This meeting has no authority to make a decision like this. A possible slaughter programme won't be decided out here. It's a political hot potato. It will have to be discussed at ministerial level. After submissions from appropriate national experts and the Government's Chief Medical Officer.'

'A decision needs to be made quickly,' Manville reminded him.

'I'm aware of that,' Allardyce snapped. 'I'll be taking all necessary steps as soon as I get back to London. You will, of course, be kept fully informed on all relevant matters.'

He stood up and, with a curt nod at the others, left the room.

'Well,' Manville said in the silence that ensued, 'I think that puts us in our place. We'll await a decision from our masters in Whitehall then.'

Housman sipped his coffee. 'Let's hope it doesn't come too late.'

10

It was lunch-time before David Seymour got a chance to take a look at the file he'd surreptitiously brought up from Central Records. He waited for Baxter and his other colleagues to go to the canteen. When he was finally alone in the laboratory, he took out the folder from his briefcase.

Derapur was a small provincial town in the Uttar Pradesh region of northern India, a poor subsistence farming area where the staple crops were rice, millet and, increasingly, potatoes. Transgenic Biotech had set up a research centre there in the mid-1990s to conduct trials into various transgenic crops, including potatoes. Potatoes were of particular interest to the company because, after rice, wheat and maize, they were the most important food crop in the world and because they were highly amenable to genetic manipulation. Commercial production of traditional potato cultivars depended substantially on the use of chemicals – insecticides, fungicides and nematicides – as the plant was susceptible to a number of pests and diseases. The company had experimented with several different cultivars, genetically modified to confer resistance to the Colorado beetle, certain herbicides, potato virus Y and – the subject of the file on Seymour's desk – potato leaf roll virus, PLRV, which produced unsightly black spots in the tubers. These blemishes were unacceptable to both the household consumer and, of greater importance to the company, the potato crisp and frozen chip industries which were huge buyers of potatoes.

Seymour had not been actively involved with any of the programmes – when they'd first been set up he'd still been completing his PhD at St John's College – but the results had obviously been shared with the plant breeders in Cambridge who were doing similar work. Seymour remembered reading the report when he joined the research team. The PLRV-resistant cultivars bred in Derapur and also the early crops grown in the UK had contained unusually high levels of glycoalkaloids. Not dangerously high, but enough to adversely affect their taste. Changes to the way in which the potatoes were modified had eradicated the problem and Seymour had not encountered it since.

But it wasn't just the glycoalkaloid problem he remembered from the report. There were other, ancillary effects which had been noted by the researchers – effects beyond the transgenic constituents of the potatoes which might, or might not, have been in some way influenced by the GM field trials. That was what worried Seymour as he read through the pages in the file.

By the time Baxter returned from lunch, Seymour had digested most of the salient facts in the report. He saw the research director enter the laboratory and slid the folder off his desk into his briefcase. Baxter came across the room.

'How's it going, David? The Eastmere samples.'

'On the tests so far, we have nothing to worry about. Solanine and chaconine levels are well within acceptable levels.'

'How big a cross-section did you take?'

'One from every sector of the crop. Whatever happened at Marsham Grange was nothing to do with us. I'm pretty sure of that right now.'

Baxter nodded. 'Cliff McCormick will be glad to hear that.'

The research director turned to go back to his office.

'Dennis . . .'

'Yes?'

Baxter swung round, waiting expectantly for Seymour to continue.

'Have you got a minute? There's something I wanted to talk to you about.'

McCormick's office was on the top floor of the research centre, a spacious corner room with big picture windows on the south and east sides that gave him a panoramic view out over the surrounding fields. The outlook was important to him. When the architects were drawing up the plans for the building he'd made sure this particular corner was reserved for the managing director's suite. His ego demanded an office that reflected his exalted status, but mere size and the richness of the furnishings were not his sole concerns. He wanted a corner room because he wanted plenty of windows and plenty of light. He'd spent too many years in ancient, dingy laboratories, struggling to work in the gloomy conditions. Now he was in charge, he was going to make sure – weather permitting – that the sunlight was always with him.

The other reason for the precise location of the office was that the company's growing sites were all on the eastern and southern sides of the building. McCormick liked to stand at his windows and see the crops in the fields: the wheat turning gold in the summer, the dazzling yellow carpet of oilseed rape flowers, the acres of polythene protecting the young vegetable seedlings from the frost which made it look as if the land was flooded with water. He still got a thrill from seeing the plants sprout and develop though he'd long since stopped working in the fields. Occasionally, he felt a pang of nostalgia for his time as a breeder – the long days in the fresh air, collecting seed and examining plants under the baking sun and in the pouring rain. But like most nostalgia, it was less a longing for the actuality of times gone by – much of which he'd found tedious and unrewarding – than a sentimental lament for the passing of his youth.

He was at the window, taking a break from his paperwork and watching two young researchers making their way through one of the wheat sectors, when his secretary came in and said that Dennis Baxter wanted to see him urgently.

'Dennis, come on in,' McCormick called, seeing the research director hovering just outside the door.

McCormick walked back to his desk and sat down, gesturing at the chair on the other side. Baxter perched himself on the edge of the chair, sitting stiffly upright, tugging at the hairs of his beard as if he wanted to pluck them out.

McCormick read the signs. 'Something on your mind, Dennis?'

'One of my team. David Seymour. He works on the potato programme.'

'Yes?'

'He's doing the checks on Eastmere you asked for.'

McCormick's eyes narrowed. 'He's found a problem?'

'No, no,' Baxter replied hurriedly. 'Everything's fine at Eastmere. He wanted to speak to me after I came back from lunch. About Derapur.'

McCormick didn't move. His gaze was fixed on Baxter's face. Then his tongue flicked out across his dry lips, licking them once and then disappearing back inside his mouth like a snake testing the air.

'What about Derapur?'

'He's a little concerned about some of the similarities with Marsham Grange.'

'Marsham Grange is nothing to do with us.'

'He knows that. But the glycoalkaloid poisoning . . .'

'He knows about *that*?' McCormick was almost out of his seat, leaning across the desk.

Baxter recoiled, shaking his head. 'Not at Derapur. He knows nothing about the Derapur incident. But he knows we had problems there. He saw the report a few years back – the PLRV trials report.'

'The report doesn't mention anything about poisoning.'

'But it does deal with excess glycoalkaloid levels in the tubers – the same problem they had at Marsham Grange.'

'Is he crazy? Marsham Grange and Derapur are six thousand miles apart.'

'I told him that. He's not suggesting it has any connection to us. But he thinks we should notify MAFF, make them aware of the similarities. In the public interest.'

'There's no way we're telling MAFF about Derapur. It was four years ago and we dealt with it at the time. It's a closed case.'

McCormick saw the look of doubt on Baxter's face.

'What?'

'It's not just the glycoalkaloid problem,' Baxter began.

'There's something else?'

'The hens.'

'Shit! That's in the report too, isn't it?'

Baxter nodded.

'And he remembers this from when?' McCormick demanded.

'Three years ago, he says. The people here needed to know about the results. I'd forgotten about the other problem until he reminded me just now. Cliff . . .' Baxter hesitated. 'I have to ask this. Genesis II. There's nothing I don't know, is there?'

'Of course there isn't. You're the bloody research director. You know as much as I do.'

'It's just that . . . well, Seymour may have a point.'

'Where's the Derapur file kept? Your office?'

'Central Records.'

'Leave this with me.' McCormick stood up.

Baxter stayed in his seat. 'He's a good worker,' he said.

'Enthusiastic, conscientious. He's a valued member of the team.'

'I'll handle it, Dennis.'

McCormick came out from his seat and ushered Baxter to the door. When the research director had gone, McCormick returned to his desk and picked up the phone.

'Rick? Two things. I want the file on David Seymour, he's one of Baxter's team. And I want the file from the basement on Derapur. You know the one I mean. Bring them both to me ASAP.'

McCormick hung up and went back to the window, too much on edge to sit down. The fields outside were bathed in the afternoon sun. The two researchers, in T-shirts and shorts, were crouching down in the rows of ripening wheat, taking samples from the ears of grain. McCormick studied them, momentarily envying them the stress-free simplicity of their jobs. But only momentarily. He liked being the boss, for all the pressures it brought. He'd known right from the start of his career that he wasn't going to spend forty years hunched over a bench in some smelly laboratory. Intellectually, the world of research had had a lot of attractions for him, but he was too ambitious to confine his horizons to being a small cog in a very large wheel. He wanted his own wheel, and he wanted to see it turning.

He'd done his degree in biochemistry and genetics at Imperial College when the science of plant genetic modification was still in its relative infancy. Staying on to do a doctorate in plant genetics, he'd begun to see the potential of transgenic breeding and studied everything he could on the subject. He could have remained in academia following his PhD, but his sights were already fixed on a more challenging goal. Finding a job as a research scientist at the UK base of a Swiss agrochemicals company, he'd begun to study in his spare time for an MBA from the Open University. It had taken him six years to complete the degree, by which time he felt confident enough to branch out on his own. With the help of his father, a well-connected City broker, he had raised the money to start a small biotech research company which had expanded so quickly that in less than three years McCormick had been able to raise more finance to buy the ailing plant breeding concern, Walmington Horticulture Limited, which its owners were desperate to get rid of. A relic of what McCormick regarded as the Dark Ages of plant technology, Walmington hadn't made a profit for five years and was suffering from decades of underinvestment and rock-bottom staff morale. McCormick had pensioned off the unenterprising management, recruited new, younger scientists and pumped in millions to rejuvenate the business and move it from traditional to transgenic breeding research. He had called the new company Transgenic Biotechnology International.

The gamble had paid off for several years. Biotechnology was a red-hot investment. Financiers were trampling on each other in their rush to get a stake in the industry. Then the general public, briefed by a resurgent environmental lobby, had suddenly become wary of GM foods. Biotech companies, almost overnight, became pariahs. Transgenic Biotech's stock price plummeted. The company, once valued at six hundred and twenty million pounds was now worth, on paper, less than half that. McCormick was still angry and frustrated by the abrupt change, and not solely because it had damaged his own personal wealth. He still believed that genetically modified food was as safe to grow and eat as any other food. And he still believed, as a scientist and a businessman, that it was the only viable future for agriculture and for the global environment. Pesticides and other chemicals were poisoning the earth, the world's population was growing too fast to feed, the amount of cultivable land shrinking every year. Without new hybrid crops, bred to withstand drought or heat or salty terrain, bred to need fewer chemicals, to resist killer diseases, there was no way that population could be supported in the twenty-first century.

The future is out there, McCormick thought, watching the two young researchers in the field. Growing before my very eyes. GM technology was the greatest leap in agriculture since man first progressed from being a hunter-gatherer to growing his own food himself. McCormick's own future was out there too. He wasn't going to stand by and see the company he'd built put in jeopardy. By anyone, or anything.

He was still at the window, engrossed in thought, when Rick Cullimore came in holding a grey personnel file in his hands.

'David Seymour,' Cullimore said, tossing the file down on to the desk. 'He in trouble?'

McCormick returned to his chair and slumped down. He leant back, rocking gently on the chair's sprung seat. 'Give me his background.'

Cullimore opened the file and glanced at the contents. 'He's twenty-nine years old. Been with us four years. Joined straight from university. BSc – first-class honours in biochemistry – and PhD from St John's, Cambridge. Academically brilliant. Work progress good. His annual appraisals look fine. Baxter seems very happy with him.' Cullimore looked up. 'A model employee as far as I can tell. We could do with more like him.'

'Personal life?'

'He's married. Got hitched shortly after joining us. Wife works as a secretary in the Chemistry Department at the university. She's expecting their first child in the autumn.'

'Did he do a psychometric test when he started?'

'Of course.' Cullimore flicked to a different page. 'Came out A1. Stable, well adjusted, disciplined, reliable. Fits our recruitment parameters perfectly. Is there a problem with him?'

'Give me the rest. The security report.'

Transgenic Biotech carried out regular, thorough checks on all its employees. This included scrutiny of their financial and personal affairs, compulsory drug testing every three months and, in some cases, surveillance outside the office. Mail and e-mail were vetted, without the employees' knowledge, and in the Security Control Room there was a second switchboard through which Cullimore or one of his team could monitor, and if necessary record, the phone calls coming in and out of the building. McCormick didn't regard any of this as intrusive or paranoid. He paid the wages, he had a right to know what his employees got up to.

'Clean living and boringly wholesome,' Cullimore said with a touch of disappointment. 'No skeletons in any cupboards. Not that we could find, at least. No serious debts or vices. Mortgage for ninety-five thousand on a small house in Soham. Doesn't smoke, drink or gamble . . . has sex with his wife once a week, missionary position only.' Cullimore smirked. 'Just guessing. Seems the type. What's he been doing?'

'Asking Baxter about Derapur.'

Cullimore closed the file on his lap. He nodded and ran a finger over his grizzled moustache. He knew all about Derapur. He was the one who'd gone out there to sort it out, his briefcase bulging with dollar bills from the company bank account in Lucknow. That was one thing he liked about the Indians: they knew the value of hard currency.

'Did you find the file?' McCormick said.

'It wasn't there.'

'What do you mean?'

'It wasn't on the shelf where it's supposed to be.'

'Has it been signed out?'

Cullimore shook his head. 'But interestingly enough, Seymour was down there this morning. Took out a file on Eastmere, according to the log.'

'I think I'd better have a chat with Mr Seymour. Get him up here, Rick, then stay down there. Go through his desk, his brief-case. If Baxter wants to know what you're doing, refer him to me. I want that file found.'

*   *   *

Seymour had never been in the managing director's office before, but it was pretty much the way he'd imagined it. McCormick had a reputation for high living: a Rolls-Royce Corniche as his company car, a yacht on the Italian Riviera, a house in the Caribbean which he visited every few months to top up his millionaire's tan. That his office should be so vast and opulent was no real surprise.

'David, take a seat,' McCormick said warmly. 'Would you like a drink?'

'No, thank you.'

McCormick went to an antique walnut cabinet whose front was veneered with an elaborate marquetry pattern in silver and ivory and opened the doors to reveal an array of bottles and crystal glasses. He poured himself a malt whisky and glanced round. 'You're sure you won't have one?'

'Quite sure, thank you,' Seymour replied politely.

He let his gaze rove around the office. The drinks cabinet was something of an anomaly, a personal touch in a room which looked as if it had been furnished by a committee of designers who had an unlimited budget but couldn't agree on what to spend it. The desk was huge, like a conference table, with nothing on it except a computer terminal, a telephone and a gigantic blotter with an embossed leather surround. The chairs were all expensive but didn't match, the sofa and armchairs in one corner were uphol-stered in a bright green and yellow fabric that jarred with the thick maroon carpet, and the paintings on the walls were a mixture of modern abstract art and ornate gold-framed Renaissance scenes which wouldn't have looked out of place in the Uffizi.

'Thank you for coming up, David,' McCormick said. He was back behind his desk now, the glass of whisky on the surface in front of him. 'Dennis tells me you've been expressing concerns about what happened at Derapur.'

'I mentioned it to him, yes,' Seymour replied warily.

He wasn't fooled by the managing director's easy demeanour – the welcoming manner, the offer of a drink. He knew he hadn't been summoned upstairs for just a friendly chat.

'We appreciate those concerns,' McCormick went on, flashing a quick smile. 'But I can assure you they are completely groundless. The Derapur business was a long time ago. It's in the past. It's irrelevant now.'

'Is it?' Seymour said, then wished he hadn't as he saw McCormick's eyes harden.

'Yes, it is irrelevant, David,' McCormick repeated. 'I'm sure you realise that. Or will come to realise it. You know what I'm saying?'

Seymour took a moment to reply. There was an undertone of something in McCormick's voice. What was it? Menace? Was that really what he was hearing? He felt a need to explain himself.

'All I said to Dennis was that what happened at Marsham Grange seemed to be similar in some ways to what I understand happened in India.'

'And what do you "understand" happened there exactly, David?' McCormick said. He used Seymour's Christian name not as a sign of informality or equality but more as a way of reminding him of the difference in their positions, the way a master might address an under-butler or one of his gardeners.

'Well, there were problems with the glycoalkaloid levels in the early crops of potatoes. And at the same time a number of hens kept on the adjoining land died of some unspecified disease. It's close enough to what occurred at Marsham Grange to make me wonder if MAFF shouldn't be told about it.'

'Let me tell you what happened at Derapur,' McCormick said. 'The problem with the potatoes was relatively minor, something you would expect in the early stages of any breeding programme. You know yourself that there's a large element of trial and error in the development of any new cultivar, transgenic or otherwise.'

He took a small sip of his whisky, pursing his lips as if he were assessing the taste. Then he continued, smooth and reassuring. 'As for the hens, there was never a shred of evidence that their deaths had any connection whatsoever with our field trials. This is India we're talking about. Hens and other animals die all the time from unspecified causes. The farmers next to our land are very poor. They see a rich European company open a research facility nearby and they want to milk it for all they can get. That's understandable. Their hens died, probably from malnutrition or old age, and they accused us of doing something to them. We paid them compensation as a gesture of goodwill. It's not our country. We want good relations with our neighbours. It was only a small sum, nothing to us, but it smoothed away the problem, kept the farmers sweet. But the claims were entirely bogus, I have no doubt about that. Does that put your mind at rest?'

'A little,' Seymour replied.

'But not altogether?'

Seymour shook his head. 'Marsham Grange still concerns me.'

'Marsham Grange is not our worry,' McCormick said sharply. 'The crucial difference between it and Derapur is that *we* are not growing potatoes at Marsham Grange.'

'Somebody is. You don't grow transgenic potatoes by accident. If it's not us, another breeding company must be involved.'

McCormick shrugged. 'That's MAFF's problem, not ours. I believe they're looking into that very question, but it's not something we need to concern ourselves with.' He paused, toying with his glass of whisky. 'Do you have any of the files on Derapur?'

Seymour didn't hesitate. 'No.'

'You seem very well informed about it.'

'I read the report a few years ago.'

'You must have a good memory.'

McCormick was studying him shrewdly. Seymour didn't flinch.

Some instinct of self-preservation had made him lie. The same instinct that had persuaded him it was wise to remove the file from his briefcase and place it somewhere less obvious. 'I have,' he said.

McCormick looked away first. He took another sip of whisky, staring at one of the paintings on the wall. 'I place a very high value on loyalty, David,' he said. 'Company loyalty. It's something I expect, something I'm *entitled* to expect from all my employees.'

He turned his head back. Seymour noticed a subtle change in the managing director's expression. Any pretence of warmth was gone.

'My loyalty isn't in question,' Seymour said defensively. 'But don't you think we have a duty to ensure we're doing the right thing?'

McCormick's lip curled. 'I don't pay you to have principles. I pay you to do as you're told. I don't want anybody stirring up trouble for us. Derapur is behind us now. Nothing will be served by bringing it up again. I remind you of the confidentiality clause in your contract. If anything were to leak out about Derapur or any other aspect of our business, I would take a very grave view of the situation. I would see it as gross misconduct warranting instant dismissal. Do I make myself clear, David?'

'Yes,' Seymour answered.

'That's all. You may go.'

Seymour stood up and walked out of the office. He was angry – at the humiliating manner in which he'd been sent away, at the threat which McCormick had so clearly made. He was angrier still when he got back to the lab. There were no really obvious signs, but from the position of his briefcase, the papers on his desk, he knew for certain that in his absence someone had searched through his belongings.

*   *   *

'Well?' McCormick demanded.

Cullimore shook his head. 'Nothing.'

'How thorough were you?'

'As thorough as the time allowed. It's not in his desk, his brief-case, the bench drawers. Did you ask him if he had it?'

'He denied it.'

'You believe him?'

'I don't know. I want you to keep an eye on him, Rick. I'm not sure I trust him.'

McCormick still had the glass of whisky on his desk. He picked it up and drained it. Then he flicked the rim of the glass with his fingernail, listening to the ping resonate around the office.

'What about the other file?' he asked suddenly.

'The . . . ?' Cullimore took a moment to work out what he meant. 'Oh, they checked out the kid's flat again. No mistakes this time. He hasn't got it.'

'And the search of the wood?'

'Nothing so far.'

'I want every inch checked.'

'The kid might have gone back for it. Hidden it somewhere else.'

'That's a possibility. But maybe he hasn't. Maybe it's still there. Under a log, buried in a hole, under leaves.'

'It's a big wood,' Cullimore said doubtfully.

'Don't give me problems,' McCormick said impatiently. 'Give me solutions.'

There was an unpredictable quality to the study of medicine which Housman found both fascinating and frustrating. Like all doctors, the more he discovered about the human body the more he realised how little he really knew. It seemed sometimes as if Nature were watching him, unseen, from the wings of a great stage, prompting him occasionally as he stumbled around the boards with his white coat and stethoscope, laughing as he fumbled his lines or bumped into the furniture, and waiting glee-fully for him to fall flat on his face.

When Phoebe and Jeff Harrison had been admitted to Addenbrooke's, he would have given strong odds on the father coping better with illness than the daughter. As a general rule, in most cases, that was how things worked out. Children were more vulnerable, had less developed immune systems than a fit, fully grown man. Yet in the end Phoebe's tiny, immature body had fought off the disease more successfully than her father. And Karl Housman had no idea why.

He'd examined her again that afternoon. Her temperature was well down, almost back to normal. She was still weak, still on oxygen to assist her breathing, but Housman was fairly confident that she was out of danger. And yet, when she'd arrived she'd been potentially a much more serious case than either her father or Caroline Malcolm, the other flu patient who was in a critical condition in the adjacent room, for Phoebe had also had the glycoalkaloid poisoning to contend with. Housman wondered if that had somehow worked to her advantage. Had the toxic substances in her bloodstream in some way helped combat the flu virus or was she just innately more resistant to the disease? Once again, Nature seemed determined to highlight his ignorance and make a fool of him.

He pondered the question at length when he returned to his office and it was then that he remembered the potatoes he'd had removed from the pigshed at Marsham Grange and taken away for analysis. Curious to know the results, he rang the Ministry of Agriculture laboratory and was put through to one of the tech-nicians. Housman explained who he was and why he was calling.

'Have the potatoes been tested yet?' he asked.

'I'm pretty sure they have,' the technician replied. 'Not by me, but I think they were completed yesterday morning. Hang on a sec.' Housman heard the technician shouting to someone. 'Jack! Those potatoes, Marsham Grange, what's the story? Yeah. When? Okay. ' The technician came back on the line. 'Dr Housman? Yeah, the report's gone upstairs. You want to speak to the director, Tony Fowler. I'll put you back to the switchboard.'

Housman was in limbo for a moment before the switchboard operator answered. Then he was put through to the lab director's extension.

'Fowler.' The voice was curt, harsh, unattractive.

Housman went through his introduction and explanation again. 'I was interested to know what the analysis found,' he said.

'It hasn't been done yet,' Fowler said.

'I'm sorry?'

'It hasn't been done.'

'What do you mean?'

'It's quite simple,' Fowler said rudely. 'The potatoes haven't been tested yet. Okay?'

'But I've just been told the tests were completed yesterday morning.'

'Told by whom?'

'One of your technicians. I don't know his name.'

There was a brief silence. Then Fowler said tersely, 'He had no business telling you anything. Everything comes through me. You should have come here first.'

Housman was bemused rather than angry at the lab director's belligerent tone. He couldn't understand why he seemed so hostile.

'So have the tests been done, or not?' Housman inquired.

'Who are you again?'

'My name is Housman. I'm a consultant at Addenbrooke's Hospital. The little girl who may have been poisoned by potatoes from Marsham Grange Farm is one of my patients.'

'You're not on my list of authorised recipients.'

Housman made a great effort to keep his cool. 'Then I think I should be, don't you?'

'It's not my decision,' Fowler said evasively.

'Then whose decision is it?'

'I take my instructions from MAFF in Whitehall. You'd better talk to them.'

'But you can tell me if the tests have been done, surely?' Housman persisted. 'I was told the report had been sent to you.'

'Speak to Whitehall. They're handling it.'

Housman hung up, puzzled and annoyed. There was something peculiar about this. He rang MAFF in London and after a couple of abortive conversations with people who clearly had no idea what he was talking about, resorted to trying Tristan Allardyce's office. Allardyce was in a meeting with the Minister, and his secretary was anything but helpful.

'We haven't received any report here,' she said.

'Perhaps you could ring your lab and tell the director there to give me the results,' Housman suggested.

'I don't have the authority to do that.'

'Then could you ask Mr Allardyce to do it?'

'He's very busy.'

'I need to know.'

'You'll have to wait until we get the report.'

'And when will that be?'

'I don't know.'

'Tell me,' Housman said, 'are you naturally this obstructive or have you done a course in it?'

'Pardon?'

He put down the receiver and took a deep breath. Having spent all his working life in the public sector, he was much more a believer in cock-up theory than conspiracy. Errors, inefficiencies, crises were nearly always due to incompetence or oversight. Rarely were they the result of some concerted clandestine plot.

But in this particular instance he was beginning to wonder. The evasiveness he was encountering seemed more than just the usual ingrained bureaucratic aversion to answering questions.

He sat absorbed in thought for several minutes, going over the two phone conversations in his head. Then he picked up the telephone and rang Marsham Grange.

'Is something wrong with the food?'

'Sorry, what was that?'

'The food. You're not eating.'

'Oh, no, it's fine.'

Seymour took a mouthful of chicken and chewed it pensively. His wife Jenny watched him from across the table, aware that he was with her in body but not in spirit.

'Do you want to tell me about it?' she said.

'Is it that obvious?'

Jenny nodded. 'Did something happen today?'

He described his interview with Cliff McCormick, the anger returning as he repeated what the managing director had said to him. 'He threatened me, treated me like some kind of servant.'

'You're sure you didn't imagine it?'

'He didn't bother to disguise it. They searched my desk too. That's what really got to me. And they did another random search of my briefcase when I left to come home.'

'Can they do that?'

'They can do what they like. They do spot checks every so often. It's never happened to me before but I know other people have been stopped on their way out. The security chief, Cullimore, is a real bastard. He likes to throw his weight around and McCormick gives him free reign.' Seymour gave a humourless chuckle. 'Still, they didn't find the file. I'm keeping that safely out of their way.'

Jenny looked at her husband, worried. He'd had bad days at

work in the past – who hadn't? – but she'd never seen him this upset. Of the two of them, he was usually the calmer, the phlegmatic scientist who took everything in his stride.

'Are you sure it's wise to hang on to it?' she asked. 'What are you going to do with it?'

Seymour pushed some rice around his plate with his fork, but didn't eat any of it. 'I mentioned it to Baxter because I was concerned,' he said. 'I thought I ought to, out of a sense of responsibility. Then I'm called upstairs and treated like some kind of criminal. It makes my blood boil. Do they think I have no integrity? That they can do what they like to me? You know what McCormick said to me? "I don't pay you to have principles." That's what he said. As if I was some kind of prostitute. It makes me wonder what I'm doing there. It makes me wonder about that company. Maybe I am a prostitute.'

Jenny stretched out her arm and placed her hand over her husband's. 'Don't let it get to you. You've done what you thought was right. Maybe McCormick has a point. It was several years ago, on a different continent. It's not important now. Perhaps you should forget all about it.'

'If it's not important, why did he react like that? You know, he seemed . . . scared.'

'It's his company. He doesn't want any bad publicity.'

'Are you taking his side?'

'Of course I'm not. But we need your job, David. In three months' time we'll be down to one income. Don't do anything foolish.'

'You think concern for the truth is foolish?'

'It is when your employer wants it concealed.' Jenny paused. 'I'm sorry, I didn't mean that.'

She stood up and came round to his side. She was six months pregnant now, her swollen belly getting more pronounced. She was starting to feel the extra weight, the discomfort. Moving around was becoming more difficult, particularly in the hot summer weather. Seymour pulled her to him, remaining in his seat. He put his arms around her waist and pressed his head gently against her abdomen. Sometimes he could feel the baby moving. Jenny stroked his hair.

'Your conscience is more important to me than your salary. You know that,' she said. 'What are you going to do?'

'I don't know. I think I'll sleep on it. See how things look in the morning.'

It was Sandy Harrison's sister, Angela, who answered the door. Housman stayed outside on the step, having second thoughts about whether this was such a good idea. Jeff Harrison had been dead only twenty-four hours. A visit from the doctor who'd failed to save his life was perhaps not what the family needed at this time.

'Is it all right for me to come in?' he said.

Angela nodded. 'Sandy's in the kitchen. Lucy and Tim are in bed.'

She stepped back to let him enter.

'How are they?' Housman asked though he knew it was a silly question. He could imagine the answer.

'As well as can be expected,' Angela replied. 'It's been a busy day.'

Housman followed her through into the big farmhouse kitchen. Darkness was falling outside and the room, with its stone-flagged floor and high ceiling, had a chilly feel. Sandy was sitting listlessly at the table. She looked hollow-eyed and tired.

'Would you like some tea?' Angela said.

'Thank you.'

Housman sat down on one of the pine chairs. This was something he'd never experienced before: seeing a bereaved family at home after the death of one of his patients. It was unsettling.

Being confronted with the consequences, the effects, not just giving out the bad news and being able to walk away from it.

'I won't take up too much of your time,' he said.

Sandy gave a brief nod. Housman wondered if she blamed him for her husband's death. Sometimes the bereaved did. When the initial blow of shock and grief had passed, that was when they often started to feel angry.

Sandy seemed to read his mind. 'I know you did all you could,' she said. 'It was . . .' Her voice petered out and she shrugged as if to say, what's the point, it's over now.

'Your daughter's making good progress,' he said, glad to have something positive to say.

'Phoebe?' Her eyes brightened. She leant towards him eagerly. 'Is she?'

'She's over the worst, I would say.'

'Can I visit her?'

'We'll see how things are tomorrow. She's making a good recovery.'

Sandy sighed and sagged back in her chair, her burst of energy suddenly waning. Her sister put a mug of tea on the table in front of her and handed another to Housman.

'Do you take sugar?'

'No, thank you,' Housman replied. What would the English do in adversity without the humble pot of tea?

He waited a short while before broaching the subject that had brought him out there. 'Your potatoes,' he began. 'The ones Phoebe ate on Sunday night. Have you any left from the same batch?'

'I threw them away,' Sandy said. 'As soon as your colleague said they might be poisonous I came home and dumped the lot in the bin.'

'Are they still there?'

She shook her head. 'The binmen came Tuesday morning.'

That was a setback. He should have expected it.

'You said they were your own potatoes. Do you have more of the same stored somewhere?'

'The Ministry people took them all.'

'Ministry people?'

'MAFF. They were out here this afternoon, asking questions. They took all the potatoes from the barn, said we were prohibited from harvesting any more.'

'Unpleasant blokes,' Angela said. 'Very rude and insensitive considering what Sandy's going through.'

'What kind of questions were they asking?'

'What type of potatoes we grew, where we got the seed, how we planted them, how we stored them. I wasn't much help to them. Jeff took care of all that.' Sandy swallowed. 'We're finished. They're going to spray the fields. Kill everything . . . that's the end.'

'I don't follow,' Housman said.

'The Ministry's ordered the crop to be destroyed,' Angela replied. 'Sprayed, then dug up and incinerated.'

Sandy gave a sob. 'We're ruined.'

'Destroyed? But why?'

'They said the potatoes are potentially toxic. All of them. They're coming back tomorrow to get rid of them.'

'I'm sorry,' Housman murmured lamely. He could think of nothing else to say.

A tear trickled down Sandy's face. 'What are we going to do? This is all we have. This is our life.'

'Can they do that?' Housman asked.

Angela nodded. 'Apparently, yes.' She put her hand on Sandy's shoulder. 'It's okay, we'll get through it.'

'Maybe I should go,' Housman said, putting down his mug of tea and standing up.

'I'm sorry we couldn't help you,' Angela apologised.

'No, I'm sorry to have troubled you. I didn't realise . . .' Housman stopped. Something had occurred to him. 'This is an organic farm, isn't it?'

'Yes.'

'So you recycle your kitchen waste. Your potato peelings.'

Sandy lifted her head and rubbed her tears away with the back of her hand. 'We have a compost heap round the side of the house.'

She came with him, a torch in her hand as the light was fading fast. The compost was divided into three slatted wooden bins according to the age of the decomposing waste. Sandy shone the torch into the nearest bin which had used tea leaves and vegetable matter on the top.

'Have you eaten potatoes since Sunday?' Housman asked.

'No. We've kept off them.'

'So any peelings near the top are probably from the weekend?'

'I suppose so.'

Housman bent down and carefully picked apart the heap. A few inches down, moist and putrid, was a layer of rotting potato peelings. He pulled out a handful and deposited them in a plastic bag he'd brought. Then they went back inside.

Housman was washing his hands at the kitchen sink when Angela came in from the hall. Housman turned and saw her face, the look of anxiety, almost of sickness.

'What is it?' Sandy said.

'Tim called out while you were outside,' Angela replied. 'He says he doesn't feel very well.'

11

Seymour had a restless night, lying awake for a long time thinking about Derapur and McCormick before finally dozing off into a troubled sleep. He was a loyal employee. He'd shown his commitment to the company over the past four years and took very seriously his contractual obligation of confidentiality. He understood the importance, particularly in his area of work, of maintaining a low profile and revealing nothing about what went on within the research centre. The GM ship was an unstable vessel, holed in several places by environmental activists and public opinion. No one who worked on board it wanted to rock the boat, it was too close to capsizing already.

But he wasn't a poodle. He had a brain, a conscience, and no one, not even his employer, was going to dictate how he used them. McCormick's reaction had surprised as well as upset him. Far from assuaging his doubts about the Derapur affair, the managing director's overtly bullying tactics had simply re-inforced his concerns. Something had happened in India. Something that neither Baxter nor McCormick wanted made known. Seymour found that disturbing. He believed in science as a form of truth. It had rules, principles that were inviolable, that couldn't be corrupted by man's self-interest and arrogance. It was perhaps a naive view, but he believed scientists should admit their mistakes and come clean when things went wrong. He wasn't going to allow himself to be tarnished by McCormick's dis-honesty. The question was what, if anything, should he do?

He was woken at first light by Jenny getting up to go to the toilet. As her pregnancy progressed, she was needing to go several times during the night. Even when she was lying down she was constantly twitching and rolling over, trying to get comfortable. It was hard for both of them. They woke up tired and irritable. Seymour looked on it as training for the arrival of the baby, when they would get even less sleep.

For a while he lay there, staring up at the shadows on the ceiling and listening to Jenny shuffling around on her side of the bed, the mattress springs vibrating under his back. Then he slid out from the duvet, threw on a pullover and went down-stairs to the kitchen and made some tea.

Drawing back the curtains, he looked out into the back garden. The view was what had persuaded them to buy the house. And the price. They'd wanted somewhere in Cambridge, but you could barely buy a kennel there for less than a hundred thou-sand. The Science Park and booming high-tech industries had seen to that. For anyone on a basic research or academic salary the city was out of the question. Even prices in the outlying villages were becoming ridiculous as property inflation spread out like ripples on a pond. Soham wasn't exactly picturesque, but they'd been lucky to find a house there they could afford. It was small and damp and poky, only just big enough for the two of them. But it was on the edge of the village and from the back windows they looked out over the green fields of Soham Mere. It was a flat, fairly dull vista, but Seymour found it restful. It was quiet, rural, calming.

He took his mug of tea through into the sitting room and sat down in an armchair, pondering his options. He could do nothing, of course: return the Derapur file to Central Records and forget all about it. That was the simplest choice. But he couldn't do that. He couldn't abdicate responsibility, pretend it was none of his business. It would always prey on his mind if he took that way out.

McCormick's attitude had made him determined to do something, a resolve that had been strengthened by one other factor in particular. Seymour had bought the *Cambridge Evening News* again on his way home the previous day. In it had been a short report on the death of Jeff Harrison. The news had shocked Seymour. This was more than just a farming story now. It wasn't simply an outbreak of flu with an ancillary problem of high glycoalkaloid levels in potatoes. A man had died. And another woman was seriously ill. He couldn't walk away from that.

He drank some of his tea. He could contact the Ministry of Agriculture and talk to them about his worries. That seemed a sensible, logical approach. But he had reservations about it. MAFF and Transgenic Biotech had very close links. To an outsider they might have seemed too close. The Ministry wasn't a truly independent body: it had been in the pocket of the farming and agrochemicals industries for years. In any conflict between farmers and consumers, MAFF was notorious for always siding with the farmers, and they had a strong vested interest in supporting the GM foods business. They would not be keen on hearing anything that might be detrimental to one of their favourite biotech companies, particularly fears as vague and inchoate as Seymour's.

There was always the press, of course. Seymour rejected immediately the idea of contacting a newspaper. He had nothing of real, proven substance to give them. Journalists wanted facts not tenuous theories and, besides, he didn't trust the media. He'd seen too many of their distortions about his own science used to whip up a witch-hunt against the transgenic breeding industry. They would use him for their own ends, then hang him out to dry.

Whatever he did, he knew he would be exposing himself to

damaging consequences. Whistleblowers, however well-inten-
tioned, always paid a high price: loss of job, of reputation,
sometimes of family and friends. No one ever applauded them
for their honesty. And Seymour had a wife and an imminent
new baby to consider.

He needed to be able to talk to someone in confidence.
Someone who understood the implications of these things and
could give him sound impartial advice. A lawyer. A face came
to him almost at once. A woman on a television screen. Dark-
haired, articulate, making a statement to the cameras outside
Cambridge Magistrates' Court. He tried to recall the name. King.
Something King. She was representing the hooligans who'd
ripped up the rape plants, who'd destroyed his lab, but that
seemed to give her the independence he was looking for. That
would reassure him that anything he did had a higher motiva-
tion than mere anger or pique.

Madeleine. Madeleine King. That was her name.

He took his mug of tea out into the hall and picked up the
telephone directory.

Madeleine was packing her briefcase, preparing to walk over to
Lion Yard, when her secretary put through the call.

'My name's Seymour, David Seymour.' He sounded breathless, a little nervous. 'I work at Transgenic Biotech.'

Madeleine put down her papers, giving him her full attention
now. 'Yes?'

'I'd like to talk to you. I *need* to talk to you.'

'What about?'

'Not on the phone. It's difficult. I need some advice.'

'Are you in trouble?'

'Can we meet? Some time today.'

Madeleine did a swift mental breakdown of her schedule. 'I
can make lunch-time. Do you know where my office is?'

'I'd rather not come to your office. Could we meet on more . . . neutral territory?'

Madeleine hesitated. She had a policy of never meeting clients except in her office or on premises linked to the criminal justice system – a police station or the court precincts. Given the dubious nature of many of the people she represented, and the seamy circles in which they moved, it was a wise precaution to make them come to her, to locations where she was in control. But David Seymour didn't sound like one of her usual clients. He was well-spoken, probably middle-class, educated. And he worked at Transgenic Biotech.

'Has this anything to do with the break-in at your research centre?' she asked.

'No.'

'It's a personal matter?'

'Not exactly.'

'Does it concern the company?'

'Look, I haven't much time. I'm in a call-box. Can we meet?'

His tone, the sense of urgency, of something important, swayed her judgment.

'Where did you have in mind?' she said.

'There's a pub on the A10. Near Waterbeach. The White Swan.'

'I know where you mean.'

'I can be there for half-twelve.'

'All right. Half-twelve.'

'Thank you.'

'Mr Seymour . . .'

The line went dead. Madeleine replaced the receiver slowly. She was intrigued. But in the pit of her stomach was a slight gnaw of anxiety. She wondered if she was doing the right thing.

Housman was given the news the minute he arrived at the hospital. Caroline Malcolm had died during the night. Cause of death: pneumonia and multiple organ failure. There had been nothing the team of doctors and nurses on duty had been able to do. Sometimes the human body was simply not capable of sustaining itself.

Housman wasn't surprised. When he'd come in late the previous evening with Tim Harrison, Caroline Malcolm had been in a bad way. She was being kept alive with every medical support the Isolation Unit could provide, but he'd realised then that it wouldn't be long before her diseased, exhausted body gave up the fight.

The statistics weren't looking good. Tim Harrison now had the virus – Housman had confirmed the diagnosis with an immunofluorescence test on the child's nasopharyngeal fluids, seen the virions for himself under the electron microscope. That meant four people had contracted the disease. Two of them had died, a mortality rate of fifty per cent. It was a misleading extrapolation, based as it was on such a small total, but it was chilling nonetheless. No flu strain Housman had ever encountered had a death rate of one in two.

Half an hour later, the total changed. Stephen Manville called to say that two more people had gone down with what appeared to be the same influenza. A man of sixty-three and a thirty-eight-year-old woman, both from Great Dunchurch. They were being sent by ambulance to Addenbrooke's.

'Have you told Allardyce?' Housman asked.

'I've faxed his office.'

'What about the cull? Have they made a decision on that yet?'

'Not to my knowledge.'

'I thought they were going to do it yesterday.'

'This is Whitehall, Dr Housman. Nothing ever happens yesterday. Tomorrow, next week, next month, but never yesterday.'

Housman smiled sardonically. Manville and he were on the

same wavelength. Unfortunately, no one else was tuning in to listen to them.

'These two new victims,' Housman said. 'Do they have any connection with farming or pigs or hens?'

'We're checking. We got the notification from the GPs. I've sent someone out to talk to the families, see if we can identify the source. I'll let you know as soon as we get more information.'

Housman rang off, then phoned Mill Hill, hoping for better news. Fitzgerald was downbeat. He and his team were making little headway.

'We've cultured enough to do a couple of tests for the haemagglutinin,' he said. 'It's not an H4 or H5. We got no reaction from the antisera.'

'No reaction at all?'

'I'm afraid not.'

'We need a result, Ian.'

'We're doing our best. The virus grows very slowly. You know how long it could take to run all the tests.'

'I know.'

'Is it spreading?'

'Only six cases so far. Two dead.'

'*Two*?' Fitzgerald cursed under his breath.

'It's virulent,' Housman said. 'But it seems to be contained. At the moment. If it takes off . . .'

He didn't finish the sentence. There was no point in speculating. They both knew what they were dealing with here.

'We'll get there, Karl,' Fitzgerald said. 'We just need more time.'

'Okay, I'll keep in touch.'

Housman hung up, reflecting grimly that time was probably the one thing they didn't have.

* * *

Allardyce had kept the meeting deliberately small. Just three men: the Agriculture Minister, David Coldwell; his junior, Max Vector; and Allardyce himself. Whitehall was notoriously leaky, the House of Commons even worse. Allardyce didn't want a word of what they discussed to go beyond the oak-panelled walls of the Minister's office.

'Right, Tristan,' Coldwell said. 'Where do we stand?'

Allardyce took a sip of his coffee to wet his lips. A sip was about all he could stomach. The Minister insisted that nothing but Nicaraguan coffee should be served in his office: a hangover from his days as a local councillor in the self-styled People's Republic of South Yorkshire when he'd been a vociferous supporter of the Sandinista revolution. He'd toned down his left-wing views since becoming an MP, even more so after he'd joined the Cabinet, but although just about every one of his socialist principles had been jettisoned in the interests of his career, he was still a hardliner when it came to coffee. Allardyce, who prided himself on his refined palate and had his own special blend of Old Government Java and Blue Mountain made up for him at Fortnum and Masons, had no particular doctrinal objections to Nicaraguan beans. He simply couldn't abide their taste.

'Well, we now have the written submissions from the Chief Medical officer, Dr Cameron,' he began. 'I believe you've both had a copy.'

'Perhaps you'd give us a précis of his views, Tristan,' Coldwell said.

'Of course, Minister.'

Coldwell, like every other minister Allardyce had served, preferred a brief verbal outline to a detailed written report. It was so much easier to let someone else pick out the important bits.

'As you know, after our meeting yesterday, the Chief Medical Officer consulted with a number of experts on swine and poultry diseases. He summarises their opinions here on page two of his report. In essence, there seems to be no unanimous view on the course of action we should take.'

Coldwell frowned. 'You mean he's made no recommendation?'

'He's leaving the decision to you, Minister.'

That was the last thing a politician wanted to hear.

'We asked him for a recommendation. What's he playing at?'

'He's putting both sides of the argument. For and against a cull.'

'That's no bloody use to us,' Coldwell snapped. 'What do *I* know about fucking chicken flu? I don't want opinions, I want a clear and unequivocal recommendation.' He shook his head contemptuously. 'The trouble with Cameron is that he's too indecisive to give us a lead. He can't bloody well make up his mind on anything.'

Coming from someone who had weals on his backside from sitting on the fence, that was just a little bit rich, but no one commented. Allardyce gave a soothing murmur which, over the years, he'd developed as a response to ministerial anger. It signified nothing, neither agreement nor dissent. It was simply a noise, like the meaningless cooing of a mother over her screaming newborn baby.

Coldwell decided to pass the buck around a bit. 'Max, what's your view of the report?'

Vector fingered the sheaf of papers. He was a slim, elegant man with black slicked-back hair and rather delicate features. In private, the civil servants called him Max Factor because of his penchant for wearing mascara on his long dark eyelashes. Allardyce knew one or two even more interesting things about him, courtesy of a classified MI5 file on the MP, but he was too discreet to reveal them – at least for the time being.

'I think we should be wary of panicking the public,' Vector

said. 'Salmonella, BSE, CJD, E Coli, filthy abattoirs, foot-and-mouth, all the rest of it. Now flu. They'll begin to think nothing we produce in this country is safe to eat.'

'They're probably right,' Coldwell admitted. 'But the farmers will be dead against a slaughter programme. I don't want the bloody NFU on my back yet again.'

'But at the same time, if we try to play it down, keep it under wraps, it may spread and we'll be accused of being irresponsible. I think we should come clean. Be completely open about the whole thing.'

'Now let's be careful here,' Allardyce jumped in quickly. If anything was guaranteed to start a civil servant foaming at the mouth it was mentioning the word openness. 'We still only have one farm affected. The dead animals have been disposed of, the waste buried, the premises disinfected. That might be the extent of the outbreak. It might be over. Killing healthy animals on neighbouring farms might be completely counterproductive. It will alarm people unnecessarily. And the farmers will demand full compensation.'

'That's one thing you can be absolutely sure of,' Coldwell remarked sourly.

He was an urban MP, representing a city constituency in the north of England, and he resented the hold the farming lobby had over government. Whatever they did, farmers always felt they had a right to be compensated. They poisoned people with salmonella-infected eggs and chickens, they fed their cattle with scrapie-infected sheep remains, passing on BSE to their herds and CJD to the human population. Any other industry which killed its customers would have been prosecuted, but farmers were given millions of pounds in state handouts instead. Coldwell knew it was outrageous, but the farming community had powerful friends and no Minister for Agriculture was going to take them on. It would have been political suicide.

'So you're saying we shouldn't cull, is that right, Tristan?' Coldwell asked.

Allardyce was far too smart to fall for that one. 'I'm not saying anything, Minister. This is a political decision. I'm merely outlining the problems it may cause.'

'Thank you, Tristan,' Coldwell said with just a hint of irony. 'We take note of your views.'

'They aren't my views, Minister. They're in the Chief Medical Officer's report.'

Coldwell stirred his cup of coffee, wondering if his favourite policy of wait and see could be applied in this instance.

'What's the position on the human victims?' he asked.

'Another two new cases this morning. One more death overnight,' Allardyce replied.

'All linked to this one farm?'

'I don't know about the new cases. The death is linked to Marsham Grange, yes.'

'Have you got to the bottom of this GM mystery?'

Allardyce shook his head. 'Not yet.'

'What about the lab report?'

'We're holding back on that.'

'I want it buried,' Coldwell said. 'Good and deep.'

'Is that wise?' Max Vector interjected.

'It's irrelevant to the question in hand,' Coldwell fired back at once. 'The outbreak of bird flu is completely separate from our biotech policy. Let's not confuse the two. Can we bury it?'

'If that is your wish,' Allardyce said. 'We have no obligation to make it public.'

'Do it. It only muddies the waters. I know I'll have the PM's backing on that.'

'Which leaves the question of the slaughter programme,' Allardyce reminded them.

'Yes.'

Coldwell drummed his fingers on the surface of his desk. There was no escaping this one. No way that he could see of passing responsibility on to someone else's shoulders. He reviewed all his options, looking to see what the fallout from each one might be. And where it might land. The first rule of ministerial office was ensuring you were out of range when the shit hit the fan.

The sudden jarring noise of the telephone interrupted his concentration. He snatched up the receiver. 'I thought I said we weren't to be disturbed,' he barked. 'What?' He listened for a time. 'Yes, thank you.'

He put down the receiver and glanced at the others. 'There's been another outbreak of flu. Pigs and hens all dead.'

'Where?' Allardyce asked.

'Great Dunchurch again. I think that makes the decision for us, don't you?'

Madeleine glanced impatiently at her watch. It was nearly noon and the magistrates still hadn't come back into the courtroom. She looked across at Tina Martin, slumped dejectedly in the dock, and gave her a brief encouraging smile though there was very little to be positive about. The young girl was back before the Bench for yet another breach of bail conditions. Madeleine was pretty sure that this time she'd be remanded in custody. The clock on the courtroom wall ticked round to twelve o'clock. Madeleine watched it uneasily. There was no way she was going to make it to Waterbeach for half past.

Going out into the vestibule, she rang her secretary on her mobile and asked her to look up the number of Transgenic Biotech. Then she called the research centre and was put through to Seymour's extension.

'Hello?'

'Mr Seymour?'

'Yes.'

'It's Madeleine King.'

'You shouldn't ring me here. What is it?' His voice was hurried, so low it was barely audible.

'I'm running a little late. Could we put back our meeting until one o'clock?'

'Yes, I'll be there.'

He rang off abruptly. Madeleine put away her mobile, wondering about the note of anxiety she'd heard in his tone. She continued to think about it until the magistrates came back into the courtroom and asked Tina to stand up in the dock.

'Miss Martin, we have considered your case and your solicitor's submissions very carefully, taking into account your particular circumstances. However, you have twice been in breach of your bail conditions, both breaches in the space of a week, and we have no guarantees that you will not do it again. We therefore feel we have no option but to remand you in custody . . .'

Madeleine looked away, angry at the stupidity of it all. A girl – and that's all she was – like Tina shouldn't be in prison. What would that achieve? An unwanted pregnancy forced through to its full term, another unwanted child taken into care. Madeleine clenched her fists under the table. She wanted to take the magistrates, those three comfortable middle-class, middle-aged justices, outside and introduce them to Wayne. Show them the grotty flat where Tina lived, the few pounds a week that her pimp permitted her to have, the squalid streets she was forced to walk in her tight skirt and boob tube. Give them a brief taste of something Tina would be choking on for probably the rest of her life. And all because of a few sordid men – Wayne included – who wanted a quick fuck.

Madeleine gathered up her files and left the courtroom. Wayne was outside in the vestibule. He curled his lip and sneered at her.

'You got her sent down, you twat.'

'I beg your pardon?' Madeleine said incredulously.

'You heard. You got her sent down. You're a fucking useless lawyer.'

Madeleine stared at him. Then she walked away quickly before she took out her mobile phone and rammed it down his throat.

'I think you should listen to this.'

Cullimore placed the portable tape recorder on McCormick's desk and adjusted the volume control.

'It came through to David Seymour just a few minutes ago.'

Cullimore pressed the 'play' button and sat back, watching McCormick's face as he listened to the recorded telephone conversation. The managing director frowned, concentrating on the brief exchange.

'Madeleine King? Isn't she the . . .'

'The solicitor acting for those kids who trashed the lab.' Cullimore turned off the tape recorder. 'You want to hear it again?'

McCormick shook his head. He was still frowning, the signs of anger spreading to the rest of his face, his mouth, his jaw.

'And she's meeting Seymour?' he said.

'You know what I think? He's been in league with those environmental bastards all along. It was probably Seymour who told them the security routine, when the fields were checked, how often. He probably told them how to get into the lab too. The little shit's working for the other side.'

'Get him up here, Rick,' McCormick said. 'Get him up here now.'

Seymour knew he was in serious trouble from the moment Cullimore burst into the lab and marched over to his desk. The security chief's expression, his body language were aggressive. He gave the impression that it was only the exercise of a fierce self-control that prevented him hauling Seymour out of his chair and beating him to a pulp. McCormick too, when they entered his office, had the demeanour of a man spoiling for a fight.

Seymour was intimidated, but he was too busy trying to figure out what was going on to let it get to him – until they played him the tape. Then he felt sick. Sick and scared, but also indignant. They'd taped his phone conversation. Taped a private call. That stunned him. He wondered at his own naivety. He'd worked for the company for four years, had thought it a benign organisation. Now he was seeing the true nature of the beast.

'Do you have anything to say?' McCormick said when the tape had finished.

Seymour kept silent.

'I said, do you have anything to say?' McCormick repeated more forcefully.

Seymour looked the managing director in the eye. 'That was a personal call. I don't think it's any of your business.'

McCormick came up out of his chair, the veins standing out in his forehead, his hands gripping the edge of his desk. 'None of my business?' he exploded. 'It's none of my business when one of my employees is meeting the lawyer representing the hooligans who vandalised my fields, my lab? Caused thousands of pounds worth of damage. That's none of my business? Well, think again.'

'It has nothing to do with what happened in the lab,' Seymour said quietly.

'Oh no? You expect me to believe that? You know what I think? You told them how to get into the lab. You told them when to attack the field so they'd miss the routine security checks. You betrayed us to a bunch of ignorant yobs. You sold us down the fucking river.'

'Why would I tell them how to break into the lab?' Seymour asked. 'It was *my* work they destroyed – *my* research.'

But McCormick wasn't in the mood to listen to reason. 'Was it money? Is that why you did it? Did they pay you? Or maybe you had a grudge against us. Is that it? You wanted to get your own back for something.'

'I've never spoken to any of those eco-protesters.'

'But you've spoken to their lawyer. What about? What have you told the bitch?'

Seymour sensed Cullimore coming up beside him, leaning down so close he could feel the heat of his breath.

'He asked you a question, dickhead. What's the answer?'

For an instant, Seymour was sure Cullimore was going to hit him. The security chief wanted to, that was obvious. But at the last moment he got a grip on himself and pulled back, flexing his biceps to dissipate some of the pent-up tension.

'What have you told her about this company?' McCormick demanded, his face flushing through his smooth suntan. 'What secrets have you sold? There are plenty of people who would love to know what we do here.'

'I've sold nothing,' Seymour said.

He knew he was finished, that protestations of innocence were useless. The phone call was all the evidence they needed.

'That's crap. You're a lying prick, Seymour.'

McCormick came out from behind his desk, into the open so they faced each other. Nothing in between.

'You're a fucking idiot too. You had a bright future here, a good career, good prospects. You've just thrown it all down the toilet. And don't think for one minute you can go elsewhere. This is a small world. I'll put the word about and make sure you never work in this industry again. Ever. I never forget people who cross me. I'm a fucking elephant when it comes to betrayal.'

McCormick licked his lips, panting like an asthmatic. 'You're fired. As of now. Your contract's terminated, but the confidentiality clause still applies. You breathe one word about your work

here and my lawyers will destroy you. You understand? Now
get the fuck out of my building.'

Seymour stood up. He was dazed, taken aback by McCormick's
fury, the crude hostility of his words. But he was furious too.
They'd monitored his phone calls, spied on him, then subjected
him to this unfair, undeserved harangue. He was tempted to
retaliate, to tell them why he was seeing Madeleine King, but
that seemed a childish tit-for-tat gesture. He didn't have to justify
himself. Besides, he had no intention of revealing his hand now
they'd dismissed him.

He walked out of the office with as much dignity as he could
muster. Cullimore remained behind, looking anxiously at
McCormick.

'He knows about Genesis II.'

'I know.'

'If he blabs . . .'

McCormick walked away from his desk to gaze out of the
window. In business, as in every other aspect of life, you looked
after your own.

'He won't blab though, will he?'

McCormick turned and looked at Cullimore. Cullimore nodded.

On the way downstairs to the lab Seymour had a sudden, frightening realisation of exactly what he'd done and what it meant.
He thought fleetingly of Jenny, the baby, the mortgage, his career,
the future, and blanked them all out ruthlessly, knowing he
couldn't cope with the worry at this moment. What concerned
him now was how he was going to get the Derapur file out of
the research centre.

A security man named Clark, who'd been waiting outside
McCormick's office, accompanied him all the way back to the
lab, to watch him clear his desk and then escort him from the
building. Seymour emptied the contents of the desk drawers.

They contained very few personal possessions: a coffee mug, a diary, a few photographs and an electronic calculator. That was about all. He packed them into his briefcase and clicked it shut as Cullimore came into the lab.

'You finished?' Cullimore said.

'I'm just going to say goodbye to Dr Baxter.'

'You've got two minutes.'

Seymour picked up his briefcase and walked the length of the room. Baxter watched him coming through the glass walls of his office. There were other people in the lab, colleagues, friends. They glanced at Seymour as he passed, instinctively moving away as if he were tainted by some contagious infection. 'What's going on, David?' one of them asked. Seymour was too abstracted, too focused on other matters to even hear the question, much less reply.

Baxter stayed seated behind his desk when Seymour came into his office. His eyes flickered from Seymour to the two uniformed security guards standing sentinel out in the lab.

'I've come to say goodbye, Dennis. I've been fired,' Seymour said.

Baxter showed no sign of surprise. He'd already worked out what had happened from watching Seymour clear his desk.

'I'm sorry, David. You were a valued member of the team.'

'Was I?' Seymour said bitterly.

Baxter couldn't meet his gaze. He stared down at his desk, picking nervously at his beard. His conscience troubled him a little – if he hadn't gone to McCormick? – but not enough to inconvenience him. He wasn't a fighter. He'd do nothing to keep Seymour on board. They'd replace him easily enough. Baxter did as he was told and kept his mouth shut. That was how McCormick liked it.

'I just wanted to say thank you for everything you've done for me,' Seymour said. 'I appreciate it.'

Baxter nodded. He didn't want to prolong the conversation. His eyes shifted across to the security guards again. Seymour looked round. Cullimore and Clark were still waiting by his desk. But they were getting impatient.

'Well, goodbye then,' Seymour said.

He held out his hand and, somewhat reluctantly, Baxter shook it.

Seymour went out through the door. On the first bench, just outside the office, was an electric propagator, a glass-sided heated container for germinating seeds. Seymour lifted up the lid of the propagator and pulled out the tray of seedlings inside, aware that the two security guards were watching him intently. Watching, but not reacting. In one swift movement, he whipped out the rubber mat in the bottom of the propagator and removed the thin cardboard file from underneath.

'Hey!' Cullimore shouted, suddenly realising what Seymour was doing.

The two guards started to run down the lab. But by then, Seymour had flung open the door next to Baxter's office and was through into the adjoining laboratory. File and briefcase clasped under his arm, he ran for the door at the far end of the room. As he reached the door, he glanced back and saw Cullimore and Clark coming after him. He tore open the door and sprinted down the corridor, round the corner, then straight ahead. Just seventy metres to the fire exit at the front of the building. He covered the ground in seconds, barely noticing the exertion. Ramming the metal bar on the fire exit, he burst out on to the driveway and headed round the side of the centre to the car park. He fumbled for his keys as he approached his car. Found the lock, pulled open the door. Threw in the file and briefcase, then jumped in after them. No time for a seat-belt. No time for anything except escape. Cullimore and Clark were twenty metres away. Seymour turned the ignition, released the handbrake. He rammed the gear lever into first and floored the accelerator. The two guards dived out of the way as the car came straight for them. By the time they picked themselves up, Seymour was on the drive heading for the main road.

At the end of the drive, Seymour braked. He looked in the rear-view mirror. Cullimore and Clark were climbing into one of the company Land-Rovers parked outside the front entrance. Seymour didn't wait to see any more. He turned out on to the road and accelerated away. It was five miles to Waterbeach. He checked the dashboard clock. It read nearly ten to one. He might just be on time for his meeting. He glanced sideways. The Derapur file was on the passenger seat next to him. Was it worth it? he thought briefly before turning his attention back to the road.

There was nothing in front of him. The road ran in a straight line to the horizon, flanked on either side by fields of wheat and oilseed rape. Perhaps half a mile ahead a raised earth embankment crossed the road at right angles, the carriageway disappearing through a notch in the slope like the V-sight on a sniper's rifle. Seymour fixed his eyes on the gap and put his foot down. The speedometer climbed above fifty, then sixty. His old D-reg Allegro wasn't capable of much more. Already he could feel the chassis vibrating beneath his seat. He looked in the mirror. The Land-Rover was out on the road behind him. He knew it was a more powerful, faster vehicle. In a straight race it would easily overhaul him. But he had four hundred metres start. Maybe that would be enough to keep him in front until he reached Waterbeach.

He raced through the break in the embankment, keeping to the middle of the deserted road. He was gripping the wheel so hard his arms were aching. He took another quick look in the mirror. The Land-Rover was gaining on him. He was sure of it.

The road started to bend to the left. Seymour eased off a little on the accelerator, feeling the force pushing him sideways into his door. Then the bend straightened out and he saw a cross-roads a quarter of a mile in front. The signposts were too far away, too small to read, but he knew the left turn was the most direct route to Waterbeach – the shortest, but not necessarily the quickest. If he kept straight on he would hit the A10 further north, a longer distance but on faster roads. He weighed up the options. *Make a decision.* The Land-Rover was closer now, there was no doubt about it. Should he keep going and try to outrun it, or turn off?

He kept straight on. He couldn't risk slowing, having to nego-tiate the sharp turn and then building up speed again. The Land-Rover would be on him before he'd gone any distance. Already it was frighteningly close. A hundred metres behind, perhaps less.

The road went over a narrow bridge across a drainage ditch, then started to turn in a long righthand curve. Seymour saw a lode on his left, a broad strip of gleaming water edged by steep grassy banks. The carriageway stayed almost parallel to the lode, only a few metres away. Seymour watched the Land-Rover looming up in his mirror. He accelerated, pushing his car to the limit. The speed crept up to seventy, higher. The curve of the road increased. Seymour clung on to the wheel. The Land-Rover dropped back a little. Seymour looked ahead and suddenly saw why. A farm tractor was coming round the bend towards him, its trailer so wide it straddled the centre of the road. Seymour braked hard. His wheels locked into a skid, the tyres screaming. The car veered sideways. He wrenched hard on the steering wheel, his right foot still jammed on the brake pedal. For a second he thought he was going to make it. Then the road disappeared from sight and he felt the car shoot out into space. As the front bumper hit the lode, Seymour was flung forwards, his body smashing through the windscreen and out over the water.

At the wheel of the following Land-Rover, Clark slowed almost to a standstill.

'Keep going!' Cullimore yelled at him.

He looked to the left as they swept round the bend, the tractor pulling off on the other side. The Allegro was sinking slowly into the lode, its bonnet and sides submerged. And floating face down a few metres away was a crumpled body, the water around its head turning pink, spreading slowly out like a halo.

12

Walking through the streets of Cambridge it was hard not to feel oppressed by the shadows of history that lay like a mantle over the city. Every building, every narrow passageway, every open space seemed to echo with the footsteps of former residents, the great men whose achievements were beacons of enlightenment in the dark annals of time, whose genius was a constant, daunting benchmark for future generations to measure themselves against – and find themselves lacking.

The names were a roll-call of scientific, political and artistic accomplishment: Newton, Darwin, Pepys, Keynes, Cromwell, Pitt, Byron, Milton, Wordsworth, Tennyson. They had all left their unique stamp, not just on the city and their old colleges, but on the wider world outside. They were giants of their disciplines, familiar names to every schoolchild in the country, but posterity would perhaps look back and confer the greatest significance on two lesser-known fellows of the university, Francis Crick and James Watson who in 1953 unravelled the structure of DNA, the key to life itself.

The Eagle pub on Bene't Street had been one of Crick and Watson's favourite haunts, a dark, gloomy watering-hole where they'd spent many hours discussing their research. Housman had also been a frequent visitor during his undergraduate years at King's, and whenever he went through the doors into the wood-panelled bar he could almost sense their ghostly presence, two faint spectres looking down in wonderment, and perhaps horror, at where succeeding generations of geneticists had taken their work.

But he hadn't been there for several years. It was always either full of noisy students or weary tourists, two groups he made a point of avoiding if he possibly could. Today was no different. The front bar was jammed with young men and women. Many of them still had exams to sit, but that didn't seem to stop them spending half the day in the pub. Housman squeezed his way past them and looked around.

The Eagle was an old pub, but very little of its décor was authentic. Tarted up by the brewery, it had a huge open fireplace surmounted by a blackened oak beam, earthenware jugs displayed on shelves and worn leather bridles and horse harnesses hanging from the brick walls – all carefully contrived to convey the ambience of a simple rustic inn, though it was unlikely that any ploughman had ever set foot in the place.

Housman studied the list of wines chalked on a blackboard over the fireplace for a few minutes, then saw Jeremy Blake come in through the door. Housman waved him over. 'What'll you have?'

Blake surveyed the row of pumps on the bar. 'A pint of Old Speckled Hen.'

Housman ordered the beer and a tonic water for himself. He never drank alcohol at lunch-times. It didn't do much for a patient's confidence if his doctor came back to the hospital reeking of booze.

'Any chance of a seat?' Blake said, peering around the throng.

But all the tables were occupied, three of them by a party of Japanese tourists who looked glazed-eyed and footsore, the classic symptoms of Heritage Fatigue from which all tour groups in Cambridge eventually suffered.

Housman picked up his glass and they moved out into the galleried courtyard at the side of the pub. They sat down at one of the wooden picnic tables, a hanging basket overflowing with impatiens, petunias and trailing ivy dangling just above their heads.

'Thanks for coming,' Housman said.

'My pleasure. It's been a while.'

They were old friends from their university days. They'd shared a staircase at King's in their first undergraduate year and remained in touch ever since. The contact had been intermittent during Housman's time at Mill Hill, but since his return to Addenbrooke's they'd met every few months for a drink or a meal. Blake wasn't a medic. He'd read botany for his degree, got a first and then stayed on to teach and do research into plant chemistry. He had a fellowship at Pembroke College, a growing international reputation in his field, but still somehow managed to look only a little older than his students. He was helped by having a round boyish face almost untouched by lines or wrinkles and he dressed much younger than his forty-four years. With his collar-length blond hair and jeans and leather jacket he looked nothing like the usual stereotyped picture of a Cambridge don.

'How's things?' Housman said. 'You still with, what was her name, Rachel?'

Blake shook his head. 'That finished in the spring.'

'And the new one, what's she called?'

Housman knew there would be a new one. Blake was one of those men who moved effortlessly from woman to woman. Whenever he split up with one girlfriend there always seemed to be another one waiting in the wings to take her place. Housman wondered how he did it. The technique, the gift, whatever it was, had always eluded him.

'Rebecca.'

'Student?'

'Postgrad.'

'So not quite cradle snatching, just pushchair snatching.'

Blake grinned. 'She's very mature for her age.'

'Which is?'

'Twenty-three.'

'One of yours?'

'Yeah.'

Blake's girlfriends were invariably students he taught. The allure of the pupil-teacher relationship. Or maybe they were just too scared to turn him down.

'And you?' Blake said.

'Me?'

'You found anyone yet?'

Housman shrugged. 'You know . . .' he mumbled vaguely.

'You work too hard. And that Sellotape on your glasses – it doesn't do much for your sex appeal.'

'Mmm.'

'Don't you miss it?'

'Sex? I don't know.'

The truth of the matter was he didn't miss it. Since his divorce three years earlier he'd been comfortably celibate. Starting over again was something he couldn't face at the moment. Women were such hard work. He didn't know where Blake got his energy.

Blake drank some of his beer. 'So what was this favour you wanted to ask?'

Housman picked up the carrier bag he'd placed by his feet and opened it to show Blake the contents. 'Could you run some tests on these potato peelings for me?'

'Tests for what?'

'Glycoalkaloids.'

'This is a bit outside your normal field, isn't it?'

'I have a patient who came in suffering from glycoalkaloid poisoning. I'd like to know a bit more about the potatoes she ate. The hospital lab doesn't have the expertise to run checks on vegetables.'

'Glycoalkaloid poisoning? That's unusual.'

'I know. That's why I want them tested.'

'What about MAFF? You tried them?'

Housman sipped his tonic water. Why were non-alcoholic drinks in pubs so revolting? He put his glass down on the table and wiped his lips. 'I gave some to MAFF . . .' he began.

'And?'

'They seem very reluctant to give me the results. I have no idea why.'

'So you want a second opinion?'

Housman nodded. 'If you can find the time.'

'It won't be my time,' Blake replied. 'I'll get a technician to do it.'

'This is unofficial, Jeremy. I don't want anyone except you to know the peelings came from me.'

'Okay. I won't be able to arrange it until after the weekend.'

'Whenever you can fit it in.'

Sitting by herself in a pub usually made Madeleine uncomfortable, but the White Swan – according to the sign outside – was a 'family-friendly inn', catering specifically for parents and children. It had a restaurant – Toby's Tuck-in – with posters of a garish clown character called Toby Tickler grinning down from every wall and a special Kids' Menu which, as far as Madeleine could judge from the one on her table, consisted entirely of junk food. She wondered why it was that with an adult population increasingly concerned about a healthy diet, it was assumed that children could only cope with fish fingers and chips.

Beyond the open French windows, in the garden at the rear

of the pub, was a children's play area: swings, a see-saw, a round-about and a huge fibreglass tree trunk with a face painted on one side and a slide emerging from its open mouth. A group of mums was sitting at a picnic table, drinking and laughing while their kids clambered over the play apparatus. Madeleine watched them, wishing that places like this had been around when Graham was a toddler. She might have felt less isolated, less trapped, been a happier mother.

Where was David Seymour? She checked her watch again. It was a quarter past one. She was starting to feel embarrassed. There was nothing threatening about the atmosphere in the bar, but she was acutely aware of being a woman on her own, was beginning to imagine that everyone was watching her. She took out her mobile phone, partly to give herself something to do, and rang the Transgenic Biotech research centre.

'David Seymour, please,' she said.

'Who's calling?'

'I'd just like to speak to him, please.'

She was put on hold, listening to *Eine Kleine Nachtmusik*, then another voice came on the line, a man's voice this time.

'Who is this?' he enquired bluntly.

'I was wanting David Seymour.'

'He's not here. Who are you?' His tone was aggressive, confrontational.

'Do you know where he is?' Madeleine asked.

'Why do you want him? What's your name?'

Madeleine broke the connection. What was that all about? She was puzzled by the man's rudeness. Unsettled by it too. She put her phone away in her bag and stood up. She'd waited long enough.

There was a cardboard cut-out of Toby Tickler by the exit. Madeleine glanced at it as she went out and almost shuddered. He had presumably been designed to appeal to the very young, but he was not a reassuring figure. With his vivid green wig, thick make-up and leering grin he looked, to her, like every mother's nightmare image of a child molester.

She went to her car and sat for a moment, thinking about the exchange she'd just had on the telephone, then recalling her earlier conversations with David Seymour. He'd phoned her from a call-box. She should have remembered that and not rung him back at work. Perhaps she'd compromised him in some way? But even so, why hadn't he met her as arranged?

Madeleine started the engine and, on impulse, decided to drive out to the research centre. It was only a few miles.

She headed north up the A10, then turned off east, winding down the window to let the breeze blow in. It was a clear, warm afternoon, the visibility near perfect for driving. After a few minutes she noticed blue flashing lights ahead of her. Drawing nearer, she saw a couple of police cars parked at the side of the road, an ambulance next to them and a police breakdown lorry completely blocking the carriageway. She slowed and came to a halt next to a uniformed constable who was standing in the middle of the road.

'You'll have to turn round, madam,' the constable said, leaning down to her window. 'The road's going to be closed for quite some time.'

'What's happened?'

'Car gone off into the canal.'

'Anyone hurt?'

'One dead.'

Madeleine could see two paramedics lifting a body bag on to a stretcher and wheeling it round to the back of the ambulance. Another man, in dark blue overalls, was down by the edge of the water, fastening a cable to the rear of a car which was half submerged in the lode. Its roof and the tops of its windows were just visible above the surface.

Curious, Madeleine opened her door and climbed out. It seemed ghoulish to stand and gawp, but she found the scene irresistible. Someone else had also stopped. There was a man who looked like a farmer standing next to a tractor and trailer just in front of her. Painted on the side of the trailer was the legend, 'H.D. Steadman, Goose Fen Farm'. Madeleine studied the man and revised her first impression. Maybe he hadn't stopped to watch. He was talking to another uniformed constable who was making notes in his pocket book as if he were taking a statement. And, more peculiarly, the farmer's clothes were soaked from top to toe. He was standing in a puddle of water, his shirt and trousers dripping wet.

'It looked to me as if they were having a race,' the farmer was saying.

'A race?' the constable said, looking up from his notebook.

'Driving like madmen they were. Belting along the road, stupid idiots.'

'There was another vehicle involved?'

'Right behind the one that crashed.'

'Can you describe this vehicle?'

'Land-Rover. Dark blue. Bastards never stopped. They saw the other fellow go off into the lode and just kept going. Despicable thing to do.'

'A Land-Rover, you say?' the constable asked.

'Aye. From the Transgenic Biotech place. Research centre. It's a couple of miles from here.'

'Are you sure?'

'You can't miss them. Security guards. They wear uniforms. The company name was on the side of the Land-Rover.'

The farmer turned his head, distracted by a sudden clanking noise. The drum on the back of the recovery lorry was turning, winching in the cable attached to the car. The vehicle emerged gradually from the lode, water pouring off its sides.

The windscreen was shattered, but apart from that it showed few signs of damage.

'Madam . . .'

Madeleine glanced round. The first constable was at her shoulder.

'Would you move your car, please, to let the ambulance past?'

'Of course.'

Madeleine climbed back into her car and reversed a few metres, pulling in on the dirt verge beside the road. She waited for the ambulance to go, then took a last look at the scene, the crashed car being winched up on to the back of the recovery lorry, the farmer talking to the police officer. Then she did a three-point turn and drove back the way she'd come.

Late afternoon, the slaughter programme began. It could have started earlier, but there were last-minute logistical details to be worked out: a compensation package for farmers to be hurriedly agreed between the National Farmers' Union and MAFF, a timetable and map of the programme to be finalised, a press conference and media briefing pack to be organised, all of it subject to the approval of the Minister.

The actual cull was straightforward in comparison to the political and bureaucratic manoeuvrings that necessarily accompanied it. Killing animals was easy. Persuading the media, and the public, that it was only a small precautionary measure and nothing to worry about was rather harder.

The well-greased Whitehall press machine was cranked up and set in motion, spin-doctors from MAFF, the Department of Health and Downing Street dispatched to briefing rooms, phone lines and various bars at the Houses of Parliament in an attempt to play down the significance of what was happening. The scale of the operation belied its supposed lack of importance, but that in itself was cunningly misleading, for every political correspondent in the country knew that the greater the emphasis placed on a story by government, the less its interest to the general public. The really controversial news was never given out at press conferences and in television interviews, it was slipped out at midnight on Christmas Eve or during the FA Cup final when the politicians knew no one, particularly the journalists, would be around to question it. So a small-scale cull of farm animals in an obscure corner of East Anglia was never going to be one of the day's main headlines, and that was exactly the way MAFF wanted to keep it.

There were five teams from the Ministry's Veterinary Service, all equipped with mobile extermination units: essentially canisters of lethal gas, protective clothing and equipment for burying the carcasses and disinfecting the animal quarters. Each team was accompanied by an official from the Cambridgeshire Public Health Department and a police car and two constables in case of trouble. The selected farms had all been notified by telephone, but no one was ruling out the possibility of individual farmers trying to obstruct the programme.

In total, eighteen farms had been chosen, all of them within a ten-mile radius of Great Dunchurch. Most of them were arable or small mixed agriculture outfits with only a modest number of animals, but one was a specialist pig farm with more than two thousand sows and weaners. Two of the MAFF teams were sent there, the other three dispersed around the remaining farms. The plan was that by noon the next day, the teams working throughout the night, the slaughter would be over.

Stephen Manville went out with one of the units, following the white transit van in his own car as they headed north from Cambridge into the fenlands. The farm they'd been allocated had the curious, rather macabre name of Undertaker's Corpse. There were others nearby with equally strange names – Coffin Bottom Farm, Gravedigger's Ghost Farm, Skull Farm – all references to historical events that had shaped the surrounding land. In the seventeenth century, when the Fens were beginning to be drained, the entrepreneurs who put up the money for the reclamation schemes were known as 'Adventurers'. The contractors who actually carried out the work were called 'The Undertakers', a term which only later took on the more gruesome connotations of the funeral director. There was still an area by the A10 trunk road called simply 'The Undertakers' and there was an Adventurers' Fen over towards Burwell. Draining the marshes was dangerous work. If disease didn't kill you, there were other man-made hazards that might. Men drowned in the sluices; embankments burst, inundating fields with floods that took numerous lives, and even away from the treacherous waters a worker risked being crushed or buried beneath the mounds of soil and rock which were excavated to build the vast network of dykes and ditches. The farm names were a memento of distant events – bodies found in the thick peat soil, ghosts ostensibly seen walking the fields – which had made an impact at the time but which nobody now could recall.

The farmer came out of a large metal shed at one side of the yard as the MAFF team's van pulled in by the farmhouse.

'The pigs are in there,' he said, jabbing a dirty thumb over his shoulder. 'Hens round the side. I've rounded them all up for you. Save you the bother.'

His manner was anything but welcoming. His tone was short, bitter. Farmers weren't sentimental about their animals, but killing them all in one go must still have been a blow.

'There's nothing wrong with them,' he said. 'Nothing at all.'

'We can't afford to take any chances,' Manville said diplomatically.

The farmer looked at him contemptuously, with all the countryman's scorn for the urban dweller. Manville, in his suit and tie, was an outsider, a city bureaucrat interfering in matters he knew nothing about.

'Aye, well,' the farmer said. 'Get on with it then.'

'We'll need some information from you,' Manville explained. 'Numbers, ages. You'll have to sign a few forms as well.'

'There's always bloody paperwork, isn't there? You'd better come inside.'

The farmer turned towards the farmhouse. Two young boys, presumably his sons, were peering inquisitively out of the kitchen door.

'Get back in,' the farmer barked at them. 'You stay out of the way.'

Manville followed him into the house. Glancing round, he saw the MAFF team unloading cylinders of poison gas from the rear of their van and wheeling them towards the animal shed.

The door was answered by a middle-aged woman who, Madeleine guessed, was probably either David Seymour's mother or his mother-in-law. She was tall and thin with short greying hair and a washed-out, pallid complexion which might have been her normal colouring or might have been the result of shock. Probably the latter, Madeleine surmised. The woman's eyes had a dull, staring quality to them and her manner was vague, unfocused, as if her mind were elsewhere.

'I know this isn't a good time,' Madeleine said. 'But I wonder if I might talk to Mrs Seymour?'

'To Jenny? Are you a friend? I'm sorry, I don't . . .' The woman's voice trailed off.

'I'm not a friend, no. My name's Madeleine King. I'm a solicitor. I was due to meet Mr Seymour at lunch-time. Is it possible for me to see his wife?'

'Well, I'm not sure. I don't quite understand what . . .'

'It's all right, Mum.'

Jenny Seymour had come out of the front room into the hall. Madeleine noticed she was pregnant and felt a sudden pang of pity – for her, for her unborn child.

'Come in.'

Madeleine followed her back into the sitting room. 'I'm sorry to intrude.'

Jenny gave a brief nod but didn't reply. She eased herself down into an armchair and gazed impassively at Madeleine. Her eyes were red and pained, a look of bewilderment seeping out through the grief. She seemed as if she'd been in an accident herself. She was dazed, almost concussed by her husband's death.

Madeleine sat down on the sofa. David Seymour's fatal accident had stunned her too. It hadn't occurred to her initially that the car she'd seen being salvaged from the lode might be his. But the conversation she'd overheard between the farmer and the constable had aroused her suspicions. Later, when she returned to her office, she'd made another call to the Transgenic Biotech research centre. The same man had answered. He'd been just as rude and evasive as before. Madeleine had called the police to ask about the accident, explaining who she was, her worries about a client going missing and not showing up for their meeting. An hour later, after the next of kin had been informed, the police had called her back with Seymour's name. The news had shocked her. She hadn't known him, but the fact that he'd been killed on his way to see her gave her a personal interest in his death. She began to wonder about the timing and the circumstances of his accident.

'I heard what you told my mother,' Jenny said. 'David never mentioned anything about seeing a solicitor.'

'He only called me this morning. About nine o'clock.'

'Why?'

'I was hoping you might be able to tell me that.'

Jenny crossed her hands on the swell of her belly, finding comfort in the feel of the warm, bulging mound. 'I'm not sure,' she said. 'He had things on his mind.'

'He sounded worried on the telephone,' Madeleine said. 'He said he needed some advice.'

'Legal advice?'

'I assumed so. I'm a solicitor. Did he have a legal problem?'

'Can this not wait?' Jenny's mother interjected. 'Is it important now?'

'I'm sorry,' Madeleine said. 'You're right. It's not important. I shouldn't have come.'

'No, wait,' Jenny said. 'Don't go.' She thought for a moment before continuing. 'He was upset last night. Things were bothering him. Things at work. He'd had a bad day, an argument, a confrontation with his boss.' She paused and swallowed. 'David had a lot of integrity. He wasn't someone who would ever do something he knew was wrong. He always believed in doing the right thing. People say a lot of horrible things about the scientists involved in plant breeding, in transgenic crops.'

'That's what he did?' Madeleine said.

Jenny nodded. 'But he believed in his work. He believed what he did was going to be important for our future. For feeding people.'

She sniffed and pressed a finger to her nostrils as if she were about to sneeze. A tear trickled out of the corner of her eye and she wiped it away.

'But you say he had things on his mind?' Madeleine said.

'Yes.' Jenny sighed. 'It's very hard to explain. I didn't understand it myself. David had a file, a company file on something that happened a few years ago in India.'

'India?'

'A place called . . . let me think. Derapur. I don't know where it is. Somewhere in the north, I think. The company has another

228

research centre there. Something went wrong with a potato crop.
I'm not sure what. There was a problem . . . poisons . . . I'm
sorry, I'm not thinking very clearly. Glycoalkaloids, that was it.'

'What are they?'

'You get them in potatoes. They're . . . I don't know . . . toxic
chemicals, something like that. It happened here too. That's what
David was worried about. Similarities. He wasn't very clear.'

Jenny rubbed her eyes. 'I'm sorry, I'm getting all confused.'

'Are you all right, Jenny?' her mother asked anxiously.

'I'm fine. Yes, I'm fine.'

'It happened here too?' Madeleine said.

'What?'

'You said it happened here.'

'Did I? Oh, yes. It did. Near here. A farm . . .'

She was breathing heavily, pearls of sweat beading her forehead.

'I'll get you a drink of water,' her mother said, standing up
and leaving the room.

'I'm sorry,' Jenny said apologetically. 'It's the heat. I find it
hard in my . . . you know.' She touched her abdomen.

Madeleine nodded sympathetically. Graham had been a
September birthday. It was a long time ago, but she could still
remember how exhausting the last few months of pregnancy
had been in the full heat of summer.

Jenny took the glass of water from her mother and sipped
some.

'Perhaps you should lie down,' her mother said.

'I'll be all right.'

Jenny took a deep breath. Her mother shot a pointed look at
Madeleine who took the hint and stood up.

'I'd better be going. This file you mentioned. Did your
husband have it here?'

'At the office.'

'And the farm? Do you know which one?'

Jenny shook her head. 'Somewhere near Great Dunchurch.'

'Thank you for your time,' Madeleine said. 'I'm sorry about your husband.'

Jenny looked at her. 'How did it happen? How? He was normally such a careful driver.'

'I don't know,' Madeleine said. She knew Jenny didn't expect her to know. She was just articulating the confusion in her mind, the questions that would keep tormenting her but would probably never be answered.

Jenny drank some more water. Then, quite suddenly, she began to cry. She covered her eyes with her hands and sobbed, her shoulders heaving with emotion. Her mother moved across and sat down on the arm of the chair, pulling her daughter close and holding her in her arms.

Madeleine felt an intruder on a very private sorrow. She went to the door and let herself out. The heart-rending sound of Jenny Seymour weeping drifted out through the open windows and accompanied her to her car.

The car seemed to come from nowhere. Appearing suddenly round the corner, its arrival hidden by the foliage of the hedge bordering the fields. It was moving much too fast for the narrow, potholed farm track, its driver showing as little concern for any oncoming traffic as he was for his vehicle's suspension.

Madeleine was taken by surprise. She was forced to brake hard and pull off on to a patch of mud by a five-barred gate. Even then the other car barely slowed. It shot past, its tyres spitting up a salvo of grit which rattled like bullets along the bodywork of Madeleine's Golf. She caught a glimpse of the driver and his passenger. Two men in grey suits. Beefy men with short hair.

Madeleine spun round.

It was a Rover saloon, navy blue. She just had time to take in the number plate before the car disappeared from sight around a bend: it was the same as on the photograph Frankie had shown her.

She waited a few minutes, her heart beating a little faster, before driving on down the track to Goose Fen Farm.

Henry Steadman's wife showed her in to the kitchen where the farmer was finishing his evening meal. He spooned up the last of his treacle tart and custard and washed it down with a long gulp from his pint mug of tea before he showed any sign that he'd noticed Madeleine's presence. Then he simply sat back in his chair and gave her a cursory glance, his fingers rummaging in a creased leather pouch, pulling out a wad of tobacco to fill his pipe.

Madeleine waited for him to finish, wanting him comfortable before she said anything. He was pressing the tobacco down into the bowl of his pipe. The stem, long and curved, was capped with a chewed bone mouthpiece that was as yellow as the farmer's nicotine-stained teeth. He struck a match and held the flame to the tobacco, his cheeks puffing in and out like bellows as he sucked on the mouthpiece. The ritual complete, he settled the pipe in the corner of his mouth, a cloud of pungent smoke wafting across his face, and looked directly at Madeleine.

'Solicitor, you said,' he murmured indistinctly, the pipe clenched between his teeth.

'That's right,' Madeleine replied.

She'd got the number of the farm from Directory Enquiries and telephoned him on her mobile before coming out. She hadn't said much, just that she wanted to talk to him about the accident at the lode.

'I gave a statement to the police.'

'I know you did. Would you mind telling me exactly what you told them.'

Steadman pulled the pipe out of his mouth and examined the bowl. His hands, like his face, were rough and weatherbeaten, the skin raw and cracked as if it had been sandblasted by the harsh fenland winds. His fingernails were chipped and ingrained with a residue of dirt and oil which no amount of scrubbing would ever fully remove. Farming, for all its mechanisation, was still a job of hard manual labour. He put the pipe back in his mouth and eyed her warily.

'Why do you want to know? Is this for legal things, proceedings, court, all that kind of stuff?'

Madeleine shook her head. 'Not at the moment. The man who died, David Seymour, was on his way to see me. I just want to know what happened.'

Steadman studied her, screwing up his eyes a bit, a man who couldn't think without giving some physical indication of cogs turning, very slowly. 'You were there, weren't you? I thought I'd seen you before.'

'Yes. But I didn't see the accident. Your clothes were wet. You tried to save him, didn't you? That was very brave.'

The farmer shrugged, but the praise seemed to take some of the edge off his caution. Madeleine sensed him relax.

'It didn't do no good,' he said laconically. 'It was all over by then.'

'You saw him crash?'

'Aye. He was driving like a lunatic. He had no chance of taking the corner at that speed. Damn near hit me too. He went straight out over the water . . . through the windscreen. No seat-belt on, you see. Poor sod.'

'You pulled him out?'

Steadman nodded. 'Waded in. The lode's not more'n chest deep there. But I could see it was too late.'

He puffed on his pipe. It was warm in the kitchen. The windows and back door were open, but Madeleine could feel the heat from the Aga behind her. Intermingled with the smell of tobacco was the sweet odour of manure from the yard outside.

'What about the other vehicle?' Madeleine said.

Steadman went rigid. His teeth were clenched tight around his pipe. 'What other vehicle?'

'I couldn't help overhearing what you said to the police officer. The Land-Rover that was behind the car that crashed.'

'There was no Land-Rover.'

Madeleine blinked. 'The Transgenic Biotech Land-Rover. You told the police officer it seemed to be having a race with Seymour.'

'You must have misheard. I didn't say anything about any Land-Rover.'

'But I heard you quite clearly,' Madeleine insisted. 'A dark blue Land-Rover with Transgenic Biotech's name on the side.'

'There was no Land-Rover,' Steadman repeated.

Madeleine stared at him. He blew a cloud of smoke across the table and drank some more of his tea.

'Is that all?' he said. 'Only I've work to do.'

'So you're saying there was no Land-Rover, or any other vehicle, behind Seymour when he crashed?'

'How many times? There was no one else there. Okay?'

He pushed back his chair and stood up.

'Who were the two men I passed coming down the track to the farm?' Madeleine asked suddenly.

Steadman wasn't prepared for that. 'What? What men?'

He wasn't a natural liar. Perhaps not a willing liar.

'In the Rover saloon.'

'Oh . . . oh, them,' Steadman stammered. 'No one.' Then he added defiantly: 'What business is it of yours, anyway?'

Madeleine didn't pursue the issue. Steadman was flustered, defensive. Maybe worried too, she could see the signs in his eyes. She dug into her handbag and took out one of her business cards.

She placed it on the table. 'If you have second thoughts about any of this,' she said, 'give me a call.'

She went back out to her car and drove away down the track. Before she reached the road, she stopped, handbrake on, the engine still running. She thought for a time, then took out her mobile phone and rang Parkside police station.

The sun was perched on the horizon, a floating orb of golden light, when she pulled in outside Frankie Carson's cottage. She'd never been there before, but she recognised his car on the gravel driveway – a dented grey Cavalier which had always struck her as far too drab and dull for a man of Frankie's flamboyant sartorial tastes. Maybe that was the point: who wanted to be upstaged by their motor?

There was no answer when she rang the doorbell so she walked round to the back of the house. She stopped, taken aback by the vista. She knew Frankie was a keen gardener, but she hadn't expected anything quite so impressive. There was a bank of shrubs and trees to her left: lilacs, azaleas, ceanothus, buddleia, a dozen others she didn't recognise. A wisteria laden with dense violet blossom smothered a wooden pergola that formed an arch over the gravel path and beyond it, in another border, there were delphiniums, shrub honeysuckles, escallonia, choisya and a dazzling mock orange tree heavy with fragrant white flowers.

Madeleine walked across the closely mown lawn, noticing how soft it was under her feet, how smooth and green its surface. There was not a weed, not a patch of moss or clover in sight. She knew from her own apology for a garden that maintaining a perfect lawn was nigh on impossible without meticulous dedication, not to mention a total absence of children and pets. The pure horticulturist, the plantsman, was not generally interested in grass, but Frankie seemed as devoted to his lawn as he was to his borders.

'Frankie!' she called.

'Over here,' came a voice from beyond a dense barrier of bushes.

Madeleine followed a path round past a cascade of yellow climbing roses, their powerful scent stinging her nostrils and removing the lingering remains of Henry Steadman's tobacco smoke. Frankie was over by a beech hedge, tending to his hives. He was wearing what was, for him, an unusually subdued outfit: a sleeveless cream T-shirt with a pink designer motif on the breast and matching cream shorts which were so tight around the crotch they were positively indecent. He had thick gloves on his hands and a veil over his face but his plump, tanned arms and legs were bare. The bees were buzzing around him, settling on the exposed skin, but they didn't seem to be stinging him. Madeleine kept her distance. Bees and wasps made her nervous.

'Maddy! Hi,' Frankie said in surprise. 'Be with you in a minute.'

He pulled a frame out of a hive and examined it, the bees clinging in clumps to his gloves like some malignant black growth. Madeleine looked at the small lake at the bottom of the garden. The sun was lower now, the shadows lengthening. The surface of the water was streaked with skeins of light that danced and shimmered as the gentle breeze rippled across it. A sleek green drake and his harem of females paddled silently towards the reeds. The stillness, the quiet was absolute, broken only by the angry droning of the bees.

'Sorry,' Frankie said, walking over to join her.

He was holding a couple of wooden frames in one hand. A few stray bees were still clinging to the honeycombs but he shook them off and waved them back to the hives. Madeleine stepped away instinctively as the bees circled around their heads. Frankie grinned at her.

'Don't like bees?'

235

'Not much.'

'I could get you a veil and gloves, show you the hives.'

'No, thanks.'

'Perhaps as well. In those clothes they'll think you're a bear.'

'Why would they think that?' Madeleine asked.

'Your black suit. They think anything black is a bear come to steal their honey. That's why I always wear pale colours when I lift the frames.'

Madeleine looked at him, unsure whether he was kidding her. 'There aren't any bears in England,' she said.

'Ah, but these aren't English bees. There are no native English bees any more. They died out years ago. In the past they didn't use hives, they kept bees in baskets. The only way to get the honey out was to kill all the bees with smoke and then squeeze the basket until the honey dripped out. Bloody stupid, but they didn't know any better. All our bees are foreign now. Like everything else in this country.'

Frankie turned and looked at his hives. 'I could watch them for hours, you know. Sometimes I do. I come out here with a chair and just sit and observe what they do. It's the most relaxing occupation in the world. You should try it.'

'I don't have time to sit and watch bees,' Madeleine said.

'The female of the species. Work, work, work, it's all you do. Jobs, homes, families, kids. Bees are the same. The females do all the work. The males, the drones, do nothing. They just laze around, stuff their faces with the honey the workers make and wait for a chance to shag the queen. They only get one shot. They mate, then they explode and die. Must be a hell of an orgasm, eh?'

Madeleine laughed. 'There are worse ways to go.'

'You don't mess with female bees. Before winter, to conserve the honey stocks, they pull the legs and wings off the drones and toss them out of the hive to die. You like that idea?'

'You think I hate men?'

'Well, you've never made a pass at me.' He gave an exaggerated wink, in case she thought he was being serious.

'What about that one? That doesn't look very active,' Madeleine said, indicating a hive that was set apart from the others.

Frankie's face darkened. 'They all died. I don't know what of. A virus of some sort probably. It's happened to a couple of other bee-keepers I know. Come on, I'll make you a cup of tea.'

Madeleine followed him back up the garden, averting her eyes from the rear view of his wobbling frame; the thick arms and thighs, the folds of fat hanging down over the top of his shorts which were stretched to breaking point across his ample buttocks.

They made a detour into the shed on the way for Frankie to dump his gloves and veil and Madeleine noticed the two audio speakers screwed to the walls on either side of the window.

'You play music out here?'

'Not for me. For the bees. I open the window and turn up the volume. They love it.'

'They have ears?'

'Sound receptors. I find music increases their honey production. The right kind, of course. They don't like pop music or anything atonal. I played them some Schoenberg once and they went berserk. I thought they were going to swarm.'

Madeleine gave him a sideways glance, trying to decide if this was another joke. She gave him the benefit of the doubt. 'So what music *do* they like?'

'The human voice. And the violin. Bach unaccompanied partitas, they love those. There's something very pure about Bach. They like opera too – Rossini, Mozart, but not Wagner. Cecilia Bartoli, you heard her? Italian mezzo. They adore her. And Barbara Bonney, she has such a beautiful tone. But they hate Lesley Garrett. They have taste, you see.'

He held out one of the wooden frames he'd brought in with him. Madeleine touched the side of it.

'It's all sticky. Is that the honey?'

'Propolis. They make it from tree resin, to sterilise the hive and fill up any gaps. It's a natural antiseptic. If I get a cut or a mouth ulcer I dip a finger in propolis and rub it on the wound. Heals it immediately. It's amazing stuff. The ancient Egyptians knew all about it. They were great bee-keepers, thought the bee was created from one of Ra's teardrops. They coated their dead with propolis before they wrapped them in bandages, to preserve them.'

Madeleine peered down at the thousands of tiny cells filled with amber liquid. 'How do you get it out?'

'Centrifuge. This is my production line.'

Frankie indicated a bench bearing a tall metal canister with a handle on the top, various arcane instruments and a stack of empty glass jars. He put the frames into a mesh cage inside the metal canister and clicked it shut.

'I'll do it later. You like honey?'

'I don't eat it very often.'

'I'll give you some to take away.'

'It's okay, Frankie, you don't need to.'

'No, believe me, you'll be doing me a favour.'

It was only when they walked into the kitchen of his cottage that Madeleine understood what he meant. The room was lined with shelves – above the worktops, the sink, even over both the doors – and on the shelves were hundreds upon hundreds of jars filled with honey. Frankie lifted down half a dozen and placed them on the table.

'There you go.'

'I can't eat that much.'

'It'll keep.'

'Honestly, Frankie, it'll take me a year to get through six jars.'

'So?' Frankie filled the kettle with water and switched it on. 'When I said it'll keep, I meant it. It really will. The Egyptians I mentioned, their tombs have been opened up and they've found three-thousand-year-old honey good enough to eat. Pure honey never goes off, unless you contaminate it with something. I'll give you a tip, if you ever see a sell-by date on a jar of honey, don't touch it. They've added something to it, adulterated it. Real honey doesn't have a sell-by date because it doesn't need one. Here, try some of it.'

'It's all right, Frankie.'

But he wasn't going to be deterred. He cut her a slice of white bread and spread butter on it. Then he took a spoon and dipped it into the honey.

'Another tip. Never put your butter knife in the honey. That really will make it go off. Always use a clean spoon.'

Madeleine watched him spreading the honey, amused by the fuss he was making. This was a side of him she'd never seen before: Frankie in his own home, in his element, contented and domesticated. It was rather endearing.

'Try it.'

He waited in a pose of frozen expectation while she took a bite. She was no connoisseur of honey. In fact, she didn't really like it very much, but she made all the right noises and was delighted to see the pleasure her reaction clearly gave Frankie.

'It's very good,' she said, licking her lips in a show of appreciation.

'It's mixed flower. My grandfather kept hives on the Derbyshire moors, made the most wonderful heather honey. You ever tried borage honey? That's really good too. Unfortunately, round here there are too many different flowers, too many different crops: oilseed rape, cabbages, potatoes, sugar beet, beans. You can only make a mixed honey.'

'I like it.'

'Take more than six jars.'

'No, six will be enough, thanks.'

Frankie poured boiling water into the teapot and covered it with a knitted green, pink and yellow cosy which Madeleine noticed matched both the tea towel hanging by the sink and the oven gloves on the surface beside the cooker.

'So what brings you all the way out here?' Frankie asked.

Madeleine waited for him to select a couple of shiny gold mugs from the cupboard and sit down before she answered.

'You like curry, don't you, Frankie?' she said.

13

Jake Brewster could trace back his interest in environmental matters to a chance meeting with a girl in a Mill Road whole-food shop. Cycling home from somewhere one Saturday, he'd stopped off to buy a sandwich. Catriona had been behind the counter, small, dark-haired, pretty. She'd been talking to another customer, handing him a leaflet about some kind of environ-mental protest. Jake had picked up one of the leaflets and read it while Catriona made him a mozzarella and sun-dried tomato baguette. It detailed a plan to build an out-of-town shopping centre on a greenfield site in north Essex which had been given the go-ahead by the local council, and urged people to gather at the site the following Saturday to stop the developers proceeding. 'You interested?' Catriona had said. 'A few of us are going down in a van. There's room for more.'

Jake had taken her phone number and thought about it for a couple of days. Thought about *her* for a couple of days. He couldn't get her out of his head. He didn't really give a toss about the shopping centre development but the thought of spending a day with her was appealing. What a man would do to get laid.

He'd gone down with her and her friends in the van, a smelly clapped-out old Ford Transit with foam rubber mattresses in the back. None of them seemed to see the irony in going off on an eco-protest in a vehicle that was an environmental hazard in itself. He'd stuck close to Catriona – Cat, as she liked to be called – all day and then spent the night with her, although not in quite the way he would have liked. She'd chained and padlocked them both to a beech tree to prevent the builders felling it and they stayed there for eighteen hours, half frozen to death, until on Sunday morning the bailiffs arrived with bolt-cutters. They'd been arrested for obstruction, but the police let them off with a caution. It was Jake's first brush with the law.

Cat was different from any other girl he'd ever met. She was active, committed, passionate about everything. She not only had opinions, she did something about them. They'd started to see more of each other. Within a few weeks Jake had moved in with her and thrown himself into the various protest campaigns she espoused. Cat had long since given up on democracy and craven politicians and decided that confrontation was the only way to tackle the Establishment. The ballot box was a farce. Direct action was the way to get your voice heard. Jake went on marches with her, joined road protesters, sabotaged hunts. Gradually, he became as committed a believer as she was.

He started to take a particular interest in the genetic modification of plants which he regarded as the most dangerous threat to the environment since the advent of nuclear power. He read everything he could about transgenic biotechnology and began to campaign against it independently of Cat. Maybe that was where he went wrong. The pupil was suddenly no longer a beginner, the disciple no longer a follower but a leader in his own right. Or maybe she just got bored. Whatever the reason, after eighteen months, Cat dumped him and found herself a new boyfriend. Jake was devastated by the split. For a few months he wallowed in a pit of depression and self-pity. Then he pulled himself together and, like any other young man, went back out on to the field to play. He'd had a couple of attempts on goal deflected but had got nowhere near scoring. Until tonight.

She was at the bar in the Three Feathers where he went regularly on a Friday night. He vaguely remembered seeing her there before but had never spoken to her. She was younger than he was – about eighteen or nineteen – with straight shoulder-length brown hair and big eyes. Pretty, in a soft, doll-like way. She made the opening move.

'You were on the telly, weren't you? Earlier this week,' she said.

Jake shrugged nonchalantly, aware that his arrest and court appearance had given him a certain notoriety, a certain kudos amongst the young crowd with whom he socialised.

'Yeah, that was me,' he admitted, trying to sound bashful.

'What was it like? Being locked up.'

'All right.'

She looked at his face. The bruises hadn't healed up yet. 'They beat you up?' she asked.

'Yeah.'

'Badly?'

'I survived.'

'I'm Jackie, by the way.'

'Jake.'

'I know.'

She smiled at him. She was wearing a tight top that hugged her small breasts like cling-film. Jake sensed a mutual attraction, a stirring of interest.

'It's scary, isn't it?' she said. 'This GM stuff. Someone told me you can take genes from anything and put them into other plants or animals.'

Jake nodded. 'You can. There's no distinction between genes from different species. You could take a gene from a human, a whale, a grain of wheat or a bacterium and you wouldn't be able to tell which came from which. What makes species different is how many genes they have, what types and how they're put together. You can literally mix genes from any number of different species and create God knows what.

'They've taken anti-freeze genes from flounders and inserted them into tomatoes to make them resistant to frost. They've put a firefly gene into tobacco plants to make the leaves glow in the dark, they've put chicken genes into potatoes to increase disease resistance, they've fused goat and sheep embryo cells to make a sheep-goat monster.'

'Why?' Jackie asked, open-mouthed.

'That's a good question. Because they can.'

That was the driving force behind science. Scientists did things not because they were necessarily good or desirable, but because they *could*. That was the only justification they felt they needed. And once something was discovered or invented it was here to stay. Nothing was ever de-invented. Man was incapable of rejecting knowledge, even knowledge that was potentially harmful. He had to push innovation to the limits and keep pushing. It was the characteristic that had taken him out of the cave into the air-conditioned skyscraper with a jacuzzi, a microwave and a television in every room. But it was also the characteristic, Jake believed, that had the potential to destroy both mankind and the planet.

'Because they can,' he said again. 'And because they can make money from it. Companies can patent human genes. They don't do anything to them, they don't create or add anything. All they're doing is identifying them and that gives them the right to claim ownership of those genes and exploit them commercially. Can you believe that? They *own* our genes. If you or I have a particular gene, an unusual gene and they identify it, then they can patent it and charge other people for using it. We get no say in the matter. It's not ours any more. They're reducing human beings to just a series of proteins which they regard as commodities to be traded on the open market.'

Jackie was impressed by his knowledge, Jake could tell. He glanced at her breasts again. It was obvious she wasn't wearing a bra. Her top had ridden up a little to expose an inch or two of white midriff. Jake wondered if he was going to get lucky.

'So are you going to do it again?' Jackie asked. 'Rip up crops.'

'You bet,' Jake said vehemently. 'These biotech companies have to be stopped.'

'Can I come with you next time?'

She was looking at him with her big doe eyes. She was very pretty, her admiration for him apparent in her expression. She was the doting, malleable kind. Jake liked that. Adulation hadn't been one of Cat's more manifest characteristics.

'If you like,' he said. 'You could get arrested, you know.'

'I don't mind that. It sounds fun. How do you fix it?'

'There's a special website. You need to know where to look. I'll show you, if you like.'

She was with two female friends, but she left them in the pub and went back with him to his bedsit. Jake made them coffee then went across to the PC on his desk. Jackie stood over him, watching as he logged on to the Web. He was aware of her, the smell of the scent she was wearing. One of her hands brushed his arm then came to rest on his shoulder.

He found what he was looking for and read the cryptic message on the screen.

'That doesn't make sense to me,' Jackie said.

'That's the intention. You have to know the code, what the symbols mean. We have to keep ahead of the police, the biotech companies' internal security people. They're always trying to pre-empt any attack.'

He moved the mouse and clicked it. Then typed in another address. A single line of text appeared.

'That's the time and date of the strike.'

'Sunday the seventeenth, that's this weekend,' Jackie said.

Jake clicked the mouse again. 'And that's the rendezvous. You don't know the target until you meet the others. It's more secure that way.'

'Are you going?'

Jake suddenly remembered he was on bail, the conditions he'd agreed to comply with. He hesitated.

'Go on,' Jackie said. 'For me.'

Her hand was stroking his shoulder. He turned his head. Her breasts were level with his eyes. Close enough to touch. Jackie leaned down and kissed him. His hands moved across her body, up under her thin cotton top. He felt reckless. She had expectations of him. He didn't want to disappoint.

'Yeah, why not?' he said.

Karl Housman stopped off to pick up a Chinese takeaway on his way home from work – fried chicken with green pepper and black bean sauce and a portion of egg fried rice. It was something he'd noticed he'd been doing more frequently in recent months. If he didn't stay on at the hospital and eat in the canteen, he invariably brought back a Chinese or a pizza or fish and chips. They weren't the healthiest of meals but he couldn't be bothered to buy in provisions and cook anything better for himself. Besides, he was a doctor. He was allowed to ignore all the medical profession's warnings about fat and salt.

He dished out the cartons and poured himself a beer from the fridge, then put a CD on the portable player he kept in the kitchen: Joshua Rifkin playing Scott Joplin piano rags. Housman played the piano a little himself. He hadn't had lessons since he was a teenager, but he liked to sit down and tinkle now and again. He found it relaxing. He'd tried Joplin without much success. The music looked easy enough on the page but was actually bloody hard to execute. Joshua Rifkin made it sound so simple. Housman had seen him play live once. It had been a strange experience – watching this scholarly, bearded American coming out and rattling off the 'Maple Leaf Rag' for a polite, middle-class English audience. Housman wondered what it would have sounded like in a smoky honky-tonk with Joplin himself at the keyboard.

Rifkin was on the 'Elite Syncopations' now. Housman listened, shovelling down his Chinese without much enjoyment. Food to him wasn't something to savour, it was simply fuel. The music eased his sombre mood. It was easy to get depressed living on your own. He hadn't been absolutely honest with Jeremy Blake in the Eagle pub. It was true that he didn't really miss the sexual side of his marriage, but he missed the companionship, having someone else around to talk to. What a sad, middle-aged admission that was, he reflected. But then he'd never been particularly sexually active, even in his youth. As a junior doctor at Addenbrooke's, when his colleagues had been frantically screwing everything in a uniform – nurses, auxiliaries, physiotherapists – he'd had one, maybe two fairly short-lived relationships with long gaps in between. He'd never had much luck with women. He was too diffident, too scared of being rejected by them. Doctors weren't renowned for their lack of confidence. The selection process, the training, the nature of the job favoured the extrovert. But professional confidence and personal confidence weren't quite the same thing. Housman had plenty of the former, but the assurance he showed in his job didn't always carry over into his private life. With women he was basically shy. Joanne, his ex-wife, had made all the running both before and during their five-year marriage. Housman had allowed himself to be carried along by her, drifting through those years in a kind of vague haze. He'd been preoccupied with his work and barely noticed his wife, even when she left him. She'd just drifted away like a cloud of vapour. He hadn't even realised anything was wrong until she'd gone, moving out to live with one of her work colleagues with whom she'd been having an affair. Housman had given up on romance since then, sublimating his sexual desire into his work. It was several years since he'd last been out on a date with a woman. He couldn't seriously see himself doing it again, he'd lost his nerve.

He finished his meal and cleared away his plate and the foil takeaway containers. He was making a pot of tea, listening to 'Solace – A Mexican Serenade', when the telephone rang. He turned off the CD and waited a moment before he picked up the receiver. He guessed what the call was about. He'd been expecting it. It was his Senior House Officer informing him that another flu patient, Arthur Wainwright, had died.

Housman closed his eyes momentarily, his shoulders slumping. 'Thanks for letting me know.'

He cradled the receiver and poured himself some tea. Wainwright was the sixty-three-year-old retired accountant who had been admitted to the Isolation Unit only that morning, the fifth victim of the mysterious flu virus. His condition had worsened during the day with a horrifying rapidity. There had been no way to stop it, no drugs or medical assistance that could halt the inexorable decline. When he'd left the hospital, Housman had suspected that Wainwright wouldn't last the night. The end had been more sudden than he'd hoped, but he wasn't surprised. The virus was the most virulent influenza strain he'd ever come across.

The day's other new admission, thirty-eight-year-old Wendy Bullingham, had also been hit hard by the virus. She was on a ventilator in a critical condition.

Housman didn't give much for her chances of survival. Tim Harrison, on the other hand, seemed to be holding his own. He was still seriously ill but had so far shown no signs of either viral or bacterial pneumonia, the secondary complication that had killed the others, including his father. Housman found that fact ominous. The two children, normally among the most vulnerable to influenza, were proving to have the highest resistance to the disease. That was uncannily like the pandemic of 1918 when the flu virus had killed an unusually large number of men and women in their prime.

Housman was restless. The weariness he'd felt when he'd got home had been dispelled by the phone call from the hospital. He knew he wouldn't sleep, he was too wound up.

He finished his tea, picked up the phone and called Mill Hill. Ian Fitzgerald was taking a break from the lab.

'How's it going?' Housman asked.

'Slowly,' Fitzgerald replied. He sounded tired. And jaded.

'You could use some help?'

'We can always use help, Karl.'

'I'll be there before midnight. Get the coffee on.'

Madeleine stayed up late, drinking wine and watching television, waiting for Graham to come home. He'd left no note again and she had no idea where he was.

At half past eleven her mobile phone rang. She snatched it up. Something had happened to him, she knew it.

'Yes?'

'It's Connolly.'

Madeleine relaxed. Jack Connolly was the police officer she'd called earlier from Goose Fen Farm. Years ago, when Madeleine had been a young, inexperienced solicitor, Connolly had been a custody sergeant at Parkside. He was now a plain-clothes inspector: not a close friend of Madeleine's, but a police contact she knew she could trust.

'You said to call whatever the time.'

'I know. Thanks, Jack. Anything?'

'I gave the Road Traffic boys a bell, they're handling the case. There's no statement on file from Henry Steadman.'

'Nothing at all?'

'No. That doesn't mean he's not going to make one. It may happen later.'

'What about the notes from the officers at the scene?'

'The accident report mentions him as a witness. But there's nothing about any other vehicle being involved.'

'What's the time on the report?'

'Eight-thirty this evening.'

'For an accident that happened at 1 pm? That's a bit slow, isn't it? I don't suppose you could talk to the constables who were there?'

'That won't be easy. They're off shift now. And they're on leave from tomorrow.'

'For how long?'

'Two weeks.'

'Both of them?'

'It would seem so.'

'How convenient,' Madeleine said.

'They're treating it as a straightforward RTA. There's no evidence on the file to indicate otherwise. Sorry I can't be more help.'

'Thanks, Jack. I appreciate it.'

Madeleine rang off and stared pensively across the room. Frankie had been right to warn her. She wasn't at all sure now she wanted to get into this.

14

Frankie hated flying. The boredom, the ghastly food, the re-circulated air saturated with other people's germs were bad enough, but it was the lack of space that really got to him. Airline seats – in Cattle Class, at least – had been designed for thin people with very short legs. For Frankie, all six foot two and seventeen stone of him, anything longer than a short-haul hop in an aeroplane was purgatory. And Delhi was nine hours away.

He hadn't wanted to go. He disliked foreign travel, particularly to places where the food and climate were significantly different from England. He'd been on trips to Spain and Greece and enjoyed them, but the hotels he'd stayed in had been isolated enclaves of British, German and Dutch holidaymakers, cut off from the local populace and fed on a bland diet of international cuisine from which all traces of ethnic influence had been carefully removed. India was different. India was the Third World. Dirty, squalid, alien, a land of heat and dust and diarrhoea. Frankie had grave reservations about going there.

But Madeleine was a very persuasive woman, and Frankie had a soft spot for her. He didn't like to let her down. She'd worked on him subtly over tea and bread and honey in his kitchen, telling him what she wanted and why. He'd resisted at first, reluctant to embark on such a long, arduous journey, but Madeleine had persisted, flattering him, cajoling him, finally begging him to help her. In the end it was the question of money that had brought him round. Not the quantity, but the lack of it.

'Who's paying for this?' he'd asked.

'I am,' Madeleine had said.

'Out of your own pocket?'

'Yes.'

'Why?'

'David Seymour was killed on his way to see me. That crash wasn't an accident. He was as good as murdered.'

'You don't know that.'

'Something funny's going on, Frankie. The farmer told the police at the scene that Seymour was being pursued by a Transgenic Biotech Land-Rover. He said they seemed to be having a race. I heard him. I was only a couple of yards away. Yet when I go to see him he denies the whole thing. And I see a Rover saloon, the same one as in your videotape, coming away from the farm. What would you think?'

'Yes, okay, it's suspicious,' Frankie had conceded.

'They weren't having a race. The Land-Rover was chasing him. It was chasing him because he had something to tell me. And I want to know what it was.'

'You're paying all expenses for a trip to India because you're *curious*?' Frankie had said.

He knew Maddy didn't have very much money. She was a solicitor and people tended to assume all solicitors were well-off. But Maddy's work was all Legal Aid. In fifteen years of practice she'd probably had only a handful of clients who'd paid their own bills. With office expenses and overheads, Frankie doubted she took home much more than twenty-five thousand a year, not a great deal in an expensive city like Cambridge.

Madeleine had taken her time replying, toying with a crust of bread smeared with honey. Then she'd licked her fingers and said: 'Not just curious. Guilty.'

'About what?'

'About my role in it all. I called him at his work, gave my name. That might have been foolish.'

'It wasn't your fault, Maddy. You weren't driving the car.'

'It's on my conscience. It'll only take you a couple of days. What do you say?'

'You know how to put a guy under pressure, don't you?' Frankie had said. Then he'd sighed. If it meant this much to her. 'Okay, I'll do it.'

He'd located Derapur after she'd left, then bought an air ticket over the Net, a last-minute cancellation for £230 rather than the standard five hundred plus. He'd chosen Economy to save Madeleine money, but had a little trick up his sleeve that he'd used once before on a long-haul flight to New York. There was no way he was spending nine hours squeezed into a seat with his knees up around his eyeballs. That was taking self-sacrifice too far.

Frankie was a collector of business cards. He had drawers full of the things at home. He was given them by people he met in the course of his work, or simply picked them up. None of them he threw away. You never knew when they might come in handy. A number of them he'd adapted for his own use. It was a straightforward thing to do. He just scanned the business card into his PC, then used his graphics package to overwrite the name on the card with his own and printed out a dozen or so copies of the new version. They were never exactly the same as the originals, but they were close enough to fool most people. In Frankie's line of business it was often advisable to pretend to be someone else to obtain information he needed. Or to let others think he was someone else.

His ticket was waiting to be collected from the British Airways desk at Heathrow on Saturday morning. Frankie went up to the counter and smiled at the woman on duty, a good-looking brunette in her mid-thirties – about the age airlines deemed a woman over the hill and moved her off cabin attachment to something more sedentary on the ground. But she still had the inch-thick make-up and fixed grin of the stewardess.

'Good morning, sir.'

Frankie introduced himself, polite but not ingratiating. He'd dressed down for the trip and was wearing a pair of tan trousers and a dark blue jacket and shirt. No tie. He drew the line at wearing a tie. He wanted to look casual but businesslike. He didn't want to be mistaken for a tourist or – with his pony-tail – an ageing hippy.

'You have a ticket for me, name of Carson,' he said.

The woman checked through a drawer and pulled out a slim ticket wallet.

'Mr F Carson, Delhi?' she said.

'That's the one.'

'Do you have some identification, sir? Your passport.'

Frankie reached inside his jacket pocket. 'How full is the plane? Any chance of an upgrade to Business?' he said casually. 'A guy my size – you know – Economy gets a bit cramped.'

'I don't think that's possible. I'm sorry, sir,' the woman said, though she didn't sound very sorry.

Frankie shrugged. 'That's okay,' he said pleasantly. 'Now . . . oh, yes, my passport.'

He took his wallet out of his pocket and extracted his pass-port. As he pulled out the document, a wedge of business cards, carefully planted for the occasion, flew out, scattering over the counter and the floor by Frankie's feet. He bent down to pick them up. In the centre of the cards was the BBC logo – a genuine reproduction from a card Frankie had once been given by a producer at the broadcaster's London studios – and at the bottom the television centre address at Shepherd's Bush. Printed in between the two in black ink, Frankie had added the words:

'*The Holiday Programme. Francis Carson, Producer.*' Frankie straightened up slowly, giving the woman plenty of time. She'd gathered up the cards he'd sprayed over the counter and was holding them out to him. He knew from her face that she'd read what was on them.

'Thank you,' Frankie said, taking the cards back and stowing them away in his wallet.

'If you'd like to wait a moment, sir,' the woman said, moving to the far end of the desk where she had a muted conversation with another, older woman. Frankie turned his back on them, counting silently to himself. There was nothing technically fraudulent about this little scam, or any of the others he'd worked with different business cards. He never actually said he worked for any of the organisations. But if people wanted to assume he did, that was their affair.

In less than half a minute the brunette was back. 'About that request for an upgrade, sir . . .'

They gave him a seat, not in Business but in First Class, at no extra charge. A big seat like an armchair with his own personal video screen on the back of the seat in front and enough leg room for an octopus.

Frankie waited until the 747 was airborne and the stewardesses were circulating with trays of drinks and canapés before he lifted his glass of chilled champagne and offered a silent toast to the British Broadcasting Corporation.

Allowing for the four-and-a-half-hour time difference between London and Delhi, it was gone ten o'clock at night when Frankie arrived in India. Even that late he noticed the heat the moment he stepped off the plane. A warm, cloying embrace that drew beads of sweat from the crevices of his body and filled him with foreboding for the suffering he knew the full sun of the day would bring.

Regretting immediately the rash impulse that had made him say yes to Madeleine, he collected his luggage from the carousel and made his way through Immigration and Customs. The concourse of the arrivals terminal confirmed all his worst prejudices about India. The place was absolutely packed with people, a pulsating throng of strange faces, of curious eyes, of small boys swarming towards him, grabbing at his baggage trolley, clamouring for the job of pushing it for him. Frankie waved them away but they clung to him indomitably, undeterred by his hostile manner. He felt like a celebrity, mobbed by photographers, except that even the world's most persistent *paparazzi* had nothing on these kids. They buzzed around him like mosquitoes, their movements and gestures accompanied by the insistent drone of their tiny voices – *carrybagsir, pushtrolleysir, youwantaxisir,* the words merging together into a hubbub of incomprehensible gibberish. Frankie ignored them, forcing a path through the pack to the nearest exit where a row of identical grubby white taxis was waiting. One of the drivers swatted the urchins away and loaded Frankie's case into the boot of his car. Frankie climbed in and closed the door, sagging back on the upholstery, relieved to be away from the unfamiliar chaos of the world outside.

He cheered up a little when he got to his hotel, part of an American chain whose bland, sanitised, air-conditioned accommodation spanned the world, each hostelry designed to be hermetically sealed off from the local environment so you could travel the globe without ever realising you were abroad. Hamburger hotels, Frankie called them. Thank God for American culture.

His room had everything he'd come to expect from a Western chain: a double bed, telephone, an en-suite bathroom with little plastic bottles of shampoo and paper-wrapped bars of soap, made especially small to deter both pilfering and washing. The only indication of where in the world he was was a framed photograph of the Taj Mahal on the wall above the bed. In the Paris branch they no doubt had pictures of the Eiffel Tower, in London Big Ben and in New York, well, in New York they probably had a Big Mac and fries.

Frankie stripped off, took a shower and changed into fresh clothes, then went downstairs to the restaurant and had a T-bone steak and apple pie. The meal over, he went back to his room, opened a chilled Budweiser from the mini-bar and watched truck racing from Indianapolis on satellite television. He was starting to like India.

He went to bed at 1 am and asked for an alarm call at six. When it came, he was deep into a heavy sleep, his body still four hours behind the local time, but he forced himself to get up. He had another shower and, after a breakfast of coffee and rolls, took a taxi to the central railway station where a scrum of small boys, so similar to the ones at the airport that Frankie thought they must have been following him around, enveloped him the instant he stepped out on to the pavement. He knew what to do this time. Resistance was futile. The only sensible course of action was to go with the flow, not fight against it. He singled out one particular boy in a red shirt.

'You, carry my bag,' he commanded.

The boy stepped forward from the mêlée and grabbed hold of the suitcase the taxi driver had unloaded. The other kids continued to crowd round, but the boy yelled at them angrily and they gradually drifted away in search of a new target.

Frankie strolled into the station concourse, walking very slowly to let the child keep up with him. He was only a small boy and the suitcase was very heavy, but he struggled along with it gamely, holding the handle in both hands so low the case was almost scraping along the ground.

They went to the ticket office and waited in line for half an hour. The heat inside the station was insufferable. Frankie's face was drenched and he could feel the sweat running down his crotch and the middle of his back. He bought a first-class ticket to Lucknow, in the province of Uttar Pradesh, two hundred miles away to the south-east, and went across to the platform, the boy still accompanying him with his suitcase. They waited another twenty minutes for the train to arrive then Frankie paid the boy off and found himself a seat.

Even in First Class the four-hour journey to Lucknow was gruelling. The windows were wide open but all they did was let in a breeze that was almost as hot as the air in the compartment. Frankie sat in the shadiest corner, away from the direct glare of the sun, feeling as if his body was melting and dripping away slowly on to the floor.

From Lucknow it got even worse. A further hour's journey in a suffocating local bus crammed with people and stacks of luggage: boxes, trunks, bundles of firewood, chickens in cages and something unidentifiable in a canvas sack which smelt like a rotting corpse. The stench and heat made Frankie feel sick, the nausea exacerbated by the constant bouncing and swaying of the bus as it belched along the dusty country roads.

Derapur turned out to be a smallish town on a sun-baked plain, its buildings an ugly mixture of concrete and mud-coloured brick. Frankie got off the bus in the central square and brought the whole place to a standstill. Passers-by stopped and stared openly at him, this huge white-skinned pony-tailed westerner so sodden with perspiration he looked as if he'd taken a shower in his clothes. Lucknow was a minor tourist centre, but very few foreigners ventured this far off the beaten track, and certainly none who appeared quite so exotic as Frankie.

Frankie looked around, basking in the attention he was receiving. Then from nowhere another small boy materialised and offered to carry his bag.

'Is there a hotel around here?' Frankie asked.

'Hotel, yes, sir. This way.'

The boy staggered off with the suitcase. Frankie sauntered after him, pursued by a huddle of curious onlookers. The hotel was down a side street, an unprepossessing building which must once have been white but was now a shade of dirty yellow. There were wooden shutters over the windows, bleached and cracked by the sun, and above the entrance, written in faded black paint, were the words, Hotel Majestic. Frankie's spirits sank a little as he looked up at the dilapidated frontage. There'd be no truck racing here.

The boy was ahead of him, going up the steps into the hotel. Frankie followed. At the end of a narrow hallway was a desk manned by a middle-aged man in a loose white cotton jacket and trousers. He squinted quizzically at Frankie as he approached the desk.

'Do you have a room?' Frankie said.

'Yes sir. I am Mr Shah, the manager. I will see if I have one available.'

He turned and scanned the board behind the desk. From the number of keys hanging on their hooks it looked as if the hotel was entirely unoccupied, but Mr Shah made a great show of checking his register before selecting one of the keys.

'I believe number eight is free. This way, sir.'

Mr Shah shooed the boy away from Frankie's suitcase and picked it up himself. Frankie gave the boy a tip and followed the manager upstairs.

His room was at the back of the hotel, overlooking a yard festooned with lines of drying towels and table linen. It looked basic but clean, a single bed with a lamp on a table beside it and a washbasin in one corner.

'I hope this is to your satisfaction, sir. The WC is downstairs.'

'How much is it?'

'Two hundred and fifty rupees a night, sir.'

Frankie converted the sum into sterling in his head – about five pounds – suspecting the price had quadrupled the moment he walked through the front door.

'Is there anything else, sir?'

'No, thank you. Actually, yes. Do you know a place near here, an agricultural research centre belonging to a British company?'

'Transgenic Biotechnology? Yes, sir, it's about two miles outside the town. You work for them, sir?'

Frankie shook his head. 'Are there any taxis in the town?'

'Of course, sir. Would you like me to call you one?'

'Thank you.'

Frankie washed and changed his shirt, rinsing out the old one and draping it over the window-sill to dry. He'd just finished when there was a knock on the door and a skinny little boy – presumably Mr Shah's son – poked his head in to announce that the taxi was waiting outside at the front.

Frankie went downstairs. The taxi was a light blue car of a design Frankie found familiar but couldn't immediately identify. Only when he saw the chrome marque on the boot did he realise it was a Ford Popular, a make he remembered vividly from his childhood but which had become obsolete in England nearly thirty years earlier.

The driver was leaning on the side of the car. He was slightly built with sleek dark hair and a thick black moustache. He stepped forward and introduced himself enthusiastically.

'Good day to you, sir. And how are you? I am Panjit. Where would you like to go?'

Frankie told him and climbed in the back of the taxi. Bright red and green cotton sheets were draped over the seats and there was a scent of flowers or herbs, not unpleasant, which Frankie realised as they drove out of town was Panjit's hair oil.

'You don't have a meter,' Frankie said, alert to the possibilities – probabilities, he was sure – of being ripped off.

'No, sir. I charge one hundred rupees an hour. Flat rate. I am the best-value taxi in Derapur. I will look after you, sir. Just tell me what you need.'

Frankie converted the rupees into sterling again. Roughly two pounds. That seemed fair enough. Frankie passed over a hundred-rupee note. 'That's for the first hour,' he said. He handed Panjit a second hundred-rupee note. 'And that is a retainer for future services.'

Frankie had learnt to be generous with money. It oiled a lot of wheels that would otherwise have remained inaccessible. In a foreign country like India it was going to be useful to have a few friends, and Frankie had no illusions that his charm and good looks alone were going to be enough.

'You are here on business, sir?' Panjit asked, swerving to avoid a bullock cart loaded with straw which was coming along the road towards them.

'Something like that,' Frankie replied vaguely. He wound down his window and let the warm breeze dry the sweat on his face.

The countryside around the town was flat and agricultural, divided up into small plots, each with its own tumbledown shack. The patchwork of fields was dotted with figures, men, women and children bent double in the rows of rice, vegetables and other crops Frankie didn't recognise. Every tiny scrap of land seemed to be cultivated.

The Transgenic Biotech research centre was hard to miss, even from a distance. In a landscape where most of the houses were little more than shanties, the tall concrete-and-glass building stood out for miles around, an incongruous edifice that was as alien to the surrounding plain as a shopping mall.

'You are visiting the centre?' Panjit said.

'No. Just drive past it and pull over.'

They stopped at the edge of the road and Frankie swivelled round to look back at the building. A high wire fence ran all the way around the compound, extending beyond the centre and its car park to encompass a broad area of fields.

'What do the local people think about this place?' Frankie asked.

Panjit shrugged. 'It does not concern them. They grow crops, like everyone else.'

'What crops?'

'Rice, millet, potatoes. I don't know what else. They test things there. They don't grow anything to sell.'

'Do they provide jobs for local people?'

'Some day labour. Some work in the kitchens, I think. They are all scientists in there. Educated university gentlemen.'

'Indian?'

'Mostly. Some western gentlemen. We don't see much of them. They eat there, sleep there. They keep themselves to themselves.'

'Any scandal?'

'Scandal, sir?'

'You know, gossip about what they do there. Has anything ever gone wrong? Maybe something to do with potatoes.'

'Potatoes, sir? No, I've heard nothing about potatoes.'

'Okay. Let's go back to town.'

Panjit continued up the road until he found a place to turn around, a rutted track that led across a dried-out stream bed to a cluster of mud-walled huts. He reversed into the track and pulled back out on to the main road. But he stopped again almost immediately, twisting his head round to look at Frankie. He was frowning, drawing something out from the depths of his memory.

'There *was* something, sir. A few years ago. I can't remember the details.'

'About potatoes?'

Panjit shook his head. 'No, sir. I think it was chickens.'

The offices of the *Derapur Times* were in a narrow street off the central square, sandwiched between a tailor's shop and a garage whose forecourt was cluttered with old cars in various stages of repair, some of them propped up on jacks with a mechanic underneath, others stripped down to little more than their chassis. Frankie recognised a couple of the models – a Triumph Herald and a Morris Traveller, the world's only half-timbered car. Long since consigned to the scrap heap in Britain, they lived on here, giving the streets a strangely anachronistic feel as if they'd been dressed for a Sixties period film.

The front office of the newspaper was technically closed to the public, this being a Sunday afternoon, but Panjit – no doubt because of his job – seemed to know everyone in the town and he'd somehow wangled permission for Frankie to go in and look at the cuttings library. Library was rather a grand word for what was basically a large walk-in cupboard filled with brown manilla envelopes containing clippings from the newspaper – another misleading term, for the *Times* had more the look and content of a parish newsletter than a proper newspaper. It was published weekly, in English, and consisted of eight pages of news, comment and advertisements. Its circulation – proudly proclaimed on a handwritten notice in the front window – was 3,162.

Transgenic Biotechnology International had its own thick envelope full of yellowing cuttings. Frankie sat on a stool and leafed through them slowly. They didn't seem to be in any sort of chronological order so he had to check every one. There were stories about the building of the research centre, and about the planning rows that preceded it. There were articles on the work that was being conducted there and an interview with the centre's director. Most of it was straightforward factual reporting, but there were several pieces of editorial comment that dealt with the secrecy surrounding the facility, and which the paper's editor clearly thought was excessive and unnecessary. Frankie had already seen the fence around the site but it transpired there were also guards patrolling the area who did not take kindly to trespassers. On a number of occasions local people had been ejected from the property and, once, a young boy who'd climbed over the fence claimed he'd been beaten up by the guards, an allegation which the company strongly denied.

After twenty minutes Frankie found what he was looking for: a piece from 1997 headlined 'Mysterious Death of Chickens'. On farms immediately adjacent to the research centre, hens had started dying from some unidentified cause. In a three-day period, twenty-six birds on four separate smallholdings had keeled over and died. The farmers, bewildered by the loss, had blamed the company. A Transgenic Biotech spokesman had denied responsibility, saying that nothing they did at the research centre could have had any adverse effects on local farm animals.

Later articles updated the story. The farmers, still accusing the company, had demanded compensation for the deaths of their hens, and Transgenic Biotech, continuing to protest its innocence, had agreed to make a payment 'as a gesture of goodwill'.

Frankie made a note of the name of the farmer who seemed to be the leader of the group – Vijay Patel – and replaced the envelope of cuttings on the shelf.

Panjit was waiting for him outside at the front of the building, talking to one of the oil-smeared mechanics from the garage next door.

'I'm thirsty,' Frankie said. 'Is there anywhere I can get a drink?'

Panjit took him to a teashop he frequented in the depths of the town. The street outside the teashop was impassable for vehicles because it was crowded with market traders, so they left the taxi parked on the pavement on the main road and went on foot, picking their way past the baskets of produce, the mounds of potatoes, onions, tomatoes, polished green chillies. The traders, squatting beside their brass weighing scales, looked up and followed Frankie with dark, inquisitive eyes.

The teashop was dim and thick with acrid cigarette smoke, but it was the coolest place Frankie had been all day. He knew one thing about India – never drink the water – so he asked for one of the bottles of Coke he could see on a shelf behind the counter. Panjit drifted off, touring the tables and chatting to his friends, making the most of the celebrity status temporarily conferred by his association with this striking Englishman. Frankie drank his Coke. It tasted very sweet and slightly odd but it quenched his thirst. Then they went back to the taxi and drove out to the research centre again.

Locating Vijay Patel's smallholding wasn't difficult, even though none of the plots was identified by a name or a sign of any kind. Frankie knew it was adjacent to the Transgenic Biotech site so it was just a simple matter of going round all the farms outside the fence until they found the right one. At the third farm they tried, Panjit came out of the mud-walled hut and nodded at Frankie.

'This is it.'

'Is he there?' Frankie asked.

'His wife is sending one of the children to fetch him.'

They went inside the hut which consisted of just a single tiny room. The floor was bare earth covered with woven straw mats. A woman in a dark blue sari was squatting by the open hearth, the glowing embers of the wood fire casting flickering shadows over her dark, careworn face. She stood up and offered Frankie a stool, the only seat in the house, saying something in a language Frankie didn't understand.

Panjit translated. 'She is asking if you would like tea.'

'Tell her, thank you but no,' Frankie replied. He didn't want to use up provisions which would be better spent on the family.

He sat down on the stool and flicked the flies away from his face. In a basket to one side, wrapped in a sheet, was a sleeping baby about five or six months old. The child seemed to be the only family member with a proper bed. Everyone else, Frankie guessed, slept on the mats on the floor.

Five minutes had elapsed when a young boy with stick-thin arms and legs ducked in through the back door of the hut. He was followed by a grown man in a tatty pair of trousers and shirt. Vijay Patel was clean shaven, his dark brown, almost black, skin coated with sweat and dust. He glanced at Panjit and Frankie and said something to his wife. Panjit interjected in the same language before the woman could reply. Patel gave a nod and squatted down on his haunches, his gaze fixed on Frankie.

'What do you want to ask him?' Panjit said.

'About his chickens. Can he tell me exactly what happened to them?'

Panjit relayed the question. The farmer shrugged indifferently and rattled off a reply in Hindi.

'He says it was a long time ago. Why do you want to know?' Panjit translated.

'Why? That's difficult to explain.'

Panjit shook his head. 'He doesn't really want to know why. He wants money.'

Frankie felt in his pocket and pulled out a handful of coins. The farmer stared at the change with bright, greedy eyes.

'Not too much,' Panjit warned.

Frankie held out a five-rupee coin. The farmer snatched it quickly, as if he feared the offer might be withdrawn, and slipped it away under his clothes. Then he started talking, Panjit repeating what he'd said in English.

'They were healthy birds, good layers. He kept them out in

front of the house. Six of them. They wandered around where they wanted to, sometimes over by the fence around the company's fields. Then one morning they all died. All of them. Suddenly.'

'At the same time?' Frankie said.

Panjit put the question to Mr Patel. He nodded and elaborated briefly in words which Panjit again translated.

'Within minutes of each other. One moment they were standing, the next they'd toppled over on to their sides, bleeding through their beaks.'

'Bleeding?'

'That's what he said.'

'Did this happen to the other farmers' hens too?'

Another brief exchange in Hindi.

'Yes. All of them bled. His were the first to die, then the Kumars, followed by the Bhatias and the Rajendras. All four farmers lost all their hens.'

'Ask him why he thought Transgenic Biotechnology was responsible.'

'Because something like that had never happened before,' Panjit explained after the farmer had given his answer. 'Before the research centre was built, no one lost any hens in that way. And it was only the farms next to the centre that suffered. The ones further away lost none of their hens. What else could have caused it? He says the farmers are very suspicious of the centre. They don't like it. He says they spray things on their crops, have lights on in their glasshouses all night. No one knows what they do there.'

'Has anything similar happened since?' Frankie asked.

Panjit translated the question and Patel shook his head.

'No.'

'What about potatoes?' Frankie continued.

Out of the corner of his eye, he noticed the young boy, who'd been crouching down beside his mother, start violently. Frankie turned to look at him. 'You speak English?'

'A bit,' the boy replied hesitantly.

'From school?'

'Yes, sir.'

'You know something about potatoes?'

The boy glanced warily at his father. 'No, sir.'

'Are you sure?'

Patel barked angrily at his son and the boy fell silent, bowing his head.

Frankie didn't press him, turning instead to Panjit. 'Does he grow potatoes? If so, has he ever had any problems with them? Disease, fungus, anything.'

'Yes, he grows them,' was Panjit's translation of the farmer's reply. 'No, he hasn't had any problems with them.'

'Thank you,' Frankie said, standing up.

He walked out through the door, screwing up his eyes as the blinding light hit him full in the face. He wished he'd brought sunglasses or a hat. His pale, exposed skin was prickling in the intense heat. His forearms and the bald patch on the top of his head felt as if they were being lightly toasted under a blow torch.

He squinted around. The perimeter fence of the research centre was only a few metres away across the dusty patch of earth outside the Patels' hut. On the other side of the fence was a strip of uncultivated land perhaps two metres wide and beyond it a rectangle of what looked like maize. There were blocks of other crops too, some covered in fine green nets, all of them separated by more strips of bare soil. In the distance the sunlight glanced off the windows of the research centre so that they gleamed like mirrors.

There was no shade anywhere. A few scrawny hens, replacements for the ones that had died, were pecking around in the dirt. Frankie found it hard to breathe. The burning air seemed starved of oxygen.

Panjit and Patel had come out of the hut behind him. Frankie held out another five-rupee coin. 'Tell him I'd like to speak to his son.'

The farmer took the coin and called to the boy who emerged cautiously through the doorway and avoided Frankie's gaze.

'Over here,' Frankie said, walking away down the track. He stopped after a few paces and waited for the boy to catch up with him. 'What's your name?'

'Sushil, sir.'

'This is just between the two of us, Sushil. No one else, including your father, will know what we talk about. Do you understand me?'

'Yes, sir.'

'You can trust me. Here. This is for you.' Frankie turned his back to the hut, blocking the view, and slipped the boy a two-rupee piece. Sushil gaped at it in amazement then hurriedly stashed it away in his pocket. 'There's another one of those for you if you answer a few questions for me. Now, what is it you don't want your father to know? About potatoes.' The boy's dark eyes flickered towards the hut. 'Don't worry, no one can hear you except me.'

Sushil took a moment to reply, perhaps searching for the right words in English. Frankie guessed he probably didn't have many hours of schooling a week. Out here education was a luxury most children would have tasted only intermittently when they could be spared from the fields. Sushil obviously helped his father. There were tiny fragments of vegetation, leaves, bits of straw in his hair and on the back of his ragged shirt. He must have been eleven or twelve years old. It was difficult to tell accurately, he was so emaciated. Frankie wondered where the other Patel children were. There surely had to be several between Sushil and the sleeping baby in the basket.

'We take some once,' Sushil said.

'Took some? You mean potatoes?'

The boy nodded. 'From there.'

'The research centre? From a field?'

'Yes. A friend and me. Vidya Prakashan. He live up the track. We climb over fence one night.'

'When was this?'

'We were small. A few years ago. They have many potatoes. Big green plants. They have lots of water there. They have those, I do not know what they are.' He motioned with his hands.

'Sprinklers,' Frankie said. 'They spray water over the fields.'

'Yes. We dig up the potatoes. They have so many. And we . . .'

'I understand.' Frankie nodded sympathetically. 'You're not going to get into trouble over this.'

Who could blame them, Frankie thought. Scratching a living from this thin, tired soil, their crops deprived of nutrients and water. And next door an oasis of plenty. Irrigated, fertilised, out of reach. It was a wonder the local people hadn't smashed the fence down by now.

'Just a few,' Sushil went on. 'It is dark, but there are lights. The men see us. We run. We get to fence and throw potatoes over. Then start to climb. But the men catch us. They beat us with their . . . what is this round here?' He indicated his waist.

'Belts?'

'Yes. Then they send us away. We find potatoes and go across there by stream. We make fire and cook potatoes. They taste not good. Not like our potatoes. I don't eat. But Vidya, he eats. They hurt him. He is like this.' Sushil screwed up his face and clutched his hollow belly. 'I am frightened. What to do? I help Vidya back to his house. Over there, not far. He is crying. I tell his mother what we do. She is angry. I go. Vidya, he die.'

Frankie was concentrating so hard on the kid's fractured

English that he took a second to realise what he'd said. Then he thought he must have misunderstood. 'What do you mean? You're saying he died?'

'Yes.'

'From eating the potatoes?'

'Yes.'

'Jesus,' Frankie breathed. 'What happened then?'

'I do not know.'

'You told his mother where you got the potatoes?'

'Yes.'

'And what did she do?'

'I do not know. But the men, in the building, they dig up potatoes. All.'

'Did anyone from the company, from the building, come to you? Asking questions?'

'No. Why? I feel good. I did not eat.'

'Who else knows about this?'

'Vidya's mother and father.'

'You didn't tell your parents?'

Sushil shook his head vigorously. 'They beat me.'

'What about the police? Did they investigate Vidya's death?'

'The police?' A look of fear flitted across the boy's face. 'No. No police.'

'They didn't question you about what happened?'

'No, sir.'

'Vidya's house,' Frankie said. 'Tell me exactly where it is.'

Sushil pointed along the dusty track that ran between the fields, connecting the scattered farms with the main road. 'Up there. On right. First house.'

Frankie gave him the two rupees he'd promised and walked back to Panjit. The track was narrow and deeply pitted, but the Ford Popular was small and robust enough to negotiate it. About a quarter of a mile further on they came to the Prakashan house.

It was considerably bigger than the Patels'; not just one room but several by the look of it. Adjoining the house was a wooden stable containing two bony black bullocks.

Frankie waited outside by the taxi while Panjit went into the house to talk to the family. It was now late afternoon, but the fierce heat showed no sign of abating. Frankie's shirt was sticking to his back, his trousers clinging to his buttocks and thighs as if they'd been welded on. He walked around a bit because standing still was unbearable. His feet were soaked with sweat. He could almost hear them squelching in his shoes.

The Prakashans' house was built on a slight incline, a small mound on the plain which, although only low in height, afforded a good view of the surrounding countryside. Frankie could see all the neighbouring houses and was struck by how similar they looked: basically one-room mud brick or wooden huts with either straw or rusty galvanised iron roofs. The Prakashans' home was the exception. He could see no other house of a comparable size. It was only relative, of course. The signs of poverty and deprivation were still apparent here, but they were less extreme than elsewhere in the landscape.

Panjit came out of the house accompanied by a small barefoot man with a face like crumpled leather and eyes so deep set they appeared to have black rings around them like a lemur.

'This is Mr Prakashan,' Panjit said.

Frankie gave him a friendly nod and reached into his pocket, preparing to bring out his loose change again.

'Tell him I'd like to ask him a few questions about his son, Vidya.'

Panjit translated the request. As he did so, a strange transformation came over Prakashan. His face, up till then quite open, if a little curious, seemed to shut off as though a visor had slammed down in front of it. His expression became hostile and Frankie saw anger, and maybe fear, in his dark eyes. Prakashan

272

waved an arm and snapped out a few words of Hindi. Frankie didn't need a translator to understand the message. But Panjit told him anyway.

'He wants us to go.'

'Why won't he talk to us?'

Panjit repeated the question, getting embroiled in an increasingly heated exchange with the farmer. Finally, Panjit threw up his hands in exasperation and turned back to Frankie. 'You'll get nowhere with him. These peasants . . . You're wasting your time.'

Prakashan pointed at the taxi and gesticulated back down the track, his meaning clear without any words.

'Okay,' Frankie said, holding up a placating hand. 'We're going.'

The farmer glared at them as they climbed back into the car and turned to drive away up the track. Only when the taxi was a cloud of dust in the distance did Prakashan take his eyes off it and return to the door of his house. He shouted at someone inside and a tiny, pinch-faced girl came out. He jabbered at her urgently, giving instructions, and the girl nodded. Then she took off at a run, heading through the fields towards the research centre.

The back issues of the *Derapur Times* were kept in a cramped basement room which was as hot and airless as a tandoori oven. Frankie had undone his shirt to the waist and left the door open to let in a draught, but he was still sweating profusely, the atmosphere in the room like a steaming towel which had been wrapped around his throat and was being slowly tightened.

He'd already checked the cuttings library, but there was no entry in the index for Prakashan. As he knew there'd been nothing in the Transgenic Biotech envelope about a young boy dying, he'd had to resort to searching through the complete back issues of the paper to see if it had been reported. It was a slow, painstaking task. He had no idea exactly when Vidya Prakashan had died. 'A few years ago,' was all Sushil had said.

Frankie started with the 1997 issues and worked his way through them, scouring the headlines for any mention of the incident. In the June editions he found the articles about the dead hens which he'd read earlier in the cuttings file. He glanced again at them and moved on.

Then something caught his eye.

A small headline which read simply, 'Bees die'. The two-paragraph story below it described how a farmer named Bhatia had lost three hives. The cause of the deaths was unknown. The farmer had just gone out one morning and found all his bees dead in the honeycombs. Frankie studied the article for much longer than its length merited, then turned to the next issue.

That was where he found it.

A child dying of a mystery illness.

Only there was no mention of potatoes, and the child's name wasn't Prakashan, it was Patel. And it wasn't just one child, it was three.

Patel was a common surname, but Frankie knew intuitively it was the same family he'd visited today. And he knew now why there'd been no more children in evidence at Sushil's house. His three younger siblings, aged seven, five and three, had all died. Died within a few days of each other. In India, the death of a child wasn't news. Millions died every year, from poverty, disease, malnutrition, none of them deemed of any importance except to their families. What made the Patel children's deaths newsworthy was the fact that they were not alone.

Frankie went carefully through the two issues from the second half of June 1997, making notes on the pad of paper he'd borrowed from the newsroom upstairs. In the space of that fortnight, sixteen people had died. All had fallen ill with a fever whose symptoms were similar to influenza. And all had died within four or five days of contracting the disease. Apart from the Patels, there seemed to be six other families affected . . .

Frankie stopped writing.

Just a minute.

There was something familiar about three of the names. One was Bhatia, the same as the farmer who'd lost his bees. Two others were Kumar and Rajendra. Frankie thought back to his conversation with Vijay Patel, recalling the names of the other farmers whose hens had died. It might be a coincidence, of course. There might be other families with the same surnames. But Frankie didn't think so. Of the four farmers who had lost hens to what they believed – rightly or wrongly – was some mysterious infection from the Transgenic Biotech research centre, three were now dead.

15

Deep in thought, Frankie went back upstairs to the newsroom where Panjit was slouched in a chair drinking tea with the Editor of the newspaper, a short, dumpy fellow with thick horn-rimmed glasses and a mop of dark hair streaked with grey which was so luxuriant he looked as if a small skunk had curled up and gone to sleep on his head.

'Did you find what you wanted?' the Editor enquired. Both he and Panjit were smoking Indian cigarettes which gave off the foul smell of burning tar.

'I'm not sure,' Frankie replied.

He'd found nothing about Vidya Prakashan or toxic potatoes, but the other deaths from fever had aroused his curiosity. He asked the Editor if he recalled the cases.

'Fever?' the Editor said dismissively. 'People die of fever all the time.'

'This was sixteen people. All living near each other.'

'That's how fever spreads. It's not unusual for whole families to catch it. Many of them die.'

'You obviously considered it newsworthy enough to report.'

The Editor shrugged. 'I don't remember it. Maybe it was a slow week. My readers are mostly in the town. Those people out there, farmers, they can't even write their own names.'

'Would they have seen a doctor?' Frankie said.

'A doctor?' The Editor was incredulous. 'Those peasants out in the fields? This isn't England, you know. How would they afford a doctor?'

'No one cares,' Panjit said harshly. 'They live, they die. Why should you, someone from thousands of miles away, care either?'

The truth was, Frankie didn't care. He hadn't known them, their deaths hadn't touched him in any way. Yet he felt he ought to have cared. Or made a pretence of caring. Maybe that was the problem. India seemed a hard country, but perhaps they were just more honest here.

'What's your opinion of the Transgenic Biotechnology research centre?' Frankie asked the Editor.

'Opinion?'

'I got the impression from some of your editorials that you weren't one of its greatest fans.'

'That's true. I'm suspicious of it. So are a lot of people. I don't trust what they do there.'

'Why not?'

The Editor tapped the ash off his cigarette and sat up straight, his eyes bright and alert. 'Because they've come here to exploit us. Companies like Transgenic Biotechnology want to control our agriculture. There are many of them here, British, American, Swiss, German. They have bought up Indian seed companies, introduced their own brands of seed which the farmers have to buy from them along with the expensive herbicides and chemicals that go with the western way of farming. They have even patented the genetic codes for things that have been with us for thousands of years – basmati rice, turmeric, black pepper, even our sacred neem tree are now owned by the Americans. How can that be right?'

The Editor turned his head a fraction. The light from the window glinted on the lenses of his glasses, turning them opaque. He looked back at Frankie with a passionate intensity.

'And now they are experimenting with genetically modified crops. They come here, buy land, build laboratories, set up trial sites and try to persuade the Government and farmers that these crops are the best way to feed our growing population. But all it will do is make us even more dependent on these companies. To many people it feels as if we're being occupied by a foreign power interested only in making money out of us. That's why I don't trust them. That's why I'm suspicious of what they do at that research centre up the road.'

'Do you believe what they're doing is harmful?' Frankie asked.

'I have no evidence of that. But one thing I know for certain, and this applies to all these companies, the welfare of the local population is not of paramount importance to them.'

'What if I told you a child had died after eating potatoes from one of their fields?'

The Editor stiffened. 'What child?'

Frankie repeated what Sushil Patel had told him.

The Editor listened closely, frowning with concentration. 'This is all news to me,' he said eventually. 'You have talked to the boy's family?'

'They refused to speak to me.'

'The father got very angry,' Panjit added. 'A rude, vulgar fellow.'

'Refused?' the Editor said. 'Why?'

'My guess,' Frankie said, 'and it's only a guess, is that they've been paid to keep quiet. They seem to have a lot more money than any of their neighbours.'

The Editor nodded reflectively, sucking on his cigarette. 'I can believe it. That's how these companies work. Indians are very cheap to buy.'

'Can you do anything?' Frankie asked.

'What do you suggest? It was several years ago. There's no medical evidence, nothing to link the death conclusively to the potatoes. If the family won't talk to you, they certainly won't talk to me. Transgenic Biotechnology employ expensive lawyers in Lucknow who have threatened me before. I'm not going to allege the company killed a child without proof. That would destroy my newspaper.'

'So they get away with it?'

The Editor gave a fatalistic shrug. 'Don't they always?'

'Let's go back to the hotel,' Frankie said.

It was growing dark outside. Frankie noted the change with relief, wondering when – if ever – the heat would finally become bearable. He was still leaking through every pore of his body, his skin moist and slippery under his damp clothes. The window of the taxi was open and it seemed as though he could smell the heat as they drove through the streets – a ripe, slightly sweet odour laced with dust and dung and the lingering tang of exhaust fumes.

The Editor's words left a nasty taste in his mouth, but he knew the man was right. There was nothing to prove that the potatoes killed Vidya Prakashan – no autopsy, no doctor's records, no body to examine for toxic residues. The evidence was purely circumstantial, based entirely on the recollection of another child. What newspaper wouldn't have reservations about such a story?

They were approaching the hotel when they got stuck in a slow-moving line of traffic behind a large lorry. In a yard set back from the street Frankie noticed two men filling glass bottles with dark syrup and topping them up with water from a hosepipe attached to a rainwater tank. He realised with alarm that the bottles bore the unmistakable shape and trademark of the Coca-Cola Corporation.

'Panjit,' he said calmly, his eyes never leaving the two men, 'that Coke I bought in the teashop. It *was* imported, wasn't it?'

Panjit glanced across into the yard. 'Only the name, sir,' he said with a grin. 'The rest is made in India.'

At the hotel, Frankie climbed out of the taxi and gave Panjit a hundred-rupee tip. 'Thanks for your help.'

'If you need me again, sir,' Panjit handed him a grubby card with a name and phone number on it, 'I can be contacted there day and night.'

They shook hands and Frankie went upstairs to his room. He tried the light switch inside the door. Nothing happened. Feeling his way past the bed in the semi-darkness, he clicked on the table lamp. Again nothing happened. He tilted the lamp to see inside the shade. There was no bulb. Not that it would have made much difference if there had been, for on closer examination of the walls he discovered there wasn't a single electric socket in the room.

He stripped to the waist and washed in cold water at the basin, then changed his shirt for the third time that day. Within minutes, he was sweating as much as he had been before. Whether it was the heat, or possibly the psychological effects of seeing the local Coca-Cola bottling plant, he suddenly felt his bowels loosening. Locking the door, he went downstairs quickly, following the signs to the toilet. It was further than he'd anticipated: through the hall by the reception desk and down a corridor towards the back of the building. Emerging into the open air, he found a door marked WC and realised he was in the yard just below his bedroom window. He pulled open the door and stepped inside. The stench almost knocked him out. He peered around in the gloom, trying to hold his breath, but couldn't see a toilet anywhere. Then he looked down and saw the hole cut in the wooden floor. Shit, one of those.

He didn't linger. The smell was bad enough, but it was the clouds of flies and mosquitoes that really made him hurry. The thought of a mosquito bite in the wrong place . . . He got out rapidly and went back upstairs to wash his hands. He was hungry. He'd had nothing to eat since breakfast. Going back to reception, he rang the bell on the counter and asked the small boy who came out from a curtained doorway if the hotel provided any food.

'Oh, yes, sir,' the boy replied. 'We have full dinner menu. Please to come this way.'

Frankie followed the boy into what seemed to be a dining room. There were tables and chairs crammed into a small space, none of them occupied. Frankie appeared to be the only guest in the hotel. He sat down with a sense of misgiving. This didn't look very promising, but the thought of wandering around the town looking for somewhere else to eat was too much to contemplate. There were no lights in here either. It was too dim to read a menu, which was fortunate as there didn't appear to be one.

'What would you like, sir?' the boy asked.

'What have you got?' Frankie countered.

'Whatever you would like, sir.'

Realising this conversation could go on for a long time, Frankie summoned up all his knowledge of Indian cuisine and tried to recall the menu at The Jewel in the Crown, the restaurant on St Andrew's Street he went to regularly back home.

'How about an onion bhaji for starters?' he said.

'Pardon?'

'An onion bhaji. You have that?'

'No, sir. No onion bhaji.'

Frankie couldn't think of any more starters so he moved on to main courses. 'What about a chicken tikka masala?'

The boy looked at him blankly. 'What is that, sir?'

'Never mind. Let's try a chicken korma. Do you have that?'

'No, sir.'

'Chicken vindaloo?'

'No, sir.'

'Chicken dupiaza? Chicken biryani?'

The boy shook his head. 'No, sir.'

'This isn't a restaurant at all, is it?'

'Pardon, sir?'

'Well, it does seem to be noticeably uncontaminated by food.'

Frankie considered what to do. India was a big country. He knew vaguely that there were many different types of cooking. Maybe he was in the wrong area for these dishes.

'What about a balti?' he ventured and saw a scintilla of recognition in the boy's eyes. 'You have a balti?'

'Yes, sir. We have balti.'

'Excellent. I'll have one of those.'

The boy looked at him without moving. 'You want balti now?' he said.

'Yes, now.'

The boy disappeared into the kitchen and came back carrying a large metal mop bucket which he offered to Frankie.

'What's that for?' Frankie asked.

'You say you want balti. This is balti.'

This wasn't working. Frankie tried a different approach. 'I tell you what, why don't you tell me what's available first. Then I'll choose.'

'Very well, sir. We have dhal.'

'And what's that?'

'Lentils.'

'Anything else?'

'Rice.'

'No meat?'

'No, sir.'

'Is that it?'

'Yes, sir.'

'Okay, I'll have the rice and lentils.'

'And to drink, sir?'

'What is there?'

'We have Coca-Cola.'

'No Coca-Cola,' Frankie said hurriedly.

'Or other American drink. Seven-Up, Sprite. Or tea.'

'I'll have tea,' Frankie said.

The food arrived so quickly and was so lukewarm it must have been sitting around in the kitchen for some time. Apart from the dhal and rice there was an unidentified mush on the plate that smelt strongly of spices and was hot to the taste. Frankie never usually touched vegetarian food – vegetables were things that came with meat, they had no *raison d'être* on their own – but he was hungry enough to eat anything.

It wasn't bad, plain but filling. Periodically, other small children would poke their heads out of the kitchen and stare at him, but Frankie didn't mind. Halfway through the meal the electric overhead light flickered on suddenly. Frankie wished it hadn't as he could see what he was eating. But it didn't last and he finished in the same enveloping gloom in which he'd started.

He went to bed early. Derapur didn't strike him as a town with much of a nightlife. He lay on top of the bed wearing nothing but his underpants, the window wide open, but it was too hot to sleep. He rolled around restlessly. The rice and dhal were heavy on his stomach. Once or twice he got up and splashed cold water on his torso and face. It didn't make much difference. He still felt as if he were in the steam room of a sauna.

He must have dozed off eventually for he was in a shallow, troubled sleep when something woke him abruptly. He sat up in a panic, not sure where he was, and stared around the darkened room. What was it? He listened. His heart was racing, his skin clammy with cold sweat. He could hear nothing. The moving shadows settled back into the familiar outlines of door, window, bed. Frankie took a few deep breaths and relaxed. He never slept well in strange places. Looking at the luminous dial of his watch he saw that it was 1.20 am.

He lay on his pillow and closed his eyes again. Slowly, he

became aware of a different sensation, the same one he'd felt earlier – a pressure in his abdomen, in his bowels. He tensed his muscles, hoping it would pass, hoping he could last until morning. But it only got worse.

He swung his legs off the bed, praying he could get there in time. He pulled on his shirt and trousers and thrust his feet into his shoes, then hurried out of the room. On the staircase the pressure intensified, almost a pain now. He held on tight, concentrating hard on muscle control as he headed down the corridor and out into the yard. He tore open the door of the WC, his hands fumbling with his trousers. The release came with an explosion that drew a low cry from his lips. The flies and mosquitoes didn't bother him this time. It was just a blessed relief to be there.

He was standing up, fastening the clasp on his trousers when he heard voices outside in the yard. Two men, speaking softly in Hindi. Frankie froze, his fingers gripping his waistband. His first thought was that it was someone else coming to use the toilet, but there were two of them. And they were coming into the yard from the street at the rear of the hotel. He listened to them talking. Maybe it was Mr Shah returning home after a night out with a friend. Frankie kept quiet, waiting for them to go into the building. He was too embarrassed to want to be seen emerging from the lavatory. But they stayed in the yard.

Frankie peered through the gap around the ill-fitting door. The men were only a few paces away. They were big, well-built compared to most of the Indians he'd encountered so far. It was too dark to make out much of their faces, but light enough to see that they were each carrying something in their hands.

Frankie pulled back from the door and held his breath.
Shit!

They were carrying wooden clubs. Long, tapered clubs about the size of baseball bats, swinging loose by their sides. Frankie had a sudden, terrible premonition as to why they were there. He heard them pad across the yard on their bare feet and pressed his eye back to the gap, watching them as they climbed up a drainpipe and in through the open window of his room. What would they do when they discovered he wasn't there? When they felt the bed and found it still warm? They'd come looking for him, of course. And they'd try the most obvious place first.

Frankie zipped up his fly and eased the door open cautiously. He glanced up at his bedroom, saw a figure flit across the window. There was no way of telling whether he'd been spotted. He stepped through the doorway into the corridor and crept along it to the hall, pausing to consider his next move.

The stairs creaked. They were coming down. Frankie dropped to a crouch and crawled behind the high reception desk, pressing himself deep into the shadows under the counter. He heard rather than saw the men descend to the hall. They exchanged a few whispered words before heading off down the corridor. Frankie peered out round the side of the counter. The men were out of sight in the yard. He knew he had to make a swift decision. The reception desk was the first place they'd check when they came back in. His room? They'd almost certainly hear him going up the stairs. That left only one option. He straightened up and stumbled across the hall into the dining room. There was nowhere to hide there, but he pushed open the door to the kitchen and slunk softly inside.

A faint glimmer of moonlight penetrated the tiny windows high up on one wall of the room, grazing the table and worktops below and making the cheap metal pots and pans on the stove shine like polished silver. Frankie looked around for a hiding place. Apart from under the table, an exposed and hazardous location, there was nothing. A door on one side, he guessed, gave access to another part of the rear yard, but Frankie didn't really want to go outside. The yard was even more risky than staying in here. Away from the sanctuary of the hotel he had nowhere to go. Then he saw the second door, in the wall at the far end of the kitchen. He walked across and pushed it open. It was some kind of pantry about two metres square. On the ceiling-high shelves that lined the walls he could discern the shapes of tins and boxes. There was a strong smell of onions and garlic and spices. He went inside and pushed the door shut behind him.

He waited, trying to control his pounding heart. Maybe the men would give up and go away. He knew that was a slim hope. They would search until they found him. They would finish the job they'd been sent to carry out. Frankie didn't let his mind dwell on exactly what that job was. He was frightened enough already.

It wasn't the first time he'd been in such a position. He'd taken a couple of bad beatings on jobs in England, narrowly avoided a few more. He was big enough to look after himself in most situations, but he didn't fancy tackling two men with clubs. He wished he'd picked up a weapon in the kitchen; a knife, a pan, something he could use to defend himself. He hadn't been thinking clearly. There was nothing in the pantry. He ran his hand along the shelves. Perhaps he could use a tin or a glass jar. His fingers encountered something metal, a bowl of some sort. There were several of them next to each other, all containing some kind of fine powder. He took a pinch of the first and sniffed it. It was a spice, but he couldn't identify which one. The second bowl he recognised, dabbing a few grains on his tongue. It was chilli powder.

The kitchen door squeaked. Frankie went very still. Had he imagined it? He could hear no further sound. Surely even bare feet would make some slight noise on the tiled floor. He listened intently. Then he started. *Jesus*. Very slowly, the pantry door was swinging open towards him. Frankie dipped his fingers into the bowl of chilli powder and took a good handful. The door opened wider. Frankie didn't wait. With one hand he whipped the door back and with the other flung the chilli powder into the face of the startled man outside. The man gave a shriek of pain and raised both hands to his eyes, dropping his club to the floor. Frankie kicked him hard in the stomach and knocked him sideways with a right hook. Then in one movement he picked up the club and swung it down on the man's back. The man scrambled away, still blinded by the chilli, fumbling past the table to the door where his companion had just appeared. Frankie gave a blood-curdling yell and lunged for them both with the club. The two men turned and fled across the dining room and down the hall. Frankie chased them out on to the street and let them go. When he returned to the reception desk, Mr Shah was scurrying down the stairs in his underwear, his hair dishevelled. Frankie pulled out the card Panjit had given him from his trouser pocket and placed it on the counter.

'May I use your phone?' he said.

16

Madeleine didn't often get angry with the clients she represented – it was unproductive as well as unprofessional – but this was one occasion when she let her feelings get the better of her occupational detachment.

'What the hell do you think you're playing at? You're an intelligent boy. How could you do something so stupid?'

Jake kept his eyes fixed on the surface of the table between them. He couldn't meet her gaze, couldn't face up to the contempt he could hear in her voice.

'You're on bail for an offence and you go out and commit exactly the same offence again. I don't believe you did that. What were you thinking of? Did you think you wouldn't get caught? Why? Why did you do it?'

Jake wondered too. He knew the answer, but didn't want to admit it. Not to himself. Certainly not to his solicitor. She would never understand.

'You gave an undertaking to the court,' Madeleine continued. 'You agreed not to go near any GM crops.'

'No, I didn't.' Jake looked up, trying to defend himself. 'I agreed not to go near any property owned by Transgenic Biotechnology. This field was a Xenotech trial site.'

'The difference is going to be academic to the magistrates, believe me. You've reoffended whilst on bail. They take a very dim view of that.'

'What right do they have to judge me?' Jake flared up suddenly. 'They're just a bunch of middle-class, middle-minded Establishment puppets. Pillocks who enjoy locking people away as a hobby. And we're stupid enough to give them the power.'

'Who they are is neither here nor there,' Madeleine replied in exasperation. 'They just enforce the law.'

Jake lifted a hand and rubbed his eyes. He felt dirty and tired. His hands and face were smeared with grime and sticky resin from the stalks of transgenic maize he'd helped rip up from the earth. He wanted a hot shower and something to eat, but the Norwich police seemed in no hurry to offer him either.

'They're going to send me to prison, aren't they?' he said resignedly.

Madeleine softened a little. He was just a boy. A foolish boy who was going to pay a heavy price for his Sunday afternoon outing to Norfolk. 'I'm afraid they almost certainly are,' she said.

'For how long?'

'Until the case comes to trial.'

'That could be months.'

'Quite possibly.'

Jake blinked. Christ. He'd expected the worst, but having it spelt out for him made him feel sick. He didn't know how he'd cope with prison. He thought briefly of Jackie. A bitter, resentful memory of a single night's pleasure. A fumbled, hurried coupling on his lumpy sofa, both of them too horny, too impatient, to move over to the bed. It was easy to blame someone else. He knew his own vanity and lust were partly responsible, but Jackie was as much at fault as he was. And she'd got away unscathed. That didn't seem fair.

What had he been thinking of? On Friday night he knew all too well what he'd been thinking. But afterwards he could still have reconsidered and backed out. Except that his male pride, his testosterone-fuelled conceit hadn't let him. Even in the field he'd felt compelled to strut his stuff. When the police had arrived he'd been the last to flee, lingering behind so Jackie could see what a daring guy he was. Jackie, who was too busy scrambling over a fence and into the back of the van to care about his pointless posturing. And when he'd finally run, it had been too late. The van had gone, the rear doors swinging open as it raced away down the country lane. He'd seen Jackie looking back at him, watching as the coppers closed in and dragged him to the ground. He could still feel the ache where the beefy sergeant had accidentally on purpose stuck his boot into his groin. In different circumstances he might have found something apposite about that rough justice: punishing the part that had caused all this trouble. This was what came of thinking with your prick.

'I'm going to ask for bail,' Madeleine said. 'It's always worth a try, but I don't hold out too much hope. I've no idea what the magistrates up here are like.'

'Where will I go?'

'If you're remanded? I'll ask for Bedford Prison. That's where the remand prisoners from Cambridge Magistrates' Court are usually sent. It'll be more convenient for you if you want any visitors.'

It was more convenient for her too. She'd already wasted half her precious Sunday driving up to Norwich. She didn't want to have to do it any more often than was absolutely necessary.

'When's my court appearance?' Jake asked.

'Tomorrow morning.'

'You'll be there?'

Madeleine heard the note of anxiety in his voice and nodded.

'Of course. I'm here to help you, Jake. I just wish you'd done more to help yourself.'

'We have to take a stand against these crops,' Jake said.

'Not when you're on bail for another offence. That doesn't make sense. Leave it to others to make the stand.'

'That's what everyone does. They leave it to other people. It's our national disease, apathy. We let things happen without protest, without fighting back.'

'You're not going to do much fighting from Bedford Prison,' Madeleine retorted harshly.

Jake sat back, momentarily thrown by the comment. Then he shrugged. 'Why not? Getting jailed might draw more attention to the issue. It might serve a purpose.'

'Is that what you want? To become a martyr to the cause?'

Jake looked at her searchingly. 'Where do you stand on this issue? What do you believe in?'

'Let's leave me out of this. I'm your solicitor, my views are irrelevant.'

'But you must have some.'

'We're wasting time,' Madeleine said. 'The police are waiting to interview you. We'd better talk through your case.'

'I bet you're opposed to GM foods, aren't you?'

'Jake.'

'Okay, whatever you say.'

Madeleine turned to a clean page in her notepad and picked up her pen. He'd acted like an idiot, but she had to concede there was something she could admire in Jake Brewster. In this cynical age it was tempting to mock the idealism of youth, but Madeleine wasn't cynical. Not underneath, though she saw plenty to be cynical about. She'd always fought for her clients as a matter of personal and professional pride. Once, long ago, she'd fought for other causes. She'd written letters, been to meetings, joined the occasional march, perhaps even believed that it would achieve something; that protest could ever achieve anything. She wasn't sure whether she believed it now. She wondered whether she would have the guts to go out and tear up transgenic crops, risk going to prison for something she believed in. Growing older brought a complacency that often masqueraded as realism, a justification for doing nothing. Madeleine had seen too many causes lost to truly believe she could make a difference to the world, but Jake still had the stars in his eyes. He knew a cause only became lost when you gave up the battle.

'I spoke to the custody sergeant,' Madeleine said, more comfortable now they were getting down to the legal procedures. 'They're going to charge you with criminal damage again.'

'I intend to plead not guilty,' Jake replied. 'On the grounds that I was acting to prevent serious damage to other crops and the environment by genetic pollution from the GM maize pollen.'

Madeleine gazed at him pensively. 'It's a defence that's worked before. But a lot depends on the jury you get.'

'What the hell,' Jake said. 'I'll take that chance.'

The struggle to identify the influenza virus was taking its toll on Ian Fitzgerald. Long hours, stress and lack of sleep had all left their mark on the scientist's face which was ashen and lined with fatigue. Arriving at Mill Hill late on Friday evening, Housman had been shocked to see the transformation that had come over his old colleague. He was bleary-eyed, unsteady on his feet, beginning to exhibit the lassitude, slurred speech and lack of co-ordination that presaged breakdown from exhaustion.

Housman had hauled him out of the laboratory – quite literally dragged him physically into his office – and made him lie down on the couch.

'You shouldn't be doing this, Ian.'

'I'm okay.'

'You're not okay. You should be going home and getting a proper night's sleep.'

'We need to find out what it is.'

'You have a team for that. Younger people who are better

equipped to cope than you. Let them do the all-nighters.'

'You don't lead by staying in bed and letting others do all the work,' Fitzgerald replied stubbornly.

That was how he'd always been. It was one of the reasons he commanded such respect and real affection from his colleagues and assistants. But he wasn't looking good. The last time Housman had seen him this run down was in central Africa fifteen years earlier, and neither of them wanted to dwell too much on what had happened then though it was carved indelibly on their memories.

They'd been in the remote interior of Zaïre, studying an outbreak of Lassa fever, a killer viral disease spread by the *Mastomys* rat which was endemic in that part of the world. Travelling round the isolated rural villages in a Land-Rover, they'd found one community where half a dozen people had died of the disease and another eight, all sick with fever, had been dumped in a hut and left to fend for themselves. Fitzgerald, taking a blood sample from one of the semi-conscious victims, had momentarily lost concentration. The hypodermic syringe full of infected blood had slipped, the needle piercing the protective rubber gloves Fitzgerald was wearing and breaking the skin on his right forefinger. He'd bathed the wound immediately with disinfectant and prayed he'd caught it in time. But the Lassa virus was amongst the most virulent on earth. Three days later, Fitzgerald had started to show the first signs of the illness: sore throat, shivering, high temperature.

With no hospital close to hand, certainly no hospital he trusted, Housman had taken the decision to get his friend out of the country. He'd put Fitzgerald in the back of the Land-Rover, wedged between their equipment, and driven two hundred and fifty miles non-stop to Kinshasa Airport, a drive that even now, a decade and a half later, could still bring him out in a cold sweat when he recalled it. There were no metalled roads in that part of Zaïre and the driving conditions were atrocious. But worst of all, the Zaïreans believed that they saved fuel by not using the lights on their vehicles. Heading at night along the pot-holed jungle highway surrounded by huge invisible trucks and lorries, it had been little short of miraculous that they had made it to the airport in one piece.

They'd been flown back to England by the RAF and Fitzgerald had been put in an isolation room at the London School of Hygiene and Tropical Disease. His temperature had been 40 degrees Celsius, his blood pressure sky high with red and white blood cells draining from his cardiovascular system into his urine at an alarming rate. And that was only the start. His temperature later rose to 42 degrees, his throat became so inflamed he couldn't swallow his own saliva and he lost all control of his muscles as the virus attacked his central nervous system. For more than a week Fitzgerald had teetered on the brink of death before his body fought back and he gradually recovered. The headaches and dizziness remained for several weeks after and he never fully regained his hearing. As soon as he was well enough to return to the lab at Mill Hill he'd called Housman in and told him to make arrangements for them to return to Zaïre. 'You're going back?' Housman had said in disbelief. 'Of course,' Fitzgerald had replied. 'I'm immune.'

He might have been immune to a second attack of Lassa fever, but he wasn't immune to the passage of time. He was sixty-four years old now and his legendary stamina was beginning to wane. Watching him slumped on the couch, his eyes closed, his breathing laboured, Housman had felt a stab of sadness for the inevitable decline of youthful vigour.

'I'm calling for a taxi,' he'd said. 'Sending you home.'

'I have a car.'

'You're in no fit state to drive. You go home, Ian. And you don't come back here before noon. That's twelve hours.'

'You can't order me around,' Fitzgerald had protested weakly, but he'd gone quietly in the end. He knew he was no use to anyone if he didn't get some rest.

It wasn't until Saturday afternoon, when Fitzgerald returned to Mill Hill, that they sat down together in the office and talked through what progress had been made. They'd been testing the virus since Tuesday but none of the antisera had given a positive result. The problem with antibodies was that they were very specific – like a key that would only fit one lock. They either reacted to a virus or they didn't.

'Are we going to get a match?' Housman asked.

'I don't think so. We're running out of options. It's entirely new, that's my feeling.'

Housman nodded grimly. They'd both been hoping that somewhere in all the antisera they'd been trying there would have been one that would have caused a reaction – proof that the virus had already shown itself in an outbreak of the disease, however small, elsewhere in the world. An entirely novel strain was bad news, for no one would have an acquired immunity to it.

'A new bird flu that can infect humans. That scares the shit out of me,' Housman said.

'The slaughter programme might just contain it.'

'And if it doesn't?'

Fitzgerald didn't bother to reply. He took some sheets of thin photographic paper out of a file on his desk and pushed them across to Housman. There were rows of tiny marks on the sheets, narrow bands of dark and light ink like elongated bar codes. They were genetic printouts of the virus, a breakdown of the RNA that made up its genome.

'The ninth strand of RNA,' Fitzgerald said. 'It hasn't split off from one of the other eight.'

'You're sure?'

'I've been over the printouts a dozen times. Had the computer check them. Whatever it is, it codes for a new gene.'

'Doing what?'

'That's the question.'

'What is it, a peculiar reassortment?'

'I don't think so. The other eight strands could be a typical H5. They're complete and wholly avian. They don't seem to have changed in themselves.'

'What are you saying?'

'That the flu virions have been infected by some other virus. A virus that isn't influenza.'

Housman stared at him in silence for a long time. It was one of the basic rules of virology that there could be no genetic interaction between unrelated viruses. Two different strains of influenza could combine but influenza and a disparate virus, say measles or rabies, could never mix. It simply wasn't genetically possible.

'It reproduces true,' Fitzgerald went on. 'I know it's hard to believe, but each generation is identical. The genome has been changed.'

'How is that possible?' Housman breathed.

'The results stunned me too.'

'And the additional strand of RNA? Where the hell has that come from?'

'I don't know, Karl,' Fitzgerald said. 'But I think we ought to find out.'

Late on Sunday evening, Housman received another blow. He was in the Mill Hill lab, just preparing to finish off what he was doing and get ready to drive back to Cambridge, when the telephone rang.

'It's for you,' one of Fitzgerald's assistants said, holding up the receiver. 'A Stephen Manville.'

'The hospital told me where you were,' Manville explained when Housman came on the line.

'Another case?' Housman said.

'I'm afraid so. A forty-three-year-old woman.'

'Great Dunchurch again?'

'Yes.'

That was something at least. The disease was still being contained within a narrow geographical area.

'What's her condition?'

'Like the others. The GP saw her this morning, called an ambulance immediately.'

'She's at Addenbrooke's?'

'In the IU.'

'Background?'

'She's a close friend of Wendy Bullingham, the patient who was admitted on Friday. I went out there this afternoon myself, did the checks . . .'

Manville paused. Housman felt a cold shudder run the length of his spine.

'And?' he prompted.

'She's on a low-cholesterol diet,' Manville continued. 'Never touches eggs. Hasn't had chicken for more than a fortnight. But she was round at Wendy Bullingham's house on Thursday afternoon.'

Housman leaned back on the bench. His legs had gone suddenly weak.

'You sure? This is important,' he said.

'I'm sure,' Manville replied quietly. 'She's had no contact with hens or eggs or any other farm animals. Just with Wendy Bullingham.'

Housman touched his forehead, feeling the sheen of sweat which hadn't been there twenty seconds earlier. Fitzgerald was watching him intently from further along the bench. Housman put his hand over the mouthpiece of the phone and turned to look at him.

'It's found a way to transmit from person to person,' he said.

17

David Coldwell was the last to arrive, sweeping majestically into the conference room with Tristan Allardyce and two other civil servants trotting along in his wake. He paused for effect at the head of the long mahogany table, glancing around the faces of the other men in the room, before taking his seat. Allardyce and the other civil servants took up positions away from the table, perching on chairs behind and a little to the side of the Minister.

'Good morning, gentlemen,' Coldwell said smoothly. 'Are we all here?'

For television and newspaper interviews he exaggerated his mild Yorkshire accent to emphasise the bluff man-of-the-people image he liked to project, but this morning he was the epitome of the metropolitan politician: urbane, softly spoken and, beneath the false smile, as benign as a crocodile.

'Let's do the introductions, shall we? Make sure we all know who we are.'

Allardyce, who'd organised the meeting, did the honours, going round each seat at the table and identifying its occupant: Housman, Fitzgerald, Manville and the Government's Chief Medical Officer, Alistair Cameron.

'Mr Manville, perhaps you'd like to begin,' Coldwell said.

Manville cleared his throat nervously. 'I'm not sure how much you know already.'

'This is Whitehall,' Coldwell said. 'It's always best to assume we know nothing.'

He flashed a smile and Allardyce chuckled loyally though he'd heard the joke at least a dozen times before.

Manville looked down at his notes and briefly outlined the situation at Great Dunchurch.

'Just give us those figures again,' Coldwell said at the end. 'How many cases?'

'Seven.'

'And three dead?'

'That's correct.'

'What condition are the other four in?'

'Dr Housman can answer that better than I can.'

'One of the children, Phoebe Harrison, is out of danger,' Housman replied. 'Her brother Tim is making good progress. I expect a full recovery. The two adult patients, however, are in a critical condition.'

'Will they survive?'

'I wouldn't like to say either way at the moment. On the basis of the other patients who've died, the prognosis is not good.'

'Three out of seven dead. That's a high mortality rate,' Coldwell said. 'This is some flu bug. Do we know what it is yet?'

It was Fitzgerald who answered. 'We know it's influenza A and avian in origin – a strain we haven't seen before anywhere in the world. That makes it potentially very dangerous.'

'Because it's new, or because it comes from birds?'

'Because it's new. There has never been a new strain of influenza A which hasn't been pandemic: 1918, 1957, 1968, the three major flu pandemics in recent memory, were all new strains of influenza A.'

'This is hardly on the same scale,' Coldwell pointed out. 'Seven victims in one tiny geographical area.'

'That's because in order to contract the disease, the victims had to have had some contact with either hens or eggs or pigs. Until yesterday.'

'When you discovered it had spread directly from one person to another?'

'Yes.'

'Are we sure about that?'

'As sure as we can be,' Manville replied. 'The victim, Marjorie Wilson, is too ill to speak but I've checked with her family, examined her diet, her movements and contacts over the last few days, the incubation period of the virus. As far as we can tell, the only credible source of her illness is her friend Wendy Bullingham, one of the other victims.'

Coldwell's fleshy mouth puckered as if he were about to whistle. He stroked the smooth line of his jaw and turned his gaze on Fitzgerald. 'Is this medically possible? For a bird disease to be transmitted between people?'

'It hasn't happened before,' Fitzgerald replied. 'But the flu virus is constantly adapting. Genetic reassortment, we call it.' He paused, wanting to keep things simple. There was no point in getting too technical with people who knew nothing about orthomyxoviruses. 'But there is no scientific reason why avian flu, given the right conditions, can't become endemic amongst the human population.'

The Minister for Agriculture let the information sink in. He was annoyed that he'd been landed with the unwelcome job of chairing the meeting. This affair was partly the Department of Health's responsibility now, but the Secretary of State and his junior were on some junket in Washington and wouldn't be back for two more days. Coldwell was acutely aware it made him politically vulnerable. If something went wrong, it would be a MAFF cock-up not a DoH.

'Is it going to spread further?' he asked.

Housman accepted the challenge 'I think we have to work on the assumption that it will.'

'Why?'

'Because it always does. Influenza is highly contagious, spread by droplets of saliva or mucus in the breath or a sneeze. If Marjorie Wilson has caught it, you can bet she's not the only one.'

'How fast?'

'That's impossible to say. We've been lucky so far. It's been confined to a very small area. The slaughter campaign probably helped to limit the outbreak, but now it can jump from person to person, the door's wide open. How quickly it spreads will depend on a number of factors. How mobile the population of Great Dunchurch is, how much contact they have with outsiders, how robust the virus is.'

'Can we stop it?'

Housman shook his head, not saying no but simply declining to answer.

'Can we protect the population? Give them something, drugs, a vaccine? Are there drugs?'

'There's one called amantadine,' Housman said. 'It can be used for both prophylactic and therapeutic purposes. It's not a cure, but if you administer it early enough it can alleviate some of the symptoms. I emphasise *can*. I gave some to both Caroline Malcolm and Arthur Wainwright and they died all the same.'

'Not a very persuasive advertisement for it,' Coldwell commented dryly. 'Is that all we have?'

'There are a couple of other newer drugs which have been shown to be effective, but neither of them is licensed for prophylactic use in Europe.'

Coldwell stared at Housman. An illness as common as influenza and all there was to combat it was a single drug which didn't seem to work. 'Well, can we give everyone in Great Dunchurch a shot of this . . . amantadine?'

'That's not good clinical practice, Minister.' Alistair Cameron, the Chief Medical Officer, spoke for the first time.

'I don't give a damn what it is. Will it help?'

'In the short term, possibly. In the long term it may do more harm than good.'

'Meaning?' Coldwell, like most politicians, looked no further ahead than the next general election. In the long term they were all out of office.

'Administering a medicine on a large scale to people who may not need it is not sensible,' Cameron explained. 'All that will happen is that the virus will find a way around it and you'll lose the effectiveness of the weapon when you really need it.'

'So what about a vaccine? You can vaccinate people against flu, can't you?'

Housman and Fitzgerald exchanged glances. They'd known this was bound to be raised. Coldwell was looking at them expectantly.

'Well?'

'There are problems with a vaccine,' Fitzgerald said slowly.

'Problems? What do you mean? We vaccinate millions of people every winter.'

'That's true. But the vaccines are prepared for months prior to that. Mass production of a vaccine takes a certain amount of time.'

'What if we just make enough for Great Dunchurch? That's not very many. What's the population of the place?'

Allardyce leaned forward over the Minister's shoulder. 'We believe it's about three hundred and fifty, Minister,' he said.

'Three hundred and fifty! We can make three hundred and fifty doses quickly, surely?'

'It's not quite that simple,' Housman said. 'Vaccines are not something you can knock up overnight in a lab. It would take weeks, probably months, just to make a few doses. You need a licensed facility, a major drug company on board, and with a virus like this there are very great risks involved in the actual manufacture of a vaccine.'

'What risks?' Coldwell snapped.

'The virus is a killer. To make a vaccine you would normally need to find a non-pathogenic surrogate strain – a similar flu virus which isn't deadly – to use in the process. We don't have such a surrogate strain.'

'Why do you need one?'

'Because you have to grow millions and millions of live viruses in fertilised hen's eggs. You then purify them and inactivate the virus with formalin or beta-propiolactone, but in those initial stages, when the virus is live, someone has to handle it. There's a high risk those people will contract the disease and die.'

'Flu vaccines are also expensive to manufacture,' Fitzgerald added. 'They're usually done on a worldwide basis. Is the Government willing to pay for the UK to go it alone on this particular virus?'

Coldwell was silent for a time, his forehead creased into a deep frown. Money. It always came down to money. 'So what do you suggest we do?' he asked eventually.

His eyes roved around the table. The wood was so highly polished he could see the others' faces reflected in the surface. Fitzgerald met his gaze.

'We have to seal off Great Dunchurch,' he said. 'Allow no one in, and no one out.'

Coldwell stared at him, his eyes unblinking, wide open with shock. 'You mean quarantine the place? Like a plague village?'

'It's not the term I'd use.'

But it's the term the press will use, Coldwell thought in alarm. Jesus, does he realise what he's suggesting? There was a village in Derbyshire, not all that far from Coldwell's South Yorkshire constituency – the village of Eyam. In the Great

304

Plague of 1665–6 it had been one of the few settlements outside London where the deadly disease had taken hold, transported there on fleas in a consignment of cloth sent up from the capital. The local vicar had sealed off the village. Food had been left by a water trough on the outskirts. No one had been allowed to enter or leave. The inhabitants had been left to their fate. Two hundred and sixty people, more than half the population, had died but the plague had been contained. It had not spread to any of the surrounding area. But that was three hundred and fifty years ago, when people did what the church told them, when they were more fatalistic in the face of terrifying disease. No modern populace was going to stay put and wait to either die or survive. They'd be in their cars getting the hell out, demanding medical attention, drugs, lobbying Parliament. The consequences didn't bear thinking about.

Coldwell swallowed. His mouth was dry as sawdust. 'That's not a viable option,' he said hoarsely.

'Hear me out,' Fitzgerald said. His entire working life people had never taken flu seriously. He was going to have to spell it out in terms a layman could understand. 'I don't mean to be melodramatic, but if we let this virus get loose in the wider population the results could be catastrophic. If it turns out to be another 1918 – and I'm not predicting it will – it will kill more people in a year than cancer, strokes, heart disease, lung disease, Alzheimer's and AIDS put together. That's how potentially virulent it is. It will also destroy the chicken and egg industry in this country. Better to take decisive action now while it's confined to just the one locality.'

'What are you suggesting?' Coldwell asked in horror, the colour draining from his plump cheeks. 'We call in the Army, close the roads and arrest anyone attempting to leave?'

Fitzgerald nodded grimly. 'The alternative is much worse.'

*   *   *

McCormick got up from his desk and paced across the office in front of the window. He was too agitated to stay seated. He could feel the knot of tension in the back of his neck, the dull ache spreading upwards over his cranium as if his skull were being compressed in a tight crash helmet.

'So he found out about the boy?' he demanded.

'That's not what I said,' Cullimore corrected him. 'He went to the house and started asking questions. But Prakashan sent him packing, refused to speak to him.'

'He must have known something. Why else did he go there?'

'Perhaps,' Cullimore conceded.

'Why else was he in India? That's a long way to go without a bloody good reason. You got a name?'

'Carson. Francis Carson. I did some checking. He has an office in Cherry Hinton. Ex-copper, good reputation.'

'Working for?'

Cullimore shrugged. 'Who knows?'

McCormick turned to look at him, his eyes like splinters of steel. 'Find out, Rick. That's what I pay you for.'

Cullimore shifted awkwardly in his chair. He nodded. 'You want me to check out his office?'

'Don't bother me with details. Just get me the information. Where is he now?'

'No one seems to know. He left the hotel in the middle of the night.'

'That's great, just fucking great,' McCormick spat.

The ache in his head was getting worse. He went to the ornate drinks cabinet and helped himself to a couple of paracetamol, washed down with mineral water.

'They're trying to track him down, but he seems to have disappeared,' Cullimore explained, aware that the excuse sounded feeble. When McCormick was in one of his moods, everything sounded feeble.

'He seems to have disappeared,' McCormick repeated sarcastically. He walked back to his desk but didn't sit down. 'On reflection, I think that's probably as well. What were they intending to do to him?'

'Warn him off.'

'Christ, haven't they heard of the word subtle out there? They should have left him alone. Said nothing, done nothing. Now he knows for sure we've something to hide.'

'He can never prove anything.'

'That's not the point. A mere allegation, a rumour will be sufficient to put the spotlight on us. If the Government finds out about Derapur . . .'

McCormick paced away from the desk again, his feet moving soundlessly over the deep-pile carpet. He stood by the window, looking out over the fields. He'd always had a nose for trouble, an instinct that told him when he should fight and when he should cut his losses and run.

'I want the harvest at Eastmere brought forward,' he said.

'To when?'

'Now. Tell Baxter.'

'You mean abandon the crop?'

'Of course not. We'd be lifting it in a few weeks anyway. Get it out of the fields and into a secure store. Immediately.'

The news from India had rattled him. If a private detective was asking questions six thousand miles away, how soon would it be before he started poking his nose in closer to home?

'It's just a gut feeling,' McCormick said. 'Playing safe. I want all evidence of that crop removed.'

'You want a coffee?' Jeremy Blake asked.

'No, thanks, ' Housman replied. 'I have to get back to the hospital.'

'Busy?'

307

'You could say that.'

Housman didn't elaborate. He was feeling the pressure. He had his regular workload to contend with, plus the influenza patients in the Isolation Unit, but he was also supposed to be coordinating with Stephen Manville on the quarantine measures for Great Dunchurch. The politicians, prevaricating to the last, had yet to make a decision on whether to go ahead. Coldwell was in further discussions with the Department of Health and the Cabinet Office. High-level political consultations was the official description. Housman suspected that Coldwell was simply spreading the responsibility around, hoping someone else would make the decision for him. Either way, the public health teams had to be in place and ready to go if they were needed.

'I got a result sooner than I said,' Blake explained. 'Technician came in on Saturday and did the analysis.'

He shuffled some sheets of paper around on the bench in front of them, looking for one in particular. They were in one of the laboratories in Blake's department. The wooden surface of the bench was scarred by chemicals, Bunsen burner scorch marks and the carved initials and expletives with which generations of students had recorded their passage through the university.

'He checked the glycoalkaloid levels in the potato peelings, as you requested. The levels were off the scale.'

'How high?' Housman asked.

'Well, the MAFF recommended levels for total glycoalkaloid content are 200 milligrams per kilogram. The peelings had a level nearly fifty times greater. Potato skins always contain more solanine and chaconine than the tubers, but not that high.'

'Fifty times? Making them poisonous, I assume?'

'That level of glycoalkaloids would be highly toxic.'

'How toxic?'

'Enough to cause serious illness. Perhaps even death in large quantities.'

'How abnormal is that?'

'Very. But then the potatoes those peelings came from weren't normal.'

'Weren't normal in what way?'

'They were genetically modified.'

Housman stared at him without speaking.

'You didn't know?' Blake said.

'No. They came from an organic farm.'

'Not those potatoes. There's no question. They're transgenic.'

Blake pulled out some other sheets of paper covered with tiny printed sequences of what looked like smudged ink blots.

'This is what the genome of a normal potato looks like. And this . . .' He referred to a second set of papers '. . . is what the genetic profile of those peelings looks like. See the differences – here, here and here. They've altered the genome. Added genes.'

'Genes to do what?'

'You can't tell from this. There are a few standard ones they use, of course, so I could take an educated guess as to what's been added. There are only a certain number of diseases and pests which afflict potatoes. All the GM work I'm aware of has been targeted at those problems.'

'Like what?' Housman asked.

'Colorado beetle for one. That's a huge problem in the States, less so here. But they've created and already marketed a potato resistant to Colorado beetle. They add a gene from the bacterium *Bacillus thuringiensis* which codes for an insecticidal protein known as Cry3A. The protein is expressed in the potato leaves and it wards off the beetle. They've done similar things to stop potato virus Y. They take the replicase gene from the virus and add it to the plants, giving the potatoes a natural immunity to the disease.'

'So what would account for the high level of glycoalkaloids in the peelings you tested?'

'My guess is something has gone wrong. No one would deliberately engineer a potato to be poisonous. These are commercial breeding processes. The whole point is to produce a better plant.'

'Gone wrong?'

Blake shrugged. 'Genetic modification isn't the exact science you might think it is. It's a fairly hit-and-miss business. You can add a gene to a plant but you can't control exactly where in the genome you put it, and you can't be absolutely sure what it will do once it's there. Adding a gene is a complicated process. You always need a promoter, some kind of messenger to get the gene into a plant's cells. With potatoes the promoter is usually the cauliflower mosaic virus or the figwort mosaic virus.

'But even once the gene has been inserted it's impossible to predict exactly what effect it might have on the rest of the plant's genome. The new gene might not get "switched on", some other genes already present might be changed by the new arrival. All manner of things could go wrong. In this case something has clearly gone haywire with the mechanism for producing glycoalkaloids. I'm not an expert on potatoes, but maybe the gene which codes for glycoalkaloid production has not been "switched off" at the right moment. Maybe there's some other gene which should have been "switched on" to control the glycoalkaloids but hasn't. Once you start messing with the genome there's no telling what exactly might happen?'

'Are you saying these transgenic breeders don't know what they're doing?' Housman said.

'I'm saying they're experimenting. It's how all plant breeding works, not just transgenic. You try something. If it doesn't work you try something different. Breeding is inherently unpredictable.'

'Somehow I don't find that very reassuring.'

'It's been going on for thousands of years.'

'Not with genes from completely unrelated species. Don't you find it worrying? Someone has accidentally bred a deadly potato – a potato that could kill. I find that deeply disturbing. Will you do something for me, Jeremy? Put this in writing. Give me a written report detailing what your analysis found.'

'Sure, no problem.'

Housman was sure the Ministry of Agriculture analysis had come up with the same results. So why hadn't they told him?

He drove back to Addenbrooke's in a state of mental turmoil. The telephone rang almost the instant he stepped into his office. He snatched it up.

'Housman.'

'Dr Housman?' A woman's voice, clear, confident. 'My name is Madeleine King. I believe you're the consultant handling the flu cases from Great Dunchurch.'

'That's right, I am.'

'I think we should meet. As soon as possible.'

18

Madeleine had given birth to Graham in the Rosie Maternity Annexe situated just behind Addenbrooke's, but it was years since she'd been in the main hospital building itself. The change was quite startling. The central foyer, which she remembered as an open space covered with shiny linoleum and rows of uncomfortable plastic chairs, had been taken over by what looked like a shopping mall. There was a Burger King outlet, a coffee shop, sandwich bar and pizza parlour; a newsagent's, convenience store, florist's, hairdresser and branches of Sock Shop, Body Shop and Barclays Bank. There was even a travel agency, a solicitor's office and a mortgage broker and estate agency. You could eat here, pay in a cheque, have your hair cut, buy a house and sue your doctor, all without moving from the hospital. And if you were lucky, you might just get a bit of medical care thrown in as well.

Madeleine followed the instructions Housman had given her on the phone, taking the lift to the ninth floor and walking down the corridor until she located his name on a door. She knocked and a voice from inside yelled out, 'Yes?'

Madeleine entered. Housman was on the telephone. He waved her in and stood up, the receiver clutched between ear and left shoulder to leave his hands free to remove a pile of files from a chair. He gestured to the seat and moved back behind his desk, still keeping up his phone conversation. Madeleine sat down and looked around, reflecting how revealing a person's work environment was. How it seemed to mirror the personality of its occupant. Housman's office was chaotic and cluttered, papers and folders and dog-eared medical periodicals stacked untidily on the window-sill and on top of the scratched metal filing cabinet. She knew better than to make snap judgments, but the disorderly mess certainly seemed to match Housman's dishevelled appearance. His shirt and trousers were creased and his mop of dark hair uncombed and unruly. He smiled at her and pushed his glasses back up his nose with a finger. He was tall and ungainly, Madeleine thought, but not bad looking. She liked his voice. Deep, reassuring, decisive. A good voice for a doctor. It was authoritative, efficient, belying the sloppy jumble of his office.

'Sorry,' he said, putting down the receiver. He reached across with a hand the size of a plate. 'Karl Housman.' His grip was warm and firm.

'Madeleine King.'

'Can I offer you a drink?'

'No, thanks.'

Housman looked at her. That just about exhausted his store of small talk. 'So tell me about India,' he said.

The call had come at around midnight British time, 4 am in Lucknow which was where Frankie had fled after leaving his hotel in Derapur, driven there in the middle of the night in Panjit's taxi. He'd been breathless, shaken, but quite coherent. They'd talked for nearly half an hour, Frankie telling her everything he'd found out, telling her there was no way he was returning to Derapur. He was taking the train to Delhi at first light and flying home later that day.

Madeleine repeated all this to Housman. She'd already given him the gist on the phone, but now she filled in the details, recounting exactly what had happened in Derapur and why she'd asked Frankie to go there in the first place.

'This fever these people had,' Housman asked. 'The flu-like symptoms. Do you know what they were?'

'No. Headaches, aching muscles, the usual, I suppose.'

'Did anyone examine them, take blood samples, or tissue from their bodies after they died?'

'As far as I know, they didn't get any kind of medical treatment. They were poor farmers.'

'So no autopsies. And no doubt their bodies were cremated.'

'That's the Indian custom.'

'And this child who ate the potatoes. Did he see a doctor?'

'Frankie didn't know. The family wouldn't talk to him. He died very soon after eating the potatoes. I doubt there was time to get him to a doctor, even if they could have afforded one, but I don't know for certain. It's the same, isn't it? The flu, the hens dying, the toxic potatoes.'

'It's persuasive,' Housman said noncommittally. 'Without some medical evidence that's all it is. In India there are dozens of fevers that can be fatal. There's no proof it was flu.'

'David Seymour's widow said Transgenic Biotech had had glycoalkaloid problems during their trials at Derapur. That's what Seymour was going to tell me himself, I'm sure of it. But he died before we could meet.'

'There are certainly several similarities,' Housman admitted. 'But with one important exception. The company's research centre in this country is nowhere near either Marsham Grange Farm or Great Dunchurch where the outbreaks of flu have occurred.'

'It's not the research centre that counts,' Madeleine replied. 'It's the fields. Transgenic Biotech are breeding transgenic crops. Maybe they're growing them near Marsham Grange.'

Housman studied her pensively. When she'd rung him he'd

thought at first she was a crank, a nutter inflicting him with absurd conspiracy theories about a distant village in India he'd never heard of. He'd been curt with her, very nearly hung up before she'd had a chance to explain herself. Something in her voice, a clarity, a conciseness, had made him hear her out. He was glad he had now. Seeing her in person, listening to her face to face, she was as far removed from a crank as it was possible to get. Intelligence, common sense and sanity were ingrained in her face and everything she said. Housman looked at his watch.

'How are you fixed for time?'

'I've nothing on I can't cancel. Why?'

'I'm going for a drive in the country. I'd like you to come with me.'

Sandy Harrison met them at the back door of the farm, watching them with tired, worried eyes as they climbed out of the car and walked across the yard.

'Phoebe, Tim . . . which is it?' she said, her voice choking with emotion.

'They're both fine,' Housman answered.

She didn't believe him. 'I need to know. I want the full picture. Even if it's bad.'

'That's not why we've come.'

'Then . . .'

'Come inside and sit down.'

Housman took her arm and guided her gently into the kitchen. 'Phoebe is just about ready to come home,' he said. 'And Tim is over the worst.'

Madeleine watched the transformation that came over Sandy's face. It was like a spotlight moving across her features, only the illumination came from within, spreading out from her eyes until it glowed from every pore of her skin. It must be wonderful to be a doctor, Madeleine thought, bringing such joy into someone's life, until she remembered there was a flip side and it wasn't always good news a doctor brought.

'Come home?' Sandy said. 'Come home when?'

'She can probably be discharged tomorrow.'

'Tomorrow?' Sandy echoed, looking anxiously for confirmation.

'She'll be weak for a few days, perhaps longer,' Housman replied. 'But she'll make a full recovery.'

'Thank God.' Sandy sagged back in her chair, the invisible burden lifted from her shoulders. 'And Tim?'

'He'll have to stay in for a while longer.'

'But he'll get better? He's not going to die?'

'He'll get better,' Housman reassured her.

'Thank you.'

Sandy's mouth quivered. For a moment it seemed as if she might burst into tears, but she bit her lip and turned her head away, blinking hard.

Housman pulled out a chair and sat down beside her. 'This is Madeleine King,' he said. 'She's a solicitor.'

'A . . . is there some trouble?' The anxiety was back in Sandy's expression.

'Relax, Mrs Harrison,' Housman said soothingly. 'We just want to ask you about the potatoes Phoebe ate. We need to find out where they came from.'

'I told you before, they were ours. From our fields.'

'They can't have been. They must have come from somewhere else.'

'Jeff brought them in. I saw him. They still had the soil on them. They were fresh from the ground.'

'Are you absolutely sure?'

'Positive. You think we run a potato farm and go out to the supermarket to buy someone else's? Why are you asking?'

'Because the potatoes Phoebe ate had been genetically modified.'

Sandy gaped at him in astonishment. Then she shook her head firmly. 'Impossible. That's completely impossible.'

'I had the peelings tested. There's no doubt about it. They're transgenic.'

'You're mistaken. How could they be? This is an organic farm. Soil Association certified. You know how strict they are? How thoroughly they check a farm before they give it their stamp of approval?'

'I know, Mrs Harrison. Nevertheless, they were transgenic potatoes.'

'What are you saying?' Sandy demanded indignantly. 'That we cheat. That we lie about what we grow here?'

'I'm not saying anything like that. I'm just trying to establish where they came from. Somehow you must have planted some transgenic plants. Where does your seed come from?'

'We retain most of it. Keep back a part of the crop to plant the following year.'

'Do you buy any in?'

'Some, I think.'

'From where?'

'I don't know. Jeff took care of all that.'

'Did he keep records?'

'Of course. They're in the study.'

She led them out into the hall and through into a small room at the side of the house. It had a desk in front of the window and shelves of box files on the walls. Jeff Harrison appeared to have been an organised, meticulous farmer. There were files labelled VAT, Inland Revenue, NFU, Sales, Buildings and Maintenance and perhaps a dozen more. Sandy scanned along the shelves and removed one marked 'Suppliers'. Opening it, she leafed through the contents.

'Why don't you let us do it?' Housman suggested. 'How about a cup of tea?'

318

He waited for Sandy to leave, then sat down at the desk and inspected the file. Madeleine watched over his shoulder. It was only a small room and Housman seemed to fill it with his enormous frame.

'You think the potatoes came from an external supplier?' Madeleine asked.

'It seems a good place to start.'

'But why would a seed company be selling transgenic plants? It's against the law. There are no commercial GM crops of any kind in this country. Just a few small-scale trials carried out by the biotech industry.'

'I know. It's puzzling. Either they've been sold by mistake, the product of a research trial that's accidentally been released into a batch of normal seed, or they're the product of some kind of contamination.'

'You mean pollen from a GM potato plant cross-breeding with a normal plant?'

Housman nodded. 'The environmental nightmare scenario.'

He took a wad of papers out of the box file and split it into two, handing one half to Madeleine.

'See what you can find in that lot.'

Madeleine leaned over the desk and studied the documents one at a time. They dealt with the purchase of various agricultural supplies: machine parts, organic feedstuffs, fertilisers, organic manure. Madeleine found invoices for cauliflower and cabbage seeds from an organic seed merchant in Boston, Lincolnshire, but no mention of any potatoes. Housman finished sifting through his pile and shook his head.

'Nothing.'

'Same here,' Madeleine said. Then she thought of something. 'Did you have the top or the bottom of the pile?' She reached out and examined the dates on the other invoices. 'These are all at least two years old. There must be another more recent file.'

She checked the shelves but could see no other box marked 'Suppliers'.

'That's peculiar.'

The door opened and Sandy entered with two mugs of tea.

'Are these all your files?' Madeleine asked her.

'Yes. Why?'

'There doesn't seem to be one for purchases in the last couple of years. It wouldn't be anywhere else, would it?'

'It shouldn't be. I can't think why Jeff would have taken it out.'

Housman took his mug of tea and stared out of the window. He could just see one end of the barn where the Harrisons' potatoes had been stored. The barn that the team from MAFF had emptied . . . He twisted around abruptly. 'The men from MAFF who were here, asking questions. Did they come in this room, look at the farm records?'

'Well, yes, they did.' Sandy paused. 'You're not suggesting . . .'

'Can you remember a name?' Housman asked. 'A seed company, a supplier your husband might have bought potatoes from. Did he use the same supplier regularly?'

'I'm sorry. I left all the farm business to Jeff.'

'He must have talked to you about it.'

A ghost of a smile touched Sandy's lips. 'He probably did, but I wasn't listening. The details of the farm have never inter-ested me much. If anything comes to me, I'll let you know. I wish I could be more helpful.'

They drank their tea and went back out into the yard. Housman walked past the car and stood for a moment looking out over the surrounding fields. Madeleine came up to his shoulder and followed his gaze. The first field was lined with rows of cauliflowers, their creamy white crowns poking out from the green foliage. But in the distance the ground was either bare or covered with brown, shrivelled potato plants.

'What's happened over there?' Madeleine said. 'They're dying.'

Housman didn't seem to hear her. His eyes were locked on to the horizon. 'Surely not,' he murmured. 'Is it possible?'

'Dr Housman?'

The words broke his trance. He glanced round at her. 'Did you say something?'

'Are you all right?'

'Yes, I'm fine.'

He frowned, a mixture of puzzlement and concentration. Then he strode across to the car and pulled open the door, reaching in to pick up his mobile phone.

'I think I may have worked out where the flu virus came from.'

19

Housman said almost nothing on the journey back to Addenbrooke's. Madeleine left him alone, though she was intrigued to know more about the enigmatic comment he'd made at the farm. He was keyed up, clearly excited, and driving so fast she didn't want to distract his attention from the road. She wasn't usually a nervous passenger, but his speed and reckless disregard for traffic regulations scared her half to death. It was a relief when they finally pulled into the hospital car park and Housman was forced to slow to under fifty for practically the first time since they'd left Marsham Grange.

Upstairs in the Infectious Diseases Department, he made a detour into his secretary's office and came out holding a sheet of paper which he carried to his desk and studied avidly, oblivious of Madeleine's presence. She sat down and watched him patiently. The sheet of paper was obviously a fax, Madeleine could tell from the type of paper, but it bore no text or other message – it was just a slightly blurred photograph of some object she was unable to identify, particularly as she was looking at it upside down.

At one point Housman broke off and searched through his desk drawers, producing another photograph which he placed next to the fax. Taking a magnifying glass from a tray on top of the desk, he peered more closely at the photographs, apparently comparing the two.

'Ha!' he grunted. 'I don't believe it. I don't fucking believe it.' He glanced up apologetically. 'Sorry. Just stunned. Completely stunned. This is incredible.'

There was something a little old-fashioned and appealing about him, Madeleine thought. The rumpled clothes, the broken spectacles, the boyish enthusiasm for something he had yet to explain. He didn't fit the image she had of NHS consultants: the smooth, overbearing, arrogant, self-regarding demi-gods who swanned in and out of hospitals, claiming their hundred grand a year from the taxpayer but devoting most of their energies and all of their bedside manners to their private patients. She couldn't see Housman in Harley Street or any other private practice, he was too creased around the edges.

'Take a look at these,' he said, his eyes gleaming. He turned the photographs around and pushed them across the desk.

'What are they?' Madeleine asked.

'Micrographs.'

'And what are micrographs?'

'Photographs taken through an electron microscope.'

Madeleine looked down at them. They certainly weren't photographs of anything she recognised. The fax showed a strange collection of tiny balls with a distinctive mottled surface. The other photograph was of a group of spherical objects with tiny spikes sticking out from their surfaces.

'What am I looking at?' Madeleine enquired.

'That one there . . .' He indicated the micrograph he'd removed from the drawer '. . . is a flu virus. And the other is a cauliflower mosaic virus. A friend of mine, a botanist, who tested the potato peelings from Marsham Grange, faxed it through for me. That was the call I made at the farm.'

Madeleine was bewildered. 'Dr Housman . . .'

'Karl, please.'

'I don't quite see the significance of all this.'

Housman leaned across the desk and put his forefinger on the micrograph of the flu virus. 'This is the virus that's caused the outbreak at Great Dunchurch. You see here, on the surface, the antigens? No, they're not particularly clear. Try this one instead.'

He stood up and walked across to one of the blown-up photographs on the office wall. Madeleine had thought the prints adorning the room were some kind of weird modern art. Now she realised they were close-ups of diseases.

'This is a different strain, but it's still flu,' Housman said. 'These are the haemagglutinin antigens, these are the neuraminidase. Okay?'

Madeleine regarded him dryly. 'Is English your first language, Karl?'

'What? Oh.' He chuckled ruefully. 'Sorry. Am I talking gibberish?'

'I have no idea what an antigen is.'

'A substance that stimulates the production of an antibody. You know what antibodies are?'

'Yes, I know that much.'

'Well these protrusions on the capsid – the outer casing of the virions – are what cause the body to fight the virus. They produce a hostile response, if you like. They're basically proteins which the virus uses to lock on to human cells and penetrate the cell wall. You want any more detail?'

Madeleine smiled. 'You're looking at someone who failed Biology O-Level.'

'All you need to know is that influenza virions have two types of protein protruding from their surface. These ones that look like spikes are haemagglutinin. These that look like mushrooms are neuraminidase. Now take another look at that micrograph on the desk. Use the magnifying glass.'

Madeleine studied the print.

'You see something else?' Housman said. 'A protrusion that looks like a small mottled ball?'

'Yes.'

'Now check that with the other micrograph.'

'They're the same.'

'Exactly!'

Housman came back to the desk and sat down. 'The mottled ball protrusion in the flu virus shouldn't be there. We haven't been able to work out what it is or where it's come from. Now we know. It's a cauliflower mosaic virus.'

Madeleine looked at him blankly. 'You're losing me. What's a cauliflower mosaic virus?'

'A plant virus. It grows on cauliflowers – turns the leaves yellow and makes them wilt – but it's also used as a promoter in the genetic modification of plants, including potatoes. They first insert the new genes they want to introduce into the potato into the cauliflower mosaic virus and then they infect the potato with the altered virus. The virus breaks into the cells of the potato, taking the new gene with it and altering the potato's own genetic make-up.'

'You're saying this cauliflower mosaic virus has joined up with a flu virus?'

Housman nodded. 'That's what it looks like to me. But how? *How* has it happened?'

'Let me get this straight,' Madeleine continued. 'You think this new strain of flu, this deadly strain, has been caused by genetically modified potatoes?'

'Not directly, no. The victims didn't contract flu from the potatoes, by handling them or eating them. But indirectly there's a link. There has to be. The flu didn't originate in people, it's avian. Then it was transmitted to pigs. The human victims caught it from either the pigs or the hens.'

'And where did the pigs and hens get it from? The potatoes?'

326

'I can't see it. The pigs at Marsham Grange ate potatoes, but how did the virus get into their respiratory tracts? You catch flu by breathing, not by ingestion. And anyway, the hens at the farm certainly didn't eat potatoes and they all died of flu.'

Housman picked up the magnifying glass and examined the micrographs again. 'It's the same, there's no doubt about it. It's a cauliflower mosaic virus.' He stared at the wall, thinking out loud. 'Two viruses – one plant, one avian. How do they meet? How does one infect the other? How do their genes combine?'

'I thought you could mix genes of any species together,' Madeleine said.

'But that's a deliberate process. It doesn't happen accidentally. Someone has to remove the genes from the first species and insert them into the second species. There has to be a promoter like a bacterium or a virus, or some other vector.'

'Vector?'

'A carrier of the disease. Like an insect . . . shit!'

'What is it?'

Housman leapt to his feet and rummaged through one of the piles of papers on his desk. 'Fuck, where is it?' He went to another stack on top of the filing cabinet and searched through the documents, tossing them down on to the floor one by one. 'It's here somewhere.'

He checked the window-sill, riffling urgently through the mounds of files, dropping each one in turn as he glanced at the cover and rejected it, until the floor of the office was awash with paper. Finally, he noticed a pile under his desk and got down on all fours to examine it more closely, emerging triumphantly with a thin cardboard folder clutched in his hand.

Throwing himself back into his chair, he opened the folder and flicked through the contents. Then he lifted his eyes to Madeleine and smiled. 'The autopsy report on the dead pigs and hens from Marsham Grange,' he explained. 'One of the hens had swelling on its neck. Inflamed tissue with a puncture in the centre identified as a bee sting. And bees, of course, collect pollen from potato flowers.'

'The bees transferred the virus?'

'It seems a good bet. They collected pollen from a transgenic potato plant which had been genetically modified using the cauliflower mosaic virus promoter and somehow became infected with the virus themselves. One of them then stung a hen and passed on the virus which reassorted with an avian flu virus to create a new hybrid strain. That was passed on to the other hens. The pigs caught it from them, probably from their droppings. The hens at Marsham Grange were free range. They went where they pleased, including the field where the pigs roamed. And then the farmer and his kids caught it from either the pigs or the hens.'

'Is all that scientifically possible?'

'Theory and practice are two very different things. It's theoretically impossible for a bumble-bee to fly, but it does. If you play around with genes, theory goes out of the window and anything is possible.'

'Doesn't it scare you, all this? It makes me go cold. The thought of all those scientists playing God with Nature.' Madeleine realised it was a phrase Jake Brewster had used. 'It's irresponsible. Worse. It's criminal. That farmer, the other victims, they *died*. They died because a scientist added a virus to a common potato plant. And no one . . .' She stopped. 'Bees . . .'

'What?'

'Frankie mentioned that one of the Indian farmers whose hens died – and who himself died of fever – had lost three hives of bees at around the same time.'

'Lost them to what?'

'Frankie didn't know. It was just a short report in the local paper. There's something else too.' Madeleine paused again. Was this worth mentioning? 'It's peculiar, a weird coincidence, but

328

Frankie also keeps bees. And he's also lost a hive. All the bees killed by some unknown disease or virus.'

'A virus?'

'And he's not the only one. Other bee-keepers he knows have had the same problem.'

'Where is he now?' Housman asked.

'Frankie?' Madeleine consulted her watch. 'In the air some-where. He was catching a flight from Delhi at two pm local time, that's about ten am here. He won't be back until later tonight.'

'I'd like to talk to him. Where does he live?'

'Out in the Fens.'

'Anywhere near Marsham Grange or the Transgenic Biotech research centre?'

Madeleine shook her head. 'Ten, fifteen miles from either.'

'Mmm.' Housman chewed the knuckle of his thumb rumina-tively. 'We're still faced with the same questions. If I'm right about the source of the flu outbreak, we need to know where the bees picked up the cauliflower mosaic virus, where they collected the GM pollen.'

'At Marsham Grange, surely they collected it from the farm's own fields,' Madeleine said.

'I mean the original source. I believe Sandy Harrison. She isn't lying. They aren't knowingly growing GM potatoes there, it's an accident. But how did part of their crop become transgenic? It must, at some point, have cross-bred with a GM potato plant, been fertilised by pollen from a GM plant. That's why I wanted to know where their seed came from. Any cross-fertilisation wouldn't be apparent immediately. It would only manifest itself in subsequent generations. It might take a few seasons to produce the kind of abnormal genome, the abnormal glycoalkaloid levels, found in the peelings I had tested.'

'There must be a GM trial site somewhere near Marsham Grange.'

'Or somewhere near the organic farm that produced the seed used at Marsham Grange,' Housman added. 'How do we find out that kind of information?'

'It's published. The Department of the Environment, MAFF could probably tell us. Friends of the Earth too. We could phone them.'

'Not at this time,' Housman said, glancing at his watch. 'Outside office hours.'

'In the morning then.'

'Why wait? The Net never sleeps.'

Housman switched on the computer on his desk, logged on to the Net and typed in an address.

The Friends of the Earth home page appeared on the screen. Housman scrolled down the index and found a heading 'GM Test Sites'. He clicked on it. A map of the country came up, marked with small black dots, followed by a list of farms and their addresses. There were four in Cambridgeshire, colour coded according to the crop they were testing: blue for sugar beet, pink for fodder beet, green for forage maize and yellow for oilseed rape. None of them was growing GM potatoes.

'What about this one?' Housman said. He clicked on one of the black spots and the address of a farm in Norfolk appeared. 'That's the nearest potato trial. Fakenham. That's sixty miles from here. There's no way bees carried pollen sixty miles to Marsham Grange so the cross-breeding has to have occurred on the seed farm. There must be a list of seed-potato suppliers somewhere. I wonder if we can find it.'

Madeleine stood up and walked round behind the desk, watching over Housman's shoulder as he surfed the Net, trying various key words in an attempt to locate the information he wanted. After a few abortive searches he finally found the website of an organisation called the British Organic Seed Merchants'

Association which gave a list of all their members and the types of seeds in which they specialised. Housman narrowed it down to just those who dealt in potatoes and printed off the list. There were eight names on it. One of them was in Cambridgeshire: Fodder Creek Farm, near Ely.

Housman went back into the Friends of the Earth website and printed out the locations of the GM trial sites. Then they compared the two lists.

'What do you think? My geography's not too reliable,' Housman said.

Madeleine studied the addresses. 'I don't know. I'm not sure exactly how far away from each other some of these places are, but I'd say there wasn't a GM trial site within ten miles of these eight seed suppliers.'

'Too far for the wind to have dispersed the pollen. Can bees fly ten miles?'

'I have no idea.'

Housman frowned, disappointed at the outcome. Then he brightened a little. 'Of course, there might be organic seed-potato growers who aren't members of this association.'

'That's true. Or there might be GM trial sites the Government isn't telling us about.'

Housman gave her a look, weighing up the possibility. 'You have a very suspicious mind.'

'I'm a lawyer,' Madeleine replied.

She'd guessed from the moment she'd first set eyes on Housman that he wasn't married – or if he was, he was living apart from his wife. No woman could have resisted doing something to tidy up his appearance: making him get his hair cut, fixing his glasses for him, buying him some shirts which didn't look as if they'd been left over at the end of a jumble sale.

It was only when they were in the restaurant – eating savoury pancakes with a chilled white Burgundy – that she had her guess confirmed.

'Divorced. Three years, I think. I forget exactly,' he said, obviously not wanting to discuss it much. 'You?'

'The same.' She had to think how long, relating it not to any milestone in her own life but to how old Graham had been at the time. That's how she remembered everything. She had vivid recollections of Graham starting playgroup, Graham getting chickenpox, his first day at school, crashing his bike into the river, passing his GCSEs, coming home late smelling of beer. Her own experiences were a blur, a fog of missing years and dim memories which had somehow failed to leave any lasting impression on her mind. It was as if she'd done nothing of any importance herself in seventeen years except give birth to a son.

'Six years,' she said. Graham had been eleven at the time, just starting secondary school. Madeleine had been prepared for the split, had seen it coming for years, but Graham had been pole-axed by his father walking out on them. He'd withdrawn into a shell. The sunny, affectionate boy had turned into a taciturn, uncommunicative teenager. How much of it was due to the divorce and how much to the onset of puberty Madeleine never knew, but for three or four years afterwards she'd struggled to cope with his moods and sudden outbursts of aggression. She suspected – no, she knew – that, perversely, Graham had blamed her for the separation, blamed her for somehow failing to hold on to his father. Perhaps he still did.

'You see your ex-husband still?' Housman asked.

'Yes. Graham – my son – stays with him every so often.'

Not very often these days. There'd been a time when Graham had gone to his father's every other weekend, but now it was only once a month, sometimes less. Graham found it boring being away from his friends and his computer, and Edward,

Madeleine's ex, didn't like the disruption the visits from this
truculent son he hardly knew caused to his perfect, sanitised life.
Edward had always liked things to be organised; the sort of man
who wanted his meat and two veg on the table at six o'clock
sharp every evening. Madeleine, on the other hand, was chaotic
and disorganised. She'd gone back to work a couple of years
after Graham was born, but had never managed successfully to
combine a career with both motherhood and the demands of her
husband. To be honest, she hadn't seen why she had to. Graham's
needs had been her first priority and her work imposed a timetable that was to a large extent outside her control, so inevitably
Edward had had to make do with what was left over. He hadn't
liked that. He expected to be looked after, pampered. The idea
of cooking or ironing shirts for himself had been anathema to
him, and childcare – changing nappies, bathtime, even playing
with his son – was something he had participated in only reluctantly.

Madeleine wondered now how they'd lasted nearly twelve
years, how she'd endured it for all that time. They'd been incom-
patible from the beginning. They'd met at law college in Chester,
a hard graft of a year in which there had been almost no time
for anything except study and sleep, moving afterwards to
Cambridge where Edward had joined a commercial law firm
and Madeleine had taken articles with a criminal law partner-
ship. What had she seen in him? Even as a student he'd been
pompous and opinionated, but as he passed into his thirties he'd
become an insufferable prig. She'd fallen out of love with him
after six or seven years of marriage though the physical side had
died long before. Edward had never been particularly interested
in sex and Madeleine's libido had wasted away under the weight
of exhaustion and domesticity. Inertia had been the only thing
that had kept them together. Inertia and a fear of being alone.

Edward had remarried since the divorce. His new wife, Julia

– as he'd told Madeleine several times – was everything Madeleine hadn't been. A deeply conventional, bossy housewife with an immaculate house and a firm belief in the supremacy of the male provided he did what you told him, Julia was, in Madeleine's view, the female equivalent – in both looks and personality – of the Regimental Sergeant-Major. Dropping Graham off once, Madeleine had strayed into the kitchen and noticed a menu pinned to the noticeboard, the week's evening meals neatly typed and printed out on a home computer. Julia did things like that; made lists, planned food days, probably weeks, in advance. Madeleine suspected she did the same with sex, specifying the exact time, location and position in which they were to have it and posting it in triplicate on the noticeboard. That would have suited Edward. He could have put it in his diary at work, got his secretary to remind him: 'You're in court this morning, client conference this afternoon and this evening you're rogering your wife.' Occasionally, in her more prurient moments, Madeleine had imagined the pair of them in bed together, Julia lying back looking at her watch saying, 'Go on, get it over with then.' But mostly she never gave her ex a single thought. He was out of her life and their years together had faded into a distant haze like a long-forgotten dream.

'How about you? Any children?' Madeleine asked.

Housman shook his head. 'Thank God. It gets messy with kids.'

That was true, Madeleine reflected, but she wouldn't have wanted to be without Graham.

'How're your pancakes?' Housman asked.

'Good. Yours?'

'Mmm.'

Madeleine drank some wine. As soon as they'd sat down at the table it had rapidly become clear that Housman wasn't much of a one for social chit-chat. She wondered why he'd suggested they went for something to eat, why she'd agreed. Probably because it made a pleasant change. She rarely ate out, even more rarely with a man. She'd liked the idea of some company, some conversation, but it was proving harder work than she'd anticipated.

Only when they moved on to his job did he become more talkative. Madeleine listened with interest. For a doctor he was remarkably self-effacing, for a scientist surprisingly entertaining.

They'd finished their pancakes and moved on to ice-cream with hot chocolate sauce when they got back on to the subject of the flu outbreak.

'How bad is it going to get?' Madeleine asked.

'I don't know.' The question reminded Housman that he hadn't heard from Stephen Manville. No doubt the politicians were still trying to make up their minds. 'The mortality rate is very high. That's one of the things we don't understand. Also, why have all the deaths been fit adults? Usually the elderly and the young are most vulnerable, yet Jeff Harrison died and his kids survived. That's what happened in the 1918 pandemic.'

'You think it's the same virus?'

'No, 1918 wasn't avian, although no one knows for sure exactly what it was. It's never been conclusively identified, what we call "typed". There was an expedition to Spitzbergen a few years ago. A group of Norwegian coal miners died of flu there in 1918. The scientists on the expedition thought the miners had been buried in the permafrost and there was a chance of finding some of the virus frozen in their tissues. But they were above the permafrost, in the topsoil which freezes and thaws every year. A similar search in Alaska also failed to find any trace of the virus. There's a research team in America studying a sliver of lung tissue from a 1918 victim which was preserved in paraffin wax and kept in a military pathology store, but so far they haven't managed to type it, and they certainly haven't found out what made the virus so deadly. That's still a matter of conjecture among virologists and –' He grinned at her '– like all scientists we can never agree on anything.'

Madeleine ate some of her dessert, letting the hot chocolate sauce melt the ice-cream in her mouth before she swallowed it. Housman's was melting almost untouched in his bowl. He seemed to have forgotten it was there.

'You want to try him again?' he said.

Madeleine took out her mobile phone from her bag and punched in a number, letting it ring for a long time. She shook her head.

'No, he must still be . . .'

A voice broke in on the line suddenly. 'Yes?'

'Frankie? It's Maddy.'

'Oh.'

'You okay?'

'Just tired. I've only just got in.'

'How was your flight?'

'Long. Look, can I call you in the morning? I want to go to bed.'

'Frankie, I need another favour. We need to talk to you.'

'"We"?'

'Stay up for just a while longer. We're coming out to see you.'

Frankie sighed wearily. 'Do I get a choice?'

'What do you think? We'll be there in half an hour.'

Frankie was slumped in an armchair nursing a tumbler of malt whisky and a splitting headache when they arrived. He pulled himself to his feet to let them in, then staggered like a drunk back to the chair and flopped down on the cushions. Madeleine looked at him with concern.

'You sure you're okay?'

'Yes,' Frankie replied irritably. 'I'm fine.'

As fine as could be expected considering he'd been up most of the previous night and had just driven back from Heathrow after a nine-hour intercontinental flight. His business card scam had not impressed the British Airways staff at Delhi airport, nor had a twenty-pound note stuffed conveniently inside his passport, so he'd been forced to fly Economy, wedged into a seat between a sweaty backpacker and a man in a suit who'd spent the whole journey tapping away on a laptop computer.

'I'm sorry, Frankie,' Madeleine said. 'For what happened in India, and for coming out here now. We won't keep you up long.'

Frankie raised his tumbler. 'Help yourselves. The bottle's over there.'

'No, thanks. This is Karl Housman. He's a doctor at Addenbrooke's.'

Frankie nodded at Housman. He was struggling hard to keep awake. 'So how can I help?'

'Your bees,' Madeleine said. 'When I was out here the other day you said you'd lost a hive to some unidentified disease or virus. You said a couple of other bee-keepers had had the same problem.'

'That's right.'

'Do you know where their hives were? Their location?'

'Yes.'

Madeleine unfolded a map of Cambridgeshire she'd brought in with her from her car and spread it out on the floor in front of Frankie. 'Show me,' she said.

Frankie lowered himself to his knees with a look of long-suffering resignation. If this was what it took to get rid of them . . .

'One is there,' he said, putting a finger on the map. 'The other is . . .' He moved his finger, searching for a landmark '. . . here. They're not near each other.'

Madeleine used a pencil to mark the two locations, then added a third cross over the location of Frankie's house.

'How far does a bee fly?' she asked.

'Collecting pollen? Depends where the flowers are. You mean how far it flies in total on one foray from the hive? Or the maximum range of a flight?'

'The maximum range.'

'About six miles. That's the generally accepted figure among bee-keepers.'

Madeleine consulted the scale marker at the side of the map. 'Two centimetres to the kilometre. What's that, about one and a quarter inches to the mile?'

She estimated the distance and drew a rough pencil circle representing a radius of six miles around each of the three points. Where the three circles intersected was open fenland crossed by a minor road marked in yellow. A track branched off west from the road leading to an isolated building. Madeleine read the name printed beside the building.

'Eastmere Farm.'

'You want to tell me what this is all about?' Frankie asked, hauling himself up off the floor into the armchair.

'Another time,' Madeleine replied. 'You get to bed now, Frankie.'

20

The decision had finally been taken at seven o'clock in the evening, but it wasn't until midnight that Stephen Manville had rung Housman.

'It's on,' he'd said. 'They're sealing off Great Dunchurch. They're printing leaflets now. One to be delivered to each house in the village by morning.'

'Saying what?'

'Outlining the problem, describing the symptoms to watch out for. Asking people not to travel unless they really have to. Giving an emergency number to call if they feel ill. The police are setting up roadblocks on the three roads into the village. They'll be stopping every car, advising the occupants not to enter or leave unless it's essential.'

'But no compulsion?'

'They got cold feet in Whitehall. They said they had no legal powers to compel people to stay. We're lucky to have got this much. The lawyers have been going over every detail of the plan, making sure it's within the law. They've only just given the green light for us to go in. There's a briefing in the church hall, eight o'clock tomorrow morning.'

'I'll be there,' Housman had said.

He arrived early, stopping at one of the roadblocks to explain who he was to the police constable on duty before driving on into the centre of the village and parking by the church. It was a cool morning, a low mist lying like gauze over the fields which stretched into the distance beyond the stone wall of the church-yard. You could feel the damp in the air, the moisture which clung to the grass in between the moss-covered gravestones and coated the roof tiles of the surrounding houses with a glistening sheen.

Built in a nucleus around the sixteenth-century church of St Mary, Great Dunchurch was a functional, far from picturesque settlement which had originally developed to provide cottages for workers on the nearby farms. Over the centuries it had expanded a little, with new buildings periodically being added on the outskirts to give an eclectic mix of architecture, the last significant development coming in the 1950s when a small estate had been established at one end of the village, the identical pebble-dashed houses with tiny windows betraying their local authority origins. After peaking during the war years, when airmen from the local RAF base had given a temporary boost to the village's economy and its birth rate, Great Dunchurch had started a decline which was only just beginning to slow. The village shops, which at one time had numbered six, had all closed, as had the Post Office and the primary school. The pub survived, bolstering its income with food and Bed and Breakfast, but there were scarcely any other employers in the area. The farms still prospered but they no longer provided more than a handful of jobs. Too plain and unprepossessing to attract tourists or other visitors, the village had been in danger of dying along with its aging inhabitants until an influx of younger residents, forced out of Cambridge by the soaring house prices, had breathed new life into it.

Housman slipped on his jacket to keep out the cool breeze and walked across the churchyard to the adjacent stone-built hall. Manville was already inside, collating sheets of paper into piles. He handed one pile to Housman.

'Briefing document. Outlines what we'll be doing.'

'It's pretty much what we discussed yesterday, I assume?'

Manville nodded. 'Twenty public health officers, ten nurses plus five doctors – you, your SHO and the three GPs from the village medical centre. Working in ten teams of three, a nurse with each group, the doctors floating loose, going where they're needed. We'll concentrate, as planned, on the families, friends and acquaintances of the existing flu victims, then widen the examination to the rest of the village.'

'Amantadine?'

'Four hundred doses. The Chief Medical Officer changed his mind. We're going to give everyone a shot as a prophylactic, see if we can nip this in the bud. What's your feeling?'

'If we're not imposing compulsory quarantine, anything's worth a try.'

'We have an ambulance on stand-by at the medical centre. Huntingdon and Ely are ready for any overflow from Addenbrooke's, with extra space available at Norwich and Peterborough. Let's hope we won't need it. What's the condition of Marjorie Wilson and Wendy Bullingham?'

'Still critical. I checked before I left home. What do you think the village reaction is going to be?'

'You mean, will they take any notice of our warnings? I'm not overly optimistic. The leaflets the Department of Health have drawn up are pretty good. They make the risks clear. The nature of the disease is the problem. If this were, say, an outbreak of Ebola or similar I think people would stay in their houses and avoid contact with anyone. But it's flu. Most people have had flu before and survived. They're not scared of it no matter how many doctors tell them it's a killer.'

'You think they'll ignore the warnings?'

'Some won't. The older residents, the pensioners, they'll take it seriously. They know flu's a real danger at their age. First sign

341

of a headache they'll be ringing that emergency number. But the younger ones, those with jobs, I'm not so sure. How many days do you take off work to prevent spreading a disease you may not have and may not get? I reckon most of them will take today off, as a public-spirited gesture, but if nothing happens their willingness to cooperate will wear very thin very quickly.'

'That could be disastrous,' Housman said. 'If they start travelling about the country . . . I know, I'm preaching to the converted.'

'This is as far as the politicians are prepared to go,' Manville replied with a shrug. 'They don't want to blow it out of proportion. They're terrified the press is going to overreact, start a panic.'

'They're briefing them?'

'Press conference in Whitehall at ten. Two camera crews allowed into the village thereafter. One from the BBC, one from ITN, both escorted by DoH press officers.'

'They're letting camera crews in?' Housman asked in disbelief. 'The whole point is to keep outsiders away.'

'It's government by media, Karl. Ministers are shit scared of a bad press. They'll do anything to keep them happy.'

'Well, I'm not a minister,' Housman said resolutely. 'If anyone asks me, I'll tell them the truth. I'm not going to put a favourable spin on it.'

'Truth?' Manville smiled cynically. 'Whatever you do, don't mention that word to the press officers. They'll have you locked up.'

The briefing was short and to the point, Housman outlining the medical aspects of the influenza virus before Manville explained what actions they were going to take to try to contain it. At half-past eight, the teams left the church hall to start knocking on doors in their allotted sections of the village.

Housman and Manville went first to Marjorie Wilson's house, a three-bedroom semi in a cul-de-sac on the southern fringes of the village. Marjorie's husband showed them through into the sitting room. He was a small wiry man with a gingery complexion and pale, almost translucent lashes above eyes which were sore and heavy from lack of sleep.

The first thing he said was: 'Marj . . . how is she? I rang the hospital. They said there was no change.'

'That's right,' Housman replied. 'She's stable, but still very sick.'

'Can't you do something?' Wilson pleaded. 'I was there yesterday. They wouldn't let me into her room but I looked through the window. She looked terrible. Those tubes up her nose.'

'She's on a ventilator, Mr Wilson. To help her breathe. The tubes don't hurt.'

'There must be something you can do. It's only flu. Marj has had flu before. So have I.' He reached out and picked up one of the Department of Health leaflets from the sideboard. 'It says here it's new, potentially dangerous. What're you doing, putting these through people's letter-boxes? Frightening them to death.'

'It's for your information,' Manville replied. 'To let you know what we're doing here today.'

'I don't care what you're doing here today. I want to know what you're going to do for my Marj?'

'The hospital is doing all it can,' Manville said placatingly. 'You can rest assured she's getting the best medical care possible.'

'But she's not getting better. She's not getting bloody better, is she?'

Manville glanced at the nurse who was with them and nodded almost imperceptibly. The nurse stepped forward and took Wilson's arm, guiding him to a chair.

'Now don't go upsetting yourself, Mr Wilson. What's your first name?'

'Bob,' he muttered grudgingly.

'Come and sit down, Bob. We're here to help. To help you and everyone else in the village. Now, how are you feeling your-self?'

'Me? I'm all right.'

'No aches and pains? No headaches, no temperature?'

'You think I'm getting it too?'

'That's what we're here to check. Do you have children?'

'No, it's just me and Marj.'

Housman and Manville edged out into the hall, leaving her to it. Nurses were better at dealing with people than doctors.

'Do we know who else Marjorie Wilson might have come into contact with over the last week?' Housman said.

'I made a list when I was here on Sunday,' Manville replied.

'Many outside the village?'

'A few. She works in an office in Ely. Insurance brokers.'

'Seeing clients?'

'She's the receptionist.'

Housman grimaced. Almost no one lived in isolation any more, even out here in the Fens. They went to work, to the shops, to pubs and restaurants. Marjorie Wilson might have infected dozens of people, most of them untraceable. Even attempting to identify them was an impossible task. People she'd passed on the street or spoken to on a bus could have been infected. Concentrating on Great Dunchurch made sense as a starting point, but Housman was uncomfortably aware that they might well have been simply locking the stable door after the horse had bolted.

The sudden ring of Manville's mobile phone interrupted them. The public health officer answered and listened, repeating an address that had been given to him.

'We're on our way,' he said, breaking the connection and clipping the phone back on his belt.

'Someone's called the emergency line,' he explained. 'Mother of a ten-year-old boy. He's got a high temperature, muscle aches, all the symptoms.'

'In the village?'

Manville nodded. 'Just down the road.'

Kieran Mitchell was lying back in bed, his eyes closed, his face pink and shining with perspiration. Occasionally he twitched and moaned, moving restlessly on the pillow as if he were having a nightmare. Housman stood outside the bedroom door with the boy's mother and studied him from a distance.

'When did it start?' he asked.

'Just this morning. I came in and found him all hot and feverish.'

'Like this?'

'No, he's got worse in the last hour. That's why I rang that number.'

'Have you given him anything?'

'A couple of aspirin.'

'*Aspirin*? Not paracetamol?'

'No, aspirin. That's all right, isn't it? It gets the temperature down.'

'I'm going to examine him now. It's probably better if you stay out. Why don't you go downstairs? Mr Manville needs to ask you a few questions.'

Housman went into the bedroom and closed the door behind him. He didn't want Mrs Mitchell to see him putting on rubber gloves and a surgical mask. It was a routine precaution, but it would alarm her unnecessarily.

He took Kieran's temperature first – it was 40 degrees – then listened to his chest and heart through his stethoscope. He didn't like what he found. Pulling off his mask and gloves, he placed them in a disposal bag and sealed it before going back downstairs.

Manville was in the sitting room, filling in one of the standard questionnaires with which the teams had been issued. He broke off as Housman entered and raised a quizzical eyebrow. But it was Mrs Mitchell whom Housman addressed first.

'I'm sending Kieran to hospital,' he said. 'He needs medical care we can't provide here.'

'Hospital?' Mrs Mitchell was on her feet, staring anxiously at Housman. 'Is he very ill?'

'There's no need to worry. He has symptoms of influenza. We'll do tests at Addenbrooke's to confirm the diagnosis.'

'But hospital, that must be serious.'

'We're playing safe. He'll be better off in hospital. Why don't you go and pack a bag for him? Spare pyjamas, washing kit, that sort of thing.'

'Is he going to be all right?'

'The sooner we get him to hospital the better.'

'Yes, but . . .'

'Mrs Mitchell, the bag.'

She looked at him, then nodded and hurried out. Manville was already on his mobile phone, calling the ambulance.

'It's on its way,' he said. 'Is the boy bad?'

'I'm worried about complications. Reye's Syndrome. She's given him aspirin.'

Manville nodded grimly. Reye's Syndrome was a rare complication of influenza in children that caused cerebral oedema and fatty degeneration of the liver. In about a third of cases it was fatal. And aspirin predisposed to the syndrome.

'What've you found out?' Housman asked. 'Any connection with the other patients?'

'The boy's a member of the village scout troop. The scout leader is Wendy Bullingham's husband.'

'That's all we need. A whole bloody scout troop going down with flu. You got a list of names?'

'Some. We'll have to get the rest from Bullingham. This isn't looking good, is it?'

Housman heard the noise of an engine outside. He went to open the front door for the paramedics.

Rick Cullimore settled himself down in his chair and shot the cuffs of his shirt, a rapid, aggressive movement which always reminded McCormick of a bouncer getting ready to eject a difficult customer from a nightclub. There was a lot of the bouncer in Cullimore: his muscular build, his biceps and shoulders straining under the material of his dark jacket; his sleek moustache and the belligerent in-your-face snarl that was his habitual expression. He was sometimes a little too uncouth and vulgar for McCormick's tastes, but then he hadn't hired the man as head of security for his vicarage tea party manners.

'We checked the office,' Cullimore said. 'Nothing.'

'I told you, no details. I don't want to know how you did it. I don't want to get involved in that kind of stuff.' McCormick paused, looking across his polished desk. 'I hope you've got more than that.'

'I have,' Cullimore replied. 'We traced him from Derapur to a hotel in Lucknow.'

'He was there?'

'He'd checked out. Caught the train to Delhi. But he made a phone call in the middle of the night. Itemised on his bill. An international call to a UK number.'

'Yes?'

'Madeleine King's number.'

'Fuck!' McCormick felt a flutter of alarm in his stomach. 'He was working for her?'

'Looks like it. That's not good news.'

'Thank you, Rick,' McCormick said acidly. 'You have a real talent for stating the blindingly fucking obvious.'

Cullimore let the insult wash over him. He was used to McCormick's rudeness, paid handsomely to be the target for the MD's foul mouth.

'So we can assume she knows, or has some inkling as to what happened at Derapur?' McCormick said.

'I think we have to assume that. We can't afford to be complacent.'

'The tip-off had to come from Seymour. Do you think he told her about Genesis II as well?'

'That's the question,' Cullimore replied. 'Do we want to take that chance?'

McCormick gazed across his office. The flutter in his stomach had turned into a hard clench of something he wasn't used to experiencing: fear.

'You want me to deal with her?' Cullimore asked.

McCormick was tempted. But he knew fear induced panic and that was the worst state in which to make any kind of rational decision.

'Leave it with me,' he said.

'Time may not be on our side, you know.'

'I *know*,' McCormick snapped. 'I said leave it with me.'

He waited for Cullimore to leave the office, then picked up the telephone and punched in a number. He was surprised to feel his pulse throbbing like a drum inside his head.

'This is McCormick,' he said as the call was connected. 'We have to meet . . . Fuck your commitments. We have to meet. *Today.*'

David Coldwell glanced nervously around the rich book-lined room. They were alone, but he was on edge in case anyone walked in and found them there.

'I've only got ten minutes,' he said tersely. 'I have to be back in the House.'

'You've got as long as it takes.' McCormick's voice was as sharp as a razor. He was looking at Coldwell with cold, dispassionate eyes, like a vulture surveying a bloody carcass, deciding where to start first.

'What do you want?' Coldwell demanded.

McCormick took his time. He knew he was in control of the meeting. The very fact that Coldwell had shown up told him that.

'I have a problem I need to discuss.'

'Your problems aren't my concern.'

'Oh, but they are. I'm talking about David Seymour.'

Coldwell licked his lips. Again his eyes flickered around the room as if searching for hidden watchers. But the walls held nothing but rows of ancient leather-bound books. They were in the library of his club. He knew no one would disturb them here – that was why he'd chosen it for their rendezvous. The books were purely for show, historical relics that were treasured but never opened. The members came to the club to drink and gossip. They would no more have thought of reading a book than they would of admitting women to their hallowed sanctum.

'I thought we'd sorted that all out. Kept your name out of it,' Coldwell said.

'There are complications. We think he may have told a Cambridge solicitor about Genesis II.'

'Jesus! Why didn't you tell me this sooner? What solicitor?'

'Her name's Madeleine King. She's representing the vandals who ripped up our oilseed rape last week. We've taken the precaution of digging up the potatoes at Eastmere but, as you know, there are other sites. She could blow the whole thing.'

'Dear God!'

'Is that all you can say?'

'What do you want me to say?'

'I want you to say, "How can I help?"'

'That's impossible,' Coldwell exclaimed hastily. 'Completely out of the question.'

McCormick sighed. Politicians just didn't get it. They had this naive belief – or maybe it was just a foolish hope – that they could sup with the Devil and leave their spoons at home. But the world outside the cloistered Never-Never Land of Parliament didn't work like that. If you dipped your hands into a cesspit, some of the shit was going to stick.

'Perhaps Gavin didn't tell you what I said last week,' McCormick went on. 'We're in this together. We both believe in the same thing. If this leaks out, your biotech policy is going to be in shreds. I'm your only hope of keeping Britain at the fore-front of GM development. We can't let these Luddites, these ignorant troublemaking environmentalists destroy it, now can we? Particularly as you, as Minister for Agriculture, have such a personal stake in it.'

Coldwell flinched. That was cutting very close to the bone. He was a staunch defender of the biotech industry. He'd made innumerable statements supporting it, even gone on television eating a transgenic tomato to prove how safe they were. He'd given grants of £2 million to promote organic farming, but £75 million to aid biotech research – a large chunk of it to Transgenic Biotechnology. There was no doubt where the Government's priorities lay.

'And that's what's going to happen, David,' McCormick continued, 'if we don't act now. And act decisively.'

McCormick's tone was mild, reasoned, but Coldwell sensed clearly the threat beneath the words. His career was on the line. The policy was the Government's, not his alone, but he knew he would be held responsible for any failure, any damaging revelations. Downing Street would make sure of that.

'You want me to do something about this woman?' he said hesitantly.

'No, David,' McCormick replied. 'I *expect* you to do something about her.'

21

'The CPS sent over the Brewster file this afternoon. I put it on your desk,' Madeleine's secretary told her as she walked into the office.

'Anything else?'

'Just a message from a Dr Housman, asking you to call him. I've left you a note with his mobile number.'

'Thanks, Eileen.'

Madeleine went through into her own office and sat down behind her desk, kicking off her shoes and stretching her toes. Her feet were hot and sore from standing up for most of the day.

The Crown Prosecution Service had been remarkably efficient in sending her the papers relating to the break-in at the Transgenic Biotech research centre. Normally it could take weeks for the prosecution documents to arrive. She glanced through the stack, running her eye down the list of witness statements. Accompanying the paper evidence were copies of two CCTV videotapes, one labelled 'Research Centre Rear Exterior' and one 'Ground Floor Laboratory G1'. Madeleine pushed the whole lot to one side – she'd study them in detail when she had more time – and called Karl Housman.

'Hang on a second,' he said. She heard movement, a door closing, then Housman came back on the line. 'Sorry, I'm out at Great Dunchurch, in someone's house.'

'More cases?'

'Only one so far, thank God. But I've had a message from Sandy Harrison at Marsham Grange. She's remembered the name of a grower her husband bought seed potatoes from. Fodder Creek Farm. Wasn't that one of the names on the list we found on the Net?'

'I think it was. Near Ely,' Madeleine said. 'I'll check on a map. You still on for this evening?'

'Can we make it a little later? I've a lot to do here. Say half-seven.'

'That's fine. Where shall I meet you, Great Dunchurch?'

'Just outside, on the Cambridge road. By the police roadblock.'

'Roadblock?'

'You obviously haven't seen any news today.'

'I've been in court.'

'I'll tell you later. I have to go.'

Madeleine replaced the receiver and yawned, glancing at her watch. It was only five o'clock, but she felt dog tired. She had a mound of paperwork to look at before tomorrow. Cases to prepare. Somehow she couldn't face them. She'd do it later, or maybe get up early and study them before she left for work. She slipped her shoes back on and packed the files into her briefcase. She was about to leave when she remembered the Brewster papers. The two videotapes were on the top of the pile. It wasn't exceptional for there to be video evidence in a case, but it was rare enough to make a television and VCR in the office unnecessary: she always viewed them at home. Picking up the cassettes, she dropped them into her case and left the office.

For the first time in months she was home before six. She'd hoped, expected, Graham to be in. She was looking forward to seeing him before she went out later, but the house was empty. A note on the kitchen table read simply: 'Gone out. G.'

She changed into jeans and a T-shirt and watched the six o'clock news on television. There was a report on the flu outbreak at Great Dunchurch, some footage of the village's empty streets. A Government spokesman was interviewed at Westminster, explaining why the measures had been necessary, then there were brief soundbites from a local councillor and a public health official in Great Dunchurch itself. In one of the clips, Madeleine thought she caught a glimpse of Housman in the background, but she couldn't be sure.

Graham wasn't back by the time she had to go out so she left him a note of her own, thinking, this is how we communicate, with scraps of paper, impersonal messages deposited on the kitchen table.

Karl Housman was waiting for her on the outskirts of Great Dunchurch, his car parked on the verge at the side of the road, a little in front of a police patrol car. The roadblock he'd mentioned was an unobtrusive affair: no barrier across the road, just the police car and a constable in a luminous green jacket waiting to stop vehicles. Housman climbed out of his car and walked across to Madeleine's Golf, opening the passenger door and sliding his long frame inside.

'Have you been waiting long?' Madeleine asked.

'Couple of minutes.'

'Can we drive through the village?'

'Better to turn round.'

'Is the air contaminated or something?'

'No. I'm just practising what I preach.'

Madeleine did a U-turn and headed back up the road.

'The map's in the glove compartment,' she said. 'I looked up Fodder Creek Farm. It's about three miles south-west of Eastmere.'

Housman pulled out the map and navigated them north across the fenlands, across the broad plain framed with horizons of pale blue sky which were turning hazy in the evening light.

Fodder Creek Farm was a few miles from Ely, a small cluster of brick buildings beside a shallow lake on which ducks and white geese paddled lazily. A sign by the gate, underneath the farm name, read: 'Organic Seed Suppliers. Organic Potatoes and Eggs. General Public Welcome.'

Madeleine turned off the road and down the unmade track to park in the yard outside the farmhouse. Climbing out, she could see fields of potatoes on all sides and on the skyline, impressive even from this distance, the distinctive tower and octagon of Ely Cathedral.

A stout ruddy-faced woman emerged from a door in the farmhouse, wiping her hands on a towel. She smiled.

'Hello.'

'We wanted to buy some potatoes,' Madeleine explained.

The woman motioned with her head and waddled away across the yard into one of the outbuildings. Following close behind, Madeleine and Housman stepped into the gloomy interior of the building and saw sacks of potatoes stacked against the wall next to a slatted wooden bin brimming over with loose potatoes.

'How many would you like?' the woman asked. 'A sack? They're good value in bulk.'

'Just a few pounds,' Madeleine said. 'How much are they?'

'These are earlies, fresh from the field. Ninety-two pence a kilo.'

Madeleine converted the price to imperial measures in her head. Like everyone else in the country she had only a vague idea what a kilogram was.

'I'll take a couple of kilos,' she said. 'And half a dozen eggs. No, make that a dozen.'

It made her feel virtuous, fulfilling one of her regular pledges to buy more organic produce; pledges that somehow lapsed, despite her good intentions, when she walked into a shop and saw the prices.

The woman put some brass weights on a set of ancient scales and selected a few potatoes from the wooden bin.

'Are you completely organic here?' Housman enquired, wandering around, fingering a couple of tubers from the bin.

'Of course. It's all or nothing.'

'Are many farms around here organic?'

'Ours is the only one for miles. Great Dunchurch is the nearest other one.'

'Marsham Grange?'

'That's right. You know it?'

'Eastmere isn't organic then?'

The woman gave him a contemptuous glance. 'Eastmere? Barry Mullen's place? No, he's not organic. Not by a long chalk.'

'Does he grow potatoes?'

The woman tipped the potatoes into a brown paper bag and handed them to Madeleine. 'Yes, he grows potatoes. Mostly lates. Why are you interested in Eastmere?'

'No particular reason,' Housman said casually. 'How about seed potatoes? Do you supply a lot of other farms?'

'Enough. Quite a few smaller buyers too. Allotment holders, gardeners with vegetable plots.' She looked at him suspiciously. 'Why do you want to know?'

'Just curious.'

The woman walked across to a refrigerator and removed a box of eggs. 'That's one eighty-four for the potatoes, and one sixty for the eggs – three forty-four altogether please.'

Madeleine paid and they went back out to their car. Heading down the track towards the road, Housman took one of the potatoes out of the paper bag and studied it.

'Looks ordinary enough, doesn't it? I'll get my friend to check it for us.'

'Which way to Eastmere?' Madeleine asked.

Housman consulted the map. 'Left at the road, then right about a quarter of a mile further on.'

'I got the impression she wasn't very keen on the owner. What was his name? Mullen?'

Housman nodded. 'So did I.'

They saw why when they got to Eastmere and the farmer came out to greet them, though greet was hardly the right word given the ferocious scowl on his ugly face, an expression which was mirrored in the snarling dog crouched by his feet.

'What do you want?' he demanded as Madeleine and Housman climbed out of their car.

'Mr Mullen?' Housman said.

'Who the bloody 'ell are you? This is private land. Clear off.'

'We want to buy some of your potatoes.'

Mullen glared at them, his forehead creasing into a frown so deep the folds of skin seemed to hang down over his mean little eyes. Madeleine stayed close to the car, her door still open. His hostile attitude made her nervous.

'I don't sell bloody potatoes,' the farmer snapped, flecks of spittle seeping from the corner of his mouth. 'Not to the likes of you. Now fuck off!'

'You grow potatoes, don't you?' Housman persisted. 'What sort?'

'Let's go, Karl,' Madeleine murmured.

'You're trespassing,' Mullen growled, his hands, dangling down to his knees like an ape, clenched into hairy fists. 'See 'em off, boy!'

The lean black and white Border collie raced forward, barking fiercely, its teeth bared. Madeleine jumped quickly back into her seat and slammed her door. Housman, on the side nearer the dog, had less time. The collie was at his ankles, tearing at his trouser leg before he could escape. Housman pulled his leg away but the collie hung on. The material ripped and a section came away in the dog's mouth. Housman kicked the animal hard with his other foot, forcing it back momentarily, and threw himself into his seat, banging the door shut. The dog jumped up at the window, the strip of cloth clenched in its salivating jaws.

'Drive!' Housman yelled.

Madeleine twisted the key in the ignition and rammed the gearstick into first, hitting the accelerator and spinning the wheel to bring the car round in a tight circle and out through the exit from the yard. The dog chased after them in a frenzy of barking, pursuing them tenaciously for a hundred metres before giving up and trotting back to the yard. Madeleine saw it receding in her rear-view mirror and eased off on the throttle.

'Jesus!' Housman exclaimed. 'You think he didn't like us?'

'He certainly gave that impression.'

'Talk about the Missing Link. He looked as if he'd escaped from a zoo.'

Housman leaned forward and examined his shredded trouser leg.

'Did it bite you?' Madeleine asked.

'Just the trousers. Look at that, they're ruined. I'll have to get a new pair.'

'I'm sure they weren't your best,' Madeleine said ambiguously.

Housman gave her a look. 'You casting aspersions on my clothes?'

Madeleine grinned at him. 'Well, put it like this: I think the dog may have done you a favour.'

Housman snorted and turned to look out of the window. The fields on either side of the track were bare earth, recently dug over.

'Pull in when you get to the road,' he said.

'Pull in? Why?'

'The woman at Fodder Creek said Mullen grew late potatoes. They're harvested in the mid-autumn, not now. Yet these fields are empty.'

'Maybe they weren't potato fields.'

Housman shook his head. 'There's no stubble, no sign that any crop has been cut. The earth has been lifted. It has to have been a root crop.'

Madeleine slowed for the junction and turned out on to the road, pulling in to the side after just a few metres. The road was above the level of the surrounding land and from where they were parked they could look across to the farmhouse. Mullen and his dog were nowhere in evidence. The field immediately beside the road was also bare and it was clear that many others had also been recently dug over.

'That was something of an extreme reaction, don't you think?' Housman said. 'I know some farmers aren't the friendliest of people, but there was no need for any of that.'

'Some men are very aggressive.'

'But why? The swearing, setting the dog on us. He seemed like a man with something to hide. I'd like to test some of his potatoes.'

'How, if he's dug them all up? I don't fancy going back and asking to look in his barn, do you?'

'No. But I think we could always go looking for volunteers.'

'Volunteers?' Madeleine said. 'To look in his barn?'

Housman smiled. 'When you harvest potatoes, you never get them all out. It's impossible. The ones you leave behind in the soil are called volunteers.'

'You're suggesting we go and dig around in his fields?'

'You got a better idea?'

Madeleine looked out through the window. The fields were just a few metres away down a grassy embankment.

360

'Why not?' she said. 'I spend my days indoors. It's time I got my hands dirty.'

The soil in the field was loose and moist, a dark rich peat which crumbled like Dundee cake. Housman and Madeleine chose a spot at random and knelt down, dipping their hands into the earth and shovelling it aside.They dug down a foot or more, sifting through the peat to find any tubers that had been missed by the mechanical harvester.

'Anything?' Housman asked.

'Not here.'

'Move along a bit. We may have to try a few places.'

Madeleine's bare arms were covered with dirt right up to the elbow. The knees of her jeans were soiled and her hands were almost black, the earth compacted beneath her fingernails.

Crawling on all fours across the field, she selected another spot and plunged her arms into the ground, throwing the soil out to form a shallow hole. She raked through the sides and bottom of the hole, enlarging it, but there were no potatoes there, not even a tiny tuber.

She moved along a few feet and tried again. Housman was a couple of metres away, digging energetically with his large, spade-like hands.

'They've taken them all, Karl,' Madeleine said, kneeling back on her haunches.

'They haven't. They always leave some behind. Always. Keep trying.'

He scooped out more soil and rummaged beneath the surface, trawling his fingers through the earth. Madeleine leant over and dipped her hands in again, feeling the peat warm and sticky on her skin.

Then she heard the gunshot and twisted round abruptly.

Barry Mullen was on the far side of the field, coming through a gate from the farmyard. He was carrying a shotgun which he lifted to his shoulder and fired a second time. Madeleine ducked instinctively, though she couldn't be sure whether he was shooting at them or over their heads as a warning.

'Christ, he's off his rocker,' she cried. 'Karl?'

'Get back to the car.'

Housman was still digging, tearing desperately at the soil and hurling it aside. 'Go!'

Mullen was breaking open his shotgun, reloading it. Madeleine scrambled to her feet and ran for the car. As she clambered up the bank to the road, she looked round. Mullen was taking aim.

'Karl!' she yelled.

Housman glanced up and threw himself to the ground. The gun report boomed across the landscape. A hail of pellets kicked up the dirt, but Mullen was too far away to actually hit anyone. The farmer started to run across the field, shouting angrily, a tirade of abuse so furious it was completely incoherent.

'Karl!'

Madeleine had the car door open, but she was staring back down at Housman who had resumed his digging. 'Karl, the dog!'

Housman turned his head. The collie was racing across the field towards him, a sleek dark shape close to the earth, slower than a shotgun pellet but infinitely more effective. Housman's arms were buried in the soil, feeling, sieving. His fingers encountered something hard and oval. He looked up. The dog was halfway across the field. Housman clawed at the earth, pulling out a cluster of tiny potatoes. The dog was less than fifty metres away now, close enough for Housman to see the sheen of its teeth. He leapt up and sprinted for the embankment, scrambling up the slope and pulling open the car door. An instant after he'd slammed the door shut, the collie hurtled up the bank and threw itself at the window, snarling and snapping, smearing the glass with saliva.

Madeleine already had the engine ticking over. She engaged the clutch and the car skidded off the verge and away along the road. Housman looked over his shoulder. The dog was haring back to its master who was standing with the shotgun raised. Mullen fired, aiming at the speeding car, a gesture of anger and frustration rather than a serious attempt to hit it for the vehicle was well out of range. Then he turned and lumbered towards the farmhouse.

Madeleine slowed the car and let her muscles relax, taking a few deep breaths. 'Jesus,' she panted. 'He was going to kill us.'

'You okay?'

'Me? What about you? You were the one out there with that dog coming for you.'

'I'm fine. At least I got these.'

Housman held up the potatoes. There were three tubers, each about the size of a pigeon's egg. He brushed the soil off them to reveal a smooth pale brown skin. He handed one to Madeleine.

She weighed it in her hand. 'I hope they're worth it,' she said.

Three miles further on, heading away from Ely on one of the long straight fenland roads, Madeleine saw a distant flashing light in her rear-view mirror. As the light drew nearer, she realised it was attached to a police patrol car. It was moving fast. No siren, just the pulsating beacon on the roof. Madeleine slowed automatically, pulling over to give the patrol car more room to pass. But instead of accelerating, as she'd expected, the patrol car slowed, pulling alongside so the two officers inside could get a look at Madeleine and Housman. Then it drew past and the glowing red STOP sign was illuminated. Madeleine braked and came to a halt, watching the police car stop in front. The uniformed constables got out and walked back towards them.

Madeleine wound down her window. One of the constables peered in, his eyes roving around the interior.

'Is this your car, madam?' he asked politely.

'Yes.'

'Would you step out, please. You too, sir.'

'Is there a problem?'

'If you'd just step out, please.'

'Why are you stopping us? You need a reason.'

'This won't take a moment, madam.'

Madeleine sighed and climbed out on to the road. There was little point in arguing with them. Housman got out on the other side and came round to join her. Madeleine felt reassured having his towering figure next to her.

'Have you been anywhere near Eastmere Farm this evening?' the constable enquired. 'We've had a complaint from the farmer that he saw two people – a man and a woman – in a light blue Volkswagen Golf stealing potatoes from one of his fields.'

Madeleine stared at him in disbelief. Two officers, a patrol car on their tail almost within minutes of their leaving Eastmere. For such a trivial accusation. Something wasn't right.

'You're stopping us on suspicion of stealing potatoes?' she said.

'You haven't answered my question, madam.'

'Look, officer . . .' Housman began, but Madeleine cut him off.

'You don't have to say anything, Karl. This is ridiculous.' She turned to the constable. 'Are you serious?'

The constable inspected them both slowly, taking in the soil on their clothes, their filthy arms and hands.

'You wouldn't have been digging, would you?' he asked.

'Dave . . .'

The second officer was leaning inside the Golf. He lifted out two tiny potato tubers from the floor in front of the passenger seat and held them up. The first constable looked at Madeleine and Housman and shook his head sorrowfully, as if they'd somehow let him down.

'Do you have an explanation for these?'

'We have nothing to say,' Madeleine replied.

'In that case, you're under arrest.'

22

It was a strange experience for Madeleine, being on the receiving end for once. Strange, and not very pleasant. After the constable had cautioned them, they were put in the back of the police car and driven to Ely police station, the second officer following on behind in Madeleine's Golf. The custody sergeant was polite and punctilious, doing everything by the book: the custody sheets, the charges, the fingerprints, photographs and DNA samples.

'Haven't you got better things to do with your time?' Madeleine asked sourly.

'I'm just doing my job, madam,' the sergeant replied phlegmatically.

'You're accusing us of stealing potatoes worth – what would you say two minute specimens like that were worth? A penny? Twopence?'

'There were others found in the back of your car.'

'In a brown paper bag? We bought those from Fodder Creek Farm earlier this evening. Along with the eggs. Check.'

'We will, madam.'

They allowed them their one phone call. Housman declined, having no one to contact, but Madeleine rang Graham and told him, without saying exactly why, that she would be home later than she'd expected. She knew the procedure. For an offence as minor as this, and with their backgrounds, there was no reason why they shouldn't be released on police bail, which in due course was what happened. An hour after they'd arrived at the station, they were back outside in Madeleine's Golf. She was angry, and not a little worried.

'This is unbelievable,' she exclaimed heatedly. 'Completely un-fucking-believable. Two poxy little potatoes and our careers could be over. What's the General Medical Council's view of a theft conviction?'

'I don't know,' Housman said.

'I know what the Law Society's is. There's no way I can prac-tise as a solicitor with a criminal record.'

'I'm sorry. It was all my idea. I shouldn't have got you involved.'

'I was involved already.'

'I'll accept full responsibility. I was the one who dug them up, after all.'

'It won't make any difference. I was with you. They'll charge me with being an accomplice.'

'Over a couple of potatoes?'

'This isn't about the potatoes, Karl.'

'What do you mean?'

There was something slightly naive, slightly unworldly about him, Madeleine realised. That was part of his charm. Maybe it was her job, her daily immersion in the mire of criminal law, but she had no illusions about what was really going on here.

'Think about it. You can smell the fish a mile off. We lift the potatoes and within ten minutes, maybe less, there's a police car on our tail. You ever heard of the police responding that quickly to anything, never mind an allegation from some farmer that his spuds are being nicked? Please. They'd have filed his complaint and forgotten about it. Instead we get a patrol car scrambled, a hot pursuit across the countryside and we end up arrested. You think Mullen has that kind of clout? A yokel like him?'

'So what are you saying happened?' Housman swivelled side-ways in the passenger seat, staring quizzically at her.

'He phoned someone who *does* have that kind of clout. Who has an awful lot of clout. Interesting. Now who would Mullen know like that? Why would he phone them? And why would that person want to stop us taking a few worthless potatoes?'

Housman's brow furrowed. 'If Eastmere's a GM trial site the Government's keeping secret, then they're not worthless.'

'Not a trial site. It's bigger than that. You saw how many of Mullen's fields were bare. I think he's growing GM potatoes commercially.'

'But I thought no commercial licences had been issued? That's the whole point of the trial sites – to see if GM crops are safe before commercial growing is allowed.'

'That's what the Government's telling us. But I think they're just going through the motions. They've already decided GM crops are safe. The trials are nothing but PR.'

'Shit!'

Housman was silent for a while.

'We're in trouble, aren't we?'

Madeleine nodded. 'And you know what? I bet Eastmere isn't the only place it's happening.'

'Why would the Government do that?' Even now Housman couldn't quite believe it. 'What's in it for them?'

'The general public don't want transgenic crops,' Madeleine said. 'The agrochemicals and biotech companies do. So do the Americans. Which do you think the Government is going to listen to most? They're desperate to stay at the forefront of the biotech revolution. GM crops have been on sale in the USA for years. US biotech companies have a huge head start on compa-nies here. What if the Government's been levelling the playing field, giving Transgenic Biotech the chance to get ahead on the sly? And not told us anything about it.'

'So they've let them grow GM crops and sell them to the public without us knowing what we're buying. They'd pull a deception like that?' Housman paused, then answered it himself. 'Yes, they would, wouldn't they?'

He sounded resigned, deflated by the realisation. Madeleine, though, was boiling with suppressed fury.

'That's not the end of the story,' she said grimly.

'Isn't it? Where's our proof? The potatoes are gone. Even the three we found are now in the hands of the police.'

'Only two of them.'

'What? What happened to the third?'

'They don't strip-search suspects,' Madeleine said. 'Unless it's a drugs charge. They only search pockets.'

She reached down into her cleavage and pulled the third tuber out from her bra. 'Sometimes being a woman has its advantages.'

She dropped Housman off at his car by the roadblock outside Great Dunchurch. It was approaching half past ten and they were both tired. Housman didn't get out immediately. He was holding the potato in his hand.

'I'll have my friend check it over for us,' he said.

'Who is he?'

'His name's Jeremy Blake. He works in the Plant Sciences Department at the university.'

'You trust him?'

'Implicitly. We were students together.'

'Sorry. I'm getting paranoid.'

Housman was looking across at her, his expression hidden in the darkness. 'We'll work something out,' he said. 'About the theft charge. You'll be okay.'

Madeleine tried to smile, but she didn't have the energy. 'It's nice of you to say so.'

'I mean it. What we're doing is in the public interest.'

She was reminded of Jake Brewster. It was what he'd said. But the law had never recognised the public interest as an excuse for illegal behaviour. Parliament would never have sanctioned such a defence. God forbid that the public should have a say in their own laws.

Housman opened his door to climb out and stopped. Then he leaned over and touched Madeleine's hand briefly with his fingers.

'I'll speak to you tomorrow,' he said.

She wondered about that touch on the way home. Wondered about Housman. It had been a long time since she'd been attracted to a man. It was a part of her she'd deliberately put on hold until . . . until when? Until Graham left home was how she subconsciously thought of it. Was she really doomed to a life of chaste loneliness until then? Was that her lot? Or her choice? She put it out of her mind and concentrated on driving.

She could see a light upstairs in Graham's bedroom as she approached the house. At least he was home. She pulled out to pass a parked car, thinking about what she was going to tell her son. How she would explain to him where she'd been. She'd have to tell him. He would find out soon enough and . . .

The parked car.

She looked in her rear-view mirror. Saw the outline of the Rover saloon, the two men sitting in the front. Waiting patiently.

She took her foot off the brake, moved it to the accelerator and drove straight past her house, turning left a hundred metres further on and pulling into the kerb. She was surprised to feel her heart racing. I really am getting paranoid, she thought. But why were they there? To intimidate her? To frighten her? They were doing both very effectively.

Madeleine looked over her shoulder, half expecting to see the Rover creeping around the corner after her. Had they seen her drive past?

She wondered where else she could go for the night. Graham would be all right. She'd never left him alone overnight before, but he was more than capable of looking after himself. Her heart gave a jolt. Graham . . . maybe they were . . . no, that really *was* paranoid. If they'd been after her son they would have been in and gone long ago. They wouldn't still be sitting outside in a car.

Madeleine took out her mobile and punched in her home number. It rang for a long while before Graham answered.

'Yeah?'

'It's me. I'm not going to make it home tonight, I'm afraid. I'll explain tomorrow.'

'I'll be okay.'

'You sure?'

'I'm not a little kid.'

'I hope to be back at breakfast.'

'Whenever, no problem. I'll see you then.'

Was she being silly, needlessly cautious? Any other night, perhaps, she might have dismissed the thoughts – rational and irrational – that were flooding through her mind. But not tonight. Not after what had happened out in the Fens. But where could she go?

She punched in another number on her phone. Housman's voice was soft, sleepy.

'Did I wake you?' she said.

'No. Has something happened?'

'I don't suppose you have a spare bed for the night?'

Housman didn't ask any questions. He simply opened his front door and let her in, then brought a bottle of red wine and two glasses into the sitting room and set them down on the table.

'I was having a drink. You want one?'

Madeleine nodded. Housman poured her a glass and handed

it to her. She took a long gulp, almost choking on the liquid. She noticed her hands were trembling slightly and gripped the glass between her palms to steady them. Housman sat down next to her on the settee.

'You okay?' he said.

'Yes.'

She wasn't sure why she'd called him. She had other people she could have rung, friends she knew much better. Or she could have gone to a hotel. But she didn't want to be on her own, and her friends would have required more explanation than she felt up to giving. Housman understood. They'd only met the previous day but they were in this together.

'You're scared, aren't you?' Housman said.

'Yes.'

He waited, not wanting to push her.

'There was a car outside my house.' Madeleine took a sip of wine to ease the dryness in her mouth. 'Two men inside. I recognised both them and the car. I don't know who they are but they're either MI5 or Special Branch.'

'You've seen them before?'

Madeleine nodded and told him about Goose Fen Farm and Frankie's videotape.

'Why would they be outside your house?' Housman asked.

'I don't know. But it's the sequence of events, not one single event, that scares me. One of my clients found two strange men – almost certainly the two in the car – searching his flat. David Seymour was killed, the only witness to his death mysteriously changed his evidence and then we get picked up and charged with theft. I'm a target, Karl – and, yes, it scares me.'

'You fear for your own safety?'

'Yes, I think I do. And I don't think it's silly. Do you believe in the concept of a benign state?'

'How do you mean?'

'A government – not just the politicians but the whole apparatus of government – that rules for the common good. For the benefit of the many, not just the few. A guiding hand, watching over us all to preserve and guarantee our liberties. It's a nice idea, but I don't believe in it. It doesn't exist. It never has done. The whole point of government is power. Whatever form it takes – dictatorship, oligarchy, parliamentary democracy – its purpose is not to set us free. It's to control us. And it's getting worse. I've seen it happening over the years I've been in practice. A slow, stealthy erosion of rights to give government more control over us. If we go along with it, if we don't fight it, then yes, you could say we have a benign state. But the minute you raise an objection or question what they're doing then their true colours emerge and they will try to crush you. They're terrified of opposition, of anyone finding out what they're really up to. If we're on to something they want kept hidden, do you think they won't try to stop us revealing it?'

'How?'

'That's what scares me.' Madeleine sipped some more wine. 'It makes me feel vulnerable.'

'But what can they do?'

'They're doing it already. Arresting us is just the start.'

'And next?'

Madeleine shrugged, aware that she was shivering though the house wasn't cold. 'I don't want to think about it. The image of David Seymour's car being winched out of that drainage canal is still too vivid in my memory.'

Housman's gaze was fixed on her face, puzzled, anxious. 'Aren't you getting a little carried away?'

'He was *murdered*, Karl. I know he was. And no one will ever stand trial for it. They've got away with it. You think they can't get away with more?'

'Yes, but surely . . .'

'I'm serious,' Madeleine broke in impatiently. 'These are not agents of the mythical benign state I mentioned. They're agents of a repressive, intolerant, fanatically secretive government. And as far as they're concerned, we're on the wrong side.'

Madeleine swallowed and put down her glass of wine. Her whole body – legs, arms, hands – was shaking now. She tried to control the spasms, but her muscles were tensing involuntarily, vibrating violently as if an electric current were being put through them. She could feel her heart pumping, a film of perspiration on her forehead.

'Karl . . .'

Housman grasped her hands. 'You're having a panic attack,' he said. 'It's nothing to worry about. Breathe out. You're hyperventilating . . . Madeleine, breathe with me. With *me*. In, out, in . . .'

She followed his lead, synchronising her breathing with his, looking into his eyes, relaxing until the spasms finally receded. Even then he kept hold of her hands, not gripping them any more but holding them gently.

'I'm sorry,' Madeleine said, still a little breathless.

She extricated her hands, embarrassed by the incident.

'It's late,' she went on. 'Maybe we should go to bed.'

'The bathroom's at the top of the stairs. I've put out a towel for you, made up the bed in the back room.'

Madeleine went upstairs and washed. She had no toothbrush, but she squeezed toothpaste on to her finger and rubbed it around inside her mouth, rinsing with cold water.

Housman was on the landing, standing awkwardly by his bedroom door, when she came out. Madeleine gave a quick smile.

'About . . . just now,' she said. 'Thanks.'

'That's okay.'

'Goodnight.'

'Goodnight.'

Neither of them moved. They looked at each other, uncomfortable in the silence.

Then Housman said: 'Why don't you come in with me?'

It was an impulsive decision, a choice made instinctively with some part of her that was neither the head nor the heart. It wasn't thought through in a rational sense, but nor was it something purely emotional. She wasn't in love with him, wasn't overcome with the hot flush of lust, but there was something there, a gut need, a desire for contact, for companionship that made her say yes. And once she'd agreed there was no backing down. She didn't *want* to back down. But all the old fears, the clumsy inhibitions returned, threatening to paralyse her. Only when they were naked under the sheets with the light off did she start to feel more at ease – using senses other than sight, her doubts about her body hidden away in the reassuring darkness. As they kissed and touched, the weariness fell away from her and she remembered how good it felt to be desired.

'I haven't done this for a long time,' she murmured, unable even now to conceal her insecurities.

'You don't forget,'Housman said. 'It's like riding a bike.'

'Don't say that. I always fall off bikes.'

He laughed and touched her again. She liked the masculine smell of him, the taste, the way his fingers lingered on her skin. What had been a shy, tentative warmth between them began to change into a more fervent passion.

'Have you any . . . you know?' Madeleine asked.

'What? Oh, yes.'

He slipped out of bed and padded across to the chest of drawers. She heard him opening a drawer, rummaging through the contents.

'Shit, where are they?' he muttered under his breath. 'Close your eyes, I'm going to have to put the light on.'

He clicked the switch and checked another drawer, feeling under a mound of socks to pull out a new, unopened packet of condoms. When had he bought them? He couldn't remember. Probably way back after his divorce, when he'd thought he'd jump straight back into the sharkpool of dating but had never summoned the nerve to take the plunge.

He turned the packet over and examined the sell-by date printed on the bottom: 99-06. June, 1999. They were two years out of date. And rubber perished, didn't it? What the hell, he wasn't stopping now. He tried to open the packet but it appeared to be wrapped in bullet-proof Cellophane.

'Fuck!'

Madeleine opened her eyes and watched him tearing at the plastic wrapper with his teeth. He had broad shoulders, a smooth hairless back and a ripple of excess flesh around his waist. A good body, but not perfect. Like her own. It was better if you had matching imperfections.

Finally, he got the Cellophane off and pulled out a condom in its sealed sachet. He turned round and, noticing Madeleine gazing at him, glanced down.

'Now where did *he* go?'

'He'll come back,' Madeleine said.

'He'd bloody well better,' Housman replied, snapping off the light and sliding back into bed.

Madeleine ran her fingers over him. 'See?'

'It's been a long time for me too,' he said, kissing her.

'You know what you're doing?'

'Trust me, I'm a doctor.'

Housman had set the alarm for 7.30, but Madeleine was up half an hour before, woken by the clock inside her head. She left him sleeping and went into the bathroom to wash. It was a light, cool room tiled in cream and cornflower blue. There were bottles of shampoo and conditioner at the end of the bath and a canister of shaving foam and disposable razors on the window-sill above the sink, half hidden behind the Austrian blinds. The contents were masculine but the room had a feminine feel to it. It was the blinds, Madeleine decided. Cream and frilly, they were something no man she'd ever met would have chosen himself. She guessed they were the legacy of a previous occupant, or maybe his wife, and he hadn't bothered to change them. He didn't strike her as a man with a great deal of interest in interior décor.

She put back on the clothes she'd worn the previous evening – the T-shirt and jeans, both stained with soil; not an outfit she could contemplate wearing to work – and went downstairs. While she was waiting for the kettle to boil, she telephoned Graham. He took a long time answering but she was expecting the delay. Little short of a nuclear explosion was guaranteed to get her son out of bed.

'Yes?'

'It's me,' Madeleine said.

'You woke me up.'

'That was the idea. You've got school.'

'Not for hours.'

'Will you do something for me? Look out of the front and see if there's a Rover saloon parked up the street with two men inside.'

Graham grunted. The receiver clattered as he put it down. Madeleine waited, listening for his footsteps as he came back.

'No, no Rover,' he said.

'Thanks. I'll be home very soon.'

She hung up and made a pot of tea, pouring a mug and taking it upstairs to Housman. He stirred and opened his eyes as she put the mug down on the bedside table.

'I'm going,' she said.

He levered himself up on to an elbow and yawned. 'Not staying for breakfast?'

'I have to change my clothes.'

She hesitated, wondering where they went now. Then she bent down and kissed him briefly on the lips. It seemed a much more intimate act than anything that had happened the night before.

'I'll call you later,' Housman said.

He was bleary-eyed, unshaven. He reached out for his glasses. Madeleine didn't want him to see her without make-up, her hair and clothes a mess.

'I'll see you,' she said, opening the door and walking out.

'Jeff wants to see you,' Eileen said as Madeleine walked into the office.

Madeleine paused, resting her heavy briefcase on the corner of her secretary's desk. 'He say what about?'

'No.'

Jeff Appleton was the senior partner, a dour, humourless man in his fifties who spent more time on the golf course than he did in the office. A summons from him was sufficiently rare to be disturbing. Madeleine deposited her case on the floor by her desk and went down the corridor, feeling as nervous as she had when she'd come for her job interview after law college.

The firm's premises, as befitted a practice whose income came mostly from Legal Aid, were far from lavish. Even the partners' offices – like Madeleine's – were plain and rather drab, but Appleton's was bigger and better furnished than the others. His desk was a reproduction mahogany antique, his bookshelves laden with thick, embossed volumes of law reports, and the carpet – an expensive dark green Axminster – was as smooth and soft as a putting green though Appleton, ever conscious of the proprieties, would never have dreamt of practising shots in his office.

'Thank you for coming, Madeleine,' he said. 'Please take a seat.'

His manner was cool, inscrutable, no different from usual, but Madeleine already knew what he wanted to talk about.

'I wanted to see you as well,' she said, preempting the discussion.

'I'm sure you did.'

He made himself comfortable in his leather chair and straightened the blotter on his spotless desk. He was a fastidious man, particular about his appearance. His suits were always dark grey or black, nothing too colourful, his cufflinks either gold or silver, and the handkerchief nestling in the breast pocket of his jacket was always chosen to complement his tie.

'Who told you?' Madeleine asked.

'I received a phone call at home this morning.'

Madeleine didn't ask from whom. Appleton was a mason, like many senior police officers, and the masons had a communications network that would have put GCHQ to shame.

'You should have contacted me last night,' Appleton said reproachfully. There was something of the clergyman in his habitual moralising tone. If he hadn't been a solicitor, he would have made a good country vicar.

'I know,' Madeleine said. 'But it was late when we got out. I thought it could wait till the morning.'

'It's a serious allegation. I don't have to remind you of its implications for your career, should it be substantiated. Is it true?'

'I intend to plead not guilty,' Madeleine said.

'That's not what I asked. I said, is it true? Did you steal potatoes from a farmer's field?'

Madeleine hesitated. She didn't want to get into a discussion of semantics. She wanted to keep it simple. 'No, I didn't steal any potatoes,' she said firmly. In the strictest sense that was accurate: it was Housman who had taken them.

'The police think you did.'

'They're mistaken.'

'Would you care to elaborate on that?'

'I think it's better if I don't at the moment.'

She could have told him the whole story, but it was very complicated and she was aware that parts of it he would find difficult to believe. Besides, whatever she said, there was only one possible outcome from this interview.

'We will stand by you, of course,' Appleton said. 'But I'm sure you understand when I say that you cannot continue to practise with a cloud over you.'

'You're suspending me?'

'Putting you on paid leave until this matter is resolved. Give any cases you have outstanding to Gill and Clive. They'll take care of them.' Appleton frowned at her. 'What I can't work out is why the police should think a respected solicitor would go out into the countryside and steal a few potatoes.'

'Yes, it's absurd, isn't it?' Madeleine said.

She tried not to think about it on the drive home, but it wouldn't go away. It gnawed at her like an abscess, painful and relentless. The charge against her was trivial and ridiculous, but that didn't make it any less damaging. Whichever way the dice fell, she was the loser. A conviction was a certain end to her legal career, but the alternatives weren't much better. Even if the police dropped the charge, or she was acquitted at trial, some of the mud would inevitably stick. Her reputation would be sullied, a questionmark left hanging over her integrity, and what firm would want to employ a solicitor under those circumstances?

She parked on the road outside her house and walked up the drive. She was opening the front door when they came up behind her. She was so preoccupied she didn't hear them coming until they'd taken her by the arms and bundled her into the house. They dragged her through into the sitting room and pushed her down into an armchair. Madeleine looked up, feeling the bruises on her arms where they'd gripped her. There were two of them, both wearing crumpled grey suits. They were big, well-built men with short hair and thick necks, their faces hard and pugnacious. Madeleine's indignation temporarily overcame her anxiety.

'Who the hell are you?'

'Think of us as friends,' the shorter of the two men said.

'I don't remember inviting you in.'

'That's good. A bit of selective amnesia is what we need from you.'

'Get out.'

The men sat down, one on the settee, the other in the second armchair. They stretched out their legs, making themselves at home.

'Get out, or I'll call the police,' Madeleine said. 'Oh, I'm sorry, I forgot. You *are* the police. Or are you? Show me some identi-fication.'

The shorter man feigned an exaggerated yawn. 'Shut up, you stupid bitch, and listen.'

There was a hint of cockney in his accent, a London whine, but it was his abusive manner that told Madeleine he was Special Branch. The spooks at Five were a smoother, better-spoken class of thug. Not that it mattered. The distinction was purely aca-demic. Special Branch didn't so much as sneeze without Home Office approval.

'We've come to give you some advice,' the man continued.

'Like you did Henry Steadman, you mean?'

The man sighed and sat up. He leaned over casually and – before she had time to react – slapped her hard across the mouth. 'I said shut up and listen.'

Madeleine's face stung, but she resisted the urge to rub it. She wasn't going to give them the satisfaction of seeing that they'd hurt her.

'Quite a man, aren't you?' she said contemptuously.

'You want another slap?'

'You want a kick in the groin?'

He looked at her, amused. 'You've got balls, I'll give you that.'

'Which is more than could be said of you.'

'Don't tempt me, darling.'

'Please, you're not my type.'

The second man gestured impatiently. 'Let's get on with it.'

'Yes,' Madeleine said. 'I'm sure you're busy men. You don't want to keep your manicurists waiting, do you?'

'You think you're so fucking smart, don't you?'

'In present company it's an easy illusion to have.'

She knew it wasn't wise to antagonise them, but it was a defence mechanism, her way of controlling the fear that threatened to overwhelm her. She had to keep them at bay somehow. They were bullies, cowards underneath the veneer of toughness. The worst thing she could do was to show any sign of weakness.

'Say what you have to say and get out,' she said dismissively.

The shorter man stared at her with mean, malign eyes.

'Let me ask you something,' he said. 'Where does a struck-off solicitor find a new job?'

'I could try Special Branch, but I don't fancy a lobotomy. You got any other ideas?'

'There's always the street corner.'

'I don't think so. One meeting with you is more than enough.'

'Think about it. You've got a nice house here, a good job, a car, a future. Why throw it all away? Think about your son too. What's his name? Graham, isn't it? Lower Sixth at Netherhall School. Seems a nice kid.'

Madeleine's blood turned to ice. 'You bastards.'

The man smirked at her. 'Not so clever now, are you? We've got your tits in a vice and we're going to squeeze them nice and slowly.'

He liked that image. He made an obscene motion with his hands, leering at her.

'You need help,' Madeleine said.

He shook his head, sensing he'd found a chink in her armour. 'No, it's you who needs help. That's why we're here.'

'You're going to offer me a deal, aren't you?'

It was the second man who answered. 'We can arrange for the theft charge to be dropped.'

'And what do I have to do in return?'

'Keep your mouth shut, and your nose out of other people's business.'

'Do you want to be more specific?'

'We don't have to spell it out for you. You know what we're talking about.'

'And if I say no?'

'That's the wrong answer.'

Madeleine didn't give herself time to think about it. Once you started to compromise, the canker of betrayal would eat away at your integrity, consuming it slowly from the inside until there was nothing left but a worthless shell.

'You can go to hell,' she said.

She stood up and went out into the hall to open the front door. The two men followed.

'I'd think about it if I were you,' the shorter man said.

He gave her a friendly pat on the cheek. Madeleine knocked his hand away angrily.

'You know the good thing about the English legal system?' she said. 'Anything said in court has absolute privilege. You can say what you like and the press can report it without fear of being sued. I've got a lot to say and I'm going to enjoy saying it.'

'If you make it to court,' the man said and walked out.

Madeleine slammed the door behind them and turned the key in the lock. Then she went through into the kitchen and took a bottle of vodka out of a cupboard. She poured herself a shot with trembling hands and gulped it down.

Housman wasn't sure exactly when the ache began. It hadn't been there when he woke up, when Madeleine came in to say goodbye, nor afterwards when she'd gone and he'd lain back on the pillows wondering why she hadn't stayed longer. He didn't remember it when he'd gone into the bathroom to shave and wash, but it must have been there, creeping slowly to the surface, for when he got downstairs he'd become aware of a dull throb behind his eyes. A throb which soon progressed to a distinct ache spreading across the whole of his head.

He'd found it annoying, but nothing more. He'd taken a couple of paracetamol and left for the hospital. He hadn't felt like breakfast – a bad sign – but it was still only a headache. On the drive to Addenbrooke's it got worse.

He felt dizzy. The ache no longer seemed confined to his head, but was seeping into other parts of his body. His arms and legs were heavy and a hot flush rolled over him like a wave, leaving behind a patina of sweat which clung to his skin, cooling rapidly in clammy streaks. He started to shiver. Another wave, this time of nausea, pulsed through him. He slowed the car, wondering if he was fit to drive. His arms were so weak it was an effort to turn the steering wheel and his vision was becoming erratic. He realised, with alarm, what it was.

Fortunately, it was a short journey, one he could do almost in his sleep. He parked in another consultant's space and hauled himself out of the car. For an instant he thought his legs were going to collapse, but from somewhere he found the strength to stagger into the hospital. Three times on the way to the lifts he had to pause, supporting himself on the wall, as more hot and cold waves broke over him and then ebbed away.

His secretary stared at him as he stumbled into her office.

'Are you all right, Dr Housman?'

'An envelope,' he mumbled, holding out one hand, the other propping himself up on her desk. 'Call the IU. Get a nurse up here with a dose of amantadine.'

He snatched the envelope from her hand and tottered through into his own office. Sagging down into his chair, he took a few deep breaths, then scribbled a note on a piece of paper. He slid the paper into the envelope and had to rest for a moment before he had the energy to write Jeremy Blake's name and address on the front. The aches were getting worse. His muscles felt as if they were being wrung out like strips of wet cloth. He'd never felt this ill before.

From his pocket he took out the small potato tuber Madeleine had managed to save and sealed it in the envelope. Then he dragged himself to his feet and staggered back into his secretary's office.

'Send this . . . by courier . . . immediately,' he gasped.

He held out the envelope, then the room started to spin. A dark shutter came slowly down over his eyes and he crumpled to the floor in a heap.

23

Madeleine sat for a long while in an armchair in the living room. Doing nothing except staring at the wall. The vodka had calmed her nerves a little, but her pulse was still racing. Occasionally, a shudder passed through her body and she had to grip the arms of the chair to steady her trembling limbs.

In her mind, she ran over every detail of her conversation with the two men. Every nuance, every undertone. They'd forced their way into her home, slapped her across the face, but it wasn't the physical violence that frightened her: it was the other, more intangible threats they'd made. Nothing specific, nothing overt. Threats were always more effective when you left it to your victims to fill in the gaps. When you left them alone with their imaginations.

The front and back doors were locked and bolted. She had positioned herself so that she could see if anyone came up the drive to the house, and on the table next to her was a chopping knife from the kitchen. She knew she'd never use it, even in the most dire emergency, but having it there made her feel better. It eased the sense of powerlessness which gnawed at her insides, chewing a hole through which her resolve was slowly dripping away.

Doing nothing was a mistake, she knew that. It was dangerous to sit still and ponder, to let the mind dwell too much on what had happened. Fears fed on indecision and inactivity, swelling and spreading until they poisoned the whole system. Yet she didn't know what to do, didn't have the energy or the nerve to rouse herself.

More than anything, she felt alone. A dark, debilitating loneliness that made her cold inside, the way contemplating your own death made you cold. And perhaps that was what it was: a simple fear of extinction, the final black nothing.

The men had threatened her life. How else could she interpret their last few words? *If you make it to court.* She'd twisted them around, looked at them from every angle since they'd left. What else could they have meant? But still a part of her wondered whether she might be wrong. This was England, they were coppers, and the two things – despite her experience to the contrary – merged together into the comforting stereotype of the benign bobby. Things like that didn't happen here. Did they?

But then she thought of David Seymour being lifted, limp and dripping, from the lode, his pregnant wife waiting for him at home. She thought of Jake Brewster, of Dan Cruickshank, of Barry Mullen letting rip with a shotgun. And she knew there was no comfort in stereotypes. The benign bobby, like the benign state, was an illusion, an apparition that melted into thin air the moment you tried to touch it. Those men weren't phantasms, they were real. And everything they did, Madeleine had no doubt, was officially sanctioned.

She shivered again and thought about another vodka. The alcohol would warm her throat, settle her jittery stomach, but her tolerance to spirits was low. Two shots might make her feel better, but they would also dull her senses and cloud her judgment. And right now she needed all her faculties.

She looked out of the window, noting the cars, the people that went past, watching for anything out of the ordinary. The oppressive atmosphere in the house was starting to get to her. It was too quiet. Too isolated. She felt a need to talk to someone and thought immediately of Housman. They were in this together.

Reaching down for her handbag, she took out her mobile phone. She tried Housman's mobile number first. It was switched off so she called his direct line at Addenbrooke's. His secretary was guarded.

'Can I take a message for him? He's not here at the moment.'

'I'd prefer to speak to him,' Madeleine said. 'When will he be back?'

'Who's calling?'

Madeleine gave her name. 'I can't reach him on his mobile number. Is he out at Great Dunchurch again?'

'Does this concern Great Dunchurch?'

'Not directly. Is he there?'

'Perhaps I could help you. What did you wish to speak to him about?'

'It's personal. I'm a friend of his. We met on Monday, I believe. When I came to his office.'

The secretary's tone changed. 'Of course, I remember now.' She paused. 'I'm afraid Dr Housman has been taken ill.'

'Ill? When?' Madeleine said.

'Just this morning.'

'Is he at home?'

'He's in the Isolation Unit here.'

Madeleine's heart gave a thump. 'Flu?'

'It looks like it.'

Madeleine hung up, feeling slightly queasy. She was no longer worried for herself but for Housman. The news of his illness, a shock after seeing him apparently fit and well only a few hours ago, galvanised her, shaking her out of her torpor. She went out to her car and drove to Addenbrooke's, her eyes continually flicking to the rear-view mirror. If she was followed, she wasn't aware of it.

The sister in the Isolation Unit was initially unhelpful, preventing Madeleine from going beyond the nursing station and refusing to be drawn on questions about Housman's condition. But when Madeleine explained that she was a friend, a *close* friend, the sister opened out a little.

'Yes, it's flu,' she confirmed. 'The same as the others.'

'It must have come on very suddenly.'

'This particular strain of flu seems to.'

'How ill is he?'

The sister shrugged noncommittally. 'It's still in the very early stages. Patients are always worse at this time, until the body starts to fight back.'

'Can he talk?'

'He's asleep most of the time. In a fever.'

Madeleine threw an anxious glance towards the closed cubicles, a question forming on her lips. The sister seemed to sense what she was going to ask and shook her head.

'It's impossible to tell. He's very ill, but he has every chance of pulling through.'

'Can I see him?'

'I'm sorry.'

Madeleine hadn't really expected to be allowed to visit, but nevertheless she went upstairs to Housman's office feeling disappointed. Although she hardly knew him, his illness afflicted her with a despondent unease. The one person in whom she felt she could confide was now out of reach.

Housman's secretary was typing at a word processor when Madeleine walked in. She broke off and swung her chair away from the desk, giving a brief nod of recognition. Madeleine got straight to the point.

'Dr Housman was going to send a package over to the university Plant Sciences Department. You don't happen to know whether he did, do you?'

'Well, yes,' the secretary answered. 'It was the last thing he did before he collapsed. He gave me an envelope and asked me to have it couriered over.'

'When did it go?'

'About an hour ago.'

'Thank you. Do you have a telephone directory I could look at?'

Madeleine scribbled down the number of the Plant Sciences Department and went downstairs to one of the payphones in the main foyer. She dialled the number and waited for the switchboard to put her through.

'Jeremy Blake.'

Madeleine explained who she was and why she was ringing.

'Yes, I got the package,' Blake replied. 'One small potato.'

'Did Karl ask you for an analysis, to check if it's transgenic?'

'Yes, he did.'

'How long will that take?'

'Well, that depends. We have other things on, you know.'

'This is urgent.'

'We're not some lab for hire, Miss King,' Blake said with an edge of irritation. 'This is an academic department. I did the last test as a favour for Karl. I can't keep diverting resources.'

'Just this once. It's very important.'

'Why isn't Karl ringing me himself?'

'He's got flu.'

'This new strain?'

'Yes.'

'Shit! How is he?'

'Not well. But I know if he was fit, he'd beg you to do this analysis for him.'

Blake was silent for a moment. Then he said: 'I'll see what I can do. Call me tomorrow morning.'

Madeleine drove home in a sombre mood, thinking of Housman

and of her own predicament, wondering what she was going to do. She'd been in the house only a few minutes when the telephone rang. It was a reporter from the *Cambridge Evening News*, wanting to talk to her about the theft charge against her. Madeleine snapped, 'No comment,' and slammed down the receiver. They were turning the screws on her. Releasing not only the facts of the incident to the press but also her home ex-directory telephone number. That infuriated her, but there was no point in complaining. The police would only deny they were responsible.

It wasn't long before the phone rang again. This time it was a local stringer for one of the tabloids. Madeleine hung up on him, then unplugged the phone from the wall socket. Her mobile rang shortly afterwards. It was the same stringer. Madeleine cut him off and switched off the phone. So they'd given out her mobile number too. She knew this was only the beginning. They'd brief the press, slip a few misleading titbits to 'friendly' journalists. Smear her so her credibility was shot to pieces. Then it was so much easier to dismiss whatever she said as the rantings of a disturbed, embittered woman. Madeleine knew it wasn't the first time they'd done it. When it came to dirty tricks, the Branch had little to learn from anyone. But they were playing with the wrong woman. Madeleine had no intention of rolling over and surrendering.

She made herself a pot of coffee and sat down at the kitchen table with her laptop. For the next two hours she tapped away on the computer, writing a detailed report containing everything she'd learnt since she'd first met Jake Brewster that morning at Parkside police station. She included details of what Frankie had discovered in India, her suspicions about David Seymour's death, an explanation of Housman's theory about the origins of the flu outbreak and how Eastmere farm fitted into the picture. Then she saved it to disk. She'd add the final piece of the story tomorrow when she had Blake's analysis of the potato.

Worn out and hungry, she made herself a cheese sandwich and went through into the sitting room and lay down on the settee. She was tired, but her brain wouldn't stop working, going over and over the events of the previous week.

Something bothered her. Something right at the beginning. That very first day when Jake and the others had ripped up the oilseed rape at the Transgenic Biotech research centre. She couldn't figure out what it was.

She looked at the clock on the mantelpiece. It was half past three. Better to get it over with now. Bracing herself, she went out of the house and down the road to the newsagent's. She bought a copy of the *Evening News* and, deliberately refraining from looking at it, brought it home with her. Only when she was back in the armchair did she summon up the courage to glance at the front page. The implications of the theft charge for her life and career were so enormous that it hadn't occurred to her that others might not give them the same weight. So it was with a feeling of relief that she saw no mention of her name on the front of the paper.

The lead concerned the death of a ten-year-old boy, Kieran Mitchell, from Great Dunchurch. He'd died in Addenbrooke's Hospital that morning, from acute liver failure brought on by influenza and Reye's Syndrome; the fourth victim of the flu outbreak. There was a photograph of the child, obviously lifted from a holiday snap: a smiling, tousle-haired kid posing for the camera on a beach somewhere. Madeleine thought of his mother, remembering Graham at that age. Then she thought of Housman and a chill of foreboding swept through her. She turned the page quickly and checked the other headlines.

It was on page five, a mercifully short report giving only the barest details: their names, ages, professions, the offence with which they'd been charged and the fact that they'd been released on police bail. It was brief, but Madeleine knew the damage had already been done. By now every solicitor in the city would have heard the news.

She put the paper down and gazed listlessly across the room. For an instant, she wondered if it had been a mistake to reject the deal Special Branch had offered her. They were right. She had a son, a mortgage, a future to think about. Then she berated herself immediately for her weakness. She was tougher than that, her rectitude wasn't for sale at any price. She'd fight them. And she'd win. When she produced her evidence in court, no jury was going to convict her of stealing three paltry potatoes.

Her gaze settled on the television set in the corner of the room. There were two video cassettes on top of it, their labels facing her. She could faintly make out some of the words and realised they were the CCTV tapes from the Transgenic Biotech research centre she'd brought home with her from the office.

It was then that she knew what it was that had been bothering her. Dan Cruickshank. He was one thread of the story she hadn't followed up. Frankie had discovered he'd been working for Xenotech UK, one of Transgenic Biotech's competitors, but they hadn't taken it any further. According to Jake Brewster, smashing up the lab had been Cruickshank's idea. He'd known where he was going, how to get into the building and how to get out in an emergency. Had he come up with the idea himself, or had Xenotech told him to do it? He and Jake had done a good job of vandalising the place, but that was all it had been – mindless vandalism.

What had Dan been paid £50,000 for? To wreck a lab? That seemed a lot of money for such a crude and ultimately futile act. Madeleine found it difficult to see the fingerprints of a multinational corporation on it. They were sophisticated operators. The risks of Cruickshank getting caught were high. If they'd sent him in, they would surely have had a more important reason than a simple desire to destroy a few bits of a rival's equipment.

She got up from the chair and walked across to the television set and switched it on. She picked up the video cassettes and read the labels, then inserted the one marked 'Research Centre Rear Exterior' into the VCR. Returning to her seat, she pressed 'play' on the remote control and settled back to watch the tape.

It was a good, only slightly grainy, black and white picture of the eco-protesters breaking into the field of oilseed rape and pulling it up. It was impossible to work out which of the hooded white-clad figures were either Cruickshank or Brewster until well into the tape when the security guards had arrived on the scene and were making vain attempts to catch the intruders. At that point, Madeleine noticed two figures splitting off from the others and pausing for a second to discuss something. Then they ran out through the open gates into the car park and round the corner of the building where the camera lost them.

Madeleine stopped the tape and switched the cassettes, inserting the one marked 'Ground Floor Laboratory G1'. She watched it with a lawyer's eye. It was certainly damning evidence. The CCTV camera had captured with incontrovertible clarity the two men coming into the lab and smashing everything they could lay hands on. There was no sound on the tape, but it was easy to imagine the noise as the glass bottles and other equipment were hurled to the floor. The two figures split up, one remaining in the lab, the other heading into the glass-walled office at the far end of the room. Madeleine knew the latter had to be Cruickshank. Jake Brewster was taller than that.

Cruickshank forced the locks on the metal filing cabinets with a jemmy and pulled out the drawers in turn, tossing the contents on to the floor. Brewster, meanwhile, was still trashing the lab. Then Cruickshank turned round and gesticulated at Jake, obviously saying something though his mouth was hidden behind his surgical mask. Jake joined him in the office and started dumping more files. Madeleine watched the digital clock ticking away at the bottom of the picture. Fifteen, twenty seconds elapsed before Brewster spun round. Two security guards had entered the lab. They were standing almost directly below the CCTV camera. Jake stepped hurriedly out of the office, but Cruickshank lingered behind for a moment. The guards started to run down the lab. Cruickshank finally tore himself away from the cabinets and rushed out, sprinting through another door next to the office. Madeleine waited until the guards had disappeared through the same door and stopped the tape. She'd noticed something odd, but couldn't quite place what it was. When Cruickshank lingered behind he'd been doing something. Doing what?

Madeleine rewound the tape and watched the last bit again more carefully. Then she played it a third time, crawling on to the floor to get a better view of the television. When she'd finished, she sat back on her haunches, staring at the screen, her brow furrowed in thought.

Then she stood up and took out her mobile phone. She contemplated it for a moment. Could a mobile phone be monitored? She didn't know. The house phone was almost certainly compromised. She didn't want to take any chances. She went out of the house to the payphone down the road. She made two brief telephone calls, to Parkside police station and the coroner's office, then rang Bedford Prison and asked the switchboard to put her through to the Deputy Governor. She was a regular visitor to the prison, well known to the staff. But Bedford was thirty miles away, outside the circulation area of the *Cambridge Evening News*. No one there would yet know she'd been charged by the police or that she'd been suspended by her practice.

'I'd like to arrange to visit one of my clients,' she said. 'A remand prisoner, Jake Brewster.'

'When?' the Deputy Governor asked.

'Tomorrow.'

'Morning or afternoon?'

'Afternoon,' Madeleine said.

She hung up and went back to the house to watch the tape one more time.

24

Madeleine parked on the west side of the Backs and walked up Silver Street towards the city centre, pausing for a moment to watch the punts on the Cam. It was not yet ten o'clock but already the tourists were out in force on the river. The clear morning air, laced with the scent of newly mown grass, reverberated with their excited giggles and cries, the splash of water and the thud of wood as the unwieldy boats collided with one another. A lithe young man in tennis shoes and straw boater – one of the *Brideshead Revisited* caricatures who were employed part-time by the more exclusive 'chauffeured' punt hire operations – navigated a path expertly through the clusters of floundering visitors, his vessel gliding smoothly across the still water as he imparted information to the group of camera-clutching tourists lounging on the seats below him.

Madeleine listened to the young man's loud confident voice relating the history of the Mathematical Bridge beneath whose graceful wooden arch the punt was passing. Linking the old and new parts of Queen's College, the original eighteenth-century bridge had ostensibly been designed with such skilful use of geometry and engineering that it had needed neither glue nor screws to hold it together. Legend had it that it had been taken apart as a prank one night by drunken undergraduates who, not blessed with its creator's genius, had been unable to put it back together again. Nor had anyone else, so the replacement structure had had to be rebuilt using nails, metal brackets, bolts and all manner of artificial fixatives.

Madeleine had heard the tale many times before and didn't believe a word of it. It was simply a part of Cambridge folklore that had grown up over the years, like the stories of ghosts walking the staircases of the various colleges which had no doubt been invented by mischievous students and later embroidered for the benefit of the tourists who'd been visiting the city for centuries. Yet Madeleine found something reassuring about the tale. It was familiar, comforting, like the solid profiles of the colleges lining the Backs whose weathered walls exuded the heartening glow of permanence.

She felt in need of reassurance right now. She'd passed a restless night, troubled by fears and the dark conjurings of her imagination. She'd lain awake for hours, listening to the sounds outside in the street and the disturbing beat of her own heart. The house was locked tight, her son in the adjoining room, but she knew that wouldn't deter them. If they wanted her, they would find a way to get to her.

On the drive she'd kept a close eye on her mirrors without seeing anything to worry her. Even now, walking through the busy streets, she kept glancing back, stopping to study the pedestrians behind her. Her nerves were jangling, ready to react to any threat. But nothing happened.

The university's Department of Plant Sciences was a motley collection of buildings off Downing Street. Jeremy Blake was waiting for her in his office which overlooked the back of the Museum of Archaeology and Anthropology. She'd spoken to him earlier from the payphone near her house and arranged to meet. He was in a hurry, anxious to get off to a lecture he was giving, and Madeleine found his manner offhand and peremptory.

'I could have told you this on the phone,' he said.

'I didn't want to discuss it on the phone,' Madeleine replied without explaining her reasons. 'But thank you for your time.'

'I haven't got much,' Blake said. 'Here's the technician's report.'

He handed her a sheet of paper. Madeleine glanced at it, knowing she wouldn't understand anything too technical.

'Was it transgenic?' she asked.

'Yes, it was.'

'In what way?'

It must have been a stupid question for Blake gave a dismissive shake of his head and pointed at the paper.

'It's all in there. Now, if you'll excuse me.'

But Madeleine persisted. 'I need it explaining to me. I'm sorry, I don't have a scientific background.'

'There's nothing to explain,' Blake said impatiently. 'The potato's genome – its genetic make-up – has been altered.'

'Why?'

'You'd have to ask the people who bred it.'

'I mean, to do what? What would be the results of altering it?'

'I can't tell. Look, I explained all this to Karl last time. It's too complicated to go into now. Read the report.'

Blake picked up a sheaf of lecture notes and moved towards the door of the office.

'Is it the same as the peelings Karl gave you?'

'Miss King, I really have to go.'

'Is it?'

'No. The peelings were transgenic too. But they'd been genetically altered in a slightly different way. Okay?'

'Deliberately?'

'What?'

'Had the peelings been altered deliberately? Or could the difference have been caused by some kind of accidental cross-pollination?'

Blake shrugged. 'A transgenic hybrid? Yes, that's quite possible.'

He pulled open the door and ushered her out into the corridor. Locking the door behind him, he hurried away without another word. Madeleine went back downstairs and walked across the courtyard and through the arches on to Downing Street. There were people around, some students, others obviously tourists. Madeleine felt happier in a crowd so she stayed close to a tour group as it drifted in a long straggling crocodile down to the river. By the Mill Basin, where the punts were moored in long rows, she slipped into the Anchor pub and walked down the steps to the riverside bar. She bought a tonic water with ice and sat down at a table near the window. Outside, the small terrace was crowded with tourists. Madeleine could see the weeping willows overhanging the river along Laundress Green, where the university's washing used to be hung out to dry, and hear the rush of water as it cascaded over the nearby weir.

She took out the sheet of paper Blake had given her and read it through several times. It might as well have been written in Swahili for all she understood of it. Nucleotide sequence, recombinant DNA, codons, bases, adenine, guanine, cytosine, thymine, these were words that were completely meaningless to her. Fortunately, Blake had already given her the one piece of information she needed to know: the potato from Eastmere Farm had been genetically modified.

Madeleine put the piece of paper into her handbag and left the pub, continuing back over the river to her car. Her laptop computer was in the boot. She took it out and carried it along the Backs to King's Bridge. The open expanse of grass beside the water near King's College was scattered with groups of people – enough to make Madeleine feel protected, but not so many that they invaded her privacy. Sitting down on the grass, she placed the laptop on her outstretched legs, logged on and called up the document she'd started the previous day. It took her only a few minutes to add the information about the potato she'd got from Jeremy Blake. Then she saved it to disk and stowed the disk in her handbag.

There was a Post Office on St Andrew's Street. Madeleine bought a thick manilla envelope and slipped the disk inside it with a brief covering note. Then she sealed the envelope, wrote Frankie Carson's home address on the front and posted it. By now it was almost noon. She had a sandwich and a cup of coffee in a teashop near the Guildhall and returned to her car. Before driving off she called Addenbrooke's on her mobile and asked about Housman. He was 'seriously ill but stable'; that was all the nursing sister would tell her. Madeleine threw her phone down on to the passenger seat and started the engine, heading west out of the city towards Bedford.

She'd long ago lost count of the number of times she'd visited Bedford Prison, yet she'd never got used to the cold, authoritarian atmosphere of the place. The moment she passed through the outer door into the visitor reception area, she was intensely aware of the institutional nature of the establishment, a feeling that grew more dispiriting as she was escorted through a heavy steel door by one of the prison officers and down a bare corridor to another locked gate, the only sound the thud of their feet on the linoleum floor and the rattle of the keys dangling from a chain on the warder's belt.

She had to walk through an electronic scanner and was given a rub-down search by a female officer before being shown into a windowless interview room. The room was warm and stuffy, the air tainted by a smell – a sort of mixture of boiled cabbage and disinfectant – that Madeleine always associated with prisons. It didn't matter where they were, they always smelt the same.

Jake Brewster was brought in a few minutes later.

'I'll be outside if you need me,' the prison officer said, as if Jake might be some kind of danger to her.

Madeleine had rarely seen a less threatening prisoner. Three days inside had already had an effect on him. He looked thinner, paler. His eyes were listless, the skin beneath them smudged with dark rings.

'How are you, Jake?' Madeleine asked.

'Okay,' he said with a weak shrug.

'They treating you all right?'

'I suppose so.'

The prison officers, for the most part, would have been relatively easy on him. He wasn't a thug or a thief, he was a prisoner of conscience and though the staff may not have understood his actions, they might well have been sympathetic to his cause. The other prisoners would have been Jake's real problem. An educated, articulate idealist, he would have been one of a kind in the remand wing. His fellow inmates would have been baffled by him, resentful, perhaps intimidated, and that didn't make for a smooth relationship.

'You're coping?' Madeleine continued.

'Do I have a choice?'

'You'll be fine, Jake. The first few days are always the worst.'

'How would you know?'

His bitterness was understandable. He'd brought it on himself, of course, but Madeleine wasn't going to point that out. She was used to her clients transferring their anger on to her. Some needed sympathy, others needed a kick up the backside. She suspected Jake was in the latter group. Inclined towards self-pity, a few grim realities might wake him up and help him through what was undoubtedly going to be an ordeal.

'You're here, Jake,' Madeleine said. 'And you're going to be here for a few weeks. You'll adjust better if you accept that fact.'

'Oh, yeah? What do you suggest I do? Sip wine and enjoy the view from my cell window?'

'No, but I think you'd better face up to your position,' Madeleine replied, letting his sarcasm wash over her. 'There are people on remand in here who are innocent. Who know they've been unjustly accused and who are terrified they will end up being punished for something they didn't do. Think how they feel. You at least know you're in here for a reason, whether you think it's right or not. You know you did what you're accused of, and you knew the risks when you did it.'

Jake didn't reply. He was looking down at the table between them. His lower lip was quivering as if he were close to tears.

'I know you're angry, Jake,' Madeleine said more gently. 'And I know it's hell in here. But some things we have to get through. You have to toughen yourself up. Don't let it get on top of you. Remember, you did what you did because you believed in it. Don't lose your resolve now you're in here. Okay?'

Jake lifted his head. He gave a reflective nod, then said: 'So what's happening?'

'We're getting things moving as quickly as possible. We've got the Advance Disclosure from the Crown Prosecution Service so we can start preparing your defence in detail.'

'How long will it be before my trial?'

'In the Magistrates' Court, it could be fast-tracked and dealt with in five to six weeks. If it goes to the Crown Court, there'll have to be a committal hearing, then the case will have to be scheduled. It will take a few months.'

Jake absorbed this, mulling over the comparative time scales.

'I still want a jury,' he said firmly. 'I want some ordinary people, not a bunch of narrow-minded magistrates, to hear my defence. I think they'll be on my side. No one wants these fucking crops.'

'Okay, that's your choice.'

Madeleine paused. She had to tell him. 'Someone else will be dealing with this from now on.'

'What do you mean?'

'One of my colleagues – I don't know which one – will be taking over the case. It's not my decision. Let's just say it's been forced on me by circumstances.'

'What circumstances?'

'I don't want to go into that at the moment. But whoever it is will do a good job for you.'

'You came all the way out here just to tell me that?'

'No, I had another reason. I've been looking at the CCTV tapes of your break-in at the Transgenic Biotech lab.'

Jake winced. 'Not good, I suppose?'

'You appeared to do an awful lot of damage. But I want to ask you something. When Dan was in the office, you know, emptying the filing cabinets, did he take anything?'

'Take anything? From the office? Not that I saw.'

'Are you sure?'

'Well, no. I wasn't paying a lot of attention. Not to Dan, anyway. I was too worried the security guards were going to come in and catch us. Why?'

'Take me through what happened after you left the lab. Where did you go exactly?'

Jake described the route they'd taken. Down a corridor and out through the fire escape at the front of the building. Then across the road into the wood.

'Were you with him all the time?' Madeleine asked.

'Yeah, right behind him all the way . . . hang on, no. There was a moment, in the wood, when we got separated. But it wasn't for long.'

'Separated, how?'

'I don't know. I just lost sight of him for a few seconds. Then he was there again, coming out of the undergrowth.'

'Can you remember where in the wood this was? Any land-marks, anything unusual about the terrain?'

Jake shook his head. 'It was just a wood.'

'And where was Dan knocked down?'

'Out on the other side. It's about a quarter of a mile across. There's a track where you come out of the trees. That's where the Land-Rover hit him. Why are you so interested, if you're not handling my case any more?'

'This is something different.'

He waited for her to go on, but Madeleine was already getting to her feet.

'Is that all you're going to tell me?' he said indignantly.

'I think it's better if you don't know, Jake. You're in enough trouble already.'

It was past six o'clock by the time Madeleine got to the wood. She'd gone home after returning from Bedford and changed into casual clothes: jeans, an old sweat top she used for gardening, and flat-heeled walking shoes. Then she'd driven out to the Transgenic Biotech research centre and cruised slowly past the front of the building, getting her bearings.

The wood was to the north of the research site, a dense block of broadleaf deciduous trees and thick undergrowth. Madeleine circled around, well away from the centre, and parked the car at the edge of a farm track she'd noted earlier on the OS map. From there it was less than a mile's walk across the fields to the back of the wood. Madeleine covered the ground in fifteen minutes and paused on the rough track which separated the fields from the forest. This had to be the track on which Dan Cruickshank had been knocked down, but Madeleine didn't know exactly where on it.

Scrambling up the low earth embankment, she plunged into the trees and made her way to the other side of the wood, crouching down behind some bushes as she drew near to the road. She could see the research centre in front of her and a little to the left across the carriageway. She retreated a few metres to avoid being seen and crept through the trees until she was directly opposite the fire exit on the front corner of the building. If Jake and Dan had run in a straight line across the road, this was about where they would have entered the wood.

Madeleine looked around her. Someone had already been here. Quite a few people, in fact. The ground cover was crushed and trampled as if a herd of wildebeest had stampeded through it. She chewed on a lip, wondering if she was wasting her time. But she'd come this far . . . She turned, trying to gauge exactly what line they would have taken, and began her search.

She took it slowly, working carefully back and forth across a five-metre strip, examining the undergrowth, the ground, the trees as she traversed the wood. She rummaged in the loose material on the forest floor, digging through the fallen leaves and probing any cavities underneath. How big was the file? Maybe twelve inches by eight, she guessed, though she didn't know how bulky. That wasn't a difficult size to conceal in a wood. Would he have buried it, or simply dumped it under a log or in a thick shrub? She knew he'd disposed of it somewhere. Her calls to the police and the coroner's office had confirmed that there'd been no documents on Cruickshank's body when he'd been taken to hospital. The Transgenic Biotech security guards might have removed them before that, of course, but Madeleine didn't think so. The flattened undergrowth told her that someone had already been here looking. Who else could that have been but a team from the company?

It took her nearly an hour to reach the far side of the forest. She'd found nothing. She sat down on a tree stump and pondered whether to give up now. Perhaps the Transgenic Biotech team had already found it. But she was disinclined to abandon everything without widening her search. Taking another five-metre strip to the west of the first, she went back across the wood, examining every inch of the terrain. Then she marked out a third strip to the east and carried out yet another thorough sweep of the ground and vegetation. Again she found nothing.

Emerging from the trees on to the track behind the wood, she glanced at her watch. It was nearly half past nine. The light was beginning to fade and she was limp with fatigue. Her hands and clothes were caked with dirt, her hair itching from the dust and sweat.

She slumped down on to the earth embankment and stared across the fields to the horizon. The sky was bruised in livid shades of purple and orange, glowing with a luminous intensity that made the intervening ground seem darker than it really was.

She didn't have the energy, or the willpower, to continue. She'd scoured an area fifteen metres across and close on four hundred metres in length. Surely that was enough. There was nothing there. It had either been found by someone else or buried so deep it would never be recovered.

She wiped her forehead with the sleeve of her sweat top and pulled herself to her feet. Below her the track was dried out and stony, its edges blurred by encroaching clumps of grass and weeds. There were two deep tyre marks in the surface, their ridges set solid like plaster casts. Madeleine guessed this was where the Land-Rover had braked, skidding to a halt. She stepped down on to the track and looked along it, imagining the scene that damp Monday morning: Dan Cruickshank descending the bank, maybe slipping on the loose earth, the Land-Rover coming full throttle towards him. Hitting him, lifting his body into the air . . .

Madeleine shuddered, putting the image out of her mind. She

took a final look around, disappointed and exhausted. Dusk was falling fast, but the last rays of the sun were still grazing the surface of the fields, smearing the leaves of the trees with their dying warmth. Something glinted in the ditch on the far side of the track. A puddle of water almost hidden beneath the overhanging trellis of vegetation. Madeleine glanced at it and moved away down the track.

Then she stopped.

Water?

It hadn't rained for days. The surrounding ground was parched and dusty. Madeleine walked across to the ditch and knelt down, pushing aside the brittle stalks of grass. It wasn't a puddle she'd seen, but the transparent plastic cover of a file. Very carefully, she reached down and lifted it out. She brushed off the cover which was sprinkled with soil and grass seeds. The papers inside appeared to be undamaged. Madeleine leafed through them. They were dry and clean, covered with printed text. On the title page was the heading, 'Transgenic Biotechnology International', and below that the words, 'Genesis II. Strictly Confidential'.

She guessed what must have happened. Cruickshank hadn't disposed of the file in the wood. He'd had it on him, probably tucked inside the front of his anti-contamination suit as he ran. Then when he'd been hit, his body had tumbled to the ground and the file had somehow fallen out unnoticed and dropped into the ditch.

It seemed a thin, insubstantial thing to die for. Madeleine took the file back to the embankment and sat down again. She turned to a page at random near the beginning and glanced down the text, struggling to read it in the gloomy twilight. It was a list of farms in different parts of the country: Norfolk, Lincolnshire, Yorkshire, Dorset, Sussex, several more. And next to each name was a description of the crops being grown on the farm – mainly sugar beet, oilseed rape, maize and potatoes. Halfway down the list was the entry, 'Eastmere Farm, Cambridgeshire, transgenic leaf roll virus resistant potatoes, 15 hectares.'

On other pages there was an outline of the history of the project and at the end of the file a sheaf of papers headed 'Ministry of Agriculture, Fisheries and Food'. These papers were all virtually identical, authorisations for the growing and commercial sale of transgenic crops for each of the farms listed earlier. The licences were valid from 1 January 1998. Each one was signed at the bottom, 'David Coldwell, Minister for Agriculture'.

Madeleine closed the file. It was too dark to read now, but she'd study it more closely when she got home. She slid it under her arm and stood up.

'An interesting read?' a voice said behind her.

Madeleine started violently and spun round. The two men were standing in the shadows at the edge of the wood.

'You've saved us a lot of work,' the shorter of the two said. 'We've been looking everywhere for that.'

Madeleine backed away, transferring the file to her hand. Her chest felt so constricted she could barely breathe. She stared at the men, swallowing hard, her stomach sick with fear.

One of the men held out a hand.

'I think that's ours.'

Madeleine didn't move. The men towered over her, as big and solid as the trees around them. She shook her head, unable to speak.

'Don't make us take it from you.'

Madeleine found her voice, hoarse, barely audible.

'I know,' she said. 'I know it all.'

She saw a gleam of white as he smiled.

'So?'

She knew then what they were going to do. Knew with a certainty that sent an icy breath of terror down her spine. She reacted instinctively, doing the only thing that made sense. She ran.

Along the track, her feet pounding on the rocky surface. Ran as fast as she could, stumbling a little in the darkness. The men came after her, she could hear them, but they weren't built for sprinting. A hundred metres down the track, she vaulted the ditch into the adjoining field and paused to look back. The men were thirty metres away, struggling clumsily in their suits and city shoes. Madeleine turned and raced away down the side of the field. There was a narrow strip of bare earth next to the swathe of waist-high ripening wheat. The clods of dry soil crumbled as she hurtled over them, losing her balance occasionally and swaying sideways into the wheat.

She came to a break in the crop, a low earth mound dividing two fields, and halted briefly, trying to remember which way she'd come. Her car was half a mile away, hidden in the distance, but she wasn't sure exactly where. Everything looked the same in the dark.

The men were skirting the wheat now. She could see their shadowy outlines lumbering towards her. She went left, running along the earth mound. If she could only get to her car.

Suddenly her foot slipped on the soft, friable surface and she toppled over, falling heavily on to her right hip. She got up immediately, partially winded, and kept going. But her lungs were struggling, whooping for air. She was forced to slow down. Her hip felt bruised. She ignored the ache, making herself run through the pain.

Her foot slipped again and she almost fell a second time. But she flung out her arms and regained her balance. There was no time for caution. She just had to press on blind and hope for the best. The ground was a black sheet before her. Holes, roots, rocks were completely invisible. A single wrong foot and she could fall headlong, twist an ankle or break a leg. She risked a glance back. The two men were struggling as much as she was, maybe more considering their heavy builds. The gap between them had opened up. Madeleine took heart, finding a burst of new energy. The ground began to level out and she hit a path crossing at right angles in front of her. Something about it was familiar. She turned on to it without hesitation and accelerated, heading in a straight line between two more fields of wheat. This was the way she'd come. Another quarter of a mile and she'd meet the track where she'd parked. She scanned the horizon, looking across the ears of wheat which were moving in the breeze as if being stroked by some giant hand.

There it was: the shape of a car silhouetted against the skyline. A pulse of relief, almost of exultation, shot through her. The men were far behind. She had more than enough time to get to the car and away on to the road.

Then she saw something else. She slowed. No, it couldn't be . . . the night was playing tricks with her eyes. She saw not one, but two cars. There was another car, tucked in just behind her own so the two vehicles seemed to merge into one. And standing beside them were the dark outlines of two more men.

Madeleine stopped dead, gasping for air. The men had seen her. A torch clicked on, the beam lancing over the carpet of wheat and coming to rest on her face. She lifted a hand to shield her eyes, turning round momentarily to look back down the path. The first two men were closing in on her.

The torch beam wavered a fraction. Behind the dazzling light, the men by the cars started to move towards her. They were coming from both sides, she was caught in the middle. Madeleine had only one place to go. She stepped off the path and plunged into the field of wheat.

The movement took them by surprise. The torch beam lost her. It danced around, searching desperately across the terrain for a few seconds until finally it found her again. Madeleine

sensed the light hitting her, throwing a puddle of silvery lumines-
cence over the wheat as she ran through it. One of the men
shouted. Madeleine turned her head to right and left and saw
figures stumbling across the field, heading towards her in diag-
onal lines. The torch beam followed her like a halo, striking her
body at an angle so her shadow raced along beside her, twisting
and turning in perfect unison as she tried in vain to escape.

The field was hard going. The stalks of wheat ripped at her
clothes, spiking through the material, scratching the exposed
skin of her ankles and hands. Running through it sapped her
energy. She could feel the ache in her muscles, the strain on her
lungs. She knew she was slowing and wondered how long she
could keep ahead of her pursuers.

The torch was drawing nearer, something about the intensity
of the light told her that. In a straight race they would surely
catch her. Yet she had no alternative. There was nowhere to hide
out here on the open plain, nowhere to seek refuge. A dull orange
glow on the horizon marked the position of a farmhouse, but it
was a mile, possibly two miles away. Madeleine wasn't sure she
could run that far.

Then the field came to an abrupt end. Madeleine stopped with
a jolt, almost falling into the drainage ditch that cut across the
ground in front of her like a dark gash. A ribbon of water gleamed
in the bottom, fringed by tall grass and tufts of spiky reeds.
Madeleine glanced round. The men were gaining on her. She
counted two, three silhouettes. Where was the fourth? They were
less than fifty metres away, approaching in a flanking action that
blocked off any possibility of a change in direction. Madeleine
had to keep going straight ahead.

Taking a deep breath, she slithered down the bank into the
water. The ditch was nowhere near full, but the water still came
up to her knees, then up above her thighs as she edged further
out. She could feel the cold, stagnant liquid seeping between her

legs and around her waist. The file was clutched over her head, well clear of the water, but with each step she sank lower, her feet disappearing into the soft muddy ooze at the bottom of the ditch.

Halfway across, she became aware of the noise of an engine. She turned her head and saw headlights on the farm track, a car crossing a bridge further along the drainage ditch and coming round to cut her off. She knew then where the fourth man had gone. It was too late to turn back. The other three had nearly reached the ditch. They came out on to the bank and paused, looking down at her. A wave of resignation, of defeat broke over her. She could barely lift her legs, she was so exhausted. She struggled across the remaining few metres and almost fell on to the bank on the other side. She dragged herself out and clawed at the grass, pulling herself up the bank on to the track at the top.

The car headlights hit her full in the face. She had no strength left to run. She stood there, dripping wet and panting for breath. Waiting for them to come for her.

25

The sunlight woke Frankie shortly after dawn, but he pulled the
sheet over his head and dozed on peacefully until gone eight,
sleeping off the jet-lag which still afflicted him. When he finally
made himself get up, he slipped on a T-shirt and shorts and
went downstairs. The kitchen and the patio outside were bathed
in glaring light. Frankie slid his feet into a pair of tangerine flip-
flops and strolled out for his regular morning tour of the garden.
It was warm, but fresh, a breeze blowing off the lake, rustling
the leaves of the Japanese maples, stirring the roses and mock
orange so the air was saturated with their perfumes.

At the bottom of the garden, he paused as usual to inspect
his bees. Each morning he dreaded finding another dead hive,
but so far he'd been lucky. Only the one seemed to have been
affected. The others were thriving, their occupants untouched
by whatever mysterious disease had killed their sister colony.

Back at the house, he made tea and toast and took them out
on to the patio. He spread butter and honey on the toast and
settled back in his chair, listening to the nine o'clock news on
the local BBC radio station. The lead item was another death in
the Great Dunchurch flu outbreak.

'Hospital consultant Dr Karl Housman died early this
morning, the fifth victim of the disease which has terrified residents of the tiny Cambridgeshire village . . .'

Frankie sat up, a piece of toast halfway to his mouth. *Housman*?

'Dr Housman, head of the Infectious Diseases Department at Addenbrooke's Hospital, was part of the team of health experts who were trying to contain the spread of the mystery influenza virus . . .'

Housman? Wasn't that the name of the doctor who'd come out with Maddy?

'Colleagues this morning paid tribute to the consultant who is believed to have contracted the disease while treating other flu patients . . .'

The tall, gangly one. He'd have to ring Maddy and ask.

Frankie took a bite of toast and chewed it, listening intently as the report continued. Then he heard a noise out on the road at the front of the house, the familiar engine note of the local Royal Mail delivery van. Frankie finished his toast and went into the house. There were three envelopes on the mat by the front door: two obviously junk mail and a brown manilla envelope with something bulkier inside it. Frankie tore it open and took out a computer disk. He read the covering note that came with it. Then he read it again, his pulse throbbing in alarm.

He picked up the telephone from the hall table and called Madeleine's home number. Graham answered.

'This is Frankie Carson. Is your mother there?'

'No, she's not. She didn't come home last night. I don't know where she is.'

'She didn't leave a note, a message of any kind?'

'No. I don't know what to do.' Graham's voice trembled with anxiety. 'I rang her office. Her secretary said she wasn't there. I'm worried. That's why I haven't gone to school. She's never done this before.'

'Call the police,' Frankie said. 'Report her missing.'

'Missing? You think something's happened to her?'

'Call Parkside police station. You got a pen?' Frankie gave him the number. 'Sit tight, I'll be with you as soon as I can. Okay?'

Frankie hung up and went hurriedly upstairs, the disk still clutched in his hand. He had a PC in the front bedroom. He plugged it in, then hesitated. Staying in the house didn't feel right. Didn't feel safe.

He threw on some work clothes without bothering to wash or shave, took the disk out to his car and drove to Cambridge. On the northern outskirts of the city, he turned off the main road into the Science Park. Eric Barclay was in a meeting, but Frankie interrupted him.

'I need a PC. I need it now.'

The words were still up on the screen, but Frankie wasn't taking them in any more. He'd read them so many times, with such intense concentration, that he could almost have recited them from memory. Some of the information on the disk he already knew. Other bits were a revelation. Taken together as a whole, the facts – and their chilling implications – left him numb with shock.

He glanced away, absorbed in thought, pondering his next move. Madeleine had been pushed to the back of his mind – he'd think about her later. Right now he had to make a decision. He had to look at what he knew – about what had happened, and who was involved – and make a choice. None of the options was risk-free, none either ethically or practically the right one. Whatever he did put him in danger, but doing nothing was even more hazardous.

Closing the file, he ejected the disk from the machine and walked through into Barclay's office.

'I need a favour, Eric,' he said. 'Can you make me a couple of copies of this disk and put the original in your safe?'

'This isn't a bank, you know, Frankie. I'm still holding that videotape you left.'

'Can you copy that for me as well?'

'Anything else we can do to help you?'

Frankie pretended not to notice the sarcasm. 'Actually, yes. Let me use your phone.'

He rang Directory Enquiries and asked for a number, then called it.

'Xenotech UK,' a bored female voice announced.

'Who's in charge? Who's the boss of Xenotech?' Frankie asked curtly.

'You mean the chief executive, Mr Ross?'

'Put me through to his office.'

'Can I say who's calling?'

'Just put me through. This is urgent.'

The chief executive's secretary was polite but unhelpful.

'Mr Ross is a very busy man,' she explained. 'Is he expecting your call?'

'I'm a private investigator,' Frankie said impatiently. 'Tell him it's about Transgenic Biotechnology International.'

There was a short pause before the chief executive came on the line.

'Yes?'

Frankie took a deep breath. 'Mr Ross? I have something that might be of interest to you.'

Press Association, 12 August
FIRST COMMERCIAL GM LICENCES ISSUED
By Chris Thomas, Environment Correspondent
The Government today gave the go-ahead for the commercial growing of genetically modified crops in Britain.

Agriculture Minister David Coldwell issued the first licences for large-scale production of transgenic oilseed rape, sugar beet, maize and potatoes to the Cambridge-based company Transgenic Biotechnology International.

'Trials over the past three years have shown that these crops are absolutely safe,' said Mr Coldwell. 'They are safe to grow and safe for people to eat.'

Mr Coldwell denied that there was any risk to either the environment or wildlife.

'We have looked into these questions extensively and found no evidence that GM crops do any more damage to the environment than conventionally bred species. We can also reassure the British public that these crops pose no risk whatsoever to their health.'

Mr Coldwell said the licences had all been granted to Transgenic Biotechnology, the leading British biotechnology company, because it had been at the forefront of GM research for several years and was best placed to go ahead with large-scale commercial planting. Shares in the company rose 38 pence at the news, valuing it at £720 million.

The planting is expected to start immediately on farms throughout the country. The identity and locations of the farms is being kept secret to prevent anti-GM protesters damaging the crops.

Mr Coldwell justified the decision, saying: 'We have no problem with people voicing their objections peacefully, but the campaign of unlawful violent action against the GM industry has gone too far. Independent scientific experts and numerous trials have shown conclusively that GM crops are perfectly safe, and the Government intends to continue to promote their production and sale in this country.'

Environmental groups condemned the decision to issue the licences.

A spokesman for Friends of the Earth said: 'The Government is riding roughshod over the wishes of the public who have repeatedly shown that they do not want GM crops to be grown in this country. Allowing commercial planting is irresponsible and potentially catastrophic for the British countryside.'

Press Association, 1 September
FLU OUTBREAK COMES TO AN END
BUT MYSTERY VIRUS IS STILL A POTENTIAL THREAT,
SAY EXPERTS
By Jonathan Soames
The mystery flu virus which struck a Cambridgeshire village in the summer seems to have disappeared, health officials said today.

Stephen Manville of the Cambridgeshire Public Health Department said there had been no more cases of the disease in the past two months. The initial outbreak hit the isolated village of Great Dunchurch last June, claiming 10 lives. A further 16 people contracted the disease but recovered after treatment in hospital.

Health officials placed the village, population 350, in 'voluntary quarantine' in an attempt to prevent the virus spreading.

'The precautions we took appear to have paid off,' said Mr Manville. 'We have been monitoring the residents of the village since June and have found no new cases of the disease during the past eight weeks.'

The source of the killer virus remains a puzzle. It is believed to have originated in hens on a local farm, but flu experts have been unable to identify how the hens first became infected.

Dr Ian Fitzgerald, a leading virologist at London's National Institute for Medical Research, said it was vital to remain vigilant.

'We have no idea where the virus came from or where it has gone,' he said. 'But there is every possibility it could resurface again in the future. If it does, the consequences could be disastrous.'

The Government has yet to make a decision on whether to pay for the development of a vaccine against the virus.

'Time is running out,' Dr Fitzgerald said. 'This was the most virulent strain of influenza I have ever seen. We don't know exactly what has happened to it. It may be lying dormant somewhere, waiting for the conditions to be right for it to reemerge. One thing I'm sure of, it hasn't gone away for good – flu viruses never do. And if, and when, it comes back, we must be ready for it.'

Cambridge Evening News, 16 September
GM PROTESTER JAILED
By Karen Quentin
An anti-GM protester who ripped up genetically modified crops and smashed up a research laboratory was today jailed for 18 months.

Jake Brewster, aged 22, of Bold Street, Cambridge, was one of a group of activists who last June invaded a field belonging to Transgenic Biotechnology International and tore up oilseed rape plants valued at £375. Brewster then broke into the company's research laboratory and caused £25,000 worth of damage.

He pleaded not guilty to charges of burglary and criminal damage, saying in his defence that what he did was in the public interest to prevent contamination of the countryside with GM pollen.

The jury at Cambridge Crown Court acquitted him of criminal damage to the oilseed rape plants, but convicted him of burglary and criminal damage to the laboratory.

Passing sentence, Judge James Higgins said: 'In this country there are legitimate forms of protest, but an individual, whatever he believes, cannot take the law into his own hands. This was a disgraceful act of sheer vandalism for which only a custodial sentence is an appropriate penalty.'

Cambridge Evening News, 23 September
BODY IN FENS IDENTIFIED
By Alison West
Police today confirmed that the body of a woman found in a drainage ditch north of Ely was that of the missing Cambridge solicitor, Madeleine King.

Miss King, 42, disappeared last June. Her car was found abandoned on a farm track near Waterbeach, but despite an intensive police search Miss King herself was never found.

Two anglers discovered the body last Sunday, in dense reeds at the remote Coldwater Fen. It was badly decomposed, but forensic experts used dental records to identify it.

Police speculate that Miss King, one of Cambridge's leading defence solicitors, may have gone for a walk and accidentally fallen into the drainage ditch. They said there were no suspicious circumstances.

Press Association, 2 October
GM CROPS GROWN WITHOUT PUBLIC KNOWLEDGE, CLAIMS BIOTECH COMPANY
By Jack Villiers
Britain's largest biotechnology company was today accused of secretly growing GM crops. Transgenic Biotechnology International then sold the crops, introducing GM material into the human food chain without the public knowing what was happening.

The allegations were made by the rival Xenotech Corporation which claims that Transgenic Biotechnology had the full approval of the British Government in the deception.

At a press conference in London, Xenotech's UK chief executive Malcolm Ross said: 'We have evidence that this has been going on for several years. We have identified at least eight sites where Transgenic Biotechnology has been growing GM crops – including potatoes, oilseed rape and maize – since 1998. These are not GM trial sites, but commercial operations which the company – and, we believe, the Government – has kept secret from the British public.'

Mr Ross said that a team of 10 independent investigators had spent the past three months compiling a comprehensive 250-page dossier on Transgenic Biotechnology International which they had sent to both Downing Street and the Director of Public Prosecutions.

'We are calling on the authorities to set up an immediate independent inquiry into the activities of the company. If they do not agree to our request, we will release the full dossier to the media.'

Mr Ross denied Xenotech was making the allegations out of pique after Transgenic Biotechnology was recently awarded the first licences to grow GM crops commercially in the UK.

'This is not some malicious slur on a rival corporation,' he said. 'It goes to the heart of corporate accountability to the public and has huge ramifications for the future of GM agriculture all over the world.'

In the dossier, Xenotech also demands an investigation into a number of other matters:

- Links between Transgenic Biotechnology's GM potatoes and the recent outbreak of avian flu in East Anglia.

- Incidents connected to Transgenic Biotechnology's research centre in India.
- The death in a car crash of one of Transgenic Biotechnology's UK scientists.
- Police Special Branch involvement in criminal activities, including burglary, tampering with evidence and the intimidation of witnesses.
- The mysterious death of Cambridge solicitor Madeleine King.

'These are serious allegations we are making,' said Mr Ross. 'They have been examined by our legal advisers and we believe they will stand up in a court of law.'

The allegations were brought to Xenotech's attention by private detective Francis Carson who was also present at the press conference.

'I went to them because I didn't trust the police or the Government to carry out a thorough and independent investigation,' he said.

Mr Carson said he had been in hiding for the past three months because he feared his life might be in danger.

'I'm doing this for Madeleine King,' he said. 'She was a friend of mine. Her death was no accident. I intend to pursue this investigation until the full facts are uncovered and whoever was responsible is brought to justice.'